GALATEA

GALATEA

A NOVEL BY
Philip Pullman

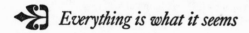 *Everything is what it seems*

E.P. DUTTON • New York

First published in 1979 by E.P. Dutton, a Division of Elsevier-Dutton
Publishing Company, Inc., New York

Copyright © 1978 by Philip Pullman
All rights reserved. Printed in U.S.A.

For information contact: E.P. Dutton, 2 Park Avenue, New York, N.Y. 10016

Library of Congress Catalog Card Number: 78-70518

0-525-11125-5

10 9 8 7 6 5 4 3 2 1

First Edition

To Nic and Anne Messenger

PART ONE

Roses from the South

One evening, the orchestra in which I played the flute gave a concert of Viennese waltzes and polkas, and when I went home afterwards I found that my wife had disappeared, without leaving a note to say where she was going.

I walked out of my job the next morning and set off to look for her.

First I went to her home town, but nobody there knew where she was. I asked our friends, but they'd heard nothing either. Finally I went back and sat in our apartment and tried to think what might have happened. No clues came to me. I stayed there miserably while two or three days went by.

Eventually a few speculations drifted together. The last piece of music I'd played had been Strauss's *Roses from the South*. Roses had been her favourite flowers. There was a song which went

> *Valencia*
> *Es la tierra de las rosas, de la luz y del amor,*

and Valencia was in the south. It was a city of business, what's more, and she had worked for a merchant banker, and taken an interest in that side of life. I had nothing else to go by; I thought she must have gone there.

I sold everything I did not need, put our furniture into store, took my flute and the little money I could gather, and set off for Valencia.

The Broker of Reality

I had a letter of introduction, which I had asked a distant cousin of mine to write for me. It was addressed to a banker and prominent financier called Lionel Pretorius. I knew nothing about

7

him, but my relative had told me that if anyone knew what was going on in the financial and social world of Valencia, it was Pretorius.

I was nervous of meeting him. I had no decent clothes and I thought I would be ill-at-ease in the company of the very rich. Furthermore I was not sure how I should present my letter; nor whether the whole thing wasn't a fool's errand.

However, on the morning after I arrived, I telephoned his secretary and made an appointment to see him. He agreed to give me a quarter of an hour that afternoon.

The Pretorius Bank was a small glass-fronted building on the Ocean Boulevard, a long wide avenue that ran parallel to the sea. On one side of the bank was a fashion house and on the other the main building of the Ministry of Marine. Inside the lobby of the bank a uniformed porter asked for my name, and spoke into a telephone.

I waited. On a table in the lobby was arranged a selection of financial journals in—I counted—seven languages; and a vase of yellow roses.

Then a girl came down in a lift.

"Mr Browning?" she said. "Mr Pretorius will see you now."

I went into the lift after her. I could think of nothing to say, and we rode upwards in silence.

It stopped at the fourth floor. She led me down a wide corridor and through an empty office. Then she knocked at a panelled door and opened it.

"Mr Browning, sir," she said.

I went inside. I blinked; the sun was full in my face. The room was enormous. It was at the corner of the building, and two walls appeared to be of glass. Mr Pretorius stood up at his desk and held out his hand. He was so far away, the room was so large, that I felt myself hurrying forward so as not to make his arm tired waiting for me.

He was in his fifties, broad-faced and fleshy, with thick brown hair. He wore glasses that were slightly tinted, and his suit was of some lightweight material that gleamed like silk. In his buttonhole was a yellow rosebud. His smile was relaxed and kindly. He had the air of a man who could afford to be anything, including kind. Power and subtlety were negotiating for dominance in his face. His movements were as clear and swift as those of an athlete.

"Mr Browning," he said. "Come and sit down over here."

8

He led me away from his desk to where two antique armchairs stood by a wooden cabinet. We sat down.

"Cigar?" He held out a gold case. I shook my head and was about to say "No thank you" when he went on. I had said nothing yet.

"So you're a cousin of my noble lord? And how is he these days?"

"To tell you the truth I hardly ever see him; but he's well, I know that. He gave me a letter—" I fished it out of my pocket.

"No hurry," he said, putting it on the cabinet beside him. "You never see him? Well, who does? I haven't seen him for months. How much money have you got, Mr Browning?"

The question came so suddenly that it seemed quite meaningless. Then I realized what he'd said.

"Very little," I said. "Enough to last me a month."

"Enough to live on for a month?"

"Yes, but I—"

"Well, you shall be my guest then. Now what did you want to do in Valencia?"

"I hardly know what to say. The fact is I'm looking for my wife. But I can't accept your offer, generous as it is—"

"Why not?"

"Because there's nothing I can do for you in return."

"But you were prepared to use your connection to meet me. Presumably you wanted something from me. And if you really have nothing to give, then whatever you get will be unpaid for, will it not?"

I blushed; his tone was courteous and enquiring.

"Yes," I said. "But I can't be your guest, all the same. If I were I'd want to behave appropriately, and I don't think I know how to. And it would cost me more to buy suitable clothes than I could afford; so it wouldn't save me any money to stay with you."

"I hadn't thought of that," he said.

"I really shouldn't have bothered you."

"Why did you come to see me, then?"

"Because I thought you'd know more about the city than most men."

"And you're looking for your wife. Do you know that she's in the city?"

"Not for certain. I've been following omens rather than clues."

"And why did she leave?"

I shrugged, and wished I'd never come to see him. There was nothing whatever I could say without feeling foolish, nothing I could hear from him without finding it patronising, nothing we had in common.

" I don't know," I said.

"No, of course. A silly question. You haven't thought—quite apart from the expense—of a private detective?"

"I want to find her myself. For a month I don't have to do anything but look for her, and that's all I want to do."

"I can't imagine how you're going to do it, on your own."

" I can't imagine how you run a bank; nevertheless you do. I shall find her eventually. I thought that with your knowledge of the city, of business in general, you might be able to advise me where to start looking."

"Business? Was she concerned with that?"

"It's her life, as music is mine. If anything—I don't know— unusual or exciting was going on, in the business world, she might want to be there. That's all I can think of."

He nodded, and said nothing for a moment. Finally he got up and went to the window.

"Well then," he said, and turned to face me. "Your behaviour is perfectly appropriate. What else I can do I don't know, but tonight it's my daughter's birthday. I am giving a ball. My son David is about your size; you can borrow his dress clothes. You may see your wife at the ball, or you may meet someone who knows where she is. Come to my house at about seven."

He took out a visiting card and wrote something on the back.

"Give this to the butler," he said. "David's clothes will be ready for you."

He handed me the card, and laughed gently. It made me laugh too.

"Thank you," I said.

"What will you do when your month is up?"

"I practise the flute every day; I shall find something to do."

"I don't know anything about music," he said, "though no doubt I employ people who do. Good afternoon, Mr Browning."

We shook hands, and he opened the door. The secretary took me downstairs again.

Salt, Flowers, Lies

The mercantile city of Valencia was holding a week-long festival of flowers, and I had arrived in the middle of it. As soon as I'd stepped off the train the night before I'd smelt flowers, mixed with the salt of the sea, and now I left the glass-fronted bank the same combination of scents came to me sharply. It was another omen to be accepted gratefully.

And in truth I hadn't known about the festival before I arrived and found myself in the middle of it. There were flowers everywhere; the air was full of scent. The breeze from the sea arrived laden with roses; the breeze from the land lifted trails of perfume out of thousands of freesias, while in the warm night the atmosphere was languid with night-scented stocks and tobacco plants, and with rarer tropical plants grown carefully under glass and brought out now with a thousand misgivings. And there were petals everywhere, in all the gutters and all the crannies, most of them bruised and rotting, but among the numberless millions it was possible to find some petals that were perfect: the blue enamelled claw of an iris, the silky crimson skirt of a rose; or even complete flowers, perfect and abandoned.

Everyone wore flowers, in their buttonholes, in their hair, pinned to a dress. Society inaugurated the festival with a Flower Ball, which was repeated with variations all the way down the social scale. Stalls were set up in the streets to sell the blooms to the tourists; the municipal parks and gardens were bright with specially arranged displays. Bands played nightly in the bandstands, and coloured lights hung in the limes and plane trees.

I wandered down to the harbour. There was nothing I could do until the evening except wander and look, and I might see my wife in the crowd. The afternoon was hot and the sun was very bright. In the open water of the harbour grey-painted warships rode at anchor, and launches and yachts came and went like swifts. Great white cruise ships and liners were tied up at quays on the far side, perhaps half a mile away.

The people were prosperous and happy. The shops were full. Business was booming; was that sufficient reason for her to leave me? Maybe it was.

We had been married for about two years. We were very happy. We had got married doubtfully, not trusting completely in marriage or even in each other. At first we were doubtful about love too; but after a few months, we had begun to love one another, we thought.

11

We admitted our doubts. There were many secrets we kept from each other.

We had little money, but we spent less than we earned, and our flat was bright and clean. It's hard to write about being happy; it seems to inhere, happiness, I mean, in not being overdrawn at the bank, and having dry walls painted with cheerful colours.

But still, there were our secrets. One of hers was why she loved me. It was easy to see why I loved her; for she rescued me from all kinds of wrongdoing and ignorance. She knew things more securely than I did. She was more wise in the ways that people behaved. She knew what was realistic and what was extravagant and fantastic, where I could see no dividing line at all. Her perceptions of the world were rock-solid and clear, whereas mine were unsafe and perilous, so I relied on her to lead me and tell me things.

I thought, as I stood and watched the great cranes dipping and rising again on the hazy horizon, that the only surprising thing about her going was that I should be surprised at it, for I could see little reason except habit for her to stay.

Don't be silly, she'd have said, you refuse to like yourself out of pride, that's the only reason.

I was optimistic; she might have loved that in me. The colours of the sea made me optimistic again, and I wandered about looking at the faces of the people in the streets until it was time to go to Pretorius' house.

It was in the richest part of the city. Large shaded gardens and quiet wide avenues seemed to exhale money into the evening air as flowers exhale oxygen, so that I felt rich too just walking along.

The house was immense. It was square in plan, Neoclassical, with an ornate flight of steps in front. The clean gravel of the drive swept past towering rhododendrons and well-clipped box hedges. The façade of the house, warm and honey-coloured in the face of the setting sun, was as elegant as a theme by Haydn. A flattish cupola was coloured that most beautiful of greens by verdigris. As I walked up to the door a lightness came into my spirits, introduced by the quiet, and by the sheer loveliness of the house in the evening sunlight, and by the thought that the evening was only beginning.

A calm butler showed me in, and took me through a large hall, where I saw depth upon depth of riches. For instance, there was a glass-fronted cabinet containing pieces of porcelain. I was no judge of the porcelain, but the wealth was visible in the taste and skill with which the display had been arranged, in the meticulous dusted cleanliness of it, in the mirror-like shine of the polished wood and the sparkling glass. All these things as well as the porcelain had to be paid for; and unlike the porcelain the cleaning had to be paid for again and again. Every inch of the house was as clean as that, I was sure.

I was taken to a room upstairs, a simpler and kindlier one, with subdued green wallpaper and carpets. The furniture was sturdy, and painted in clear pleasant colours. On the bed lay a dress shirt; the suit was hanging in a recess, whose curtain was drawn back. There was a box on the dressing-table that contained mother-of-pearl studs and cufflinks.

I took off my own clothes and folded them more carefully than I was used to doing. I thought that it would be hard to be slovenly in surroundings like that. When I put on David's clothes, I found they fitted me perfectly, even the shoes.

I rang for the butler. He came and led me downstairs into a room that led off the hall, a long, wide room that overlooked the garden. It was on the east side of the house, so the evening sun didn't enter it; and it was a dark room anyway, for the walls were lined with thousands and thousands of leather-bound volumes. One of three french windows was open. The scent of flowers from the garden and of the evening air was blended with the fragrance of cigar smoke.

At first I could see no one in the room. There were several armchairs and two big tables, and I didn't know which way to look; but I heard a voice, not that of Pretorius, from one side, talking quietly. It had not paused when the butler announced my name.

From a chair at the other end of the room, Pretorius stood up. The voice faltered and stopped.

"Mr Browning," said Pretorius. "This is my father."

Sitting in the armchair opposite him was a very old man. His face was aristocratic and his bearing patrician, but his expression was that distant out-of-focus concentration which marks the afflicted.

"How do you do, sir," I said, holding out my hand.

The old man took it in both his.

"David," he said. "Home for a day or two."

"No, sir, I'm not . . ." I broke off.

"My father is quite deaf," said Pretorius. "He thinks you're my son."

"Sit down, my boy," said the father. "Have you got a drink? Give the boy a drink, Lionel."

"What will you have?" asked Pretorius.

"Whisky, thank you," I said.

"How are you getting on?" said the father. "What are you doing these days?"

"David is at Harvard studying law," said Pretorius, pouring out a drink at a sideboard with his back to us.

"Sit down here next to me; I can't hear you if you're too far away," said the father.

I sat down where he told me to.

"Well?" he said. "Speak up."

"I'm working hard," I said loudly.

"Look at me when you speak, will you? I can't see his mouth if he looks away, Lionel," he said querulously.

"He'd better sit opposite you," said Pretorius as he handed me my drink.

"I want him beside me," said the old man. He put a hand on mine and squeezed it, trembling slightly.

"Do you want me to pretend?" I asked Pretorius.

"What are you saying?" said the father. "Speak to me, David."

"How are you, grandfather?" I said, facing him.

"Getting on," he said. "Getting on now. I can't move very far these days."

Pretorius sat down and drew on his cigar, watching us.

His father went on "Are you still hunting?"

"When I can," I said, but not loudly enough, for he leaned forward stiffly and said:

"Doesn't he *know* I'm deaf, Lionel? I can't hear him at all."

"I'm sorry, grandfather." I said. "I've had a cold but I'm still a bit hoarse."

"Caught a cold?"

"I caught it swimming," I said, making futile swimming gestures with my hands.

"Don't you go and give it to Mary," he said.

I shook my head.

"The boy's changed, Lionel. What's he done?"—then he turned to me and said "What have you done? Cut all your hair off?"

"Yes. I have had it cut."

"Change, change, all the time."

"It's not easy to know what you want."

"Know what who wants?"

"Any one. What I want."

"Don't you want to be a lawyer, then?"

I sat back and looked at the wall of books. I didn't know whether I could carry on. Pretorius said, so that his father could hear, "I'm sure he knows . . ."

"Let the boy speak, Lionel," said the old man. "Do you want to be a lawyer or not?"

I sat up again.

"No," I said. "But I think I had better be one."

The father nodded. "Yes, that would be best," he said, and he sat back and closed his eyes. All this time his hand had been resting on mine, on the arm of my chair; now he took it over to his own, where it gripped the end of the arm gently, and then relaxed.

Pretorius blew a stream of smoke elegantly above him, like a flag.

"Did you tell him I was David?" I asked in a low voice.

"Why would I have done that?"

"I don't know, but it seemed all set up."

"I assure you it wasn't. But are you easily surprised?"

"I haven't thought about it. What did my cousin mean when he told me you were known as El Cambista de la Realidad?"

"The Broker of Reality?" He laughed quietly. " It would take a while to explain. I don't deal in reality, though; quite the opposite."

"I've noticed."

"You managed very well."

I remembered that I had a drink in my hand, and sipped it.

"I've been thinking," he said. "You have enough money to last for a month. How much is that?"

"In dollars, a hundred and twenty."

"Well, you haven't calculated very well. Suppose you discover that she is in Australia? Or even in Milan? How far would a hundred and twenty dollars take you and how long would it last then?"

"Well, not long, I agree. But I haven't much choice."

"You ought to double your capital, or treble it, at the very least, before you even begin to look for her."

"I don't agree. In the first place I don't know enough about money to make it behave like that."

"Give it to me, and I'll do it for you."

" What would I live on in the meantime?"

"I'll give you a job."

"Then I wouldn't be able to spend my time searching. It's kind of you, but I couldn't accept the offer."

"With two hundred dollars, four hundred, you could look that much more thoroughly. Have you thought of that? It wouldn't take very long to make that much. I'd pay you a good salary and you could probably save most of that, or better still put it to work as well. Nor would you need to stick at four hundred. Why not accumulate a thousand while you're about it?"

"You make it sound very easy."

"And so it is. I know nothing easier."

"I'm grateful for your interest, naturally, but I hardly expected it in this degree. May I ask why you're taking an interest in my search?"

"You asked me to, by coming to see me. But apart from that, I like seeing things well done, and I imagine you do too. You're a musician, I take it; now, if I came to you with a plan to write an opera, and sang you one of the main themes, and it was dull and unpleasant, wouldn't you try to set me on the right track? Or discourage me altogether?"

"It's not a good analogy. Music is my business, but looking for wives is hardly yours."

"My dear Mr Browning, I'm not talking about what your purpose is, only about your means of achieving it. You may see this as a matter of romance. I see it as a piece of bungled economics. Your money's going to waste, and aesthetically I'm offended, as you would be if my opera were full of mismanaged or inappropriate harmonies. Would it matter what the opera was about if its manner were so bad and yet so easily corrected?"

"From your point of view your argument is overwhelming. But from mine it hardly reaches me. Nothing can alter the fact that I'd be losing time."

"One thing would alter it. Suppose I were to employ you to look for your wife?"

I fell silent, astonished, and stared at him. He was lying back in his armchair, his legs stretched out, the ankles crossed. His hands lay along the arms of his chair. His eyes behind the tinted glasses were narrowed very slightly.

I answered: "On what terms?"

And he laughed loudly. His father stirred and woke up briefly.

"Time to get dressed yet?" said the old man.

"Not yet," said Pretorius, looking at him fondly.

His father nodded and shut his eyes. Pretorius looked back at me.

"The terms," he said. "Simple enough. Look for your wife. Go where you like, do whatever's necessary, employ whom you need, and charge it all to me. I'll pay all your expenses, and send you each month wherever you are a salary of—what was your figure? A hundred and twenty dollars? If you can live on that, as you claim."

"But how shall I pay you back?"

"I'll pay myself back from your capital. If by the time you find her your money has increased beyond the amount you've spent finding her, I'll deduct that amount from it and give you back the remainder. If you find her before it's increased enough to cover your expenses and salary, I'll keep it until the two sums balance, close the account, and neither of us will owe the other anything. Can you see any flaw in that scheme?"

"It gives me a financial incentive to delay."

"I'll come to that in a minute."

"I can't see how all that could come out of a hundred and twenty dollars."

"Of course you can't, or you'd be doing it on your own. But I can."

"What would prevent me from delaying, then?"

"Inflation. If you can live on a hundred and twenty dollars a month now, you won't be able to in a few months' time, or a year; and I won't put your salary up. Nor, while working for me, will you be able to get another job, so you'd have to hurry—reasonably, that is. You'd have several months, maybe even a year, before you'd have to stop. But set that against the certainty of having to stop in a month's time from now, and the impossibility of getting to her if she turns out to be in South America or China, and it doesn't look too bad a bargain, eh? And of course working for me you'd be able to use any of the resources of the bank: credit transfer, purchase of foreign currency at the most favourable rates, and so on; plus of course the name of the Pretorius Bank behind you, which guarantees the best of any service you pay for."

"I don't know what to say."

"Think about it this evening. Who knows? Perhaps your wife herself will be at the ball, in which case everything is solved. But now I must go and dress, and so must my father." He stood up with a swiftness that startled me, and bent over and pressed the old man's hand gently. His father nodded and woke up. "Now you go and look around the garden, Mr Browning. Help yourself to cigars or drinks. When you hear music, make for it and enjoy yourself. Don't worry about introductions: half the people here are strangers on any occasion. I'll send for you later on and introduce you to my daughter; after all, it's her ball. Come along, father," he said more loudly. "Time to dress."

He helped the old man to his feet.

"Good to see you, my boy," said his father to me. "Come and see me again before you go back."

"I will, grandfather," I said.

They moved away slowly, the middle-aged man tenderly supporting the old one.

The Price Is Higher Than It Seems

I had seen depths of wealth in the house, and I saw them again in the garden, translucent depths. There was a gravel terrace outside the french window, with a lawn below it. To the left a beautiful cedar shone densely in the evening sun, and straight ahead the rhododendrons clustered protectively around the stillness of the lawn. Along the terrace at intervals were marble statues of nymphs and gods.

The gravel of the path was raked and immaculate. The lawn was clipped and rolled to perfection; not a dead leaf, not a twig, disfigured it. I thought that what Pretorius spent on keeping up the garden for one week would enable me to live for six months.

And that brought me back to his offer.

I never for a moment thought of it as a trick or a trap. Because what would be the point? I was sure he'd stated his motive truthfully. Or it might have been simple kindness, or the wish to oblige my cousin.

But I didn't know whether I could accept it. It seemed to put me under an obligation which no money of mine, no matter how it grew, could repay. Nor was I keen on searching for my wife on behalf of another man. The real tie would be between her and Pretorius, with me as the agent to bring them together.

My thoughts were confused and troubled. With an obscure shock I realised that my first conversation in his house had taken place under false pretences. I had deceived an old man, for however innocent a reason; not to put too fine a point on it, I had told lies; and it made me uneasy.

I wandered over to the cedar and put my hand on one of the branches that swept low over the lawn.

From here I could see the whole sweep of the garden. Behind the house it extended two or three hundred metres to a miniature lake, beside which a marquee had been erected. Couples in evening dress were strolling down from the house. As I stood there, with all my certainty gone, I heard from the marquee the most thrilling sound in the world: an orchestra tuning up, and falling silent, and then launching into the first bars of a waltz.

The Music Begins. A Conversation with a Damned Soul

You can't march to a waltz, you can't walk to it; the only way you can move to it is by dancing. It speaks directly to the heart and the nerves of sex.

A thrill ran through my body as I heard those first bars from the edge of the lake, and my hand involuntarily gripped the branch of the tree, and I took a deep breath and lifted my head. I left the sheltering cedar, and walked down towards the lake.

More people were arriving every minute. They were drifting down the great lawn, laughing and talking, coming out of the house and through the double doors that led on to a low balcony, and then down the steps at each end of it.

The marquee was open at the side facing the lake, and the wooden dance-floor that had been laid extended for some distance into the open. Some couples were already dancing.

At the edge of the lake, a little wooden jetty was decorated with bunting and with lanterns, as yet unlit. A number of punts and canoes were tied up to it. As I watched, a party of four, laughing, got into one of the punts and clumsily poled away.

There were a number of older people there. On the faces of all of them was an expression of wealth, something I was now beginning to recognise. The men were gathering slowly in self-involved groups, raising a hand occasionally to summon a waiter and take a drink from his tray. Their conversations, scraps of them that I overheard, concerned profits and exports and shareholders' meetings.

I took a glass of something from a waiter and went to lean on the wooden railing of the jetty. Beautiful girls and slim, handsome men walked by, all of them rich and innocent. They took no notice of me, except to smile briefly as if they might have known me.

Then a man of about fifty came and leant on the rail beside me, and stared moodily over the dark lake.

"Be careful," he said. "Don't sell Lionel your soul."

I started.

"What do you mean?" I said.

"I sold my soul to him thirty years ago and I can recognise a fellow-victim."

"Who are you?"

"My name is Roger de Witt. Lionel pays me a handsome salary to do exactly what I want to do, which is paint, with the result that I can't do it. He's perfectly content with that. That's just what he wants. My soul has been damned for thirty years! Do you wonder that I'm slightly cracked, and go about talking to total strangers?"

He had an insistent whining tone, as if he was not in control of his own fate, and knew it.

"I'm unreal," he complained. "I haven't got an economic reality. I'm a pet."

"Kill yourself," I suggested.

"Why?"

"If that's the only thing you're free to do."

"I'm only trying to warn you, that's all."

"Thanks."

"I'm not asking for sympathy, for God's sake."

His voice was getting louder, and we were beginning to attract the attention of the passers-by.

"I've gone completely rotten," he said in a lower voice, seeing people give him sideways glances. "Confidentially, that is. My psychology is fascinating. I don't even dream any more."

"Can't you break away and refuse to take any more money?"

"And live on what?" he retorted with bitter triumph.

"Yes, I see. But the fault is yours and not Pretorius'."

He leaned towards me. "You know that ridiculous name they give him? El Cambista de la Realidad?"

"Yes."

"He really does deal in it. Reality and unreality. Everything he touches becomes unreal."

"I'm sorry, but I don't understand. I think I can decide what I want to do. And if you really can do nothing else, you'll have to kill yourself. He'd never make that unreal."

20

He tried to pluck at my sleeve, but I had had enough of him, and walked away.

"All right, I *will*," he called petulantly after me.

An Important Announcement; and the Love of a Champion Cyclist
They were beginning to light the lanterns in the trees and along the jetty. The entrance to the marquee was already glowing with hundreds of coloured light bulbs. As if to emphasise the gathering darkness, floodlights suddenly came on, illuminating the Mozartian perfection of the house.

The marquee was full, the dance floor crowded. The orchestra was playing a foxtrot. The air was warm, balmy, inexpressible, full of the south. It smelt of the sea and of flowers, of oranges, and of the scent of beautiful girls, and the fragrance of tobacco. Under its influence I felt the urge to spread my arms wide, to breathe deeply, to run and swim and dance.

On the terrace above the lawn, servants were erecting trestle tables. They covered them with white linen, and then piles of gleaming plates were brought out, and box after box of cutlery. I sat on a bench near by to watch them work and admire their swift unhurried skill. When the plates had been piled neatly at one end of the table, and knives and forks laid out in shining rows, a series of chafing-dishes were brought out; and when they were set on the tables, tureens, carving boards, and great dishes with silver covers were put on them, and the rich smells of roasted meat and piquant sauces drifted out from the table. Meanwhile, wine, ice-buckets, and trays of glasses were being set out; and when all the tables were full, with every salt-cellar in place, Pretorius himself stepped on to the balcony and clapped his hands for silence.

Behind him on one side stood his father, with a woman who although she wore evening dress was plainly a nurse. Next to the father stood a middle-aged woman, probably Lionel's wife, and a slender girl, obviously his daughter. Pretorius smiled, waited for the orchestra to fall silent, as after a few seconds it did. All the guests turned to face him, and conversation stopped.

"My friends," he said, raising his voice so that they could all hear, "a few words of welcome before we eat. After all, we have several things to celebrate, the main one being Mary's birthday. She's nineteen: old enough to go her own way and be her own mistress, but she still allows me to give her birthday presents. Happy birthday, my darling! And what else can we celebrate? The Festival of Flowers, for one thing; finer this year than for a long time. And something of interest to my older friends. I mean of course business. We don't celebrate enough in business. But I propose that we drink a toast tonight to the biggest boom in trade and business that most of us can remember: that we celebrate the healthy state of world markets and the increased business each of us enjoys as a result. And a last little piece of information—I don't want to keep you away from your food, but I think you'll be interested to hear that the government of Venezuela has unconditionally approved the final stages of the Anderson Valley Project, and that only fifteen minutes ago I authorised the first ships to sail for La Guaira. But now, please come and eat!"

The last sentence was lost in the stir of excitement and comment that followed his announcement. The older men, the brokers and financiers I had noticed earlier, became quite animated; toasts were proposed, backs were slapped.

But meanwhile Pretorius and his family had turned away from the balcony and come down to the lawn. A small group instantly gathered around him, while his wife and daughter were surrounded by admirers.

Behind them, waiters were serving the crowd at the buffet; slicing hams, chickens, great joints of beef and lamb, and rich pies; helping the guests to all manner of vegetables and salads, and pouring wine.

I joined the crowd, and took a plate, and had it filled. I was hungry. When I'd collected a glass of wine I took my plate down to the jetty, as some of the other guests were doing, and sat down there to eat.

After a minute a board behind me creaked, and a voice said "Mind if I sit here too? There's no room further up."

"No, of course," I said.

I turned to look at him as he sat down. A little younger than I was, and very good-looking, with dark curly hair and very white teeth. He looked guileless and happy.

"You're not waiting for anyone?" he said.

I shook my head, and he smiled. His face was open and cheerful. "I haven't seen you before," he said, forking salad into his mouth. "Are you a cousin of Mary's? I heard she had some staying."

"No, no relation. Not even a friend. In fact I only met Mr Pretorius today."

I told him about it. He listened intently, swallowed some wine, and said "What's your name?"

"Martin Browning."

"I'm Johnny Hamid. I haven't met your wife, unfortunately. But I suppose she could be using another name."

"She could be, yes."

"I hope you don't mind telling me. I don't want to be nosy, or anything."

"I'll never find her if I don't tell people about it."

"Do you think she's in on this Anderson Valley thing?"

"What is it?"

"I don't know . . . electricity, or mining, or something. Lionel's committed to it, and all the others follow him. My father's involved, too."

We ate in silence for a few moments. Then he said "How long have you been married?"

"About two years."

"Did you enjoy being married?"

"Yes . . . that's why I want to find her again."

"Maybe she didn't enjoy it, so it wouldn't be any use."

"Well, I want to find out."

"I want to marry Mary."

"Mary Pretorius?"

"Yes. But don't . . . I was going to say don't tell anyone, but there's no point in that because they all know I do. Even Lionel."

"Does she want to marry you?"

"She likes me, but whether . . . I don't know. I haven't got a chance anyway."

"Why?"

"Well, I'm a wog, for a start. And I'm a wastrel. One or the other wouldn't matter much, because at least we're rich, but both together is too much."

"What's your form of wastrelling?"

"Bicycle racing. Hunting or ski-ing would be all right, but the best people don't ride bicycles, let alone race them."

"Do you win?"

"Sometimes."

There was another pause. I felt completely at ease with him; I

23

liked him, and I wanted to know more about him; and I wanted him to think well of me.

"What's Mary like?" I asked. "If she's the girl I saw on the terrace, she's very good-looking."

He turned to me and laughed, and swallowed the rest of his wine. His laugh was infectious.

"What do you expect me to say? She's so beautiful that I don't know what to say about her. I can't say anything."

"Of course."

"Was your wife beautiful?"

"Not especially beautiful so much as clear. Everything was clear about her. She didn't intoxicate you like wine but she was like clear fresh water. I'm not putting it very well."

"Never mind. Let's make a bargain: you help me to persuade Mary, and I'll help you find your wife."

"Really? You're not joking?"

"No, I'm serious. I want something to do."

"All I'm doing is wandering about looking. Unless . . ."

I told him about Pretorius' offer. He looked thoughtful; behind us the orchestra began to play a quiet, dramatic tango.

"You'd better not take it up," he said.

"Why? I don't think I was going to, but why?"

"He's done that sort of thing to other people, given them an allowance for no particular reason, and then they've gone to pieces. He likes tempting people."

We looked out over the lake. One or two of the boats gliding across the water had lanterns placed in the bow; the sky was now completely dark.

"Would you call him evil, then? I don't know what to make of him."

"Nor do I. I like him, but I don't trust him. Oh, maybe I would in business, but not . . . I don't know. I shouldn't be talking about him like that, as he's Mary's father."

"I shouldn't be involving you. And I don't see how I could help you with Mary, either."

"Take messages, things like that. Put my case."

There was an odd quality of femininity in some of his movements. He sat gracefully with one knee drawn up, and his head at a slight angle; his skin was so lustrous and clear, his eyes so bright, that from time to time I thought, he could almost be a girl. But there was nothing effeminate in him, nothing feeble or fluting;

24

all his impulses and unconscious movements were masculine.

"Well, if it'll help, I will. And thanks for offering your help, too."

"Good!"

He smiled, and we shook hands.

"Now you'd better tell me everything about her, and what she looks like and all the rest of it," he said. "Then we can decide what to do."

So I told him all I could think of that might help in the search. And while we were talking a servant came over to us and said "Mr Pretorius would be pleased if Mr Browning would care to join him and his family on the terrace."

Johnny cast me an ironical glance as I stood up. "You can take your first message, then," he said. "Tell Mary—no, ask her if she'll run away with me. I'll see you later."

I followed the servant up to the house. The great table was now laden with fruits and elaborate desserts. On the terrace I saw Pretorius and his family among a group of others. I was relieved to notice that his father was no longer there. How should I greet Madame Pretorius? She took the initiative, stepping out of the group and extending her hand.

"Lionel tells me you're a cousin of Lord Sallis," she said. "You must tell me all about him in a moment. Mary, dear, this is Martin Browning."

I hardly dared look at Mary, as I shook her hand.

Harlequinade

I'd looked at her with great curiosity from a distance, as I approached the terrace, now that I'd met Johnny, but as I got closer I felt increasingly nervous: she was extraordinarily beautiful.

Some of it is money, I told myself, wealth and position.

But I might as well have tried to put it down to the make-up she wore, which you could hardly notice. She informed her wealth and her position with some unfathomable grace, she lived in it, just as a vital woman can become her artifice and endow it with life; the wealth, and the rest of it, became extensions of her, living parts.

I felt it all in a second, and was in awe of her straight away.

"How do you do," she said politely and without any interest.

I looked at her.

Her face was soft, unfocussed in a way that rare faces can be

25

soft without being smudgy or blurred. There was nothing unformed about her, but she looked as if she was behind the most diaphanous and insubstantial veil, so that there was a suggestion of hiding and mystery in her.

Her skin was very white, and her hair thick and dark and wavy, and lustrous.

"You've met some odd people, I hear," said her mother after I'd stammered out some form of acknowledgement to Mary. She was a handsome woman with an oddly world-weary air. "Roger de Witt—did he tell you his life story?"

"The part that concerns Mr Pretorius, anyway," I said. "I was too curious not to listen."

"And the Hamid boy."

"Is he here?" said Mary. "No one told me! Where is he?"

"By the lake," I said.

"Hardly a lake," said her mother, "but too big for a pond."

"Is he on his own?" asked Mary.

"I left him alone, yes."

"Oh, you should have brought him too!" said her mother. "I didn't realise you were still with him."

"We were talking about the Anderson Valley Project," I said. "Your announcement sounded so exciting that I couldn't help wondering what it was all about."

I spoke directly to Pretorius because I was slightly embarrassed by his presence, and wanted him either to talk or go away. But he merely smiled and nodded.

"I don't suppose Johnny knew very much," said Mary.

"No, he didn't," I said.

"How long are you planning to spend in the city?" said her mother.

"I really don't know."

"You haven't got a drink," said Pretorius, and looked around for a servant. One came with a tray of drinks; I didn't know what they were, but took one anyway. "I surprised Martin earlier on," he continued, "by offering him a job."

"What sort of a job?" said Mary. "Did you take it?"

"You'll have to forgive my husband," said her mother. "I'm sure you don't need any sort of job. He was just being Napoleonic."

"It was the most unusual job I've ever heard of, and I'm not sure yet whether I'll take it."

"Why?" said Mary.

26

"I'm not sure that I've got the talents it requires."

I was addressing her, but really talking to him. His calling me Martin had thrown me off balance; I could hardly call him Lionel without being insolent, or anything else without being, now, more deferential than I wanted to be.

"Perhaps he'll need even more talent to refuse it," said his wife.

After that remark each of us stood silently for a moment or two, seemingly preoccupied. The light that bathed us came partly from the floodlights and partly from the lanterns; the harsh shadows cast by the first were flooded with gentle pinks and greens by the second, giving us the air of pierrots and harlequins. The music that drifted up from the marquee had changed in character: a smaller group, with an accordion, was performing *O Sole Mio*. I was close enough to Mary to be able to smell the scent she was wearing: it was heavy and musky, and it lay over the ever-present scent of flowers like filmy clouds over the moon.

There were many strands in this, and I didn't know what any of it meant, nor how it would lead me to my wife. I seemed to be getting further from her every minute.

Mary moved closer, and turned her head towards me. I was a little behind her, so that she had to tilt her head back slightly, looking over her shoulder, and the line of her jaw and neck and of her cheekbone was more tender and lovely than I could bear to see.

Pretorius stood behind us, watching.

"I want to talk to you," she said.

Without a word to her parents we walked away.

Modern Politics

And said nothing: I didn't trust my voice. We went past the cedar tree and along the lawn beyond it, where the darkness was greatest, by the rhododendrons. There we stopped, and stood face to face, close enough for me to put my hands on her shoulders if I dared. I said the first thing I could think of.

"Johnny told me to ask you if you'd run away with him."

"I won't."

"He's in love with you."

"I don't love him."

"Do you love anyone?"

"How can that concern you?"

"It wouldn't have done, half an hour ago."

27

"Then why should it now?"

"Because I've seen you."

"I see . . . no, I don't love anyone."

"Do you know what I've come to the city for?"

"Does it concern me?"

"I hope it does."

"I don't know what that means. You'd better tell me."

"Your father hasn't mentioned it?"

"Not to me."

"I came here to look for my wife."

"Were you so careless as to lose her?"

"Careless . . . Yes. I must have been."

"Do I know her?"

"If you do, you've known her under a fortnight."

"I meet too many people to remember. I may well have met her. Is she pretty?"

"I can't remember her face clearly. Not really pretty."

"What's her name?"

"Catherine."

"Why can't you remember her face?"

"If I were alone I could remember. But I can't think of her while I'm looking at you."

"Isn't that unfaithful of you?"

"I dare say it is."

"Perhaps you shouldn't have left the terrace."

"What did you want to talk to me about?"

"Things like this."

"You're very sure of getting what you want."

"Of course."

"How many men are in love with you?"

"I've no idea."

"Doesn't it interest you?"

"A little. It seems to interest you, though."

"Because of Johnny, who's one of them."

"Oh, yes."

There was a little silence which I could think of nothing to fill. She made a slight movement as if to turn away.

"Don't go," I said involuntarily.

"What do you want to do?"

"Find out everything I can about—your father, and you, and the city, and the Anderson Valley Project."

"They all have a bearing on where your wife is, I suppose?"

I recited all the omens I had been following. Even to my ears they sounded thin. She listened patiently, and then, raising her voice a little, said "Helmut!"

I was amazed . . . a man came out of the shadows only a few metres away. I couldn't see his face, but he stopped respectfully in front of Mary and said "Yes, miss?"

"Tell Mr Browning what my father's like. You've heard the sort of things he likes to know about. I'd tell you myself," she said to me, "but I hardly know him."

"Who's this?" I asked.

"A servant," she said coolly.

"A bodyguard," said the man from the shadows. "Mr Pretorius is an enterprising, imaginative and generous man, a true heir of the great banking family, a merchant prince."

All I could think of to say next was "Why does Mary need a bodyguard?"

"Who knows who you could be?" he replied. "Only last week she was kidnapped."

She was standing calmly beside me, as if from a sense of social duty.

"Were you on guard then?" I asked rudely.

"That was the reason I was appointed."

"What happened?" I asked her.

"Some men came into the garden and took me away. But my father had them chased. He saw them from the window. They didn't get far with me. My father had six cars after them and they caught up even before we were out of the city. They shot the men dead through the windows of the car."

"With you inside it?"

"I didn't have time to get out."

"But weren't you hurt?"

"Not a bit."

"They just shot them dead, just like that?"

"That's right. It was quite simple."

Since the bodyguard had stepped so calmly out of the shadows I had found it hard to think. I found the revelation that he had been listening to our conversation, with her full knowledge, far more astounding than any kidnap and gun battle.

"Can he go now?" I asked her.

She shrugged. "If you like. But he'll still hear whatever we say."

"And report it to your father?"

"I suppose so . . . do you?" she asked.

"If he asks me, I tell him what I hear," said the guard.

"There you are," she said.

"All the same, I can't pretend he's not there just because I can't see him."

She gave a short, low laugh. The servant withdrew.

"Are you tongue-tied now?" she said mockingly, after a moment.

"Do you live your life spied-on, like this?"

"Probably."

"Suppose you really wanted to be alone with someone?"

"Some things are impossible. But now you're becoming prurient."

The rebuke silenced me.

"Well, you're right," I admitted after a moment. "I can't pretend, after all."

"Don't bother. Treat him as a tree, or something."

"It would drive me mad."

"I'm quite happy to do anything I need to, or want to, in front of anyone else. I have to."

"I dare say."

We walked on slowly, like old lovers. The sexual current between us had died away and another, possibly curiosity, was replacing it.

"What is the Anderson Valley Project?" I asked.

"You'll have to ask my father."

So Much for Small Businesses

"Well now; something very large and nebulous," said the banker. "The South Sea Bubble, eh? An enterprise of great ingenuity and profit, but no one to know what it is. Something like that, no doubt."

We sat in Pretorius' library; it was late, but most of the guests were still dancing outside.

"I'd find it easier to talk to you if it were as natural for me to call you Lionel as it is for you to call me Martin; but of course it isn't."

"No doubt you would. Do you want things made easy for you?"

"No easier than they are naturally."

"I thought not; so you'll have to put up with the fact that I can patronise you."

"I'll put up with it for the sake of your conversation, but when that palls I shall go."

I spoke lightly, and he smiled. "Of course," he said. "And you have the advantage of me there, because I can hardly leave my own house if *you* become boring."

"Quite. But I'm still interested in the Anderson Valley Project."

"Why?"

The real reason was simple: Anderson had been my wife's maiden name. But that was something I wanted to keep to myself for the time being.

"I'm trying to think as she would, to interest myself in the things which she might have—preferred to me."

"Your best way of finding out about the Project is to take up my offer of a job. All sorts of things would be open to you then."

"Since you made the offer, I've met Roger de Witt, and it no longer sounds so attractive. But I must say that I don't think I'd have accepted it anyway."

"You're not equating yourself and de Witt, even in your own mind. He's got nothing to do with it."

"I won't find out anything about the Anderson Valley Project, though, without working for you? Is that what you're saying?"

"You may find out what you like, but I won't tell you anything."

"Which only makes it more interesting. May I ask you, Mr Pretorius, what you would do in my situation?"

"It wouldn't be in my nature to be in your situation. I would not lose a wife, but if I did I would weigh up more carefully than you seem to be doing what she was worth to me. And if I wanted her back I would stop at nothing and take every chance. I've learnt one thing at least in my fifty years: not to be afraid of incurring debt. Debts can be repaid, but once a chance has gone, it's lost for ever."

"What I've learnt is the opposite: some debts can never be repaid, and chances are everywhere. The world is full of chances."

"Have you got the courage to seize them?"

"Yes."

"Suppose I offered you the chance of a bet?"

"I might take it . . . what is it?"

"Your stake is your one hundred and twenty dollars, and the chance of the job I offered. If you lose, you lose them both. If you win, I keep open the offer, and pay you five thousand dollars."

"I imagine the odds are in your favour."

"Well, I'm offering the bet."

"What are we betting on?"

"I'm betting that the next person who comes in here is looking for me: you, that they are looking for you. Yes, of course the odds are in my favour, but think of what you could do with five thousand dollars. I take it you like dollars? The equivalent in any currency, if you prefer."

So I thought about it, and then, out of bravado, said "Very well."

And we shook hands on it, and then leant back in our chairs again.

"Mary was telling me," I said, "about when she was kidnapped."

There was a standard lamp on the floor beside Pretorius' chair whose shade, of rich crimson silk, acted as a kind of chimney for the smoke of his cigar, drawing it aside and upwards and letting it drift calmly out of the top. I could see it all reflected upside down in the whisky glass I held. I watched the inverted Pretorius' mouth open and the tiny hand lower itself from the arm of the chair as he gestured.

"Business," he said, "has to change, as everything else does, or it dies. There was a small firm in Valencia owned by a man called Palme. It made parts for typewriters: the keys, or the type, one or the other. The company he sold to exclusively was a subdivision of a large manufacturing corporation which I, that is to say my bank, took over early this year. We bought it because it was ailing and undervalued, and trimmed it down considerably. It's now well on the way to making a profit on its first year's trading under new management, but it no longer makes typewriters. And Mr Palme, being too specialised, had to close down. As it happened, he was heavily mortgaged to us at the time, trying to raise money to expand his business. But all his money had to go in redundancy payments for his staff, he lost his factory, he owed me one hundred thousand dollars. So much for small businesses, in this day and age."

"That's monstrous!" I said.

"Business, red in tooth and claw, eh? So he thought, too. So he decided to kidnap my daughter, foolish man. His workmen are far worse off than he'd ever have been: rent to pay, hire-purchase agreements to keep up, wives and children to feed on social security payments. Not enviable."

There was not a trace of smugness, or of concern, in his voice. Nor did he seem to have heard the voices outside the door: those,

I thought, of his wife and another woman. I felt perfectly calm, even abstracted.

"The mistake so easy to make," he went on, holding up his cigar in order to examine the ash, "is to think in terms of blame. Blame is not appropriate. I wonder what your wife would have thought? A good test of a person's capability for business is to tell them a story like that. If they react in terms of blame, wickedness, forgiveness, atonement, and so on, they're not fit for business, and will probably not make a fortune."

He eased the ash off his cigar.

"I see," I said.

The voices outside had ceased.

A moth blundered in through the open French window, and fluttered heavily around the lamp. I felt a faint stirring of air in my face, and heard a waltz beginning in the distance.

The French window was behind me. I heard a rustle of silk first, then caught a trace of musky scent.

"There you are, Martin. Are you coming to dance with me?" said Mary, and won me five thousand dollars.

Ocean's Child

Next morning was hazy and warm. The sun was in hiding, but present everywhere in disguise, in the brightness and warmth. It was going to be very hot.

I was up early, having slept for only three hours, and fitfully at that, with confused dreams. My wallet, with Pretorius' cheque in it, was under my pillow, for I didn't have my wife to tease me out of the idea.

I had a shower and dressed in my only clothes, hot and none too clean. Now I could buy some more, some cool shirts, some light trousers and sandals. The money stretched out all round me like a wide grassy plain.

With the wallet in my pocket I went out to have some breakfast. The city was clean and beautiful; the sky, a pure clear blue directly overhead and a blue-grey steely haze on the horizon, the infinitely fresh airs from the sea, the rhythm and pulse of the city beginning its day, all worked on me like wine.

In a café on the seafront (one I hadn't dared to enter the previous day, a smart, comfortable one) I ordered coffee, rolls, and butter, and bought a newspaper.

33

There was an account of Pretorius' ball in the gossip column, with a photograph of Mary dancing with some young man. And on an inside page I noticed a paragraph which said that the will of one Nils Palme, a businessman, had been challenged by his creditors. His wife and two sons were not expected to receive any money at all, despite the fact that he had left everything to them. His debts were listed as a quarter of a million dollars, and his assets as worth some sixty thousand.

Pretorius had told me that the Chief of Police had welcomed his action. A wave of similar kidnappings had weakened public confidence in the police, and a sharp warning like that would, no doubt, deter others.

I wondered about the dead Palme. What would his wife be doing, in their mortgaged home, with her husband buried, bullets in his chest? How old were his sons? My age, ready to shoulder the burdens and comfort their mother? Or frightened little children, upset by her tears?

Unless I hardened myself to imaginative scenes like that I was easily overcome. My wife had taught me another way out. Since the imagination controlled me and not I the imagination, she said, I could not refrain from imagining and it would be silly to try. What I should do was imagine, even more intensely, alternative scenes less painful. That would help them to come true, since imagination was prophetic. I trusted her completely. Now I had to do without her.

I took out the cheque and rested it against the coffee-pot as I ate. A yellow rectangle, torn neatly along a perforated edge. "Pay Martin Browning Five Thousand Dollars"; signed L. D. Pretorius, in a clear, direct hand.

While it had been his money, it had had the character of weight and authority and power. I wondered what character I would give it, since the first things I planned to buy were new clothes and the privilege of sitting in an expensive café.

Before I had left the ball, Johnny Hamid had given me his phone number. I decided to ring him and invite him to breakfast.

He arrived on his bicycle ten minutes later, speeding along, head down, and cruised swiftly to the pavement. He was perfectly balanced, elegant, light-moving. His hair was tousled; he smelt of the sun and the open air.

He ordered coffee and scrambled eggs. He was in training for a race the next day, he said, and he didn't want to eat much.

I told him about my bet. He picked up the cheque and whistled.

"What did he say as he handed it over?" he asked.

"He said 'That's taught me a good lesson and you a bad one.' Then he told me how to open an account with his bank."

"Are you going to?"

"I don't know. I don't know what I'm going to do with it."

"Don't spend it bit by bit or it'll just disappear. Use it as a lump. I don't know much about money but I know that much."

"I suppose so. I hadn't thought."

"Do you still want my help?"

"Yes, please. As soon as I think of something to do."

He ate swiftly and hungrily.

"Why are you helping me?" I asked.

"I don't know. But there you are."

I poured him some more coffee. We sat and gazed out of the window on to the seafront.

"Have you always lived here?" I asked after a moment.

"Here, and Beirut. I was born there. Well, we're part of the establishment."

"What does that feel like?"

"Very good. I'm not a rebel."

"You are in a way."

"My cycling? That's just what I'm good at, that's all. I'll take to the business eventually."

"What sort of business is it?"

"Shipping. Tankers, mainly."

"Are you the only heir?"

"Yes."

He seemed slightly embarrassed. He had become a little withdrawn. I thought it was my question, and was about to apologise, when he said "Is that a lot of money to you?" indicating my cheque.

"It's a fortune."

"Well, it isn't that, but if it feels like it, that's okay, because you won't take it sarcastically if I ask: can you imagine how difficult it is to have friends with much less money than you've got?"

Cushioned now by my money, I could view the question objectively. He was right.

"Yes, I think I can," I said.

"I'll be a multi-millionaire, if I'm not already," he said distantly. I said nothing.

"So please forgive me if I forget and make the kind of gesture that you can't afford to return. I don't know. I'm not putting it very well."

"Most people you know must be rich too," I said.

"Not most people I like; racers, mechanics, people like that."

"Do you know a lot of people?"

"Must be hundreds. And you?"

"Not many . . . Only you at the moment. And Pretorius."

"And Mary."

"And my wife."

"Do you think you'll ever find her?"

I thought carefully. "Oh, yes."

We had some more coffee, and watched the tourists walking up and down, and the yachts coming and going on the water.

Five Thousand Dollars' Worth of Power and Its Limits
Later that morning I opened an account with my five thousand dollars, not in the Pretorius Bank but in another, for I was still suspicious. Then I went out to buy some clothes. The shops took my dollars without hesitation. I spent a hundred and fifty, and ended up with almost more packages than I could carry.

I went back to my room and tried my new clothes on. I was pleased. Now I could face the city on its own fashionable terms.

So I put on my cotton slacks (wide, and of a cream colour) and my cool shirt (with a wide collar, and wide sleeves, and a design of huge white camellias) and went downstairs. I had bought some sunglasses too, a light metal-rimmed pair made by Zeiss. I put them on, and patted my pocket to make sure I had some money with me, and opened the door of the house.

On the other side of the street a chauffeur-driven American limousine was going past. It was moving slowly, and I could see the people inside clearly. Seated in the back were a young man, a middle-aged man, and between them, my wife.

I was paralysed—I tried to call out, to raise my arms. What could I do? Who were they? Why were they driving past here? Why was she with them? What had she been doing? A thousand questions. I felt a sudden terrible sense of loss. I didn't have her and these men did—to sit sit beside her, to talk to her, to listen to her!

The car was rounding the corner—it had gone. Without looking to see what was coming I ran out after it, raced to the corner. It was accelerating away. I couldn't even see the number, or make out what sort of car it was.

I tried to fix the men in my memory. The middle-aged man had been swarthy, and bulky, but not I thought likely to be tall. He had been talking, the other man and my wife listening. The other man was in his thirties, dressed like a business executive. Even at that distance and under those circumstances I caught an air of not-quite-reality about him. The sort of man who acted a business executive in TV commercials, meretriciously glossy.

And my wife, sitting grave and composed, listening carefully; she had nodded once at something the older man had said. She had been wearing a white blouse with full sleeves, and she had tied her hair up.

Who they were and what they were doing were questions which even five thousand dollars' worth of power could not answer immediately. I had to make it work first. I hurried off to meet Johnny Hamid.

Astrology

"Alexander Vrykolakas," said Johnny. He took a large bite of his hamburger, so that I had to wait until he had swallowed it to learn more.

We were in a bar near the railway station. Johnny had suggested we meet there because it was central and he knew the proprietor, who would let us use his telephone if we needed it. Furthermore this place was a favourite with his cycling friends; there might be one or two guys around who could give us a hand, he said.

He finished the mouthful and swilled it down with Coke.

"Who's he?" I said.

"Well, it might not be him," he said. "Pity you didn't get the number of the car."

"You don't have to tell me that."

"Did you see what colour his hair was?"

"Now you mention it, I think it was red."

"That's him, then. That, and the car, and the other man, they add up. But I don't know much about him. He's Greek, and he's quite well off, but without being in any business that I know of, except magic and astrology, that kind of stuff."

He took another bite of his hamburger.

"Astrology? Do you mean he tells fortunes?"

37

"All that sort of thing. Only in a kind of amateur way, at parties, these days. I think, anyway. I know he used to do it for a living."

A thin, hawk-faced man went past us, clapping Johnny on the shoulder.

"Hi, Benny," Johnny said. "What are you doing these days?"

"Sitting around," said Benny. "You got anything you want doing?"

"May have. Has that other job finished?"

"Firm went bust."

"Hey, that's bad luck."

"Well, there you go. You racing tomorrow?"

"You bet."

"Well, good luck."

"You too, man."

Benny nodded to us, and went to sit at the far end of the bar and pulled a newspaper from his pocket.

"He's a mechanic," Johnny explained. "He used to be a good rider until he broke his leg."

"What did you mean by the other man?" I asked. "You said the car, and the other man, made you think it was Vrykolakas."

The last and largest piece of hamburger went into his mouth.

"Oh, hell, it's ridiculous," he mumbled. "I heard that the other man's a zombie. Vrykolakas killed him, then brought him back to life as a zombie, to work for him."

I gaped. "You're not serious?"

"I told you, it's ridiculous. But maybe if they'll believe in astrology, they'll believe in anything."

"But a *zombie*?"

"Well, that's what I heard."

"But why?"

"I don't know, Martin! I told you, I've never seen the guy. But this girl who has said he was almost like normal. He's some secretary or P.A. or maybe boyfriend or something."

"What do you know about Vrykolakas? Where did he come from?"

"He used to live in South America, Brazil or somewhere. About ten years ago Lydia Cavalcanti took him up. She used to be crazy about seances, all that kind of thing. And he's quite well off, as I said."

"Would this Lydia woman be able to tell us about him?"

"Not much now. She's very old and she dropped all this

38

astrology stuff years ago. Though there was something—what the hell was it?"

He leant back and ran his hand through his curly hair.

"Not a scandal, but something like a quarrel or a feud, I don't know. I was too young to take it in, except as gossip I might have overheard, you know? Vrykolakas had to leave the city for a while. Leave the country, as far as I know. But the thing was, Lionel Pretorius was involved. It was him Vrykolakas had the quarrel with. A business disagreement, maybe. There was something queer about it."

"What does he do now?"

"Turns up occasionally, advises businessmen about the best time to sign a contract, what shares to buy. And their wives about how to ditch their old lover or catch a new one. People who have money without having to work for it," he said soberly, "will pay for anything."

Catherine, I thought, what are you doing with this man? In your formal white blouse, with your hair tied up? And the look of serious attention on your face, that you used to keep for me?

"Where does he live?" I asked.

"He always stays at the Metropole when he's in town."

"Well then . . . I'll write a note to her, care of him."

"Why not go and see her?"

"It wouldn't be fair to her, if she doesn't want to see me."

"What if she just tells you to go away?"

"Then I will."

He frowned suddenly. "Have you thought she may have been kidnapped?"

"Well, no, not seriously. Christ. They couldn't expect much ransom. No, she can't have been. Look, I'll go and buy some paper and an envelope and you can take the letter and wait for an answer."

"Okay," he said.

Waste Not, Want Not
Ten minutes later, he was on his way. He'd be back in half an hour, if he got a reply. Meanwhile the hawk-faced Benny had come to sit in Johnny's place and begun to talk. I bought him a beer.

"You a rider?" he asked.

I shook my head. "Just a friend of Johnny's."

"Nothing to do with racing?"

"I'm afraid not."

He sipped his drink. He was tense; every so often he gnawed his lower lip.

"Johnny told me you used to race," I said.

"That's me up there," he said, and pointed to a photo above the bar. It showed the finish of a cycle race, and a younger Benny, head high and teeth clenched, crossing the line first.

"If I'd managed to keep going till I'd saved a bit, I'd have been all right. I was only twenty-three when I broke my leg. It was set badly."

"I couldn't help hearing you tell Johnny about your job. What happened?"

"Christ knows. Something's going wrong in a place where a mechanic can't find work."

"You mean this place? The city?"

"All over. I've worked in France, Italy, Belgium. Places closing down . . . What it is, they can't afford to repair machines these days. There's no money about—you noticed that? All the goods you want, bursting out of the shops, but no money for food and rent. No one's got any money."

"But I thought business was booming."

"It is, in the circles Johnny moves in."

We both fell silent for a minute or two. We had no point of contact. Except for money; he was obviously in want, and I had five thousand dollars, and I might not need it now that I knew where my wife was.

I might easily give him half.

The thought made me flush, and I felt dizzy and embarrassed. I looked at Benny. He was preoccupied, sipping his beer, with one arm along the bar that ran behind the chair. He didn't notice my gaze, and I looked away, and let my eyes run over the rest of the café.

It was a small place with an old-fashioned zinc-topped bar. In the corner, near the door, there was a pin-table, now being played by a bulky middle-aged man in a blue overall. The photo Benny pointed out was one of dozens pinned around the walls; cyclists with the names of their sponsors on their jerseys, brewers, textile manufacturers, tobacco firms, in their heraldic business colours.

Commerce was everywhere, and everywhere apparently successful. Only that morning I'd noticed how all the shops were full. But from Pretorius I'd heard of a man being shot as a kind of penalty for failing in business, and from Benny of the underside of prosperity . . .

Nothing was plain in this city.

The thought wouldn't go away: give him half the money.

"Have you always worked for other people?" I asked him.

"Not at first. I had a little repair shop."

"How much would you need to get it going again?"

"Like I said, you can't make a living repairing things. Make them or sell them, that's what I'd do. And that would cost thousands."

"Thousands . . . Why? What would you make?"

"Couple of things I've put together."

"You mean something you've invented?"

He put his beer down and frowned slightly. "Why?" he said after a pause.

"Are you talking about things you've invented?" I repeated.

"Invented . . . yes."

"Have you tried to sell them to a manufacturer?"

"They weren't interested. They'd be in competition with things they were already producing, I guess."

"What sort of things were they?"

"Mechanical things. A kind of bearing that'd be nearly friction-less. A self-sealing tyre valve. An automatic gear-change for a motor-bike. And a few more. That sort of thing."

"Have you patented them?"

He shook his head.

"But you must!"

"Do you know how much that costs?"

"If they're worth it, I could lend it to you."

"What do you want out of it?"

"Nothing in particular. Though . . ."

"Ah."

"Though if I thought there was a chance of it succeeding I'd like to put up some money towards making some of the things. Obviously it would benefit both of us."

"You serious?"

"Of course. As serious as I can be without knowing the value of your things. But I've got a bit of spare money right now, and I don't know what to do with it."

"How are you going to know if they're any good? Do you know anything about engineering?"

41

"I'd have to ask Johnny."

"I wouldn't want you doing that."

"Why not?"

"Because a good thing about young Johnny, he doesn't buy respect, he earns it. And in return I don't treat him as a rich guy, just as a racer. Now that's worth a lot. I don't want it changed."

"We needn't tell him they're yours at all. But I don't know who else I could ask."

"Maybe that wouldn't be so bad. I don't know. I'd have to think."

"Let me have your address," I said, "so that I can get in touch with you."

He wrote his name and address on the notepad I'd bought.

"Have you made working models of the things or are they just ideas?" I asked.

"I've got drawings of most of them. I've made the tyre valve and a couple of smaller things but I can't afford to make a model of the bearing or the gearbox. That's what I'd like to do."

"But could an expert tell if they'd work from the drawings?"

"I reckon so. I can."

He swallowed the rest of his drink and stood up.

"I'm in here most days, anyway, if you want to find me. But don't involve Johnny if you can help it."

He hesitated a moment, and then leant over and shook hands with me, and then went out.

I liked his scruples. And perhaps, by acting as a businessman, I might get closer to my wife.

After a while, Johnny came back.

"It's warm," he said.

He sat down, pulling the chair out with a clatter, and handed me a cream-coloured envelope, with my name written on it.

My heart lurched as I took it, and my fingers trembled as I tore it open. A florid script in green ink said:

Dear Mr Browning, I would be very happy if you would join me in my suite here at seven o'clock tonight. I look forward to meeting you. Knowing what you are looking for, I am sure you will be able to come.

Yours very sincerely,
ALEXANDER VRYKOLAKAS

42

I looked at Johnny. He shrugged.

"I went into the hotel," he said, "and the zombie guy was sitting there. As soon as I went in he came up to me and said to go with him, so I did. We went up to the third floor and he took me to Vrykolakas' suite. And as soon as we went in, Vrykolakas gave me that letter."

"Did you give him mine?"

"I asked if she was there. 'Just take that', he said. So I gave it to him, your letter, I mean, and he just put it on the table and waited for me to go."

"You mean he had it ready without knowing who you were or who I was or anything?"

"Looks like it."

I breathed deeply, and read it again, and showed it to him. We looked at each other, and then he scratched his head in amazement.

"What are you going to do?" he said.

"Go, of course. Are you going to come with me?"

"You bet."

"What was this other man like?"

"The zombie? Yeah, he was really strange. He was quiet and polite, he smiled a lot, like a machine. But there was something else—I might be wrong, I'm not sure, but I don't think he was breathing."

"What?"

"I watched him in the lift. He wasn't breathing at all, but he didn't seem to be holding his breath. Just—not breathing."

"This is crazy."

"I know. Maybe his astrology works, too, eh?"

"Thanks for going, anyway. I don't know when I'll be able to do anything for you."

"I'll think of something before long . . ."

We arranged to meet in Vrykolakas' hotel at half-past six.

Beware of Not Looking Closely Enough! Beware of Looking Too Closely! Beware of Not Looking at All!
Those days in Valencia, when I was so full of loss I was a negative man, a hollow space in the world; and when I was in an alien society and feeling like a river fish in the salt sea; crashing through invisible glass panes of convention and politeness; trying to be blunt in order to be simple and truthful, but being dazed by

43

everything and nervous at my own presumption, and retreating into equivocation and reticence; sensible hour by hour of the fading of my wife's image, watching it grow dim and generalised and hazy; feeling at the same time new parts of me growing hard, worldly, and assured—in those days, I began to change utterly.

The world lurched into familiarity like a new acquaintance in a bar. And I had only my own eyes to see it with, and no one to tell me what was true and what was false.

Maxims to live by: See the world for what it is, or pay the penalty.

What you see is what you are.

The stronger the imagination, the closer to reality are the forms it imagines.

And so on . . .

I sat on the bed in my rented room, and took my flute out of its case. The delicate silver mechanism of the keys was all the complexity I wanted, for the moment, and perhaps all I could manage anyway. I played some scales, and then stood up to play properly.

Since I was an orchestral musician, most of the music I knew by heart consisted of the flute parts from symphonies or overtures, and sounded thin and incomplete on its own. I thought that now I was a soloist by force of circumstances I had better set about acquiring a solo repertoire, and I tried to remember some of the chamber music I had played. Loeillet, Bach, Vivaldi, Handel, and finally Debussy . . . it was still there, and I played happily for an hour and a half in that shabby little room high up above the city, with the window open and the blue sky accepting the music indifferently; until the warm air from the sea, the salt and the flowers, made me feel sleepy.

I put the flute away and lay down, closing my eyes.

After a few minutes there came a knock on the door. I stirred, too drowsy to move, and opened my eyes.

"Come in," I said.

The door opened. I lifted my head to see who was coming in.

Before I saw the visitor, I smelt him, or her. It was like a fresh breeze of utterly clean air, smelling of the desert perhaps, or snow; or even of freshly ironed cotton. But more than that, it smelt of silence and clean vast spaces.

The visitor came in and shut the door. Was it a boy or a girl?

He or she was aged seventeen or so, and slim, and very beautiful. But not with the veiled, intoxicating beauty that Mary had; this

44

had a clarity like oxygen, so that I thought: a messenger from my wife.

It seems odd that in summer, when light clothes were worn by everyone, I should not have been able to tell the sex of my visitor. Because even when I looked straight at him, or her, I couldn't. The shirt was full, and may have concealed small breasts, or it may not, and the light blue jeans were tight over hips that curved just enough to be a girl's, but not so much as not to be a boy's. The face was disturbing, calm, angelic, and utterly lovely.

So I wasn't attracted, as I might have been by a girl, or interested, as I might have been in a boy; but touched, moved by my visitor's beauty; it was my heart that felt it, like a pang.

"Who are you?" I said quietly, sitting up.

"A messenger," said he or she, in a clear warm voice, and came to stand at the foot of the bed, looking at me dispassionately, but not without friendliness.

"From my wife? What does she want to tell me?"

"That you should go home, or stay here and build up your business, but not try to follow her until you're ready."

"Ready for what? Why aren't I ready now?"

"You're too hasty. You break things. Look at the back page of your newspaper."

The paper I'd bought that morning was on the floor beside the bed. I picked it up. On the back page there was a paragraph I hadn't seen. It was headed "Would-be Painter's Suicide", and it told how the body of Roger de Witt had been found by a policeman in a city park at ten the night before. He had taken an overdose of sleeping tablets.

I dropped the paper, feeling suddenly weak.

"Was that my fault?" I said. My voice was dry.

"You'll never know," said the messenger, "and nor will anyone else. Be careful. You have to know what the world is before you give it advice about changing itself."

"Where is my wife?"

The messenger shook his or her head. At that moment I decided quite arbitrarily to think of this being as a girl. I remember making the decision with a feeling of relief, not that I'd decided how to think of her, but that I'd found it possible not to think of Roger de Witt for a moment. I watched the messenger's hair, blonde and glittering and soft, moving gently as she shook her head.

"You're not telling me?" I asked.

"That's right."

"I don't understand anything. Even if—Roger de Witt was my fault, what else can I do wrong? What is there to break?"

"Everything. She knows you well, you see. There are two ways to her, music and business. But there's no direct way; it's too difficult and dangerous."

"I wouldn't be afraid," I said.

"Dangerous to others, not to you."

I felt completely crushed.

"What about Vrykolakas?" I managed to say.

"See him for what he is," said the messenger coldly.

I lay back, while the young slight form stood in the light of the window and said nothing. A lump came into my throat, for no other reason than her beauty.

"Be patient," she said, "and make yourself ready."

And then, by intangible degrees, I fell asleep.

The Zombie and His Master

It was half-past five when I woke up. Something had happened to change me; I felt quiet, subdued, but moved and full of emotion; as if I had fallen in love. I didn't know what to make of it. I was as likely to cry as to smile with happiness.

I had a shower and dressed in my new clothes, and went out to meet Johnny at the Hotel Metropole.

It was warm but fresh, with a breeze off the sea. The hotel was right on the front, a grandiose Edwardian building surrounded with palms, and with flags flying bravely from the great mansard roof.

I found Johnny in the bar. He was drinking tomato juice, and I ordered the same, wanting to keep a clear head.

I said nothing about the messenger. I wanted to decide what I felt about it first, and I might never get to the bottom of that.

"What do we do?" said Johnny.

"Be absolutely straightforward. Tell him what I want, and why. Be honest. Then if anyone tells lies, it won't be us."

"Well, it sounds good," he said, and grinned.

"Hey, Johnny, tell me: what do you know about Benny Hagen?"

"Benny? He's a good guy. I like him. He's a hell of a good mechanic. It's a shame he's out of a job."

He sipped his drink, and looked at me directly.

"You're probably thinking why don't I fix him up with a job," he said, "and I probably could, but then he probably wouldn't take it, and if he did we probably wouldn't be friends any more. That's what I meant this morning, in the café. You know? Don't think I haven't thought about it, because I have."

"I wasn't thinking of that at all."

"I know I live an unreal life, but there you are. The other guys I race with—they're all poor, all of them. It's their way of getting out of it and making their way, and they really fight for it, they really work like hell. . . . But I take it seriously too, Martin. You can't race unless you're serious about it. I pretend I have to win, as if I was poor like them, to make a race out of it, and because . . . I'd be wasting their time if I wasn't racing seriously. And sometimes I win, and sometimes they win, and that suits us all, because sometimes we can all forget how much money I've got, and have a good time."

He stopped, embarrassed, I thought. He grinned shyly.

"What the hell," he said.

I nearly told him about the messenger then. I wanted to confide in him, in return for his telling me that. I was sure he hadn't spoken to anyone else about it. But the messenger was still too close and private; so I told him what Benny had said about him.

"Why were you talking about me?" he asked. He sounded genuinely surprised that anyone should talk about him when he wasn't there, as if he thought there'd be many more interesting things to talk about. That was one of the reasons, I suppose, that the other racers liked him.

I thought a moment, and then told him about Benny's inventions, and my plans for lending him some money.

"But for God's sake don't tell him I told you. He made me promise not to."

"Of course I won't. But I know someone you can show the drawings to. We don't actually make things but we've got some good engineers in the company."

He looked at the clock over the bar. It was nearly seven. We found a pageboy to take us to Vrykolakas' suite on the third floor, and before we knocked at the door I asked him:

"Do you know Mr Vrykolakas? Has he stayed here before?"

"I have seen him, yes, sir. Very generous gentleman."

"Is there anyone else staying with him?"

"There was a young lady, sir, but she went this afternoon."

"Went? You mean left altogether?" I asked.

"Yes, sir."

Johnny and I looked at each other. We gave the boy a tip, and waited until he left. Then I knocked at the door.

It was opened by a man I recognised as the zombie. In the room behind him, someone was playing Chopin. The light was pink and subdued.

But if ever there had been a man killed and brought back to life as a wandering corpse, this was the man. His face was rigid, making me think that if I touched him it would feel like cold clay. His eyes were filmed, his smile fixed. . . . He stood as stiff as a statue, one hand holding the door. Being as stiff as cardboard he couldn't make the little shifting adjustments in balance we make with the soles of our feet and our toes, and had always to find a third point to hold or lean against.

"My name is Martin Browning," I said.

"Come in," he said, in a low, grating voice, having had to take in sufficient air to speak—for as Johnny had noticed, he was not breathing.

He stood out of the way and let us in.

It was the sitting-room of the suite. A large, long room, with rich modern furniture: thick fur rugs, long, low sofas covered in white leather, modern paintings spot-lit on the walls. The music was coming from a white-painted baby grand, which was playing by itself. So ready was I to see magic everywhere that when, after a few moments, I remembered the Pianola, I laughed to myself.

I looked around for our host. Then another door opened and he came in, his arms open as if to embrace us.

He wore a crimson silk dressing-gown, crimson trousers, crimson slippers; his dressing-gown was open at the neck, revealing a hairy throat and·chest on which nestled a little gold cross. Clouds of perfume enveloped him. His hair was as red as fire.

"My dear boy," he said.

He took my hand; I took it away.

"Not yet," I said. "Are you Alexander Vrykolakas?"

He stepped back slightly, and made a little shrug of surprise.

"Of course," he said.

"I am Martin Browning," I said, and held my hand out. He hesitated, and smiled, and shook it. "And this is my partner, John Hamid, whom you saw this afternoon."

He nodded briskly to Johnny. He had switched off his first

48

affected persona in an instant: now he was an important business-man relaxing.

"Good of you both to come . . . Now, drinks: what will you have?"

"Plain fruit juice for me," I said.

Johnny nodded, keeping very cool.

"Felix," said the astrologer. "See to it."

The zombie's face creased like a smile and he walked to the little bar in the corner, steadying himself when he got there by leaning forward against it while he opened the drinks.

"Now, sit down, fellers. Make yourself comfortable."

He gestured at the long, wide sofas. They were placed at right angles. He sat down himself, and we followed suit. His voice was puzzling me: its register was uncertain, or fluid, as much as his personality seemed to be. Nor could I place his accent.

"I've heard," I said, "that your servant is a zombie."

"Oh, Felix is too close to be a servant."

"How did he die?"

He laughed. "Felix, tell them how you died."

"The English killed me," said Felix, "by mistake."

In the subdued light, across a large room, Felix took on that superficial executive-style gloss I had noticed in the car. His neat haircut, small regular features, even a certain boyish hand-someness, again reminded me of a male model.

"How were you brought back to life?" said Johnny.

"By the good ministrations of Mr Vrykolakas," said Felix, and made a harsh staccato coughing noise. He was laughing. Vryko-lakas smiled.

Felix handed us our drinks and then went over to the far corner of the room and sat down, slumped in absolute stillness in an armchair. His eyes were open, unblinking and filmy.

"Business," began the mystic. "You sent a letter to a Mrs Browning *chez moi*. I haven't given it to her, because she had left when it arrived. I think you're unlucky."

"Without opening the letter, how did you know who had sent it?"

"By clairvoyance."

"I see. And where has she gone?"

"It seems to be her choice not to tell you. Perhaps I should do the same. But I may be able to offer a deal."

"Why did you say *a* Mrs Browning?" asked Johnny. "Does she call herself anything else?"

49

"If I tell you her name, it's as a sample of what else I can offer, when we do our deal. She calls herself Miss Anderson."

"What's this deal?" I asked.

"A simple matter of information. You have contacts denied to me in the family of a certain banker who pretends to deal in reality. I want to know firstly who are his partners in the Anderson Valley Project; secondly where precisely the Anderson Valley is; and thirdly what part your wife is playing in it."

"You want a lot in exchange for one piece of information," I said. I'd have to think carefully: if he didn't know that I didn't know that he didn't know what my wife was doing, there might be more he'd give away by accident. But I didn't like these games, and I wished he'd simply tell the truth. "Does your clairvoyance not cover most of what's on that list?" I went on.

"And why do you want to know?" asked Johnny.

"Simple reasons of business that I won't bore you with."

"How long did my wife spend with you?"

"A few hours."

"Where did she come from?"

"Now, come on, start trading. You don't get all this for nothing."

"My father," said Johnny, "Reza Hamid, is one of Mr Pretorius' partners."

"Who else?"

"Most of this is common knowledge," I said, guessing. "If you read the financial pages of the papers you should know it all anyway. Even without your clairvoyance."

"I've been away," he said smoothly, "and I want to catch up quickly. Besides, you're mistaken about clairvoyance. You can't turn it on like a light, it's a matter of infinitely subtle vibrations, and your higher self has to be free of all disrupting influences."

"The Teixeiras are in on the Project, and so is SAETA and René Lebesque," Johnny said.

"Good," said the astrologer, beaming. "Your wife has gone to America."

"North or south?"

"Well, that depends on whether I find out where the Anderson Valley is."

"It's in Paraguay," I said.

"Ah. Well, it may not surprise you to learn that the young lady has gone to South America."

"No, I don't suppose it does. I hope you don't mind, but I'm getting a bit tired of this game. I'm beginning to think you invited me here for no other reason than to taunt me. So: why did you invite me here?"

"If I wanted to taunt you I could have done it by mail. I wanted you here so that I could study your aura."

"And what can you tell from my aura now it's in front of you?"

"That you are a very suspicious young man. You don't even trust your partner, for instance."

"Where do you see that?"

"The colours of mistrust are very distinctive. And, I might say, corrosive."

"Now you've exposed my secrets to him, you'd better convince him of the truth of them. Tell him what I don't trust about him."

Johnny was sitting back low in the sofa, ankle on knee, relaxed, but following it with a keen interest. I was sure of him; but I wish we'd prepared ourselves better.

"He doesn't trust your perceptions," the astrologer said to him. "He doesn't trust your feelings. He thinks they're not fine enough to match his own. He doesn't mind the fact that you're Egyptian, it's not because of that, but he thinks that because you're a sportsman and express yourself through the body you can't have feelings as subtle and thoughts as complex as his own. So he wouldn't express his inmost thoughts and aims to you, not because he thinks you'd betray him, but because he thinks you wouldn't understand them."

And of course I was caught.

He'd won that round conclusively; and I hadn't dreamed it, but it was true . . . A turmoil of things, shame, anger, dismay, swept through me, and I blushed. Johnny sat still, and sipped his drink before he spoke.

"But that's not mistrust," he said. "That's just good sense. I don't understand what he's doing. I *am* simpler than he is. Why should he be so silly as to pretend otherwise? I don't see what you're getting at."

"But he does pretend otherwise," said Vrykolakas.

"I don't think he does."

"But he does! He pretends! He's always pretending!"

Johnny shook his head. As simply as that, he'd won. He looked at me and laughed. I chalked up another debt gratefully.

I stood up, and Felix imitated me.

"Your various replies have been most interesting," I said. "Thank you for letting us hear them. I'm sorry you couldn't tell me where

51

my wife is. I'm sorry too that she ever came to you. But I'm sure you'll realise that we intend to protect her if need be."

"One more thing," said Johnny. "Why do you surround yourself with artificial things? Are they just toys?"

The mystic looked nonplussed. Then he grinned wolfishly. "Exactly that," he said. "But his wife thinks more of them."

"In what way?" I asked.

"There are more ways than one of dealing in reality. Maybe some people will find that out before long."

Then he turned abruptly as if he'd said too much, and went to sit down at the piano. He stilled the automatic mechanism, and began to play something intense and chromatic. Felix shuffled politely to the door.

"Goodnight," said Johnny.

Vrykolakas took no notice. We opened the door.

"Goodbye, Felix," I said.

The zombie's cheek muscles contracted in a ghastly smirk as he shut the door behind us.

Research and Development

We strolled away from the haunted hotel. The evening all around us was becoming noisy and crowded, full of tourists spending money.

In a seafront café we drank beer. I asked Johnny if he'd ring his father and find out about the Anderson Valley.

"She must be there," I said. "It's silly to think otherwise."

"You're right," he said, and went off to find a telephone.

I sat and thought about the astrologer and his revelations. He seemed to be as much in the dark as we were, unless he had been bluffing. He was in competition with Pretorius, that was clear. So was my wife against Pretorius too, since she had been with Vrykolakas? But then the astrologer had asked me what part my wife was playing in it; which implied that she wasn't directly working with him. She might even be working with Pretorius, and investigating Vrykolakas on his behalf.

And the way Johnny had defended me: so easily and naturally. I was beginning to feel something like love for him. I felt things very easily that night, in the wash left by the passage of the messenger through my emotions.

When Johnny came back, he said, "The Anderson Valley Project. He doesn't know what it's about at all. Mining, maybe, it's

52

very rich in minerals up there, apparently, or maybe not. A lot of electrical stuff comes into it too. He knows of at least three big electronics firms that are involved. And he's invested quite heavily in dredging equipment and cranes and stuff like that, and a couple of new tankers, not big ones, though. For chemicals. You don't need to take oil to Venezuela.

"Anyway, the Anderson Valley's right up in the interior, in the middle of nowhere. They're opening it all up, with roads from the coast, railways, an airport, starting now. That's about it."

"But he doesn't know what it's about?"

"That's nothing unusual."

"But there must be millions involved."

"Don't forget we're shippers. What we carry isn't our concern, necessarily."

"I suppose so. I think we'd better go and find out."

"What?"

"Well, don't you? Apart from anything else, that's your money that's paying for all this dredging equipment and stuff. And you'll have to pay later on if it all fails."

"That's true."

"Could we go and ask him more about it?"

"Sure," he said, so we left the café.

Johnny's home was a tall building in a quiet square near the centre of the city. Jaguars and Rolls-Royces and Mercedes were parked under the trees across the road. There was a light on in an upstairs room, but otherwise the house was in darkness. Johnny opened the door.

"Come and say hello to my father and then we'll have some food," he said, putting on the hall light. He led me up the wide stairway and on to the landing.

He opened a door and looked inside, and spoke softly in a language I took to be Arabic. It sounded like a greeting. A deep, soft voice responded in the same language. Then it said "Oh, bring him in by all means."

"Come and meet my father," said Johnny.

The man was alone in the large, comfortable room; he looked oddly lonely. The room was furnished with the anonymous luxury provided by an expensive interior decorator. Johnny's father was bulky, with grizzled hair and heavy-lidded eyes. He got up, looking glad to see us, and shook hands warmly.

"Mr Browning," he said. "Johnny's told me about your search

53

. . . Welcome. Come and sit down. Have you found her yet?"

"No," I said, "but I think I know where she's gone."

"That's why we came back here. Well, part of it," said Johnny. "We think she's in Venezuela."

His father raised his eyebrows. "Hence your phone call?"

"Yep. Hey, look, we're hungry. Are you hungry, dad?"

"No. But Ibrahim is away . . ."

"I'll fix something," said Johnny, and left the room swiftly.

"I'm glad Johnny told you about what I'm doing," I said. "It's the only claim I have on people's interest, and I feel rather a fool explaining it."

"If something isn't your fault, it doesn't make you a fool, I think," he said.

"I was lucky to find Johnny the other night."

"Last night."

"So it was. But he's being very helpful. Without him I wouldn't have a clue about where to look."

"He's a good boy."

"Is he your only son?"

"My only child, yes. His mother is dead, so a lot depends on him."

"Forgive my curiosity. I'm trying not to be confused about things."

"Not at all," he said. "Has he told you about Mary Pretorius?"

"Oh, yes."

"She is a lovely girl. A pity she doesn't care for him. I would be glad if they married."

"In spite of religious difference? I thought that was an obstacle?"

"You know the saying, Paris is worth a mass? These things are often quite easy to manage. But tell me why you're interested in the Anderson Valley. Surely you don't think your wife's there?"

"Yes, I do."

"But there's nothing there. The place is totally bare."

"It won't be for long, I imagine."

"Indeed not . . . but she wouldn't be able to get there, anyway. Not to the Valley itself."

"Why?"

"Because it's guarded . . . Have you any idea of the money that's involved? I'm used to handling large sums, but I can't imagine how big this is. It's inconceivable. It's engaging the largest part of budgets of a dozen, two dozen, multi-national corporations. I'm

54

sure you've heard that old claim about the budget of General Motors? That it exceeds the budgets of several countries? Well, this is much bigger than that. They're bound to guard it, and keep it out of the way."

"But what's it for? What on earth are they doing?"

"Electronics comes into it, but it's not the whole of it. A large part of it is secret."

"Secret even from you?"

"Oh, yes. My company's big enough, but it's not as big as those I mentioned. The chief executives of those are privy to it, and few others. I'm only incidentally concerned: it's no more my business what's going on than it's the business of a lorry-driver what's in the back of his lorry. As long as it's not illegal in any of the countries he passes through, or dangerous, he has to carry his cargo, and he gets paid for it."

"I see what you mean. But to get back to my wife: the clue to where she might be was provided by a man called Alexander Vrykolakas. Do you know anything about him?"

He frowned slightly. "Is he in the city? Well, by repute I know him to be a pervert, a liar, a fraud, a blackmailer and many things besides. By repute, I say again. But he has quarrelled with many of my friends, quite unpleasantly. Whether he can perform magic is open to question."

"He tried to question us about the Anderson Valley Project. He wanted to know where the Anderson Valley was, for a start."

"What did you say?"

"I told him it was in Paraguay."

He laughed. "He had no need to ask. I'm sure it's on the map."

He got up and took a vast atlas from the bookshelf that covered one wall of the room. He searched the gazetteer and then shook his head, handing the atlas to me.

"I've got maps of it in the office, and I thought it'd be in here, but it's not. This is where it is, though."

He tapped the map of Venezuela at a point south of the Orinoco, where a high mountain range spanned the Brazilian border. There were no towns marked for hundreds of miles.

"Have you never wondered yourself what it's all about?"

"Yes, of course I have. For there are moral considerations too."

I was liking him more and more. I wondered for a second whether Johnny would have the same honest gravity, the same subtle humorous weight, when he was that age. I thought not;

55

he was more dreamlike, more lightweight and airy, like me.

A little silence fell. He seemed to be lost in thought.

"What I'd like to do," I said, gently so as not to break his reverie too sharply, "is to go there myself and see what's going on. And, of course, to see if I can find her."

"You'd better decide which is your primary purpose, then."

"I suspect they're indistinguishable."

"Quite possibly, And does Johnny want to go along with you?"

"I haven't mentioned it. Perhaps he might."

"I think it would be good for him. Though it's in the middle of his racing season."

"I didn't think you approved."

"Approval is neither here nor there. But of course I want him to do well, I'm glad when he wins . . . You see that shelf over there? Those are all his trophies."

I got up to look at them; silver cups and medals, and two framed photographs of Johnny in his racing kit, one as he crossed the line first in a race, one as he strained forward, teeth clenched, in a bunched sprint.

"I'm impressed," I said. "I know nothing about cycling, but . . ."

"He's good at it," said his father. "He's had one or two offers to turn professional, and turned them down out of consideration for me. Sometimes I feel like urging him to take them up—But I'm tired, I'm wandering from the point; you were talking about going to Venezuela . . ."

He rubbed his eyes. I returned to my chair.

"It occurred to me that perhaps you could advise me," I said, rather awkwardly. "Possibly even help a little. I'm not asking it for nothing. My idea was that if you could help me get a visa and so on in a hurry, in return I could send you a report on whatever I found going on in the Anderson Valley."

"You credit me with great powers," he said.

"If you wanted someone to go there urgently, it could be seen to, I'm sure."

"So am I. In fact I do know one of the officials. Perhaps my powers *are* great." He sounded a little surprised.

"Then you could?"

"I suppose so. When do you want to go?"

"As soon as possible. While the trail's still hot."

The door opened, and Johnny came in wheeling a trolley laden with food. His father laughed.

"Well, I'm hungry, even if you're not," said Johnny. "Help yourself. I've made some omelettes, and there's some cold chicken here, if you like that."

We ate for a few minutes without a word. When we'd finished his father said "And these reports you intend to make. What would they consist of?"

Johnny looked up in surprise.

"Whatever I saw, or heard, that sounded relevant, or looked important or interesting. Everything to do with it. Maybe my wife hasn't gone there, of course, in which case I won't spend much time there. But I'll go there first, so I'll see something, at least."

"What's this?" said Johnny. "I hope I'm coming too."

"I'd be glad if you would," I said.

"In spite of your racing?" asked his father.

"The racing I can come back to, but there's only one chance of this. Of course I want to go."

"Do you want to go as official envoys of Crescent Shipping, or privately?"

"Oh, privately," I said. "We'd have to be free agents."

"I see," he said doubtfully. "I hope it's going to be worth it . . . About those visas: you'd better come to the office tomorrow morning. I'll see the man about it. You can arrange your own passage, I take it?"

"Yes, we'll see to that. And thank you."

And after that we talked about other things; about business, about sport, about flowers, and about marriage. At ten o'clock I left, and went back to my quiet room, to think about the messenger.

The Parable of the Talents Needs a Bit More Small Print

I had to pretend a confidence about all this that wasn't native to me. This business of Venezuela frightened me for a dozen reasons. I didn't want to go, I wanted to stay where I was and find a safe job playing music in this flowery city; but I had begun to risk things and begun to win. I found my courage giving out before my luck, a pitiful state of affairs.

I had to go on risking, or lose everything.

My one way ticket to Venezuela cost 720 dollars. I had 4,250 dollars left. I went to the café Johnny and I had met in the day before and looked for Benny. He was there, sitting on his own. I bought him a drink.

I hadn't much time, so I went straight into what I wanted to say.

"I want to put up some money and back your inventions."

"What? You haven't looked at them."

"I haven't got time. I'm going to South America tonight, and I've got two thousand dollars spare. I could put it in the bank, but I don't want to. Now if I give it to you, we could sign an agreement of partnership, and you could get going. I know it's not very much, but one thing you can do is to get everything patented."

"Are you serious about this?"

I took out my cheque-book and wrote him a cheque for two thousand dollars. I tore it off and gave it to him. He looked at it as if he was unsure it existed.

"When you've patented them—you'd better get a lawyer to help do that, so as to get it absolutely watertight—you could use the rest of the money to make models or mock-ups or whatever of the most likely profit-makers. Then take them round the manufacturers. Or a good idea would be financial or business journalists, get them to write about you. A brilliant idea looking for a backer, that sort of thing."

"I suppose I could," he said uncertainly.

"Of course you could. But make sure if you find a taker that you don't sell it outright. Give him a licence to manufacture, and you get a fat royalty, which gets bigger the more he makes. Then you can set up manufacturing on your own, with that money."

He said nothing.

"Do you want to take it or not?"

"Yes," he said suddenly. "But let's do it properly. We've got to sign something."

He found a piece of paper, a handbill advertising a bicycle race that was to take place that afternoon. I tore it in half, and began to write, and then stopped.

"How much of a share am I acquiring?" I asked.

He shrugged. "In terms of money, a hundred per cent. That's all the money there is in the firm," he said, pointing to the cheque.

"Shall we say that when I come back, whenever that is, I'll be entitled to claim twenty-five per cent of whatever you've made, but in any case not less than this?"

"As long as it could be taken out without harming the business," he said.

"Oh, yes."

"And why twenty-five per cent? You could claim more than that. Most people would take fifty-one per cent."

"If it succeeds, twenty-five per cent will be a lot of money anyway. And the other clause means I won't lose, whatever happens."

"Fair enough. You better write that down, then."

I wrote down the agreement in as unambiguous a way as I could, on each of the pieces of paper; and we both signed the two of them, and kept one each. Then we shook hands, and parted.

It wasn't much money, in comparison with the vast amounts involved in the Anderson Valley Project. It was minute; it hardly existed. But it was going to work. I had no idea of what I should have claimed; whether I was entitled, since I had put up all the capital, to claim all the reward, or whether Benny as the inventor should have had more than seventy-five per cent, or less . . . No idea. I thought twenty-five per cent was about right. I hoped he would do his best.

Androgyny

The day after I left the city was the day of sports. During the Festival of Flowers, every day was a climax, and this was one of them. Football matches, horse races, and a mock tournament on the water, where the great barges owned by the guilds and companies jousted like percherons of the sea.

One of the events of the early afternoon was the bicycle race on my torn handbill. It was the one in which Johnny was riding, and I thought I'd go and watch it.

The city was thronged. Police on motorcycles roared up and down, clearing the Boulevard, swinging their big machines lightly around the corners, the sunlight glinting on chrome handle-bars sun-glasses, guns. Tourists, smelling of sun-tan lotion, loitered or bustled.

I came to the square where the finish was to be. The road surface was railed off and painted with white lines. Overhead were hung banners and flags, and loudspeakers at the corners of the square blared a commentary, but so loudly that I couldn't understand it.

The press of people near the barriers was dense and excited, but I managed to find a way through.

Then they were in the square, and I had a different view of Johnny. There was a rushing sound, first, like the wind. Then the concentrating intense sound of smooth machinery, not powered by an engine, but by human muscles. The sound of well-greased chains passing through intricate combinations of gears, almost silently, but making something like a ticking noise, as each link in the chain came into contact with one of the teeth of the chainwheel. And the swift rattle and snap as the mechanism moved the chain from one gearwheel to the next.

But the rush of air, the impression of straining speed, was enthralling, as if men had become welded together by the effort into one powerful machine.

The riders' muscles were all developed in the same way. Their forearms and shoulders and particularly their thighs were heavy and powerful, dark with a summer's racing in their skin. Their legs were as smooth as a woman's legs, being shaved. Below the crossbar everything was delicacy and lightness, in contrast to the muscularity above. Their calves were slender. Their white anklesocks and black light shoes like dancers' pumps; the glittering intricacy of the naked machinery; the sun shining on the spokes, making them look like two intersecting lines of twinkling fire; the thin hard tyres, the lightness of the wheels; it was all graceful, airy, almost feminine.

Then they were gone, but in a minute they were round again. They all wore helmets made of strips of padded leather, and light leather gloves. They had numbers pinned to the bottom of their jerseys at the small of their back, and tight black shorts that reached midway down their thighs. This costume had something fixed and hieratic about it, as particular and specialised as the bullfighter's suit of lights, as unchangeable.

Johnny was right in the middle, looking cool and abstracted as he leant fiercely into a bend, snapping his chain on to a higher gear, head down, legs moving smoothly.

As the race wore on the field spread out. One rider would lead for three or four laps, and then fall back and be overtaken by another. For a time Johnny led.

When it was time for the last three laps I saw a group of riders, Johnny among them, burst forward with increased speed. They got away from the rest and sped off to race it out between themselves.

The race was to end on the far side of the square, and as the leading group entered for the last time each rider began to swerve, weaving his bike from side to side, leaning on it and swinging from right to left, out of the vertical, in order to increase the pressure on the pedals. But this was dangerous, because two of them collided and crashed, bringing down one other who was behind them.

Then the winner crossed the line, and raised his arms in a victory salute: there he was, my friend, the winner, celebrating his last day in Europe.

And the next moment, I'd forgotten all about him.

Goodbye to the City

When I turned away from the cycle race, I found the messenger standing beside me.

She was waiting for me to turn, looking at me; and then she smiled. Sometimes in a crowd you see a face that draws your attention like a magnet, with such sudden surprising beauty that your head swims, you feel short of breath as if you had been hit in the chest—has no one else noticed her? No one else has even seen her—and so on; falling in love.

And sometimes the face is accompanied by the memory of a dream, and here she is in life, and you are still in love. All the tormenting force of memory, the past, of heart-aching Arcadian dreams.

I moved closer to her, trembling.

The oxygen-clarity, the fresh ironed cotton smell, overcame me. I felt giddy and dared not say anything.

The crowd was thick. People were struggling to move away from the barriers and away towards the Boulevard. I felt as if I was leaving a trail on the world, as if it was a cloud chamber. I was charged with potent electricity. I had to touch her or burst.

I took her by the shoulders, and, very nearly sobbing, crushed her to my chest, burying my mouth in her hair and in the clean fresh smell of her neck. No one noticed. She embraced me in response. There were little flowers in her hair, rosebuds.

El Cambista had planned this, I thought, it's all unreal.

She slipped out of my embrace and took my hand. We moved out of the square and into the Ocean Boulevard. Floats covered in millions and millions of flowers were going past, bearing bathing-costumed girls called "Tulip Queen", or "Rose Queen", or whatever. Military bands were playing.

We came to a door, a bank, closed today because of the festival, locked shut. She put her hand on it and it opened.

Inside it was cool and smelt of wax polish, and of money. A dark wide corridor, with two open doors, and a leather-covered couch. As the door shut, with the heavy whisper of a great weight, we seized each other and clung like demons, afraid to move.

After a minute of tightly-held stillness we let go and sat down on the couch. I opened my mouth to speak, to say I don't know what, but she put her hand over my lips.

She might not have been a person at all. I was thinking of angels, or nymphs, not of human love. But the feeling itself was for her as an individual being, as Leucippus' was for Daphne, though she was a nymph and he a mortal. And she had not loved him, and he'd been torn to pieces when his disguise was penetrated, for he'd dressed, like Achilles, as a girl, and then the nymphs bathed naked. Sensations of intoxicating danger, similar danger, surged through my veins. I kissed her. All the time I drank deep lungfuls of the smell of her, the smell of air at a great height above the earth, of cold blue air; and her mouth tasted of infinite cleanliness, of sweet nothing.

We lay back on the couch, the cool leather that smelt of money, and held each other tightly.

What would I find when she took off her clothes? Would she have a boy's sex, or a girl's, or some inconceivable both? Or would she be blank and smooth like a statue?

I must try to say all this as clearly as I can. It was very hard to realise what was happening. She had a face and figure of extraordinary, angelic beauty and happiness; and yet, and yet, there was an air about us in that corridor, as if it arrived on a breeze of possibility, of viciousness or perversity; if those words can be understood without their connotations of disapproval.

I'll describe what we did, or what she made me do.

We were wearing similar clothes: jeans, T-shirts, sandals. So her arms were bare. They were golden and covered in the lightest of down. They had the flatness of a boy's and were as soft as a girl's. Did she have breasts? Yes, very small—my hand would seem to crush them flat, so that they weren't there at all. Her sides, her stomach, were flat and boyish, but her hips swelled slightly, so that her jeans, sky-blue, were tight over them.

When it got to the point when we would have to undress, she shook her head, and smiled. She made me leave my T-shirt on and push my trousers down to my knees. Then she lay face down on the couch, and with a swift movement unfastened her own jeans and pushed them down. She was wearing nothing underneath.

I was not to be allowed to know for certain what sex my lover was. We were to come together in the only way that would preserve my ignorance.

I tried to whisper, to caress him or her, to make love in the ways advocated by manuals of sexual conduct. But it was all inappropriate. The messenger did not move, beyond indicating in the baldest possible terms what I should do.

But then she turned and looked over her shoulder, just once. She smiled with seraphic confidence, and a flood of happiness surged into my mind. The look on her face reminded me of my wife, but that didn't matter. In some ways it even endorsed it all, because I saw my wife's expression in those eyes, her soul looking out of them. This was the message she'd sent.

But still I hesitated. I didn't know what to expect. The messenger sensed my indecision, and helped me, and we came together gently.

I dared not move, and hardly dared think. I didn't know what it meant, I didn't know anything. She had managed to evoke all the shame in my nature, and at the same time keep it at bay, where I could observe it.

And as I considered the relation our bodies were in, and reflected on the strange nature of hers, or his; the softness, the stillness; the almost tingling feeling I had, like a very cold spring, or a mild electrical current; I looked at us both, and felt utterly clean, purified, transformed.

I lay still. She was breathing gently, her eyes closed. She was still entirely a mystery. And still, now I was calm, still androgynous.

Time went by. When we were still again, she told me in a whisper to move aside and shut my eyes. I did so. I heard the rustle of cloth and the sound of a zip, and then her voice. She was standing.

"You want to know why this has happened. You'll never know, though; it might be a lesson or it might be a reward, or it might be an accident without any meaning at all.

"But it won't happen in Venezuela.

"You'll have to change a great deal if you want to find your wife. And if you find her you might discover that she's changed as well, and that nothing is what it was. And it would still be better if you stayed here."

She bent over to kiss me, and I closed my eyes. The last thing I saw was her blonde hair, with the little flowers in it. They were faultless buds, perfect and beautiful; and of all the flowers I had seen in Valencia, they were the most remarkable, because they were artificial.

63

⇥ PART TWO

Night in the Tropics
Johnny was dozing. When the plane was about to land, I woke
him up and pointed out of the window. He yawned and looked.

The lights of Venezuela lay below us. A wide curving corniche,
lit by swathes of green and gold neon, swept along the seafront.
Ahead of us were the smoky glow and the tall light-bearing towers
of an oil refinery. Through the wide harbour mouth a grand liner,
ablaze with light, moved slowly out to sea.

"That's the *Khorasan*," said Johnny. "It's one of ours."

As we circled above it all, I drank it in with my eyes, greedily.
Infinite possibilities burgeoned in the night, in the dark unconscious
hinterland and the glowing Caribbean littoral.

The plane began its final approach, the noise of the engines
sinking as we flew lower and then surging up with a roar just
before we touched the water. We touched down with a massive
hammering noise and a pounding of spray; then immediately
slowed down and became a boat, moving gently forward in the
oily water.

The pilot brought the plane to a halt about a hundred metres
from a long concrete pier, which glowed bright grey in the darkness, over its reflection. Doors opened, and the cold air of Europe
disappeared into the tropics.

The plane was tied up to a buoy. A motor-boat pulled up alongside, and the first passengers got into it. When it was full another
took its place, and it was our turn to get in; we descended the
steps shakily.

The night was huge, the stars unfamiliarly large. The scents of
the land were not only those of flowers and strange vegetation, but
of spices, of smoke, of petroleum, of pitch, of hot food, of animals,
of blood, and of salt water and fish.

In a reverie, I sat hunched in the boat. It was Johnny's turn,
then, to nudge me as we drew alongside the steps up to the pier.

65

I gathered my wits. We went into the Customs shed and waited for our luggage, with the distant clang of huge metal doors, the hum of electricity, voices shouting amiably in Spanish, a transistor radio somewhere over the water, with a disc-jockey and salty Latin music.

Then we were outside, on the wide brightly-lit concrete roadway that ran the length of the pier. And there we had our first surprise. A sleek American car drew up beside us, and a plump man in a white suit got out, beaming and extending his hand.

"Mr Hamid! Mr Browning! I am so pleased to meet you! Mr Pretorius has asked me to look after you. Would you care to come this way, please?"

Johnny said "Who are you?"

"My name is Joachim, sir, at your service. We are expecting you."

"How does Mr Pretorius know we're here?" I asked.

"Oh, come, Mr Browning! A man of his eminence naturally knows what's going on. His concern is only for you, believe me. Your rooms are booked at the Excelsior Hotel—everything laid on —you are to be his guests for as long as you stay here. And I, an accredited guide, will introduce you to the beauties and delights of this truly lovely and prosperous community."

His manner was brisk and deferential at the same time. I made up my mind and got in the car.

"Hey, man," said Johnny, "wait a minute."

"It's a free lift into town, if nothing else," I said.

He got in beside me, and said "Mm."

"Good, good," said Joachim, and got in the driver's seat and started the car.

"Where are we going now?" said Johnny.

"To the hotel. You will want to rest after your flight, no doubt. Then in the morning we decide where you would like to go, what you would like to see, all that kind of thing, courtesy of the Pretorius Bank."

"We want to go to the Anderson Valley," I said.

"Ah," he said, and nodded slowly.

"Can you take us there?"

"Well, that is not so easily done, you know, sir, at this time of year."

He stopped at a red light at the end of the pier. Traffic was flowing heavily through the port area: taxis, buses, and huge articulated trucks. Joachim gestured at it all happily.

"A beautiful thing, business," he said. "Sometimes I come here at night just to watch that flow of traffic in and out. A beautiful thing."

The light changed, and the car surged forward. Johnny looked at me, and raised his eyebrows.

"Another thing I forgot to mention," said Joachim, swinging the car out into a wide tree-lined street that led towards the city centre. " Miss Pretorius is here."

Johnny sat up suddenly. "What?" he said. "Mary?"

"Yes, yes," said the guide genially.

"Why? What's she doing here?"

"You will be able to ask her," said Joachim, "when you see her in the morning."

"I don't understand," said Johnny.

"You'll take us to the Anderson Valley, then?" I said.

"Well, as I said, it's difficult . . ."

"Then we'll find our own way, that's all."

"It may be possible. I'll see."

"Where is Mary staying?" asked Johnny.

"With a friend of her father's," said Joachim.

The hotel was large and glossy. Joachim left us when we were installed, and said he'd call back in the morning.

It was half-past midnight, but neither of us was tired. We sat in Johnny's room with a drink of whisky and tried to work out what Pretorius was doing.

"He doesn't want us near the Anderson Valley, that's obvious," said Johnny. "But how did he know we were here, anyway?"

"Oh, a man of his eminence," I said vaguely. "*That* doesn't surprise me. I'm surprised it surprises you. But I don't see why he sent Mary here."

"Maybe to split us up," he said.

"Would it?"

He looked out of the huge picture window at the view of the harbour. "I don't know," he said. "It all depends. I don't like it."

"You just don't like Pretorius," I said.

"Do you?"

"I hardly know. I don't think I hate him, but I don't think I like him either. He's out of range of all that sort of thing."

"Yes, maybe," said Johnny moodily.

"I think that he might arrange things up to a point, but then he'd stand back and watch what happened, without interfering, and

67

he might even be glad if the people he was watching took things into their own hands, or fought back, or something. That's just a feeling."

"He watches Mary night and day, and she doesn't give a bugger."

"Let him watch, then, if he wants to. I'm going to the Anderson Valley."

"Well, so am I."

He spoke as if it was the most natural thing in the world for him to come with me, and that cheered me up. A little while later we went to bed.

The Air

As soon as I woke up, I rang Joachim the guide and told him that we were going to the Anderson Valley that very day, whether or not he cared to come with us. He protested and eventually gave way.

"All right!" he said. "I'll arrange it. Miss Pretorius will have to come too, and it is not kind to her, in this hot climate. Better to leave it for a little while."

"Today. I'll see you later. Pick us up in two hours."

And when that conversation was over, I hurried out of the hotel to find some shops. I bought a rucksack, two knives, and some dehydrated rations. There were many other things that I might have bought, but I thought a poncho for each of us would be the most useful; so I bought those, and went back to find Johnny eating toast and scrambled eggs.

"He called back to say how difficult it was," he said. "But he'll be here in an hour."

I ate quickly. Into the rucksack we put everything we needed: our money, the dried food, the knives, a spare shirt each, and my flute.

"If Mary comes," he said, and then stopped.

"Yes?"

"I don't know."

"Do you want to go and get some stuff for her?"

"Like what? All this stuff? Knives and so on?"

"Well, what do you think?"

He shook his head, looking bewildered. "I don't know," he said, and sat down on his bed. "I don't want her to get hurt."

68

"She won't."

"You must be expecting . . ." He gestured at the rucksack. You expect us to have a tough time, he meant, and she's coming with us.

"I don't know what to expect. We'll look after her."

He nodded slowly, and then grinned, so that his eyes lit up. How could Mary fail to love him when he looked like that?

When Joachim arrived he greeted us reproachfully and led us down to a taxi. Mary was sitting in the back.

She was looking cool, faintly amused, and a little tired. The mystery that I'd noticed that night on the terrace was still there, but she had an air this morning of being withdrawn and detached. Her invisible veils worked even in the light of the tropical sun, I decided; she would never get sunburnt, for instance, never even slightly brown.

"Hello, Johnny," she said. "And Martin. Don't we get around."

"Mary, what's going on?" I asked.

"Oh, hush," she said. "I want to talk to Johnny."

He was bemused, hypnotised. She smiled at him, and he blushed. She leant across to him and whispered something in his ear, and not wanting to watch them I turned to Joachim, who was sitting in the front.

"Tell me about the Anderson Valley Project," I said. "Why don't you want us to go there?"

"Oh, no, no, no," he said. "Please. Haven't I arranged a flight for you? Isn't that what you want?"

"Yes, indeed, and thank you very much. But what is it? What's going on there?"

"It will be," he said, "the biggest and most exciting business project in the world, but I cannot tell you what it is. Look over there—you see that queue of men by the fountain?"

A long line of raggedly-dressed men, mostly Indians and blacks, stood patiently along one side of the square we were driving through.

"They are recruits for the labour force," Joachim explained. "We recruit workers from all over South America, Central America, Puerto Rico, all over. Many Indians leave their poor villages and farms to join us. It's good pay, you bet."

We drove past a huge baroque church. Outside it a priest was blessing a convoy of trucks, laden with machinery, and with men sitting wherever they could find room to perch. While they were being blessed, they all removed their hats, and as we drove past, they all put them on again.

"They're going there," said Joachim, "to help build a road through the mountains. The Church takes an active part in our work."

The taxi took us out of the city to a small airfield, where a two-engined plane stood at the end of a runway. It was being refuelled from a tanker; the pilot was peering into a hatch that opened into one of the engines.

Joachim paid the driver and we all got out.

Mary stood rather unsteadily by the steps of the plane. She was wearing a white flowered dress, and carrying a large bag and a floppy straw hat. She put the hat on to shade her eyes from the sun, and instantly looked even more remote and mysterious, like a figure from a cinema screen.

Johnny, solicitous, hovered beside her. He helped her up the steps, then turned to look at me with a complex and disturbed expression; and then followed her inside.

I went up after him, carrying the rucksack. It was a very new plane, clean and neat and tidy, with six passenger seats. The pilot, a slight middle-aged man, finished his inspection and came into the aircraft.

"Good morning," he said. "I am Captain Perez, and we will take off in about five minutes. You," he said to me, "you want to come and see how to fly?"

"Thank you," I said.

So I sat in the right-hand seat beside him and watched as he flew the plane. Johnny and Mary were talking, and Joachim was beaming proprietorially out of the porthole. As I listened to the throbbing of the two engines, I unfolded the noise of them in my head, just as I was used to hearing chords separate themselves into their different notes; and I heard that under the roar, the engines were not quite beating together, that the left one was a little irregular. I remarked on it to the pilot.

"Yes, I know," he said. "I was looking at it when you came. Nothing important." He was so at ease and so calm that I felt reassured, and forgot about it.

The countryside below us was flat and uninteresting at first, with farms and plantations as regular as the farmlands of northern Europe. But as the morning went by, the tameness went out of it.

After an hour we came to a broad river speckled with islands:

the Orinoco. On the southern side of it, the country was wild, and we had to climb, because mountains were rising below us. I asked the pilot if he had taken people to the Anderson Valley before.

"Many times," he said. "But only since one year. Before that, was nothing there. Now, a big landing strip, buildings, many things."

"What sort of buildings?"

"I don't know. Factories, maybe."

We flew on, and time went by. I began to feel drowsy; the sun beat full into the hot cockpit, and I hadn't slept much the night before.

Then the port engine suddenly cut out. The propellor stopped and the plane lurched. Perez grabbed the control, and pulled it back level.

"What's happened?" I said stupidly.

"The engine stop, that's all. Fuel feed pipe is come loose again. I fix it for good when we get there."

"Can we get there on one engine?"

"You see me panic? Course we get there."

I didn't see him panic, but he was sweating. So was I. I looked at the jungle again; we had lost some height and it was discernibly closer.

Joachim came forward. He spoke quickly and anxiously in Spanish. Perez grunted.

"We crash, we crash," he said and grinned at me. "I pick a nice fat tree, we land on that. Anyway, one engine is plenty."

Joachim hesitated, and then went back to his seat. Perez spoke on the radio, reporting the incident.

"Where are we?" I said. "Can I see a map?"

He handed me a transparent plastic envelope. A map inside it was marked in red ink with a circle around the Anderson Valley. He pointed to our position: a good two hundred kilometres to the north of it. There was no town, no village, nothing; just the eternal jungle.

If we get there, I thought, we'll have to stay until the plane's mended.

Time went by. Perez smoked two thin black cheroots, lighting the second from the butt of the first.

Then Johnny came up to the front. Perez repeated what he'd told me, and Johnny nodded.

Then he said "Mary's father sent her to put us off. She's supposed to keep us distracted, or something."

"Did she say why?"

"She hasn't said anything clear at all. I don't understand a thing."

"Shall I go and talk to her?"

"Yes, do. I think she's in a trance, or something."

I stood up. Johnny's expression was utterly miserable. I punched him gently on the shoulder, and morosely he nodded.

"You want to sit down, learn to fly?" said Perez.

"I know how to, but I will, thanks," said Johnny, and he took my place.

I went back and stood next to Mary. After a few seconds she turned from the window, and raised her eyebrows slightly.

"So," she said.

"So, indeed. May I sit down?"

"Don't be so fucking polite," she said graciously.

I sat down.

"What did your father tell you about all this?" I asked.

"He told me not to bother my pretty little head about that but just to keep you and Johnny occupied. I'm supposed to distract you. Am I doing that?"

She spoke in a still, husky voice, and I noticed that her eyes were shut behind her sunglasses.

"Are you all right?" I said.

"Oh, I had some bloody pill or other and it sent me to sleep. And I don't like flying, it makes me feel ill."

The pilot's cheroots weren't helping, either. She sat back, curled up and still in her seat.

"I don't know what to do," she said.

"Then come with us, come and look for my wife."

"I don't know."

"I'm not working against your father, you know. I can't imagine why he behaves as if I am."

"He's a very subtle man," she said.

But I never found out what she meant by that, because just at that moment, the other engine failed, and the plane lurched sideways. The silence was frightening. Mary gasped, and sat up. I sat up too, rigid with expectation. At any moment I anticipated a blinding crash and oblivion; then sense took over. We were flying level again, or gliding, at any rate.

Joachim was gripping the arm of his seat and staring fixedly out of the porthole. So was Mary.

"Do your belt up," I said.

She blinked, and nodded, and did so.

I went up to stand behind Perez.

"Ah," he said. "Give me a cigarillo, in that pocket there, of my coat."

I reached him the packet.

"What are we going to do?" I asked.

"Find a nice fat tree, like I said."

Johnny had been sitting stock still. He turned and said "Go back to Mary."

"Yeah," said Perez, "go and sit down. Hey, Señor Joachim," he called, "put your belt on. Go on, hurry," he said to me.

"Pick somewhere good," I said.

"Don't worry about it," he said.

We were gliding lower and lower; I could see individual trees. I collected the rucksack and sat down next to Mary, and fastened the belt. We clung on to each other's hands.

Johnny should be sitting here, I thought, it isn't fair.

I could hear the air rushing over the wings and making the radio aerial hum. Inside the plane there was no sound at all. We shut our eyes.

Vegetation and Plunder

When I woke up the first thought I had was that we had all been drowned. The light was green and sub-aqueous, and everything was cool. But my eyelids were heavy, and I fell asleep again.

And I was washed into wakefulness again a moment later. Washed in and out, like a body washed up on the shore. Eventually I was awake. I could smell things: petrol, and vegetation, and a woman's scent.

I heard the screeching cry of something, a parrot maybe, a long way above.

I smelt Perez' black cheroots.

I saw the seat in front of me, tilted at some silly angle. And there was a stiff thick odd-shaped bracket supporting the ceiling that I hadn't noticed earlier on; it didn't harmonise with the rest of the décor at all, it was art nouveau—

Well, it's a real branch, I thought stupidly.

An alarming creak came from underneath us, and the plane moved a little.

I didn't want to move too suddenly. We might be only one metre off the ground, but we might be twenty. I pressed Mary's hand, then shook her arm gently. No response.

"Johnny," I called. My voice quavered. Again no response.

"Johnny? Captain Perez? Joachim?"

No one said a word. I leant forward so that I could look past Mary and through her window, but I could see only a clump of dark fleshy leaves.

I would have to move.

Bracing myself against the ceiling and balancing cautiously, I stood up. My legs were weak.

Joachim was lying crumpled on the floor, perfectly still, his eyes open, dead. His neck was broken. In the cockpit I could see Perez' back and arms and head, resting across the instrument panel. Of Johnny I could see nothing; but through the shattered windscreen I could see the ground, a couple of metres down.

Already the jungle was claiming the plane; a fat golden spider about the size of my thumbnail marched across the floor.

I turned back to Mary and squeezed her shoulder.

"Mary," I said. "Wake up! Wake up!"

Her head moved from side to side. I shook her shoulder gently and then went forward again.

Perez was dead. His head had struck the instrument panel and his skull was fractured. He was pressed against the panel like a lover; the cheroot, no longer burning, was lodged at the bottom of the windscreen.

"Johnny!" I called.

Could he have been thrown through the windscreen? I stepped gingerly past the body of Perez and unfastened the door. As it swung open the plane lurched forward a little way, and I clung on to the seat until it was still again.

Then I jumped out and fell heavily to the ground, trembling. I stood up and looked around, pushing aside the thick fronds of some climbing plant.

Johnny was lying some way in front of the plane, his back twisted. He was dead, and a sob of fear came to my throat. Oh, many things, but fear first, and then love, anger, bitterness, affection . . . I cried, fell to my knees, and embraced his warm body.

Another screech from the trees above. An ant walked across

74

Johnny's open eye, and I stood up hastily, feeling him alien now, and beyond my reach.

I climbed back into the plane and looked at Mary. She was still unconscious. I saw a little box on the wall with a red cross on it, and opened it gratefully; but all I found were aspirins, a bottle of iodine, some quinine tablets, and a roll of sticking-plaster.

"Mary," I said despairingly.

Her eyelids fluttered. I squeezed her shoulder, and this time she woke up. Suddenly she opened her eyes wide and lay absolutely still while she looked at me.

"What's happened?" she said. "Where's Johnny?"

"I'm afraid he's dead. We crashed. They're all dead."

No reaction.

"Can you move?" I said. "Are you hurt anywhere?"

"Where are we?"

"I don't know. In the jungle. Look, try and sit up, see if you're hurt."

"They're all dead?" she muttered. She hadn't taken it in, but she sat up, with a struggle, and tried to undo her belt. Like mine, her hands were trembling; after a couple of seconds, she flapped them feebly and turned mutely to me for help. I unclipped the belt and helped her stand up.

"Where's your bag?" I said.

"Up there . . . somewhere, I don't know," she said, indicating the rack above the seats. I groped along it and found not only the bag, but a real prize: a small hatchet clipped to the bulk-head.

I gave her the bag and checked to see whether there was anything else that might be useful. Perez' lighter, obviously; and in Joachim's pocket there was a wallet stuffed with Venezuelan Bolivars. Not much use in the jungle, but we were still in Venezuela, and it might be useful later. And Joachim had something else: a gun.

It was tucked into a shoulder-holster and at first I didn't see it. It was small, blue-metalled, and very heavy. I was in two minds about it. Doubtless in the hands of an expert it would be useful, but I had never seen a real gun except in the holsters of policemen, let alone handled one.

I took it anyway. We would only regret it otherwise, and we could always throw it away. I found a spare clip of ammunition in another pocket. I put everything except the hatchet in the rucksack, and as an afterthought added the contents of the first-aid box; and then helped Mary climb down out of the plane.

"What are we going to do?" she asked.

Well?

I don't know, I thought . . .

Mary stood close to me and kept looking around her, fearfully.

The jungle was stifling. The heat was appalling; there was no breath of wind under the vast canopy, and the air was thickly laden with moisture.

I started to move, taking a direction at random, and she followed.

The trees were huge, cathedral-sized, towering so high that their tops were invisible. Their trunks were correspondingly enormous. In between them was a crowded clambering mass of all kinds of vegetation: bushes, vines, shrubs, flowers, fungi. It was all feeding on the rest, gorging and stuffing and absorbing in order to grow and bloat and wax and die, showering hundreds of seeds in the effort to make hundreds of plants grow where one grew before, and nearly succeeding.

The growth was so feverish that some seeds, unable to find a patch of soil, had lodged in the cracks of bark or the angle of a branch and started to grow there, so that one tree might have four or five different kinds of flowers, at different stages of growth, blooming on its trunk.

And then there were the insects, monstrous armed beetles, clawing laboriously at leaves; butterflies as big as my hand, fluttering languorously; dragonflies, ants, flies, spiders, their webs hung like hammocks, heavy with moisture, so that I almost expected to see their fur, too, damp with sweat; fat bourgeois centipedes, black and polished, as long as my finger; small, dandy-like frogs . . . We could not move without stepping on some life-form. We were bitten several times, but as far as we could tell, harmlessly.

Eventually we attained a sort of rhythm. I would clear a space with the hatchet, chopping through the worst of it and shoving the rest aside, and Mary, holding the rucksack, would follow into the space I had just left.

We were going upwards. It wasn't easy to sense, but every so often a gap in the encircling trees, a less tangled patch of ground, made it clear that we were climbing a slope. After about an hour

76

of hacking and chopping, I dropped the hatchet and sat down on a fallen trunk.

"It's getting steeper," I said.

She sat down beside me. She was grey with fatigue, near to collapse. I took her hand.

"Once we get to the top of this slope, it'll be easier to see where we are. We could make a fire and maybe someone'll see it."

"I'm so thirsty," she said.

So was I; I hadn't realised. Near us hung a branch laden with brownish, wrinkled, apple-sized fruits. I plucked one and cut it open. It had a mass of pink creamy flesh and seeds like pomegranate. I tasted a little, carefully. It was sweet and bland, but the seeds were like grapeshot.

We ate half-a-dozen or so and felt much better. Either the rest or the fruit had taken the greyness out of her face. She was still withdrawn and dreamy, but she stood up willingly when I did.

We moved on doggedly. The ground became steeper the further we went, the trees further apart, the vegetation less crowded. Eventually it was no longer necessary to use the hatchet, and I took the rucksack.

It was cooler here; the sun was less fierce now, the air freer to move than in the thick jungle.

It was like a calm arcade. The tree-trunks were absolutely straight and regular, towering into dimness. Stately birds, robed like rich priests, moved here and there among the pillars. An elegant jaguar, like a lady of fashion, lay on a branch, and we moved circumspectly, whispering, until we had passed her.

The ground underfoot, less crowded with tangled bushes and vines, was covered in large rotting leaves and petals. Life here moved to statelier and subtler rhythms. A jewelled snake moved across the path. We saw a giant sloth hanging upside-down, perfectly still, with moss and flowers growing among the fur on its back. There was little sound.

We trudged wearily along the floor of this vast arena. Our passing must have made no difference at all.

Ahead of us, after about an hour, we saw a lightening of the church-like gloom. It was too gradual to be suddenly noticed, but we found ourselves moving more quickly towards it in response. The sun, nearly at the edge of the sky, was full in our faces, the great beams slanting through the pillars to lie in golden-red pools on the forest floor.

Then abruptly the trees ended. Ahead of us there was nothing at all. We came out, aching with tiredness, on the very edge of a huge cliff, as the sun was about to set.

An Evening Vista

The cliff face must have been five hundred metres high, but even to my trepid eyes it did not look difficult to descend, being well furnished with ledges, hand and foot-holds, and patches of a shallower inclination. But it was what lay at the foot of the cliff that held our eyes:

A broad, cultivated valley, a kilometre or maybe more across, with, set right in the middle of it, a large, low, whitewashed ranch-house with a red roof; and, surrounding the building, paddocks, outbuildings, barns, and white-painted fences. A group of workers was engaged in some building job behind the house; others were working in the fields, cutting crops, or digging the soil.

We sat down, exhausted, and stared over it all.

"I can't climb down," said Mary, and I thought there was a sob in her voice. "I'm too tired."

"It'll be dark soon, anyway," I said. "We'd get lost and fall. We'll spend the night up here, don't worry."

After a minute I got up to gather wood to make a fire. And then we had a piece of luck, for I startled a small wild pig and stunned it with the hatchet, and killed it as cleanly as I could. When I carried it back to Mary I saw that the valley had disappeared in shadow, and the night was climbing up the cliff to meet us.

"We'd only be half-way down now," said Mary.

I lit the fire and cut the pig up. We ate the meat as soon as it was charred, and then lay down in utter weariness and fell asleep.

During the night we moved closer together, so that we ended up sleeping curled round each other like cats. We may have been cold; or we may have been dreaming of Johnny.

Zombie Farm

We woke up into a world of blue and white. Sail-like clouds floated swiftly across the intense sky. I was cold and stiff, but there was a clear angelic taste to this early morning that made my head swim with the memory of the messenger from my wife.

Mary was pressed warmly against my side. I had the vague idea

78

that it would only be necessary to take a short walk downhill and we would be presented with a delicious breakfast, welcome, and transport to the Anderson Valley. It was an agreeable fantasy.

We couldn't see the sun, but it wasn't very high in the sky. I went to the edge of the cliff and looked down at the farm. Although the valley was in shadow and the light in the air had that bloom on it that belongs to the very early part of the day, there were already workers in the fields, tending vines and clearing weeds.

When Mary was wide awake, there was nothing else to be done but descend the cliff. It was easier than it looked, but patches of scree meant that we had to think what we were doing. Mary was managing it with an an amazing degree of calmness, even disdain.

We were half-way down when I noticed that we had been seen. Someone was pointing; someone else running to the ranch-house. And, watching the pattern of work on the farm, I saw that there were two kinds of workers: there were overseers, who were carrying whips, and gangs of labouring men who were bent over stiffly at their tasks. It was the overseers who had noticed us; the others never looked up from their work, but moved awkwardly and unrhythmically, as if they were operated by some primitive kind of clockwork.

There was a wall, about two metres high, that ran all the way along the edge of the farm nearest to the cliff. At intervals along it there were gates, and as we made for the nearest of these we saw three men coming to meet us, along a gravelled path between rows of vines.

They reached the gate first, and opened it and stood just inside, waiting.

One of them was carrying a rifle. Another was holding the leash of a fierce Dobermann Pinscher. They regarded us neutrally.

"Do you speak English?" I asked when we got to the gate.

The man with the rifle, a black man who seemed to be in charge, shook his head.

"Spanish?"

"Un poco."

"Oui."

"French?"

So we spoke in French. I told him what had happened to us, and asked if we could come in and speak to the owner, and find some food and somewhere to rest.

"That depends," he said. "Herr Haibel is a busy man. He might not want to see you."

"Why not let him be the judge of that? Is this place so far from civilisation that all civilised behaviour is abandoned here? We are innocent travellers, and we are asking for nothing we are unable to pay for. Take us to your employer, and please don't waste any more time."

He laughed, and then after a moment stood aside, giving us just enough room to walk through the gate. They closed it after us, and then led us up the path and through a farmyard of unreal neatness and cleanliness. Even the tools that I could see in the open barn, even the three tractors that stood parked exactly in a row, gleamed and sparkled with polishing. The ranch-house itself was long and low, and painted white, with great clusters of bougainvillea around a wooden veranda.

We waited in the hall of the ranch-house while the man with the rifle went to fetch his boss. The furniture in there was large and heavy and vulgar; silver studs were set into the fat leather arms of the chairs, long leather whips were coiled against the gold-patterned walls.

Mary, quite composed, sat with her hands in her lap and said nothing.

Then a door was flung open and a very fat man, middle-aged, dressed in the style of a cowboy, hastened in to us. He was tall and florid. And at a second glance, most of his bulk was muscle.

"Haibel," he said, thrusting out his hand. "Hans Peter Haibel, owner of this ranch."

He had learned his English from Americans. His grip was fierce.

"Martin Browning," I said. "And this is Mary Pretorius."

"Pretorius, hey? The same as the bank?"

"Yes," she said.

He nodded, impressed. "Now my secretary told me something about a plane. That right? Sit down, come on outside now, on the veranda, we'll have a drink."

With broad, expansive gestures, he ushered us outside. We sat down in wickerwork chairs, and he rang a bell for a servant. From the veranda we could see over a large part of the valley; it looked prosperous and quiet.

"Now suppose you tell me what this is all about," he said, lighting a cigar.

I told him where we had been going, and what had happened, and said that three men had been killed in the accident, and that the authorities ought to be informed.

"Oh, sure," he said. "You leave that to Haibel. Don't you worry about a thing; there ain't no worries in this valley, not since I came. And that's a funny thing, that you're going to the Anderson Valley. That's how I started up here three years ago. Put a bit of business my way. I did them some favours—the Mitsubishi Corporation—they set me up here. Pretty neat place, huh?"

We nodded politely.

"Yes, sir," he said. "Three years damn hard work, and look at me now. You might call me the ruler of this little place. Guess you might say I was a kind of king. Ain't many men can say that."

I was wondering how all this could have been developed in only three years, when a servant came in; not the black man with the rifle, but a house servant in a white coat. And as soon as I saw him, I realised how it had been possible, and realised the nature of the slavery they practised here. For the servant moved like Felix, he had the same filmy eyes; he was a zombie.

Mary gasped. The servant's face was like wax. He leant, as Felix had done, against the wall to support himself as he waited for orders.

Haibel didn't notice Mary's shock.

"What you want to drink, you guys?" he said. "You want something hot? Coffee? Or some whisky or rum? You name it."

"Thank you," said Mary, "but I wonder if I could have a bath? I think I want to lie down and sleep."

"Oh, sure, sure," said the genial farmer. "Romero, you take this lady to Frau Haibel's room, make it ready for her, run a bath, do anything she tells you. You follow him, miss. You want anything, you ring a bell. Come on out when you're ready."

She nodded, and nervously went after the servant as he left the veranda. Haibel turned back to me.

"Didn't want to tell the little lady, but there's something special about these servants of mine, and the ranch hands. You know what a zombie is? They're all zombies. Some ranch, huh? I don't have to pay no wages, they don't strike, they don't run away, don't steal the produce. Lemme tell you something, it sure is good to see a woman about the place again. My wife died about two years ago and I miss her sorely. A man needs a woman around, but I ain't had a woman yet that stayed for long. I have a few whores in the bunkhouse for the live hands but up here I need a higher class of woman, you know what I mean?"

"Who brings the dead men back to life?" I asked.

"My secretary. That's the nigger who let you in. I have to look all over for dead men, have men in the villages around that I pay for looking, but I don't kill any. No, sir. This is a straight operation. Why should I kill a man and bring him back to life when he's worth more to me alive?"

He said this with an air of triumphant logic.

"But if he's alive, you have to pay him."

"And I pay union rates. But it's worth it. A zombie has no spirit, no initiative. Only a live hand can think for himself. That's why the foremen are live hands."

"Do they ever escape?"

"The dead hands? If they do they don't get far. The dogs tear 'em up. One thing, you can't kill a zombie. Have to eat him to stop him. But that's expensive. So we keep 'em in line, lock 'em up at night."

He fell silent, staring out over the verdant landscape.

"Yes, sir," he said absently. "Sure is nice to have a lady in the house."

His cigar had gone out; he lit it again with a lighter that looked like a miniature pistol.

"Now," he said between puffs of smoke, "you want to wash and shave? There's a shower in the guest bedroom. I'll get Romero to find you some clothes, they'll wash the ones you have on, and the lady's, don't you worry about a thing."

He pressed the bell-push again.

"Anything you want, you just ask. Now we have lunch about one, okay? Come along when you're ready. I have to get back to my desk now, a farmer these days is more like an executive than a farmer, you know what I mean? Okay, Martin."

With a genial wave he left me on the veranda.

How to Run a Profitable Enterprise

The proprietor of Zombie Farm was a talented man, so he informed us that afternoon. Luck had been against him, and although weak and disloyal men had constantly plotted to bring about his downfall, his gifts and persistence had proved too much for them.

As he showed us around his spotless domain, he explained how it had all come about.

He had left Germany in haste after the war, and gone with a little money to Brazil. There he had tried various immoral enterprises, none of which prospered sufficiently, and the last of which had led to his being asked to leave the country.

Then he went to Paraguay, and tried honesty for a while. He bought a farm and tried to breed cattle, but found that a powerful reluctance to pay wages stood between him and happiness, and that the continual obligation to part with money in exchange for service made his farm little short of a misery to him.

However, he was a man of profound and commanding imagination, and very soon a solution to the problem came to him.

"Slavery," he explained, as we surveyed a neat and fertile vineyard. "No finer system ever existed, you better believe it. I tried Indians first, but they just sickened and died. In the end I was forced back to niggers. Always has been a slave, the nigger; it's bred in. There ain't no more loyal, conservative creature alive than your nigger slave, if he's well treated."

But in this too Haibel's vision was too advanced for the age. Various tender-hearted Paraguayans betrayed his scheme to the police, and one night the farm was raided.

"It was a helluva fight," he said. In the distance a zombie who had strayed out of his field watched philosophically while a great Alsatian savaged his foot. "We held them off for hours, but they were too strong for us. And that proves what I said about loyalty. The slaves fought side by side with us. They didn't want to be liberated! They thought the police had come to kill them! How could you expect a slave to think anything else?"

By midnight everyone was dead, except for Haibel and one of the slaves. This man's name was Jean-Paul; he came from Martinique, and according to Haibel he was a real smart guy. And it was Jean-Paul who saved them, in the end.

During a lull in the fighting, he revealed to Haibel that he had the power of raising men from the dead, and suggested that he should do it there and then, in exchange for his liberty.

Being somewhat pressed by circumstances, Haibel was unable to strike a better bargain, and so agreed.

Jean-Paul then set about raising the dead. He shook some powder from a little leather flask into the mouth of the dead man, and then lay on him as a man lies on a woman; and this act made the dead man rise up as a zombie. He raised three of them, and sent them out against the police, holding on to one another for support because various bones had been shattered by machine-gun fire. This hideous spectacle, seen in the light of the searchlights that illuminated the front of the ranch-house, so terrified and demoralised the police that Haibel and Jean-Paul were able to escape in the confusion. In two minutes they were clear, and they never looked back.

"Now that nigger is my secretary," said Haibel. "We came up through Brazil, went into Colombia for a little while, made some money, came up here and bought this place. It was nothing then, just a shack and a field. But the ground was fertile and the whole valley was free, and when the first man died in the village I thought 'There's a worker'. So I sent the nigger over and he came back with him. And now here we are, in the finest little ranch in the territory of the Amazonas."

He hoisted his bulk up on to a white-painted wooden fence that surrounded a corral full of powerful black bulls.

"Only thing," he said, "I had a wife. Finally went to Caracas three years ago to find a wife; reckoned I ought to settle down, get some sons. I brought her out here—a good white woman, a lady from a wealthy family. She stayed for a year and then she died. Now I'm alone again."

"I'm sorry to hear that," I said.

"She was too fine-bred for the country life," explained the rancher. "She could never get used to the dead hands. She had a French maid, pretty little thing, caught fever and died. She missed her sorely, so I got the nigger to raise her. Should've figured women wouldn't take to the idea. She screamed—that's my wife—she screamed and hollered and called me all sorts of names, which I forgave her, but I had to lock her in for her own protection. And she pined away and died."

He shook his head, gazed out over the acres of clean sweet pasture and the docile cows, and sighed in a melancholy fashion.

"Yes, sir," he said, "I'm a lonely man."

Mary moved a little closer to me, while Haibel nodded sadly. Then he jumped down from the fence, and slapped me on the back.

"No good looking at the past," he said. "Come over this way, I ain't shown you my freezer plant yet."

And, accompanied everywhere by the saturnine secretary with the rifle, we saw over the rest of his wide and prosperous acres, encouraging our host at intervals with expressions of interest and admiration.

A Discourse on the Habits of Dead Men

A frugal man, Haibel was unwilling to let any effort go to waste; and so although the zombified French maid had proved the undoing of his wife, he was quite happy to pass her on to his secretary, for his personal use.

The resurrectionist would not live in the house with his employer, but preferred a shack of his own further into the darkness. There he lived with his zombie mistress Lisette. She performed all her tasks with efficiency and skill, but she had no grace left.

The two of them sat on their bed and let me have their one chair. A candle burned on a tin plate on the table, in front of a straw and cardboard effigy.

I had gone there to find out what Jean-Paul knew about the Anderson Valley. It was evening, and work had stopped for the night; the zombies had been herded into the long barn that served them as a dormitory, and the live hands were free to amuse themselves in the rich South American darkness.

I quizzed the secretary in my rough French. He answered me sardonically, occasionally permitting his dead paramour to put in a word from beyond the grave.

"Have you ever been to the Anderson Valley?"

"Some Japanese men came here three years ago, and gave Herr Haibel some money. In exchange for that they took me to the Anderson Valley and I showed them how I raise people."

"When they are raised, are they really alive, or is it an imitation of life?"

"I don't know. But they can move and talk, although they don't eat or shit. Nor do they piss or sweat."

"What do they know about the state they are in?"

"Ask her."

I repeated the question, addressing the ex-maid, who still wore, filthy and torn though it was, the black and frilly white costume of the traditional French maid.

Her voice, when after the familiar rasping intake of breath she began to answer me, was light and high and cracked.

"I am not dead."

"But are you alive?"

"Not that either."

"What does it feel like?"

"Nothing. Nothing to tell."

"Do you desire anything?"

"To sleep. He locks the door at night so that I don't wander away, because I can't settle down and keep still. I would like to sleep."

Jean-Paul laughed.

"What is it like to have a dead mistress?" I asked him.

"You want to try her?"

"No!"

"Every so often the boss says to send her to the house. So I wash her and dress her in Frau Haibel's clothes and take her along to him. And she makes him tea in the English way and they drink it and then he has her, and then she comes back. *He* likes it. You can do what you like with a zombie. Anything you like, what you can't do with a live girl, for various reasons. Impossible things, you can do with a zombie."

"Nothing hurts me," said Lisette. "I have no dignity. I am just flesh."

"Tell me about the Anderson Valley," I said. "When they took you there."

"It was a big city being made. Fine beautiful streets, parks, gardens, shops, beautiful, lovely city. With fountains and flowers, and wide boulevards and squares, everything. Everything new and clean. And they had an Institute, like a University, in a big park. They took me there. And they had a big room full of dead people in trays, like a big frigidaire. All kinds, disease victims, road accidents, all kinds, young and old.

"And I had my magic powder with me and they wanted to take some. So I let them have a little. What is it? Something simple, but I won't tell you. I didn't tell them. They could look and look at it and still not know.

"And they wanted me to raise some deads. So I raised about five, six, I don't know. They took films, photographs, tapes, everything, with instruments tied all over me and all over the dead. Then after a week they let me go."

"Did they tell you what they were studying?"

"What for? Would it have mattered to me? No."

"Where did you learn to raise the dead?"

"In Martinique, then in Belem, and in Georgetown. Many places."

"Is it hard to do?"

"For white people, very hard. Only one white I met can do it."

"What was his name?"

"Alexandre Légarou. A Greek with red hair. He is here now, if you want to see him."

"What? Where?"

He got to his feet and opened the door of the shack. A few metres away there was a tree covered in lights.

"That's him," said the secretary. "In Haiti where he learned his skill they can change into trees bearing lights as well as wolves."

"Wolves?"

"He is a werewolf," he explained. "He's done that now because his death is near, and he wants to hide. But I spotted him, and I gave him away to the man who'll kill him."

The leaves of the tree rustled, and the lights flickered. We went back inside the shack.

"Ça va, petite," said Jean-Paul impersonally to Lisette.

She was lying against the wall, her legs stretched straight out on the bed. She looked as stiff as a wooden doll, as wholesome as a waxwork. But suddenly I felt a subterranean movement of lust. Her legs prompted it; they were white and shapely, although filthy dirty. It was the inertness of them, and the resurrectionist's words "You can do what you like with a zombie". Pictures of what I would like to do showed themselves to my mind's eye, and I looked away hastily. I saw Jean-Paul grinning obscenely.

"Can you remember what your life was like before you died?" I asked her, trying to dispel the necrophilic miasma.

"Yes, I remember," she said. "I can't forget any of it."

"Does your flesh feel anything?"

"Very little."

"Do you feel pain?"

"I recognise it."

"And pleasure? Do you recognise that?"

"I get no pleasure from this man's embraces anyway."

Jean-Paul laughed, and slapped her thigh two or three times, in affection.

"And you," I said, "doesn't her face disturb you? With those filmy eyes and that waxy look? Doesn't it frighten you to lie down in the darkness beside her?"

"Fear, you say?" he said. "My whole life is fear."

"What are you afraid of?"

"Blood, and pain, and so on. My whole life is fear. Do I have to say it again?"

"Why are you afraid?"

"Without fear I could do nothing. It is home to me. Without fear I couldn't fuck, or eat or drink, or breathe. I have seen and done fearful things. I have eaten flesh and drunk blood, both in the jungle and in the city. White man's flesh too, in the Catholic church in Belem, but that's magic flesh. Like Lisette's. The Catholic god was a zombie, he was raised, and now they eat his flesh. But fear, you say. My father taught me fear when I was a boy, and he told me about the kings' courts in Africa, how they would kill slaves for their amusement, in all kinds of bloody ways. When I think about it I see blood everywhere, and the world is full of knives and sharp blades, and blood colours everything red; every mouth gushes blood, and the trees and the grass are sticky with it, and the air is full of screams. Always there is fear, and it is my home, as I say."

We sat quietly for a while in the gloom of the dirty shack. The night was warm; the smoke of the candle blended with the reek of sweat. But not, I remembered, the sweat of Lisette.

He told me some more about zombies. He said that they would obey any living person, because they had no will, and the weakest living will was too strong for them. And that they would never die, but that eventually their flesh would wear out, or that their bones would break in an accident, or that a wild animal would eat them. He told me that they bled little, for although they had as much blood as a living person, and that in a liquid state, it was not pumped by the heart, so it would not gush out if a vein or artery was cut, but would merely drain. If you wanted to get rid of a zombie, you had to destroy him completely, to cut him into very small pieces, or feed him to animals, or mince him, or burn him. If too large a piece was left, a malevolent spirit attaching to it would haunt the spot where it lay, and make it difficult to grow crops there, or frighten people away. So there were spirits? I asked. Oh, yes, he said, hundreds of kinds. This ranch was haunted by many ghosts, and there was a city further into the wilderness where the ghosts had almost taken over, and made life nearly impossible for the inhabitants. Here on the ranch, sometimes you could hear the ghosts crying at night, and then he was very fearful, and his melancholy grew wilder. When he died the spirits of the men he had raised, and Lisette's spirit, would take their revenge on him.

By then it was getting late. Leaving the secretary to his oceanic fears and his grave mistress, I walked back through the darkness towards the ranch-house. I paused by the light-bearing tree. Small creatures chirped among the branches. The little flames waved and tossed from their candles. I put my hand on the trunk and whispered "Well, Alexander the werewolf . . . What shall we do to you?"

A Terrible Discovery

In his grandiose drawing-room, Haibel was holding forth to Mary. He was in an energetic mood.

"I'll tell you both," he said, "I feel damn good. Matter of fact, I ain't felt half so damn cheerful all round since my wife died."

He swallowed the rest of a large glass of whisky.

"Now you come right in, Mart boy, sit down, have a drink. Help yourself, go right ahead, and we'll have some fun, okay? I got a real treat for you both to see tonight."

I looked at Mary as I poured myself a drink. She was in a curious mood; Haibel was bustling around, hardly aware of anything outside his own euphoria, talking loudly, laughing and singing, and she seemed to be encouraging it, being soft and yielding and helplessly admiring, laughing at his jokes, taking more drink in a giggly, muddled way, so that I could see him swelling with self-delight. But every so often a spasm of distaste crossed her features, and once or twice her face became a mask of pure and savage melancholy.

Haibel didn't notice. Under all his boisterousness there was a vein of hysteria, and there was a feeling of cruelty in the air. He kept looking at the low-cut dress Mary had found in the late Frau Haibel's wardrobe, and at her cool white legs.

Then he started talking about sport, about hunting and fighting, and cockfighting in particular.

"I got something mighty special laid on for you guys," he said delightedly. "Yes, sir."

He winked and put his forefinger to his lips, grinning lewdly.

"But first," he said, "I got a little surprise for you."

He pressed a bell-push, and in answer to it, there came a knock on the door.

"Come in," Haibel bawled.

The door opened. And in walked the body of Johnny Hamid, dead, with the filmy eyes and hand-on-the-wall gait of a zombie.

Mary gave a little cry. She jumped out of her chair, horror and concern all over her features, and ran to him.

I too jumped to my feet, and found myself watching what she did with fascination.

She put out her arms as if to comfort him, and made soft little consoling noises, as if to a child . . . I was amazed by her courage.

Johnny himself—or his corpse—looked as vile as any other. He had a faint grin on his lips; he was dressed in the black trousers and white jacket of one of Haibel's servants. It was heart-breaking.

Mary flung her arms around his neck, crying, "Johnny! My poor Johnny! What's happened?"

And so she was all the more startled when he gripped her fiercely with one hand and with the other pulled down the front of her dress, and thrust his hips vigorously at her, like a dog, snarling and growling, his face twisted with lust.

She screamed. I leapt forward and tore him off her. He fell to the floor and lay still. Mary, shaken, began to weep with shock. I put my arms around her.

"Make him go away," she cried.

"Tell him to go," I said to Haibel.

Haibel nodded, and Johnny got to his feet and shuffled out.

"Why did you do that to him?" she said to Haibel, her voice trembling.

"Didn't like to leave him lying around. And who'd a thought you'd mind?"

Mary shuddered, the tears flowing from her eyes. Then she pushed me away and ran out of the room.

"What's the matter?" said Haibel, surprised.

"She must be tired," I said. "Perhaps she wants to lie down."

"Yeah," he said. "I guess so."

He was mystified.

"I'll go and see that she's all right," I said.

"Don't be long, then," he said. "I got something mighty special laid on tonight. Maybe the little lady'd like to come out too."

"I'll ask her," I said.

I went to her room, and entered without knocking. She was sitting on the bed, her face set, her hands clasped in her lap.

"What are we going to do?" she said.

"Go as soon as possible. I'll find some way. But we're going to take Johnny with us."

"No, never!"

"We can't leave him here for Haibel to play with."

"But he's *dead*!"

"No, we're going to take him, and find some way of making him alive properly, or else see that he's buried or burnt. I'm not going to let him wander about for ever."

"Well, I won't come with you, if you take him. I couldn't."

"Well, what else are you going to do?"

She shrugged. Then she turned abruptly and lay face down on the bed. She muttered "My father will find me."

"Shall I go without you, then?"

"No! Please don't . . . Oh, God, I don't know *what* to do . . ."

"Well, leave it to me and do as I say."

There was a knock on the door.

"Who's that?" I called.

Another knock. "Come on," said a strange voice.

"Who?"

"You. Mista Brown."

I stood up and opened the door. A servant, one of the live hands, stood in the corridor.

"You come see the boss," he said. "The boss want to start, you no come yet."

"Stay here," I said to Mary. "I won't be long."

She said nothing. I went out and shut the door, and then followed the servant out of the ranch-house and towards the big barn, whose open door was a glow of yellow light.

I said to the servant "The new zombie, the one they found in the jungle. Where's he?"

He pointed to a long, low shed, hulked against the night.

"With all the rest, in the big barracón," he said.

And then for a moment I felt overwhelmed, as sometimes we feel dizzy when we stand up too quickly after lying down. Could I really be in the presence of men who raised corpses? Wasn't I dreaming?

I shook my head to clear it, and stood in the entrance of the barn, looking around.

There was a circle of chairs around a saw-dust covered area in the middle. All the chairs were occupied, and Haibel and a group of men were talking excitedly and placing bets on a table at the far side. There was a reek of cigars, and paraffin from the oil lamps, and of unwashed bodies.

In the centre of the ring stood two naked zombies. They were big powerful men, and they held on to each other for balance, standing perfectly still, waiting.

91

Haibel looked up and saw me, and waved.

"Okay, Mart?" he yelled. "Right, boys, no more bets? Okay, then, off we go."

He shouldered his way to the ringside, and clapped his hands three times.

Silence fell, and the zombies began to fight.

The only tearing weapons the human body has are teeth and nails, and as nails break easily, after a minute or so it's only teeth that count. So the two fighters behaved oddly, for fighters; they would struggle to get their teeth in range of the other's flesh, then sink them in and tear. It was a curiously careful and delicate process.

Soon the arena was soaked in blood, and their bodies were covered in it from head to foot, the blood not spurting but leaking steadily. Rags and clouts of flesh, imperfectly torn off, hung flapping from their shoulders, arms, back, thighs, scalps. One had a wound in his belly, and the other was trying to get a grip on it, but slipping in the blood. The crowd was behaving as if it were watching a striptease, silently, concentrating, not wanting to miss a detail, sighing.

Then the one's fingers got a purchase on the wound in the other's belly and with a tearing sound ripped it open, and a flood of slimy intestine slithered out.

No one noticed when I left.

Spontaneous Combustion
The society of dead men seemed preferable for the moment, and I had a plan; so I went towards the barracón where the dead hands spent the night.

On the way there I went past the light-bearing tree. I looked up and saw with a shock that something was hunched on one of the branches: was it a man? It looked big enough. I picked up a stone and threw it.

"That's no good, sir," said a rasping quiet voice.

"Felix," I said. "Is that you?"

In the light of his master's little flames I could just make out the shape of his body. He was perched on one of the topmost branches. His suit, made of some synthetic material, shone delicately in the gleam.

"I am instructed to bargain with you," said the zombie.

"Too late. You have to follow me now and do what I say. My first command is: cut this tree down."

"Betrayed!" said he mechanically, and began to climb down.

I left him to it, and went on towards the charnel dormitory.

I found a live hand on guard outside the door, and asked him: "Where is the key to this barracón?"

"In my pocket," he said, and stood up.

"Give it to me. Your master needs you in the barn, and I have to let the dead hands out."

He hesitated a moment, but then handed me the key.

"Now go," I said. "Quickly!"

He left.

I unlocked the door. It was pitch black inside. There was a noise of insects stirring, but man-sized insects. My flesh crawled and I stayed in the doorway.

"Dead men!" I called. "Do you want to be released?"

A simultaneous intake of breath, and a host of voices cried "Yes".

"Do you want revenge?"

The same response. They began to shuffle towards me.

"Keep still. Do exactly as I tell you. Where is Johnny Hamid?"

Poor Johnny came crabwise out of the darkness.

"Johnny, go to Mary's room and tell her to bring warm clothes and food outside and meet me by the shack down over there. Don't you touch her. You will have to keep well away from her, do you hear?"

"But when I see her I will want to touch her, and so on."

"Then don't look at her. But make her come, and remember, don't look at her, don't touch her."

"Okay," said the body of Johnny Hamid, my dear friend.

"And bring my rucksack, too," I said.

He nodded carefully, and went off towards the house, shuffling like an old man.

"Now, dead men!" I said. "You know which men are your masters and which are the men from the village. They are all in the barn. Go there and surround it and let out the men from the village, but not the others. Then I shall set fire to the barn. And if you want to be free, climb into the fire and burn yourselves away. Then the masters will be yours."

A wild, violent, melancholy cry went up, and the hundred or so dead men, holding on to one another like blind soldiers from the

93

trenches, like children, like brothers, followed me out of their grave-smelling barracón into the light of the stars.

I led my army at the best pace it could muster, and lined it up by the entrance to the barn.

Inside, the fight was approaching its climax. The audience was wild. Shouts, applause, roars of encouragement shook the walls. I could hear Haibel's high shriek above it all, and wondered if the Jews of Poland might remember that shriek.

I looked over my army. A hundred faces, waxy, cadaverous, with the gleam of rot or dew on them stared back at me. A stench arose from them, an atmosphere as sad and lonely as a swamp, as old as death itself. What could I pay them with except dissolution, these ragged mercenaries? But they had already signalled their willingness to accept those wages.

Then Johnny came back down the path.

"She wouldn't come," he said. "But I got the rucksack."

Out of it I took the gun.

"Let through only those who have not used you as slaves," I said.

I fired the gun into the air. The noise from the barn stopped in an instant.

"Haibel," I yelled. "Tell your friends: all the visitors are to leave the barn straight away and go back to their homes."

"Why?" he yelled back. "What the hell's going on?"

And he flung the door open angrily, and fell back as he saw the ranks of the dead. Involuntarily the zombies took a step towards him, now they had been promised their vengeance, and I held them back. Haibel was convinced.

He bawled something in a local dialect. Slowly the frightened farmers came out, and gasped and crossed themselves when they saw the still, gruesome ranks of dead men standing in front of them. But the ranks opened and let the first man through, and the next, and the next.

Then one of the foremen tried to get through. They seized him, choking his screams, and threw him back. He writhed on the ground at my feet, and I tried to ignore him.

More and more farmers made their way through. Finally there was a knot of live hands, and Haibel, and me, inside the ring of dead men. The man who'd tried to get through was praying aloud and crossing himself. The rest looked sullen and suspicious. Haibel was gazing wildly around for a way out.

"I'll give you all one chance," I said. "You can find out if your power over these dead men is stronger than their desire for revenge. Command them to let you go, if you can. I'm going to set fire to the barn, and they are going to immolate themselves. Possibly you too. Who knows?"

So saying, I took the dead pilot's lighter and applied it to the dry straw on the floor just outside the barn. It caught in an instant, and I slipped through the ranks of my faithful army and stood twenty or so metres away and watched.

In the hubbub that followed I could easily distinguish the live voices from the dead ones, though it all rose to a hideous pitch. Haibel was screaming "Let us through! Let me through, you filthy fucking corpses! You bloody deads! Let me out! You dirty stinking dead cocksucking sons of bitches, you dead bastards, do as I say! Move aside out of the way! I'm the boss, you do as I say! You stinking dead assholes, move, I say, move!"

And the others, the live hands, were shouting in Spanish. Then Haibel turned to German; and the crackle and snarl of parade-ground Prussian rose high above the din.

All the time a keening, grunting, rasping moan was swelling in volume from the throats of the dead men, nearly but not quite drowning the screams from the living. With their arms around each other's shoulders to stay upright, the zombies shuffled forward, step by little step, in a slow steady side-to-side rhythm that was more enduring than death; and terrible as it was to watch from behind, it must have been more so from the front. Nothing could stop it. The dead men had felt the heat of the fire on their flesh, and their cells, aching for dissolution, drove them forward.

Whereas the heat drove me back. I held Johnny by the arm, feeling him pulling towards the fire, and wondering whether I ought to let him go.

The barn was ablaze all over inside, and tongues of flame had begun to appear at the corners of the walls and at the edge of the roof, flickering like imps. And crowding to get in, shuffling in their steady deathless movement, the great mass of zombies by the door got smaller and smaller as those at the front entered the inferno and made room for those behind.

Of Haibel and his lieutenants there was no sign. They had been carried into the barn and burned to death. It was the first death I had ever been responsible for, and I was completely satisfied.

Suddenly I heard the click of a rifle-bolt, and a voice said, quite softly, "Qu'est-ce que vous avez fait, vous?"

Jean-Paul held the rifle in one hand, pointing at the ground.

"I've given the dead men the power to escape," I said.

"Maudit," he said dreamily. His face, lurid in the glare of the barn, seemed overtaken again by his visions of blood. His eyes, terribly wide, rolled upwards. And as the cries of the living and the dead sank under the crackle of flame and the crash of timbers, as the long-still blood in the zombies' veins raced, boiling, around their bodies in a ghastly mimicry of the circulation of life, Jean-Paul the resurrectionist raised the rifle to his lips, closed them around the end of the barrel, and, with a jerk of his hands, blew off the top of his head. He dropped like a stone.

I shuddered.

Then turned abruptly away as I heard my name called. It was Mary, running from the house.

"Over here!" I cried, and she stopped, looking around desperately to try and see where I was. I set off towards her, tugging Johnny. Then she saw us, and backed away.

"Oh, no," she cried. "No, I won't go with him."

"He's coming with me," I said. "And I'm going now. Come with us or stay here, it's up to you."

The flames from the barn were running along the white-painted railings, along the grass, leaping up trees and bushes, and staining the whole sky orange. I could see the corner of the house beginning to burn.

"Well?" I said to her.

"Oh, Christ," she said, and nodded, on the verge of tears.

"Come on then."

And we turned away from the holocaust and moved out into the darkness. Zombie Farm was all but destroyed, but there were two zombies whose time had not quite come, and we saw the first of them as we hurried down the path that led to Jean-Paul's shack. It was a slight figure with an axe, who was hacking inexpertly at the trunk of the light-bearing tree, heedless of the fact that his executive-style suit was blazing on his back.

"Keep going, Felix," I said as we passed.

"I was not made for manual labour," he said, "but I am trying."

The road to the village and beyond led slightly upwards, through the well-ploughed and beautifully tended fields, lying still and abstract under the light of the moon and stars. We looked back after a while. The whole farm was ablaze. There was a figure flitting from wall to fence, from door to door, a female figure. And as vaguely as a ghost I could hear "Jean-Paul! Jean-Paul!"

It was the haunted body of Lisette, and I was seized by a pang of remorse.

But she would not survive for long. Probably Felix in his courteous way would help her into the flames, and there she'd find her lover, free at last of the dykes of flesh that held back the wide grey wastes of fear from his naked soul. How would she greet him than as yet another wave that rolled over him?

And that mothlike figure, flitting here and there among the fires, was the last we saw of Zombie Farm.

On the Loose Again

So all that night, tired but calm, we wandered along the dusty road. After an hour or so we passed the village; white houses, a dry fountain, a white-washed church, all gleamed mysteriously in the moonlight. But there was not a sound. If the inhabitants were aware of the fiery end of Zombie Farm, they were letting it happen.

The road was in quite good order, dry and hard and unrutted. Probably in a rainstorm it would turn to mud, but in the dry moonlight it seemed covered in light pollen, and soon our legs and feet were covered in it too.

In order to maintain a good pace I had to give Johnny my arm to hold, so that he wouldn't fall over. We said nothing.

I wondered what thoughts lay in Johnny's cold brain, and what in Mary's warm one. The girl I had first met on the terrace of her father's house, under the carnival lights of a ball, and the friend I had made on the same occasion; it was I who had turned the one into a castaway and the other into a walking corpse. Nothing else; just me and my quest. I was an image of Western man, trudging along in the night with a dead man and an unspeakable girl, following my impossible hopes. But I belonged to the West, and I regretted nothing.

Off to the wars, it felt like; and I would have taken out my flute and played *Lilliburlero,* or *Over the Hills and Far Away,* or *Hearts of Oak,* to help us march strongly and in step. But I would have had to let go of Johnny, and we weren't marching anyway, we were ambling. So I played them in my head, and marched in tune with myself.

97

The night went by, and the three of us walked on and on. The stars swung over the sky and disappeared under the horizon.

The road was leading upwards the whole time. After we had left the valley of Zombie Farm, we found ourselves in a park-like landscape of low hills dotted here and there with clumps of trees. And for most of the time we climbed, not much, but enough to be noticeable.

When we had been walking for two hours or so Mary stopped, and said "I'm going to have to rest. I can't go any further."

"Just to the top of that ridge," I said. "Come on, it's only a few minutes."

Wearily she began to move forward again. We followed.

"If we go to sleep," I said to Johnny, "what will you do?"

"I don't know," said his body. "I can't sleep."

"Nor keep still?"

"No."

"What if I tied you up?"

"Please do."

So when we reached the top of the ridge, and Mary lay down instantly and went to sleep, I tied Johnny loosely to a sapling with the straps from the rucksack. He was quite comfortable, and it would prevent him from wandering. And then my tiredness came over me in a flood, and I lay down and was asleep in a moment.

Fashion, Commerce, Hospitality; Noble Things

When we woke up the sun was just rising. Dawn was more impressive on the plain than it had been the day before on the edge of the cliff. Now there was nothing to hide the sun from us, and as the straight rays came at us across the grass we warmed up, and I felt naked and new. Whatever happened, I was the master of things. So I must look after my subjects.

"All right?" I said helpfully to Mary. "How did you sleep?"

"Mm," she said, rubbing her eyes.

Johnny was still leaning against the little tree. In daylight he looked worse, more artificial, more dead. Either (I thought) we found a real resurrection for him, or we destroyed him. So that was the first priority.

"I want some coffee," said Mary.

I looked around for my rucksack. All I could find to give her was a bar of chocolate, but she ate it happily. Away from Zombie

Farm and its ashen proprietor, she had regained the stagelit subtlety of her earlier manner; and she sat with her legs curled to one side, leaning on the other arm, her head bent low to shade her eyes from the sun. She was wearing a green cotton dress from the wardrobe of the melancholy Frau Haibel, who died. It was in the fashion of five or so years before, and everything about her added to its effect; her pose, the very pose models of that time were often photographed in; the expression on her face, the way she moved her limbs—it was all simultaneously an exposition and a criticism of a particular style. That was where the centre of her intelligence lay, I saw, in matters like this; and she did it faultlessly.

I heard the clop of hooves, and looked around. A single horseman was riding at a walk from the way we had come. He reined in beside us and addressed us courteously in Spanish.

He was lean, whiplike, sardonic, with an eloquent, fantastical grin and a thin hairline moustache. He was dressed in dandy-like black and silver shirt and trousers, with a silver gun at his waist, elegant tooled leather boots with silver spurs, and a wide-brimmed hat. His horse was as handsome as he was, and snorted and pranced and curvetted proudly, disdaining the company its master was addressing.

The local dialect he spoke in was difficult to understand. I stood up and bowed, and he dismounted and held out his hand to be shaken. I shook it.

"Martin Browning," I said. "And Miss Pretorius, and Johnny Hamid the zombie."

"Ah," he said, nodding seriously at Johnny. He bowed to Mary. "José Maria de Valdés."

Since we had nothing else to give him, I offered him some chocolate, which he accepted with great dignity.

We all sat down and ate our chocolate in silence, while his horse cropped the grass. Johnny lay still, propped against the little tree, as dead as a stone. Meanwhile the morning continued to infuse itself throughout the visible world, and the blades of grass and the leaves on the trees began their interpretation of sunlight into nourishment, and we did the same with the chocolate.

When we had finished, the stranger began to speak. He was untroubled by the fact that we didn't fully understand him. But I caught the words "fuego", "zombi", "Haibel", and I gathered that he was congratulating us on ridding the land of a demon.

Then he got up, and out of a saddlebag on the horse's back he produced a little transistor radio.

He sat down again and switched it on. Music, for guitars and whistles, came out, tinny in the wide air.

He spoke over the radio, extolling its virtues. He had carefully unfolded a handkerchief for it to stand on before putting it on the grass, and he handled it with exaggerated care. He showed us how to change the waveband and find different stations, and how to turn the volume up and down, and how to extract a telescopic aerial from the side, to improve the reception. Only then did I realise what he was doing: he was a travelling salesman, and we were customers.

I looked more closely at the radio. It bore the name of one of the companies Johnny's father had mentioned when he was telling us who had invested in the A.V.P.

The cowboy wrote on a scrap of paper: "Bs. 300". Then he looked hopefully at me.

Three hundred Bolivars was a lot of money, nearly seventy dollars. And we didn't want a radio anyway. I shook my head. He laughed happily and stuffed the radio back in the saddlebag, leaving it switched on, so that the guitars and pan-pipes and mandolins played, muffled, as a background to our colloquy. In its place he took out a bottle of rum, and pulled out the cork, offering it to each of us.

Mary drank a mouthful, and I drank, and he asked me with a gesture if Johnny would.

"Dead," I said. "Zombie. Muerte."

José Maria de Valdés crossed himself respectfully and sat down again, talking in a friendly, open way, and passing round the rum bottle. Gradually, as the sun got higher in the sky and the fumes from the rum ascended into our brains, we found that the barriers between his dialect and our understanding were being dissolved, and that we could talk to one another freely.

After a while, by common consent, we decided to move. José offered his mount to Mary, and she accepted, hitching her dress up her thighs for comfort. We politely averted our gaze. I strapped my rucksack to the saddle and we strolled along, talking and gesticulating happily in the warm clear morning.

How I Contributed to the Cause of Electricity in a Small Way

"This dead man," said José. "Why do you keep him with you?"

"He was a good friend before he died, and I want to see whether, since he can be restored partially, there is a chance of giving him back his full life."

"Then we had better go to see my grandmother. She lives a day's walk away in this direction. She is a wise woman and can perform many kinds of magic."

"Would she be able to do this, do you think?"

"She is as gifted as she is generous," he said. "As I am myself, with one exception."

"What is that?"

"Alas! I am not skilled in business. I have been trying to sell this radio for six months, for example. But I have many other skills to console me, shooting, for instance, and throwing a knife, and with a lariat, and with a whip, and with horses, with women, with a quéna, with a charanga."

"What are they?"

"A charanga is a little guitar. A quéna is—this is a quéna."

He reached into the saddlebag and took out a reed pipe, like a flageolet or a recorder.

"Play it for us."

He turned off the radio and began to play a simple, wild little tune in waltz time. Like the music on the radio, it hovered between the major and the minor, with odd cadences. It sounded easy enough to accompany, so I took out my flute and added another part to the melody. He was delighted.

And so we went along.

At noon we came to a little village. It was even smaller than the one in the valley of Zombie Farm; just a church, a general store, a few houses. Outside the general store a couple of tables and chairs had been placed in the shade of a tree, and two old men sat down to watch us. I wanted to sit down, too, but José tied the horse up, helped Mary down, and then stood on the veranda of the shop and shouted to the people of the village to come out into the square and listen, for he, José María de Valdés, and his gifted associate Martín Bruno, would play fine music for them as an inducement to come and hear details of a new range of electrical goods, pictures of which he would display so that they could examine for themselves the intricacy of the workmanship and the quality of the materials . . . .

It was an excellent speech, and by the time it was finished, the little square was full of people.

And then he started to play. Mary sat down at one of the tables and put her head on her arms, tired out and with a violent headache, she said from the sun.

I have a quick ear, and the tunes he played were simple enough. After hearing them once it was easy to join in on the second verse with a more or less sophisticated second part. I found it a little frustrating to play continually in the same key, but there was little alternative, given the form of his pipe.

The audience enjoyed it. A few people even started to dance. Then an old man appeared with a tuba and sat down and joined in; and then came a man with a side drum, and then a guitarist, and then the whole village was dancing.

Someone brought drinks of beer and handed them up to us. We drank and played on. All kinds of tunes appeared at our lips; *Yankee Doodle, La Cucuracha, Cielito Lindo, La Paloma, Marching Through Georgia, Alexander's Ragtime Band, Perfidia,* and so on.

We played until we collapsed, deliquescing from the heat and the beer.

Platefuls of tortillas and beans were produced, and we ate greedily. Some of the villagers expressed curiosity at the sight of Johnny, but we said nothing.

When we had eaten, José began his sales talk. The radio was produced, together with an electric toaster, and a battery shaver, all from the capacious saddlebag, and they were admired by all. Then he showed them his catalogue, extolling the virtues of everything in it. Each item was described, its function carefully explained. Here was a device for heating water, consisting of a curled rod that was immersed in it, which became very hot; and here was a device for turning water, the same water, if need be, into ice. And here was a machine for so increasing the sound made by a single guitar that it would fill a valley, and be heard for many kilometres across a plain. And here was a wonderful device for looking into the sky beyond the range of a man's sight, even the most keen-eyed of men, and seeing the movements of invisible entities such as distant aeroplanes, flocks of geese, even, in all probability, angels. As the dizzying ranges of possibility opened in front of them, the villagers grew more enthusiastic and inspired; and José Maria de Valdés' order-book filled up quickly. Though it wasn't really an order-book, he explained to me, but a register of potential customers, and it was held in high regard in the local office at San Juan de Manapiare, and no doubt in Caracas also, and in New York. Later on, real salesmen would be coming, fully equipped with order forms, trading stamps, and of course the goods that were at the centre of this excitement, in an electrical epiphany. Thus did I play a small part in the chain of events that led to the electrification of the village, and aided the cause of capitalism by adding, however, minutely, to the potential customers of José's employers.

In the afternoon, worn out, we slept, first tethering Johnny to a bedpost.

We set out again in the cool of the evening, having hired horses, to ride the few kilometres to the village of José's grandmother. I was obliged to seat Johnny behind me on my horse, tying his hands around my waist, because he could not balance.

A Better Way of Dealing with the Dead

The grandmother of José was a witch, or wise woman, but she had not performed magic for many years. She lived on a farm, very old now, toothless, white-haired; and although she could, said her grandson, grow new teeth if she wished, by the operation of magic, she had no power at all over her digestion, so the milk and gruel she ate now would still be her diet even if she had teeth; so what would be the point?

She received us graciously, offering us such hospitality as she could afford, and accepting with delight her grandson's present of the little transistor radio. When we were seated around the rough wooden table, with the radio playing in the background, José explained what we had come for.

She nodded. Johnny was made to sit down while she examined him.

This took some time, and meanwhile Mary, I saw, was becoming restless and unhappy. Perhaps she sensed what was going to happen; certainly she kept looking sullenly at me, seeing quite correctly that it was all my fault. But my conscience was less powerful than my curiosity, and I watched the old woman with great interest.

First of all she examined his body in great detail. He did not seem to be broken or damaged too badly; what exactly had killed him she did not know, but it might have been shock, caused by the sudden expulsion of his spirit from his body in the crash. It often happened, she said.

Then she began to ask him a series of detailed questions about all kinds of things. She wanted to know how far he had gone into the spirit world since his death; what he had seen there; what his body, left to its own devices, would seek to do.

In answer to that question, Johnny's body looked at Mary and said, "To ravish this girl, since I cannot hope to win her love as a corpse."

Mary abruptly stood up and left the room. Johnny's eyes followed her, his dead face intense and fixed.

José said, "It's not good to speak about things like that in front of a young girl. She could be badly frightened."

"What do you want," said his grandmother, "politeness from a dead man? Dead men have more important things to occupy their minds."

I wondered if I should go out after Mary.

"What this zombie must do," said the grandmother, "is obey you," and she looked at me.

"Will that restore him to life?" I asked.

"If you do as I say. And first of all, you must persuade the young lady to grant him his desire."

"But she'll never do that!" I said, appalled.

The old woman shrugged. "I can't help that. Perhaps I wouldn't either, if I were her. It won't be pleasant, but it'll only take a minute or two, and then he'll be alive again. But she's got to do it willingly. It's no good if he takes what he wants by force. That's where you come in: you must control him. And when the time comes when she agrees, you must tell him to act like a lover, to pretend to be alive, and to treat her gently. And she will have to pretend, as well. It all depends on pretending."

"She won't do it," I said. "She won't pretend that."

"She pretends already," said the old woman. "She is good at it. She will do it, if not for him then for you. Don't give up hope. And there is an ointment, too, which will help."

"What did I tell you?" said José, proudly. "She knows all the answers."

"Yes," I said. "Thank you, señora. But now I think I'd better go and see whether she is all right. I'm worried about her, she's tired . . ."

"You're not worried," said the old woman. "But you're pretending. All right, but you had better be good at it."

Disconcerted, I got up and went outside to look for Mary. She was on the little veranda, standing with her shoulders hunched up and her hands clasped, looking out at the night. It was warm out there; the stars were bright, and it smelt of maize and sugar and coffee. Mary had been crying.

"What do you want?" she said bitterly.

"I came to see if you were all right."

"Well, great, thanks, that's really kind of you, yes, I'm fine, thanks."

I said nothing. I was worried about her, in spite of the old woman's remarks. Or perhaps I was getting good at pretending.

"I won't do it," she said.

"Do what?"

"Oh, for Christ's sake," she cried.

"You heard, then?"

"Of course." She brushed her hand over her eyes impatiently. "You think it's simple, don't you?" she said.

"No, of course not."

"You know nothing," she said, with absolute certainty. "You're no bloody use at all, you can't even keep your own wife, and you know nothing whatsoever about what you're expecting me to do, nothing whatso*ever*, not a bloody thing."

There was a wooden railing around the veranda. I moved forward and leant my elbows on it, looking down at the thin starlit grass below. I was tired, I decided, worn out, and if Mary's attack had struck home, then no doubt I deserved it. There was nothing I could say in reply.

"I won't do it," she said again.

"All right. But can you just put up with him until we get there?"

"Get where?" she said wearily.

"The Anderson Valley."

"Oh, yes, our little jaunt. I'd quite forgotten."

We said nothing then for some time. After a minute or so she came forward and leant on the rail as I was doing. And by the artificial means of adopting the same posture, our minds grew more sympathetic towards each other, though it took time. It was about five minutes before she spoke, and that is a longer time than it seems.

"Tell me about your wife," she said.

So I told her everything I knew about my wife. But I found that there wasn't much I did know, or else that to talk about a real person as if she was a character in a book was very difficult. I found myself before long talking about the messenger who'd come to me in Valencia.

"You really don't know if it was a boy or a girl?" she asked.

"A girl, I think. But . . ." I hadn't told her about the bank. I hesitated, and then did so.

"Why were you unfaithful to your wife, if you love her?"

"I don't think I was. The messenger represented her. And she could carry a message back from me to her in the same way, if she were a boy, if you see what I mean."

"And you wouldn't mind that?"

"It seems to be her choice. Of course I don't mind. I even think it might be more potent like that."

"What would?"

"Love. As if it were distilled, perhaps."

"You'll be lucky," she said, quietly.

I nodded, for she was right, and I had been talking nonsense, just letting words come unprepared into my mouth. We talked about love for a little longer, she saying more than I did, for she knew more. Love, she told me, was like architecture or music, a complex and elaborate triumph of the imagination. That was not how it had occurred to me, and I said so, but she put me right.

"You mustn't think it's something simple," she said. "Perhaps for people like you it is, I wouldn't know about that, but not for people like me and Johnny."

"What's the difference between us?" I asked.

"Our families," she said. "It doesn't matter who *you* marry, because not much depends on it, I mean not much money or power and things like that. But with us it matters a lot. So we have to think a lot more about it. We realise a lot more about what love is, because we have to create it sometimes, if it isn't there to start with."

"How can you create love?" I asked.

"It's not simple," she said. "That's what I'm trying to say. It takes a long time and a lot of skill and knowledge. It never just happens."

"For people like me it does," I said.

"You think it does, perhaps, but you're wrong. If you haven't done it consciously, you've done it unconsciously. It never just happens."

I looked out at the South American night, dusty with stars, and felt my ignorance lying heavily on me. But just then a cool breeze came down from the mountains and brushed against my face. It came from very high, where the Anderson Valley lay, and it smelt of clean, newly ironed cotton, of oxygen, of snow, of the desert.

So there were more ways than one, I discovered, for messages to be delivered. And a cool breeze was the simplest thing in the world, so Mary was wrong. Except that (as I realised when I thought about it) that cool breeze was the end result of an unimaginably complex interaction of atmospheric forces, the geology of the mountains, and gravity. So Mary was right.

But in the end, it felt like a cool breeze, and it smelt like the messenger.

Into the Territory of Another Salesman

Before we left in the morning José's grandmother gave me, in secret, a little horn box containing her magic ointment, and instructed me in its use, in case, she said, the young lady changed her mind. But I was to make sure that her desire to help was genuine, and I must not try to force her into it.

We thanked her for her hospitality, and left. José rode with us for a few kilometres, but when we reached a narrow stream he said he would have to turn back.

"It's the end of my territory," he said. "I'm not allowed by the company to trespass on the territory of another salesman. But once you have forded this stream you keep to the road until you come to the town of the *fantasmas,* the ghost town, which is called Ciudad Primero del Pueblo Ilusorio. And from there I don't know, but the Anderson Valley is at the end of the road, such as it is. God go with you."

We thanked him and said goodbye, and he reined back his proud horse so that it reared up and whinneyed, and then, curvetting elegantly from time to time, they rode away.

Mary and I urged our two horses forward. The little stream had steep banks, and we had to dismount. The water was bitterly cold. Once we were on the far side Mary galloped ahead, raising a cloud of reddish dust from the dry road.

The countryside was quiet: low hills, covered in grassy pampas, with occasional clumps of trees. The grass was waist-high. Flocks of strange parrot-like birds, and flocks of quite ordinary starlings, wheeled and screamed in the air when we passed them. From time to time I saw a movement in the grass as if some animal was passing; and once a small wild pig suddenly ran across the track ahead of us.

The road itself was a single dirt track, just wide enough for a vehicle, but unrutted, so it didn't look as if wheeled vehicles used it. It was covered in hoof-prints. Fresh horse-droppings lay scattered here and there.

I wondered about the town José had mentioned, the ghost town. A ghost town was a settlement abandoned when a mine, for instance, gave out. But he had called it the First City of the Unreal People, and called them *fantasmas*, ghosts. Maybe there really were ghosts there, but in the clear sunlight of those uplands I couldn't worry about phantoms. Had I not routed a master of zombies?

Johnny held on to my waist as we walked, or cantered; and we said nothing. If it was my fate to go everywhere with a dead man, so be it, but we could not share very much.

Every so often we passed a ruined car, or the wreck of a truck or tractor, rusting beside the road, already half-way back to nature, oxidising, decomposing; but like a zombie, they could only get half-way, the atoms being held in a firmer embrace than those of a fruit, say, or of a really dead body; and the steel cylinder-blocks, chassis members, doors and window-frames, and the glass of the windscreens and the plastic of the fascia boards and steering wheels survived like skeletons long after the few organic components of the car, the leather upholstery, the rubber floor-mats, had decayed.

I lost count of these dead cars after a while. Then we began to notice other kinds of rubbish: empty gasoline and kerosene cans, empty food tins, abandoned cookers, washing machines, a typewriter. It was all placed quite carefully. Each article stood upright, square to the road, and where the ground was uneven, a stone or a piece of plank had been put under one of the corners to keep it steady and level. The cars and trucks had been skilfully parked parallel to the road.

The effect was one of care and even artistry, as if it had been planned by a landscape gardener. And I noticed that these products of technology, in their retirement, had become gods. Garlands of flowers, withered and fresh, were decked around some of them, and inside some of the cookers had been placed dishes of fruit, or maize.

Mary was noticing them too. She had slowed her horse to a walk, and was waiting for me to catch up with her.

"I don't like this place," she said.

"Why?"

"All these things. They look like tombstones. How far is it to the Anderson Valley, anyway?"

"God knows. At least we're going in the right direction."

We moved on side by side. After a minute she said "Martin?"

"Yes?"

"Do you think I'm on my father's side?"

"I don't think you're on anyone's side, except yours."

"But you don't think I'm on yours?"

"I don't know. The only person I knew was on my side was Johnny. But there needn't be sides if you think about it. We're not competing for anything."

She was quiet for a while; and then said "It's like a rubbish dump, this place."

I said nothing. She went on. "No it isn't. I'm only saying it for the sake of saying something. Why don't you talk to me?"

"I haven't got much to say."

"Well, you could make an effort."

"Yes, I could."

"If you wanted to."

"Well, naturally. But I don't like that sort of conversation."

"All right . . . What do you think these things are here for?"

She waved a hand at the garlanded relics. I shrugged.

"Probably the salesman of this territory will tell us, if we see him."

"They might be his samples."

The further we went, the thicker they lay; until at noon we were travelling through what looked like a cemetery, with the abandoned cookers and refrigerators and washing machines looking, as she had said, like tombstones. There were many birds circling overhead, or perching on the trees and on the eye-level grills, the open lids of spin-driers, the bonnets or radiator grilles of cars. But not a single human figure was visible.

I began to be glad of her company, even if we did find it difficult to talk.

Then we saw ahead of us a motorcycle, not abandoned but new.

Gleaming and powerful, it stood at the side of the road like a quiet horse waiting for its master.

And its master was sitting beside it on the grass. He was a plump, ironic-looking man of middle age, wearing an alpaca suit and a straw hat. He was reading a magazine and smoking a cheroot; and when we came up to him he folded the magazine, put it in his pocket, and stood up, taking off his hat to Mary.

"Good day," he said. "Welcome to my territory. I am Jesús Ramon de Castillejo, poet and business representative, agent of the Mitsubishi Corporation, General Motors, Philips, the Honda Company, Standard Oil, and Du Pont Chemicals. Not necessarily in that order, but in the order in which I remember them. May I ask where you are going?"

"Good day, señor," I replied, trying to match his own courteous tone. "My name is Martin Browning, and this is Miss Mary Pretorius. We are bound for the Anderson Valley, and we understand that the road leads through a city with an unusual name. How far is it to that city?"

"Ciudad Primero del Pueblo Ilusorio lies only a few kilometres ahead of you, Mr Browning. Do you intend to stay there?"

"No. But perhaps we can find somewhere to eat at least, because we're hungry and thirsty."

"I think the city could find resources enough for that," said the salesman. "If you are agreeable, I will accompany you."

"By all means."

He started his motorcycle. It was a Japanese machine of great power, equipped with a battery of items like spot lamps, a gyroscopic compass, two-tone horns, a two-way radio; and so beautifully was it made that the engine made little more noise than an electric sewing machine.

The salesman rode skilfully along beside us, at a walking pace, adjusting his speed to that of our horses.

"Tell me," I began, "why . . ." I gestured towards the metallic shrines that carefully littered the landscape.

"Ah," he said, in a melancholy tone. "They say, in the city, that these are machines which started to become unreal, and so were moved out of the city to preserve them from the malignant effects of the Electric Park."

I thought that this was some fantastic nonsense or other, and looked covertly at him to see if he looked like a madman. But he looked merely elegant and thoughtful. He continued:

"No doubt, to experienced travellers like yourselves, we must seem like very ignorant fish in a tiny provincial pond. A year ago, when I arrived, I thought the same. But twelve months in the First City Of The Unreal People has taught me to fear unreality, and to shun it like the plague. If there were the remotest suspicion that my motorcycle, for instance, harboured the fateful germs of unreality, I would abandon it by the roadside without the slightest hesitation. No doubt there is a reason for this pestilence that lies over our fair district, but—" and he took his hands off the handlebars of his machine and shrugged expressively. The motorcycle continued docilely and mildly without wavering from its path.

"You don't know," said Mary.

"Alas," he said, "I know nothing of it."

"But señor Castillejo," I said, "you have told us that you are a poet. And, in circumstances as remote and mysterious as these, are we to believe that you poet's imagination has not speculated on the mystery? I have a theory, señor, which says that the stronger the imagination, the finer and more powerful, that is to say the closer to reality, are the forms which it creates; reality itself being the most unimaginable of things. And as the poetic imagination is the finest of all, I am inclined to think that your speculations would be very close to the truth: in short, that if you made up the story of the First City, then it would be the next best thing to the real answer."

"Your analysis, Mr Browning, is masterly; and your theory of the imagination has boldness and originality to commend it. I cannot deny that I have spent many hours in guesswork about the city . . . but guesswork is all it is. However, if it would amuse you to hear my conjectures, I would be only too happy to lay them before you."

"We would be delighted and gratified to share your knowledge, señor."

"Then I shall begin."

Poetic Speculations Concerning the History of the First City
"Wait," said Mary.

She had determined on something. Her face was fixed and slightly flushed; she looked into the middle distance.

"Leave Johnny here," she said. "I'll catch you up."

Jesús Ramon de Castillejo halted his motorcycle a few yards further on. Astonished, I merely gaped at her for a moment, and then dismounted, helping Johnny down. I gave her the little horn box and told her quickly what to do with it. I didn't know whether to say Thank you, or Do you really want to do it? or It's very good of you, though I wanted to say many trite things like that; so I said nothing. She tied up her horse to the wing mirror of a Dodge pick-up truck and waited for me to go. So I rode on, my brain teeming, and caught up with the poetic salesman.

He looked at me not curiously so much as with a slight, cultured interest.

"Your friend is a zombie, then?"

"Not for very long, I hope."

"Ah," he said.

We moved forward.

"The history of the city," I prompted gently.

"Ah yes. Now you must not confuse the unreal people with the ghosts. The ghosts were here before the people, because the land is infested with them, as some places are infested with snakes. It is unfortunate, but we live with it. No, unreality came into the city, as I guess, with the Americans.

"They set up, you see, various secret enterprises, including an electric park and many banks, in order to pursue many different lines of research that were forbidden to them in the U.S.A."

"What lines?"

"I cannot imagine," he said suavely. "But it went wrong. Money decayed in this tropical atmosphere, and some of their workers started to become unreal."

"One thing at a time, señor," I said. "How does money decay?"

"How? I don't know. But what happens is that you can no longer buy anything with it. No doubt it is a result of the heavy tropical atmosphere."

"And how do workers become unreal?"

"Ah, I shall explain that in a moment, if you can wait until the story reaches that point."

"I shall try to."

"But I can throw you a hint," he said. "The unreal people were a by-product of research. You see, in the centre of the city is an electric park, where vast currents of power are drawn out of various minerals. Or were, before the collapse. And the electric park is surrounded by a million masts and wires, aerials, I believe, for receiving electricity sent from another place. Television works on a similar principle," he explained.

"Yes," I said.

"And in the electric park they set up a great transformer—you understand the principle of transformers?"

"Vaguely," I said.

"They change things from one state to another. This particular transformer was designed to change human beings physically, so that electricity would flow in their veins instead of blood, and they would become immortal."

He stopped, as if he had come to the end of his story. We rode on in silence. A flock of heraldic birds rose, screaming, from their metallic roosts, and wheeled prophetically in the sky before re-settling. The poet's motorcycle purred competently. There was silence from behind us.

"And?" I prompted.

"That's a bad story," he said. "It leads to a dead end."

"You could imagine some more," I suggested.

"I haven't the heart to."

He sat morosely on his great machine, his lips pressed bitterly together.

"But señor," I said, "if you give up merely because you haven't the heart, how do you finish anything?"

"I am a lyric poet, not a common storyteller," he said shortly. "A hint, a perfect phrase, an image, those are my ends."

"But I like stories," I said.

"Bah!"

I remained respectfully silent.

"However," he said after a minute, "in my capacity as business representative of General Motors, Philips, etc., etc., I may be able to make a few practical remarks."

"Please do."

He was looking straight ahead. All the irony had gone out of his expression, and he now looked deeply serious, sober, level-headed, a senior and experienced executive grown wise in the ways of commerce and finance. But by comparison with Pretorius or Hamid Senior he looked like a foolish baby; and I sighed.

"This territory," he said, "is mine. It is marked thus on maps in San Juan, Caracas, Tokyo, Amsterdam, New York, Zurich . . . I administer it under the mandate of the greatest commercial organisations in the world, and consequently I have some status, you understand? Some standing in the community."

"Yes," I said, sounding impressed.

"Well, I do not care for spies."

"Spies?" I repeated foolishly.

"It was obvious the moment I saw you," he continued sternly. "By a fortunate coincidence, I was reading this when you approached."

He produced the magazine from his pocket and handed it up to me. It was a month-old copy of *Newsweek*, open at an article in the business section on new undercover work-study techniques. I read a little of it and came across a reference to the Pretorius Bank. "Europe's Lionel Pretorius, never reluctant to explore new avenues of profitable possibility, has committed his bank to a six-month feasibility study of the method. AVP execs are looking over their shoulders already."

"You don't seriously think," I said, "that I've come all this way in order to watch you selling toasters?"

"Stranger things happen every day. And if the citizens of this place see me being spied on by strangers they will revise their opinion of me, and think me less than a man, one whom his superiors do not trust, one of whom the little children can make fun of in the streets; and I will see my standing in this community dwindle like wax in the fire, and I will become nothing, unreal, illusory."

"Señor Castillejo, I swear to you on my honour as an artist that I am not spying on you. I am here for the purpose of finding my wife, who I think has gone to the Anderson Valley. As for the First City, of course I am interested in it, but it is the interest of the intelligent traveller, not the curiosity of the spy. I would not be surprised if the importance of your position attracted the attention of this kind of espionage; but, be assured, I am not one of its practitioners."

I spoke in such stately terms because I thought it would impress him. But he said nothing. We rode on at the same decorous pace, his expression signifying dissatisfaction and chagrin. After a minute he leant forward and, from a clip at the side of the motorcycle, drew a revolver. I started, and prepared to defend myself, but he raised the gun slowly to point ahead of him, his arm dead straight, took aim, and fired. The metallic emblem that crowned the radiator of a turquoise car thirty metres away flew spinning into the air, and the ricocheting bullet whined into oblivion. A chorus of panicking small birds rose into the air and shrieked.

"An artist, did you say, señor?" he asked.

"I am a musician."

"Then I accept your explanation without reserve, and offer my profound apologies."

"Which are of course accepted," I replied, and we bowed solemnly to each other.

"I remember a time," he said, "when the notion of becoming unreal would have fled from my scorn like mist from the sun."

"I think it does from mine."

"But a year in the First City, and now I dread it with great fear."

"How can a person become unreal?"

"It's a mysterious process," he said. "It begins with the contempt or neglect of others. They become pale and begin to waste away. They don't die, but reach a state in which even death is beyond their grasp. Often they become silent, and their flesh is so attenuated as to be quite transparent. Why this is so, no one knows, but we believe it is compounded by the malignant effects of the electric park. Quite possibly a virulent form of electricity still taints the place."

He described the city to me as we went on, and listed some of the many kinds of unpleasant ghost which made life in Ciudad Primero a melancholy business.

"However," he said, "we have our consolations. The city has a singular beauty, especially at night, and we endeavour to pass our time in intellectual and cultural pursuits, to relieve the anguish of life here. You must allow me to introduce you to our Musical Society. It is so seldom that we have a visitor; perhaps we can prevail upon you to play?"

"I don't want to stay very long," I said. "My friends and I are keen to move on quickly."

"But one night?"

"How far away is the Anderson Valley?"

"A week's ride, or ten days, more or less; a few hours would make no difference."

"Well, perhaps. I would certainly like to see such a curious place as your city seems to be."

"Then you must, señor, and you shall."

Resurrection and Hatred

I was also, naturally, very curious to know about what was going on down the road behind us: had Mary succeeded? How could she bear it? And so on, a thousand times.

When I heard the sound of galloping, I said to Castillejo, "Señor, may I ask if you would be kind enough to leave us on our own for now?"

"By all means," he said. He seemed to know why; at any rate, with great tact and discretion, he gave me his card, wrote on it the name of the best of the few functioning hotels in the First City, and raced off swiftly.

I turned to face them, and dismounted.

Johnny, the real Johnny, my dear friend, was riding, and Mary sat behind; and as they stopped Mary slipped down, her face stained with tears, snatched the reins from my hand and was in the saddle in a flash, and kicked my horse into a gallop and rode away. I stared after her.

Johnny jumped down, and I turned back to him. Involuntarily I grinned, and when I saw how real he was I felt tears come into my eyes; and then I embraced him, and kissed him fervently, like a girl, out of the joy of seeing him alive again. His cheeks had the flush of live blood, his eyes sparkled, his flesh was warm, and the balance and grace were restored to his movements. I could hardly speak for joy.

But his expression was serious, after our greeting.

"Martin, what's happened? Where are we? And why has Mary gone?"

So I told him. Of his sojourn in zombie-hood he remembered nothing; nothing at all until he woke up beside Mary, and found her dressing, in tears. And she would not speak to him.

"Was that what she did?" he said, appalled. "And I was like a zombie? My God, my God."

I told him about Castillejo, and the First City of the Unreal People, and of what we were going to do. He looked in wonder at the strange technological wilderness we were passing through, the innumerable dead cars, the decaying refrigerators, the electric fires, all glittering with enamel or glowing with rust, like a garden of costume jewellery. The sun was at its height, and glared madly in the still shining chrome of bumpers and glass of windscreens. As we walked along, we were lit from all sides by the heliographed reflections, and seemed to be made of light ourselves, or to be swimmers in a luminescent surf.

And in the distance, I saw the first buildings; a group of skyscraper-like apartment blocks, seeming a long way off, but in fact only veiled by the shimmering mirage-bearing haze.

And there was Mary, beside the road. She was lying on her front and hiding her face. The horse, tied up, cropped the grass quietly beside her.

"I'd better go on," said Johnny in an undertone. "She won't want to see me, I guess."

I nodded; and he mounted the horse we'd been leading and trotted on ahead.

"Mary," I said gently, and sat down beside her.

She didn't move.

"Are you all right?"

She nodded, but said nothing, and kept her face hidden.

"Johnny's alive!"

Silence. I had to say "thank you", or make some acknowledgement of what had happened, but I didn't know how to do it.

"Did he speak to you?" I asked.

"Tried to," she muttered.

"What did he say?"

"I didn't want to listen. Oh, God, Martin," and she seized my hand, and sobbed like a baby. "I'm all torn about; I won't ever look at him again, I hate him, I wish we'd killed him on the farm. Tell him to go away and never come near me ever again, ever, ever, ever."

I stroked her shoulder and muttered some soothing phrase or other.

After a few minutes she stopped crying, and sat up and asked me for a handkerchief.

"I've been learning about the city," I said. "The salesman wants us to stay overnight."

"I don't care what we do."

"What about your father? He still doesn't know you're alive."

"Of course he does. He's bound to know."

"But how?"

"Because all these salesmen and representatives are in touch with their companies, obviously. If there's one thing my father's good at, it's knowing what goes on. He'll have heard by now that we're alive, and where we are, and everything."

"I don't know how you can be so sure. Besides, if he does know, isn't he likely to try and stop us?"

She shrugged, and blew her nose. Then she began to comb her

hair; it was moist with sweat, and thick with dust, but the way she combed it, and her manner of sitting bolt upright, shaking the rich waves back, made her look like a princess, and I knew she was herself again.

"Well, what do you want to do?" she said when she'd finished.

"Me? Well, obviously, I want to get on. Why?"

"I just want to know what we'll be doing."

"You don't have to come, if you don't want to. Naturally."

"I don't want to stay here."

"Johnny's coming, though."

"Then it'll be difficult, won't it."

"You're still coming?"

"I don't want to stay here."

"But you don't want to go home? If we could find transport in this city, maybe . . ."

She was less composed than I'd thought. The pressure of my questions was too much for her, and her lips trembled and tears came to her eyes again.

"Don't keep on," she said in an unsteady voice. "Just take me with you, or leave me, do what you want, but for God's sake don't ask me what you should do. You should *know* that."

"I'm only concerned about you," I muttered. "Since you've . . ." I gestured ahead to where Johnny was riding on his own.

She shrugged. But the mention of it brought a fresh flood of tears. I felt helpless. What had she gone through, and for someone she didn't love?

"I just wanted to say thank you," I said bluntly. "I couldn't say nothing about it. And I wanted to make sure that I helped you in return. I haven't just taken it for granted."

That made her laugh in the middle of her crying.

"Why are you so bloody concerned about doing everything in return?" she said through her tears. "You always are. It's like a madness with you."

I shrugged my shoulders. "God knows. But in the financial world I came into when I met your father I feel guilty if I take something without paying for it."

"You can't always pay for things you're given."

She said that authoritatively, like a sybil, and I felt rebuked.

"And I want to come with you to find your wife," she said, in her normal voice. "I won't get hysterical again about Johnny, I promise."

"Let's go on, then," I said, relieved at her returning self-possession.

We stood up, and both of us felt dizzy for a moment in the sun, and had to cling to each other like children, or zombies.

How to Promote Tourism in a Ghost Town

This was one of the great questions in the First City; productive enterprises having failed, and international finance conservatively preferring Zurich, New York, and so on, the citizens of Ciudad Primero believed that they could promote the particular beauties of their town in the tourist market. But they were too anxious, and defeat, like a healthy bouncing child, was growing up fast in the city, and testing its strength.

The atmosphere of the place was curious and powerful. It smelt of febrile over-concern, over-activity, without roots. Competition, which, in the great seaport with its elegant boulevards where my journey had begun, was handled with irony and detachment, was here a necessary drug that had to be taken in ever-increasing doses.

Advertising posters and hoardings covered every square metre of wall space; neon signs glared and flickered in the twilight. At dusk the city looked almost poetic, but in the light of day you could see that the posters were defaced or faded and that many of the neon lights were cracked and smashed. At night, of course, you only saw the ones that worked.

The people moved like frantic ghosts, flitting urgently along the streets. They moved about in a deep, unyielding silence, which hung over the city like a curtain. There was little traffic in the streets; no horses, no cars, only the occasional truck. In the empty canyons of the American-style box-grid streets, anxiety hung like Spanish moss.

And sometimes we saw, sitting huddled in a doorway or wandering vaguely down a shadowy alley, a figure that could only be one of those unfortunates, the unreal people. They were quiet, subdued, retiring, like mental patients, or refugees without passports. And there was, as the salesman had told me, a peculiar lightening and transparency of their flesh, almost as though they were truly disappearing.

We found that if we looked at the unreals for too long (and a minute was too long) we began to shiver and feel slightly dizzy. Mary said they made her feel sick. But we found that if we didn't take any notice of them, we were safe, because they could never of themselves gain our attention, they were too shadowy, too camouflaged. Even when you caught sight of one, it never came as a shock or made you start, as it would if you saw a real person suddenly. If you came alone to your house late at night, and found as you went into a dark room that there was an unreal standing in it, you would not be startled. And after a minute you might have forgotten about him, although he would still be there.

But the ghosts were another matter.

Later that night, when I had made my South American debut under the auspices of the Sociedad Musical del Ciudad Primero, which consisted of Señor Castillejo and a dozen other cultured exiles, I went out to look for adventure, and to examine this curious city in greater detail.

The ladies and gentlemen of the Music Society were reluctant to speak of the ghosts; it seemed to be bad form to mention them. But the suave salesmen told me in an aside that I would no doubt encounter some, if I went out on my own.

I went through the empty moonlit streets towards the electric park, mentioned by the poetical agent in the story he did not finish.

The Parque Electrico was a wilderness of mystery. Gravel was being flooded by green grass, slowly, from below, but the grass was grey in the moonlight and the gravel silver. Notices, defaced by time, warned of high voltages that had never throbbed through these glinting hooks and terminals, these porcelain and glass insulators never having strained their atoms to contain vast forces . . .

Along one side of El Parque Electrico was a disused railway goods yard. But there had never been a time when it was used, and the wagons and the shunting engine that stood there under the moon were brand new, under their coats of rust. The tracks had been torn up, all but the lengths of rail on which the wagons and the engine stood, to be used for more urgent purposes such as the building of shacks for those people whose money had gone bad.

Dog Street was the name of the thoroughfare which led to this melancholy quarter. It was empty. There was a fence on each side of it, with the goods yard on one side and the Electric Park on the other.

Dog Street was burnt by the sun at noon and frozen under the stars at night; it had felt no tyres hum down its length, never since the tarmac was laid; it had never felt the drops of oil from a hot engine splash and soak, never having been painted with the iridescence of spilled gasoline; Dog Street was cracking up, and grass was appearing slyly at its edges; the street was going mad, wearing straws in its hair.

It was littered with broken bottles, empty cans, sodden and dried and sodden again and frozen paper packets, bleached, stained, bleached again, some now almost finally mad, become wild and disintegrated, others new; a nature reserve of garbage.

Glints, gleams, from the broken glass, the shiny tins, where the bits of the moon lay, cut about. This light began in the sun, was reflected off the moon, pierced the airs of the earth, was reflected again off a broken bottle, and ended in my brain. What is left of the original nature of the sun? Well, it doesn't end in my brain; here it is on the page. How much further will it go?

Ah, there is formidable poetry in places like Dog Street, never used, and decaying. Behold the end of a row of houses: new, unpainted, unroofed. And beyond them on a patch of waste ground the shack, of empty kerosene cans hammered flat, of a poor man.

A wind from the distant Andes drifts down Dog Street, lifting the light papers, disturbing the dust. In the Andes there are similar places, wonderful cities abandoned by their makers. In Europe, we don't leave cities like that. Obviously in this part of the world they are not happy in cities and don't trust them.

There were no criminals in the city, none at all. But everyone lived in fear of two things, there being no criminals to fear: first, of becoming unreal, ilusorio; second, of malignant ghosts. The unreals were harmless, but the ghosts were not. They had no physical body, but they had the power to affect people; they were more real than the unreals.

These ghosts came in many forms. There were spider ghosts, snake ghosts, ghosts like a firework, ghosts like pools of water, ghosts like bad air, ghosts like coins, like songs, like names, like books, like street-lights, like trees, like an equestrian statue, like a rumour, like birds. They had great power to hurt, and they were all malignant; not one of them but hated honest men and women.

Where they came from, or who sent them or called them up, I don't know, but the city was stiff with them. And especially at night, when the dry bone-coloured moon shone upon the wastes of the Calle de Perros, it was easy to see them, they were everywhere.

Because they didn't trouble to hide, being already disguised by their nature, by their very shapes. Who would suspect that broken bottle of being a ghost? But a ghost it was, and would cut you maliciously if you touched it, and get into your bloodstream, and haunt you. Or that song? Don't sing it! Stay away and stop up your ears, or sing another, anything else, or it will enter your brain and you'll never be free of it.

But being haunted by one ghost gave you the power of being able to recognise other ghosts, and thus avoid them. Perhaps the power to discern ghosts was worth the price of being haunted by one. As it might be worth the discomfort of living in the Calle de Perros for the sake of the wild, melancholy night views.

But how was it that I saw ghosts so clearly, unless I was haunted by a ghost myself? The ghost of capitalism, no doubt, of finance and curiosity.

Thus I pondered as I strolled, a boulevardier of the South American night, inspecting the processes of life on the Street of Dogs.

I came on a little girl, a child of nine or ten, playing with a rag doll and a cardboard box for a doll's house. I wanted to talk, but I didn't know how to address her. I stood dumbly and watched her, like a sex-murderer.

"My name is Maria," she said, when she had wrapped up her doll in a blanket and put it to sleep. "What are you called?"

"Martin," I said. "Where do you live?"

"In the Calle de Perros, and sometimes in the Parque Electrico, where I serve Las Putas Electricas."

"Have you got a family?"

"My doll Alma is all I want."

"Isn't it late to be out alone?"

"I'm not afraid of ghosts. I can see them all."

I nodded. She was so calm and so self-possessed . . . The middle of the night, a ruined, waste area, the dry shuffle of the wind and maybe rats or ghosts; the fervent moon, glowing madly over the torn walls, the empty lots, the flayed shunting-yard. But this was her happy home.

"What can you tell me about the Electric Whores you serve?"

"They are spirits of electricity, left behind by the Americans."

"Why are they called Whores?"

"Men come and try to sleep with them."

"And can they?"

"Sometimes, if the Whores want to."

"What if they don't?"

"The men become unreal."

Of course they would; people become unreal for less than that.
"Could you take me to the Whores?" I asked.
"If you want me to."

The Electric Whores

The poetical salesman had mentioned the Electric Whores to me
earlier in the evening, but I thought that he was speaking in
metaphor.

The Electric Whores were one of the two reasons (the other being
the extraordinary beauty of the ruined parts of the city) for the
place still being inhabited. They were like benevolent but fickle
goddesses, presiding with random tenderness over the destinies of
their subjects. They lived in a state of electric blessedness. Congress
with them passed on a fragment of their sanctity, or perfection, to
those fortunate enough to achieve it; and it was a sovereign remedy
against the fear of ghosts.

The giant transformers whose nature Castillejo had explained so
blandly had, it seemed, worked some miracle of transformation
with a number of the spirits of the region. Quite what had happened no one knew, but then the ancestry of the Electric Whores
was not as important as their continued presence. They were the
subject of anguished debate among those who wanted to encourage
tourism in the city; one faction urged that they be promoted as a
local curiosity, while another maintained that the awesome and
sacred nature of the Whores should set them above commercial
exploitation. But everyone was agreed that without them, the city
would be nothing, and would probably itself become unreal.

As a measure of their transcendent importance, everything about
them was the subject of elaborate ritual. And my luck had brought
me to Maria, who was the one person in the city entitled to introduce visitors into the sacred enclosure, by virtue of her innocence
and freedom from all other ties.

The approved and authentic gateway into El Parque Electrico
was where a fallen section of fencing had been pulled aside. To
apply for admission to the "real" gateway on the other side was a
confession of haste and ill-breeding. Furthermore, no one could
pass through even the authentic gateway unless he was accompanied by Maria in her capacity of Psychopomp.

Once we were inside the gravelled enclosure, which was as large
as a large field and clustered with groves of metallic structures,

Maria explained that I had to look for the Whores myself. That was part of the ritual. She would go back into Dog Street and play until I had finished, but if I had not come out till morning, she would come and look for me; because if I had not come out by then, I would have become unreal, and thus incapable of knowing when I was no longer wanted.

We walked a little way into the Park, and she directed me to the centre of it; and I thanked her politely, and she left. I went off deeper into the Park to search for the nymphs of electricity.

As I walked across the silvery gravel a little flock of papers, cigarette packets, and the like, swirled up to me and around my feet as if in greeting. If these metal trees had leaves, they would behave in a similar graceful fashion.

The bare moon of the Andes, as mad as the swirling paper leaves, floated higher in the deserted sky.

I looked around for the Whores.

In the very centre of the Park there was a sacred grove of gleaming ceramic cones and glass insulators, where the Whores were waiting. At first they were invisible, but there was a delicate susurration among the metal boughs, and the hot dry scent of electricity spread gently outwards from the secret parts of their bodies.

I stood among the moonlit, shadowy transformers and asked the Whores to show themselves to me.

But they were shy, at first, and I had to be patient. Gradually some of their whispers became clearer, and I began to learn about them; and all the time, the impulse that had taken me to the Electric Park, namely curiosity, was being changed secretly (perhaps by the nearness of the powerful transformers which had so excited the imagination of the salesman) into physical desire.

Not having flesh, the Whores were cold and impossible to kiss. But they were as naked as it was possible to be, and as soft as the air. They described themselves to me in whispers that flickered on the edge of my hearing like lightning on the horizons of summer.

My desire increased, and the voices became clearer.

"You want to see us, and touch us? Come closer, then," and I reached out to touch the chilly steel of a great switch.

They were all around me.

"How can I make love to you?" I whispered.

"Think of your wife," was the answer. "Pretend you can make love to us. Make love to yourself."

They moved around me in a dance, and I sensed where they

were by following the secret electric scent as it circled and twined.

"It's you I want," I said, "not anything else."

"Come on," they said, "pretend, it's easy."

The air around me crackled with tension. Time and again I was penetrated by shafts of electricity, like darts of scented ice, but still I could not find the Whores, and began to wonder desperately if I were not on the way to becoming unreal.

"Pretend you're not, then," came the swift reply from the air.

"I don't understand," I said.

"Pretend you do," they answered.

"What are you?" I asked.

"Spirits," they said, and whirled around me faster in their mazy dance, "produced by matter."

I felt the urge to move too, to join in their invisible dance, and began to sway lightly from side to side in time with them.

"Matter loves itself," they said. "That's how we're here."

"Why must I pretend?"

"Aaah . . ." They began a chilly keening, and the dance faltered, but only for a second. "You must. We do. Pretend you're a girl. Pretend you're a spirit. Pretend you're a broken bottle or a rusty can or the lovely silver dirt on the Street of Dogs or pretend you're the Andes, or a Whore, or an electric cable, or a ghost."

"Is that how I make love to you?"

"Yes! Yes!"

I pretended I could see the Whores, and they became visible, slim, naked, beautiful and wanton, rejoicing in their infinite grace and the amorous inclinations of matter.

"Electricity! Money! Love! Happiness! Matter loving itself, making love to itself, that's what it all is . . ."

My mind was flooded with vastness, and on its edges reared the proud snow-capped Andes. Catherine lay as clean as the snow across the sky, outlined in stars, and the planets took up their stations on her figure.

And flickering and sparkling all around me were the nymphs of the metal trees, dancing, curving their bodies, enticing me, making love to themselves, until I began to confuse them with my wife; and I pretended she was there.

Sparks crackled at the great terminals, and for a moment or two a surge of current flung itself through the circuits.

"Pretend she loves you," said the Whores, "pretend what's unreal is real, pretend there are no ghosts, pretend the world is

125

different, pretend you're rich and happy, pretend, pretend, until—"
"No!"

I flung the word unhappily into the darkness. Catherine was not there; the Whores were still.

"I won't pretend anything," I said. "I want the world as it is, and nothing else."

The Whores vanished. Nothing stood on the cold gravel but the still machines left by the Americans. The wind from the Andes moved easily between them.

But if the Whores weren't real, then nor were electricity, or money, or love, or happiness. Yet they existed. Perhaps they existed, but were unreal.

Faced with these irreducible complexities, my mind shrank back into itself. I had learnt at least that pretence was more complicated than it seemed. And one thing remained: the Electric Whores had left me, but the outline of my wife stayed printed on the firmament, dazzling my eyes; and out of reach.

Next Day, on the Open Road

When Castillejo heard that I had visited the Electric Park, he became distraught and nervous, as if he had wanted to, but dared not. He was glad to see the back of us. So we set off quietly the next morning from the First City of the Unreal People. Before we went, however, I wanted to speak, if I could, to one of these eponymous figures, to learn what I could of his origins and history, and what it felt like to be unreal.

But (so subtle and far-reaching was the influence of their doom) I found it hard to remember this wish, even when I had just conceived it; and it was not until we were at the outskirts of the city, and looking back at its empty virginal office-blocks, its never-tenanted apartment buildings, that I recalled what it was that was nagging at my attention, and reined in my horse. I told the other two to go on ahead. They were secretly doubtful about each other, but they went.

I stayed behind, in a street of once whitewashed laundries, small factories, knowing that an unreal would appear soon.

When I saw one out of the corner of my eye I made straight for him, not looking directly at him in case I forgot about him. This plan seemed to work. In a second or two I was by his side, and he was looking at me, shading his eyes from the sun.

I dismounted. "Can you talk?" I asked.

"Yes," he said, but his voice was as insubstantial as those voices you hear sometimes when you are nearly asleep; it was a hypnagogic voice.

I continued to look away from him, or away from his face. His legs in their wide trousers of white cotton looked real enough, but the light sat on them oddly, as if it were not sure whether it shouldn't penetrate. The surface seemed to flicker with indecision.

"What's your name?" I said.

"Juan," he said, after a moment of hesitation.

"When did you become unreal?"

"I lost the esteem of my friends, because I fell in love with a whore; and when she didn't return my love I went into a decline, and so became unreal."

"Could you feel yourself becoming unreal?"

"Yes, but by then it was too late to do anything about it."

"How did you become unreal?"

He sighed, and it was like the wind blowing through the grass on the graves of dead children. I caught a shrug out of the corner of my eye, but the street was so full of distractions, a dog, the weathering on a wooden notice-board, the colour of a shadow, the idea that here would be a likely place to find a recording studio in any other city, and so on.

"Do you speak to the other unreals?"

"We are as unreal to each other as we are to you."

"Are you happy or unhappy?"

"I've forgotten."

"Have you any questions to ask me?"

"May I come with you when you go?"

The idea took me aback slightly, but it didn't startle me, because unreals couldn't startle you.

"Yes," I said. "But why?"

"I don't know."

"You'll have to . . ." I forgot what I was going to say. Some condition I was going to make.

"I don't eat or drink," he said.

"That's all right. Come, if you want to."

I mounted my horse; he held the reins for me, and passed them up. He had a small bundle of possessions, a poncho, a blanket, a purse with a few coins. I stowed them in the rucksack behind the saddle.

127

"We are largely insubstantial," he said, "and I can move very quickly without needing sustenance. So do not go slowly for my sake."

I caught sight just then, in that distracting street, of a ghost. It was the ghost of a door, and it was set in the wall of the white-washed laundry. It was painted red, and the paint was peeling; quite an undistinguished and ordinary door, except that it was a ghost.

It was trying to catch me. A draught of malignancy drifted across the street.

Then came a man, carrying a brown briefcase, looking like a minor official of the municipality. He thought he was alone in the street, not seeing me while the unreal was beside me, and picked his nose. Then he stopped suddenly by the door, and looked at it hard.

Then he took out a card from his pocket and looked at that, and up at the door again, but the door had no number. He backed out into the road to look up at the wall of the laundry, to see if the number was painted there, and then went back to the corner and looked at the name of the street, and came unwillingly back to the door.

I wanted to warn him, so I shouted "Don't! It's a ghost!"

At the sound the victim turned, startled, and then he saw us and began to come hesitantly across.

But at that moment a car came around the corner, and he had to step back on to the pavement; and by the time it had gone past, he had forgotten us.

He turned back to the door, and looked guiltily up and down the street. Then he grasped the handle, opened the door, and vanished inside the doorway. The red blistered paint glowed triumphantly in the sunshine.

What had I seen?

When I say "I saw a ghost, and it was the ghost of a door, and a man was caught by it and vanished", it is not in the interests of sensation that I say it, because I know it is too far-fetched to be sensational, but in the interests of history and of my wife. *She* is the justification! She would want me to write about it.

I resisted the temptation to open the door myself and see what lay inside. It was too late to rescue the victim; he was haunted for good now. This city, I thought, had a sad air, and I wanted to go.

So I mounted my horse and rode away, out of the empty street haunted by the red door, through the straggling weed-maddened

128

suburbs of corrugated iron bungalows with wooden verandas, the dry gardens in front of each one inhabited by spiders and lizards, and all the time the flickering form of the unreal trotted at my side.

Once the last house had been left behind, I forgot about him and pushed the horse into a canter. I caught up with Johnny and Mary a kilometre or so beyond the city limits. They were moving along quietly at walking pace, on opposite sides of the road.

It was a clear, sunny morning. We were on our way again! Life was good. Complexity had been lifted from me by the electric coupling of the night before.

I was more single-minded. I wanted even more to find my wife, so that she could explain it all to me, for of course she knew about it all. I'd only submit to being taught by her, because only she would be able to command me, only her wisdom would be able to guide me. I loved her and was in awe of her.

How do you make love to such a woman? It's very hard to think about. It seems impossible, that grossness, but it's sanctified, obscenity is blessed by it. In fact the more obscene the more holy the result, if you are dealing in holiness, or the lovelier, if you're dealing in beauty. Provided, of course, that the right conditions prevail: that you are in love. When I found her, I would fall in love again.

I caught sight of the unreal again, and tried to look at him directly, but failed.

"What's your name again?" I asked, because I had forgotten.

"Juan," he said.

"Ah, yes."

My voice startled Mary's horse; it whinnied. She was startled, too, because she thought I was talking to myself until she saw him.

"What's he doing?" she said.

"Ask him," I suggested. "His name's Juan. Juan, this is Mary Pretorius, and Johnny Hamid. And I am Martin Browning."

"Are you coming with us?" asked Mary of the unreal.

"If you will let me," he said, in his voice from the edge of sleep.

"Will you always be an unreal, like this?" said Johnny.

"You can't ask things like that," said Mary.

"Of course you can. You can ask anything if you want to know the answer, and if it doesn't hurt anyone. Juan, will you become real again?"

"I don't know."

"Do you want to?"

It was like trying to recall a half-lost dream, not like talking to

129

a person. After a while, we learnt how best to talk to Juan. We had to speak casually, think of something else while he answered, or even speak ourselves over his reply, paying little attention to him; and then we found we were hearing most of what he said, and seeing most of what he did. But it was still like dreaming, or talking to yourself.

Juan hesitated, and then said "All I want is to be with people, if that is all right."

"Sure," said Johnny.

The countryside was pleasant, cultivated, undulating. Neat fields of maize, tobacco, wheat spread out around us. Occasionally we would see a farmer in the distance, behind a horse-drawn plough, or trimming a fence. There was not one motor vehicle in sight, not one that worked anyway, and the mechanical hecatombs that were so devastating on the other side of the city were much smaller here.

The salesman of this territory, as I have said, had been fearful when he learnt of my night visiting, and his gentle courtesy all ran out of him. He refused to see me face to face, and spoke only to Johnny. He gave him a map and instructions for proceeding on the next stage of our journey. It was wild country beyond the borders of his territory, he said. The salesman of the next territory was allowed more independence and autonomy, because communications were so difficult.

We rode without incident through the day. As we went on, the neat and decorous fields gave way gradually to wider enclosures, wide pastures for cattle, and to thinner crops grown on harsher soil. We were climbing slowly towards a forbidding range of hills that glowed a bitter red.

The sun was sinking behind us, so the sky ahead was a deep, dusky blue, which contrasted powerfully with the dry blood-coloured hills. These highlands were slashed with rocky gullies, but from where we were there seemed to be little water in them. I wondered whether we had better stay down on the plain for the night, and enter the next salesman's territory the next morning. When I suggested it, Mary agreed at once.

"I'm worn out," she said. "It's too hot to go on."

We hobbled the horses, gathered wood for a fire, and spread out our bedding for the night. We were in a little hollow, with a stream running near by; a good place to camp.

That evening, of all the times on our journey, was one of the strangest of all, to look back on.

It was the first tranquil time we had had. Everything was under control, and a little of the chill had gone out of the air between Johnny and Mary. He took great pains for her sake to conceal his love for her, but he couldn't hide his delight in his luck that she should be sitting, her knees drawn up and a blanket around her shoulders, across a campfire from him. As for her, innumerable fine psychic veils concealed her. She was warm, friendly even, and I began to feel through her veils something of that power to fascinate which I had first noticed on the neo-classical terrace in the great seaport. But I saw it a little more clearly now, and how closely it was involved with the artifice she lived in.

She was tenderness and grace and softness, and infinite patience and understanding, but all those abstract qualities are not what it was like at all. The physical Mary seemed to embody them perfectly, so that her flesh became them. Tenderness itself was the way her long fingers lay curled around the cup she held; grace was the way she brushed her hair out of her eyes; softness was the curve of her calf, visible where the blanket had slipped to one side, as soft as a cloud it looked, white, perfectly formed, and with that suggestion of a veil on it: something about all her flesh that made it seem that the surface of it, and the air, mingled where they met: that there was no definite boundary between them.

She saw me looking at her, and was quite happy about it, because it gave me pleasure and didn't discomfit her at all. As I watched her talk and move I thought of my wife's limbs, and how different they were.

Catherine had the arms and legs of a dancer, or a gymnast, or a nymph. They were slim and strong and brown, the skin thin and translucent, each muscle clearly defined.

With that memory came a trace of the smell of her body. She was fastidiously clean, so that when we were naked and I could smell her body, it was always fresh and new, and her sweat smelt pleasant, like grass, an active, wild, nature smell. As a nymph would smell.

After a minute or so I realised that it was Mary herself who was the cause of that hallucination. It was the scent of her flesh, transmitted by the occasional movements of a lifted arm, or a stretched-out leg . . . an odour quite different in kind, warmer, closer, but the same in origin. That Mary, the priestess of fashion and artificial grace, should smell, be it ever so slightly and sweetly, was a tiny revelation. It added another dimension to her.

Johnny, meanwhile, was sitting quietly, absorbed in cutting a piece of wood into a frame for the back of his saddle, to keep the rucksack from chafing the horse's back. He glanced up from time to time, always at her, and she seemed to repel his glances as little as she did mine.

We were talking about the city they came from, and about the history of their families.

"Do you like them?" I asked. "The city, and society?"

"The city, yes," said Johnny. "And my mother and father."

Mary leant forward and pushed a branch further on to the fire. Little sparks flared, lighting her smooth forearm with a warm glow.

"Just the city," she said calmly, as she leant back once more. She raised her arms, putting her hands on the tree behind her head, and yawned.

"D'you know what I'd like to do?" said Johnny. "I'd like to go on walking, once we'd found your wife, all around South America. I don't want to go back."

"You must," said Mary.

"What for?"

"Your father and the company."

"They can do without me for a year or so."

"You couldn't do without them, though. You'd lose the feel of it. And your racing."

"Well, that's true," he said.

"Do you want to go back, Mary?" I asked.

She shrugged. "It makes no difference where I am, he'll find me if he wants to." She meant her father. "So I may as well go where I want to."

All her life, she said, her father had known everything about her, whether or not it was secret. And he had never punished her; he remained like God, above rewards or punishments; but he knew everything.

She had grown used to it. She would behave with utter ease and openness, spontaneous and free, while being aware that there was (perhaps) a microphone in the wall, or a movie camera in a bush, or a servant in the garden, to relay all her actions to her father. I wondered if this was the source of her secret theatricality, this devoted, rapt, permanent audience.

So that night we talked like brothers and sister, and lay down to sleep side by side.

132

Into the Mountains

I awoke just before dawn. I was freezing cold. But someone was pulling my blanket around my shoulders for me and arranging it so as to cover my feet. Juan the unreal crouched, dark against the sky, keeping watch over us.

"Thank you," I muttered.

"It's nothing."

Then I went back to sleep until Johnny woke me with some coffee later on.

We ate, packed, and were moving in half an hour or less. We were at the borders of Castillejo's territory, a bare half-land of low foothills covered in scrub. The mountains rose ahead of us. Even in early daylight they gave off a harsh strident orange-red colour that hurt the eyes.

They were frightening to look at. I had seen photographs of the city of Dresden after the war, and of Hiroshima, and it was those brutalised places I thought of, and not any natural scene, when I looked at the red hills ahead. They were bare of vegetation. They were empty; there was nothing to compare them to. The whole place had an air of violence, as if the mountains had been smashed and crushed and pulverised by a mad god.

I remembered the grass growing through the concrete of Dog Street, that the street was slowly going mad: here the madness had come all at once, and totally.

The sun reverberated off the bricky rocks. The unreal flickered in and out of the corner of my eye. Johnny addressed a remark to him every so often, to be answered in that dreamlike voice with a mono-syllable. Mary was lost in a private reverie, seeming quite happy.

We climbed all morning up into the territory of the third sales-man. Eventually we came on a notice, nailed to a wooden stake that was driven between two rocks. It read:

> *Stranger! You are entering the territory of the administration of Don Alvaro Silvestre y Surtidor, magistrate of the Second City of the Unreal People, and accredited commercial agent of ITT, GM, IBM, ICI, etc. Go with care, respect our habits and customs, obey our laws.*

"How can you obey a law if you don't know what it is?" said Johnny.

"They're not his laws anyway," said Mary. "The corporations will make the laws, not him."

"What corporation can rule this place?" I asked.

It was so wild as scarcely to be believable. There was no track; the road we had followed out of the First City had long vanished. There was no track at all now. We picked our way from rock to rock. Sooner or later, I thought, one of the horses would break a leg. We walked, for riding was out of the question.

"Which way are we going?" said Mary.

"Up, I suppose," I said.

"But it doesn't even go anywhere. There isn't even a pass to aim for. It's all piled up like rubbish."

"The salesman should turn up soon, anyway," I said.

"Why?" asked Johnny.

"The other two did, as soon as we entered their territories."

I checked to see that we still had the revolver. Johnny saw what I was doing, and laughed.

"What are you going to shoot?"

"Something to eat, maybe."

It was midday, and I at least was hungry. We had some dried meat and fruit, and water in our canteens, but we had no idea how long we'd have to make it last.

We looked around us for signs of life, but apart from a few thorn bushes and a yellowy lichen on the red rocks, there was nothing. The air of the hills was inimical to life; nothing but ghosts inhabited the sun-maddened rocks.

I watched them rise like flies as we approached and then settle again after examining us in the little patch of rock or shade that they haunted. Bird-sized things for the most part, airy nothings, unlike the spectral hooligans of the First City. The desert hermits had seen ghosts like this, and thought they were demons, and feared and hated them, while courting the solitude that brought them forth.

And so we went on until noon. I called a halt by a steep overhanging rock, and we sank down to sip wearily at our water.

I wanted to find out whether the movements I had seen out of the corner of my eye, which seemed too solid for ghosts, were animals that could be shot for food. I was frightened of these savage hills. So while the others slept in the shade, I went hunting.

Juan the ilusorio came with me, at his own silent wish. When I remembered his presence, he would be company for me, and when I didn't, he could not distract me.

And as it happened, he was useful in a number of ways. Now that I had the time to search properly I saw three creatures, goats of some sort, but they were all too far away for my pistol to reach. I wanted to stalk the nearest one, to see if it could be done. So, keeping as quiet as I could, I moved towards it, Juan a few metres in front of me.

But I found that I could not keep utterly silent. Johnny might have managed it, but I was too clumsy. One of the goats bleated suddenly, and the other two darted away.

Then to my astonishment I saw the remaining goat, its high horns thrashing and its forelegs flailing in the air, being wrestled to the ground by Juan. For a few seconds the unreal looked solid, tough and undeniable, in the heat of the struggle, but then he had the creature pinned down, and it went quiet and lay still, and his firm outlines wavered again.

I hastened up to join him and pulled out my pistol and shot the goat through the head. We could cut strips of its meat, I suggested to Juan, and hang them to dry in the sun over our saddles, as the South Africans did.

I was debating whether to butcher it where it lay, and save the effort of carrying it back, or whether to make the effort in order to work in the shade, when I heard the click, close behind me, of a rifle bolt.

The sound was uncommonly loud. I was startled beyond measure, and my heart thumped, even before I turned around.

A swarthy man, dressed in loose white trousers, white shirt, poncho and sombrero, was pointing an ancient rifle at my stomach. Behind him were two others, similarly dressed, also carrying guns.

"Who are you?" inquired the brigand.

I told him my name and my business, as clearly as I could.

"You have killed a private beast," he said when I'd finished.

"I thought it was a wild beast, and fair game."

He bent over and seized one of the horns of the goat, lifting up the head to show me a nick in the ear.

"Clearly marked," he said.

"From one metre, yes, but not from a distance."

"Come with us."

"Where?'

"To apologise to the owner of the animals, and to face his justice."

"If I am satisfied that the goat was his, I shall be happy to pay for it. But I must—"

To my intense shock, he swung the rifle barrel upwards into my jaw. My head shot backwards, tears came to my eyes, and I staggered. The men laughed.

"Don't argue, just do as you're told. Come with us now."

"Who is your boss?" I managed to say.

"Don Alvaro Silvestre y Surtidor, the chief salesman and magistrate of the district. He owns all wild beasts, and receives a tribute of all domesticated cattle, so naturally he will have to decide the appropriate penalty for you to pay."

"Let me first—"

"Follow us. You are not allowed to speak. Listening and judging are not my function. Don Alvaro insists on a precise separation of responsibilities. He and he alone will listen and judge, and that only when he is ready. Follow me, and be silent."

One of the other men bent over and lifted the carcass of the goat lightly on to his shoulders. Its great curved horns swung like cutlasses as the head lolled to and fro behind him. And I began to follow them over the hot red rocks.

What Mary Did

Later on, and much further into the mountains, Mary told me the story of what she did next. That was when we were all closer to one another, and so could understand it properly.

She was asleep in the cave when Juan came back to tell them what had happened on our hunt. He could not waken her and had to tell Johnny, whose presence still frightened and dismayed her.

Johnny said "Martin's been captured!"

"Who by?" said Mary, still half asleep.

"The salesman and his men. We must set him free."

Her heart sank, because she relied on me to come between Johnny and her. I'd do that, even though I couldn't understand what had happened, she said; all I saw was that Johnny had been restored, and not that she herself had been changed in the process.

She said "But we don't even know where he is."

Juan said "But I can find out, and spy on them. And maybe let him out."

"Go, then," said Johnny, and he wished him good luck. He and Mary would wait in the cave, so as not to lose each other.

Until Juan came back, there was nothing to do. The goat was gone, so there was no meat to cut up, and the men had taken my pistol, so Johnny could not hunt another one, though he tried in the afternoon while Mary slept.

Juan came back when the sun was setting, and it shone full into his face so that they could see him for a while.

"He's in a cave," he said. "Can you hear me?"

"Yes, I can. Where is the cave?"

"Five or six kilometres away. It has a door that locks. They were talking about their city, where Don Alvaro Silvestre is."

"How far away is that?"

"Four or five kilometres further on from the cave."

"What shall we do? Shall we rescue him? I don't know what to do," she said. She felt completely alone, because the shadowy Juan couldn't keep Johnny from her, since Johnny wouldn't have noticed him.

But Johnny was talking now.

"Can we talk to these men?" he asked. "Are they reasonable?"

"They are very upright and set in their ways," said Juan. "They would arrest you too."

"Well, we'll go straight to the city then, and talk to this magistrate. If he's the agent of all those companies he must have some sense of responsibility. We'll go now."

So they got everything together and gave my horse to the shadow-man to look after. The horses were holding them up among the vicious red rocks, and they thought of leaving them to fend for themselves; but Mary, more careful than either Johnny or I about money, decided that they should keep them. And she was right too.

"Why," she asked, "are the men waiting ,in the cave if the city is only that little way further on?"

Juan said "Because they are still on patrol for the powerful magistrate, and nothing will make them return before their appointed time, which is tomorrow."

"This is Rigid Land," said Johnny, "and Rigid City."

As they moved over the hot rocks in the evening, Mary began to feel a concern about her appearance.

Obviously, she told me, you cannot keep yourself in strange lands like those as carefully as you would in the city, and she had not been caring about herself over the last day or so, ever since she had given in to Johnny's body; but now as they got nearer to the strict Don Alvaro she felt sure that he would receive them more favourably if she dressed and washed carefully, made herself up, and set herself to please him. Arts like that were second nature to her, and at the prospect of exercising her talent she began to feel a little more cheerful than she had been.

She explained it to Johnny.

"You want to find shops, and all that sort of thing? How long will that take?"

"I don't know. But I must buy a dress and have a bath."

"Here, in the middle of the wild mountains?"

"It's a city, and you don't have cities without dress shops. And the style doesn't matter. I can change my style to fit it, whatever it is."

Johnny was doubtful, but since this was the first time she had volunteered conversation, he agreed to what she said. And apart from that, it was as if some commanding idea had taken possession of her; as indeed it had, though what it was she wouldn't find out herself until later.

She had never seen mountains like the ones they were travelling through; they weren't as high as the Alps or the Dolomites, but they were far more savage. Juan took them in a detour to avoid the cave where I was being held captive, and the sun was setting behind them, so that the intense red colour soaked out of the rocks and gave the whole long journey the nightmarish glare of blood.

Mary was happily considering what she should do to make herself appear beautiful. It was no less of an art than music: a series of technical problems the resolution of which called into play the highest resources of the spirit.

She would have to be beautiful in the fashion of the city, naturally, because any other would appear false and grotesque. But it didn't matter what that fashion was; she would be able to adopt the height of it without necessarily seeing photographs or drawings of their latest ideas, without seeing a shop window or a passerby in the street. She would need only the smallest of hints: the design of an advertisement, a bread wrapper, that was all, and she could feel the rest of it by instinct. And by artifice she would arrive at whatever their fashion was, and shine in it. It was her talent, and her taste for it was faultless.

They came on the city very suddenly. It was perched on a mountain top, like the cities in medieval drawings, surrounded by a wall. There was a gate in the wall, and a porter had to look at their papers before he let them in. He didn't notice Juan.

So they found their way to the best hotel, and by then it was quite clear to Mary what she should wear, and so nothing could be simpler. There were even some shops open. So they ate first, and then she commanded Juan to come with her.

She gave him their money to carry. He could also carry the things she bought. He was glad to be of service.

She bought shampoo, soap, creams and lipsticks, nail varnish, deodorant, talc, scent; and then a set of underclothes made of silk, a silk petticoat, and two dresses, a simple floral patterned frock of the 1950's and an evening dress, mid calf length, of the early '60's, because their fashions were of those years. And some shoes to go with them, and stockings, such as she had never worn, so that she had to buy a suspender belt to go with them.

When they returned to the hotel she locked herself in and bathed. Johnny was ignored: he had become invisible, eclipsed by the obsessions and rituals of beauty.

The filth of the road was washed off, and she became as clean as a china model. Once she had seen Johnny taking a bicycle to pieces and cleaning it with love and care, every little nut and bolt and every link in the chain, and polishing all the bright parts, and that memory was the only consciousness of Johnny that she had just then; she seemed to be much more like him, doing that, than like the maid who used to massage and dress her in her father's house. But she was both the machine and the mechanic; she was a living machine. And so she could feel a double pleasure. When she washed her legs, how smooth they felt under her hands! How soft! And in the mirror they looked so beautiful. And how delicate and searching were the hands that washed them. She blossomed under the loving gaze from the looking-glass.

(She told us both this without self-consciousness; haltingly, but frowning and pausing only to find the right word, the most telling expression.)

With infinite care she anointed her legs, her arms, her face with subtle creams. She put a drop of scent, the tiniest droplet, on her breasts, and between her legs. She put kohl into her eyes, making them smart and burn and then shine brightly as the black powder lined the edges of her eyelids. And then lipstick, as pale as red could be without being pink, and clear nail varnish, after carefully shaping her nails.

The soft underclothes held her carefully, wrapped up like a jewel. The dress she put on was of the deepest lustrous brown, and it clung to her shape. She dried her hair thoroughly and, as there was no time to set it, tied it behind with a wide red ribbon, letting it fall. So there was a gypsy look about her, because that suited her colouring and her features well. And she was ready.

She caused a taxi to be summoned. It was a battered old American car. She told the driver to take her to the residence of Don Alvaro, the commercial agent and magistrate.

The house he stopped at was in a quiet square, with a fountain playing in the middle of it, and some flowers that made the air heavy with perfume. It was a night for romance. She paid the fare and the driver knocked at the door and told her name to the servant who opened it.

She was taken to a sombre Spanish room, dark and comfortable, like an old club. And from there a manservant came to conduct her into the bedroom of the famous magistrate and salesman.

He had a four-poster bed, and he was sitting up in it, with a bed-table over his lap, and on it a pile of papers. He was wearing an ornately sewn nightshirt, and his dark Spanish colouring made it look like a tragic costume, the white shirt of a martyr. Over the head of the bed hung a crucifix, and religious prints adorned the walls. But she had a shock to see Don Alvaro, because he was a midget. If he had stood he would be hardly over a metre in height. But he was perfectly shaped, and he had an expression of great sagacity and control.

Johnny's words came back to her: "This is Rigid City."

The magistrate picked up a little cane, the sort colonels carry about on parades, and pointed at a chair. She was to sit down.

He signed some documents, cast an eye over some important letters, and wrote a note for his secretary. It was interesting to see the way he wrote, because he had an instrument like tongs to hold his pen, and he wrote very deftly in spite of this curious arrangement.

Then he condescended to speak to her through an interpreter. This person was an elderly man in the garb of a monk, who remained with them throughout their discourse. What language Don Alvaro spoke she didn't know, at first, because he whispered to the interpreter, who whispered back to him.

"Why have you come to see me?"

"To pay my respects and to visit the most important man in the town as a representative of my father, the President of the Pretorius Bank."

"The least important, you should say. I am only important in so far as my position is important. I am a mask. It is not the man who is important."

"You have a very beautiful house."

"Yes. It is the magistrate's official residence. Would you like to see the rest of it?"

"Oh, yes. But are you not well?"

The interpreter held back the blankets for him to get out.

"As much as any human being can be well, I am well. I spend much time in bed, in contemplation."

The interpreter handed him a pair of crutches. So that was why he was a midget! she thought; but no. He swung himself upright on them, and she saw that they were not crutches but stilts. His feet, in gorgeous scarlet leather slippers, rested neatly on little flat platforms while the upper end of the stilt was padded like a crutch and fitted comfortably under his arms. On the stilts he had the height of a tall man.

He paused under a religious print by the door, and his feet on the little wooden platforms looked like the feet of the Christ on the cross in the picture.

"Follow me," he said.

The interpreter was carrying the cane and the tongs. Whenever Don Alvaro wanted to point something out, a valuable painting or a suit of armour, the interpreter would hand him the cane; and whenever he wanted to pick something up, the old man handed him the little silver tongs.

The magistrate's delicacy and skill were wonderful to observe. Whether holding up a Chinese jar against the light, or taking her hand to guide her along a dark corridor, he handled the tongs like a surgeon. They had velvet pads to grip with, so that no harm came to the things he held in them.

Their tour of inspection came to an end in the bedroom. He deftly stepped off his stilts and into bed, and the interpreter pulled up the blankets around him.

"In what way," he said, "do you represent your father?"

"As his daughter, and the heir to half his fortune. Some of the things in this city belong to the Bank, and so will belong to me one day. Naturally I am interested to see how the territories where I have possessions are administered."

"Very correct and proper," said the midget salesman. "Now: you understand the price you must pay for visiting my house?"

Mary shook her head. "You are mistaken if you think I have to pay anything," she said, quite calmly, because she was acting, knowing her lines to a fault. She felt cool and in command; and she knew too that the idea which was possessing her was going to be ready, any moment, to reveal itself.

"My dear Miss Pretorius, your late arrival in my city and your consequent ignorance of our rules of conduct may explain, though it does not excuse, your breaking them . . ."

He went on in this style for some time. Johnny was absolutely right. He was rigid in his own conduct, and expected everyone else to be rigid too.

"I am above your rules," Mary told him. "Because I am rich, and for another reason too, which I'll tell you later if you can't guess. Your rules can't hold me, and I came here to tell you that they are not to hold my friends either. Your men have arrested one of them and are holding him prisoner. Now I am powerful but when he wishes he can eclipse even the might of the Pretorius Bank. He is a man of great force, and out of consideration and courtesy to you he is remaining calm under your provocations. But beware."

"Tell me his name," said the magistrate, taking his pen and tongs ready to make a note.

Mary told him the details of my arrest.

"There is a heavy penalty for poaching," said Don Alvaro of the woods and fountains, for such, the interpreter told her, was the meaning of his name.

"Who made the law?" said Mary.

"I did."

"Then you can unmake it. Nothing is easier."

He threw up his hands in horror when the interpreter conveyed this to him.

"Impossible!" he said. "Only the law stands between humanity and the abyss. As a good Christian I would be blaspheming, which Heaven forbid, if I thought otherwise. The law is a blunt instrument, but thus it serves to remind man of his imperfection . . ."

He broke off, and crossed himself with the utmost piety. Then he folded his hands and closed his eyes and muttered a prayer. The interpreter murmured "Amen."

"What will happen to my friend, then?" asked Mary when he had finished.

The magistrate shut his tongs with a little snap, and lay back against the pillows.

"He will be executed," he said.

The Annunciation, the Redemption, the Transfiguration, etc., in a New Psychological Guise

But she was prepared even for that. She was an actress, which I knew and Johnny didn't; and besides, at that moment her idea revealed itself, and the future sprang into view as if a spotlight had been switched on; and she saw the possibility of release not only for me, from my captivity, but for herself, from hers.

She smiled, and bent over and kissed his forehead.

"Well done, my child!" she said to him.

To her secret pride a tremor of uncertainty passed over his stern face.

"You have done triumphantly!" she went on. "Now answer three more questions. First: has it been known for angels to descend to the earth to hold intercourse with men?"

"Yes," he said.

"And second: how may angels be recognised?"

He searched for an answer. "By their beauty, which is more than human, their cleanliness, the perfection of their forms," he said uncertainly.

"And finally: how is it that you have not recognised me as an angel?"

He fell back against the pillows, and his little mouth opened wide.

"Don Alvaro," she said, "you are a good man, perhaps the best man who is alive today. You have been chosen by Heaven to play a great role in the next stage of human history. Only a man of probity, honour, and incorruptibility could play this part, and I have searched the earth for such a man. Now I have found one. I have tempted you in various ways, and you have come through triumphantly!"

Then she told him something that shocked him. It was a pretence that God wished to create a new race to populate the earth, men and their imperfection being doomed to oblivion. And that this involved the copulation of men and angels.

So she made herself into a whore and a deceiver, with a clear

143

conscience, having discovered that the processes of pretence, of healing, of love, and of precognition are sometimes indistinguishable; since by setting the first three things in motion, she had foreseen the form that life would take in the Anderson Valley.

But that was all to come later. In the meantime, she had the magistrate to deal with; and she did so calmly and happily, knowing that I would understand that it was the answer to many things, this false sexuality.

Martin Again

Juan had told the other two of what he had overheard from my captors, but it was perhaps as well that he did not overhear them telling me of how I was to be executed. They were reluctant to tell me, at first, but finally I persuaded them that even if the method of execution was a state secret, it was one which I would never be in a position to divulge; and so, rather primly, they told me. My throat was to be cut, and I would bleed to death, after which I would be flayed.

Perhaps because of this very primness of theirs, their punctilious rigidity of manner and thought, I wasn't must disturbed by this. I had already faced Haibel and his zombies, and my friends were still at large. And I was interested to see what would happen when I met this Catholic salesman, whose mania was leading him into tyrannous ways.

According to the leader of the patrol, Don Alvaro was a man of great profundity of mind and great sanctity of life, that he heard Mass said twice a day, and so on. Since his assumption of power, immorality and crime had nearly ceased to exist in the city. But even under Don's wise administration some men and women were so abandoned as to commit offences against modesty or chastity. They were punished in an appropriate fashion, and their sin held up by the Bishop of the city as an example of the ineradicable wickedness of mankind.

I gathered that the city, whose name I had heard as the Second City of the Unreal People, was particularly troubled in sexual matters.

At nightfall the men gave me some thin soup and bread, and then tied my feet together and shackled me to a tree just outside the little cave where we rested the night. They threw a rough blanket over me and left me to my thoughts.

Before dawn I had a visit from Juan the unreal.

He found it very hard to awaken me, he said. But the guard on duty, seated by the fire, noticed nothing of the noise. Juan had hit him over the head with a rock, realising that while his own noise would be inaudible to the man, mine would not. He untied me and we went a little way off, to sit on the cold rocks in the darkness like demons.

He told me what Mary had done. He had been present as a witness, and so had the interpretor. I was to go back to the cave and be a model prisoner. Alvaro, being insanely suspicious, would ask me questions in the morning to test whether Mary had been speaking the truth. This was although he firmly believed that she was an angel.

I took it all in gratefully, and in an overflow of gratitude and feeling for Mary I put my arms around the unreal neck of my comrade and embraced him. He returned my kiss, in a light and chilly fashion.

I said that he had better take something from the camp, a rifle, blankets, anything to suggest robbery by bandits as the reason for the guard's unconsciousness. Juan took a rifle and two pistols, and went. They might even be useful to us later.

I lay down beside the fire, adding one or two more logs to make it burn up brightly. And I fell asleep straight away.

A Miscalculation; or Angels Show Their Power, All the Same
I was shaken awake in the early light of morning. The leader was shouting at me, demanding an explanation. I heard the noise of someone being sick, and sat up carefully. It was the man Juan had hit. I composed my thoughts.

"So you have been raided?" I said. "You're lucky they didn't cut your throats as you're proposing to cut mine."

"But why did they set you loose? And—"

"I set myself loose. I wanted to lie by the fire. And there was no reason for me to wander all over the mountain at night when you were here to show me the way in the morning. I intended to visit Don Alvaro anyway, and he'll receive me with honour, as you'll see."

He was very miserable about it, but there was nothing he could do. They made some coffee, and then we set off. This time they didn't think it worth tying me up, in view of my strange powers.

On our way to the city, I asked the leader who their unreal people were.

"The slaves in the mountain," he said. "The criminals."

The mountain the city stood on was, it appeared, a vast prison, containing those who had chosen to become unreal by challenging the laws. The laws were reality, so to set yourself against them, or blaspheme, was to court unreality.

The form the unreality took was a medical one. Surgeons, under the philosophical directions of Don Alvaro, performed operations of manic complexity on the poor slaves, grafting parts of one body on to another, transplanting organs with enthusiasm and finesse. The favourite operation was one to produce a hermaphrodite. These bemused creatures toiled in the hideous darkness for the rest of their days, having learnt their lesson. They were forbidden, because of the shocking and abominable nature of the distortions, ever to venture into the open air. Thus, by suppressing their unreals, did they keep order in the Second City.

We came across the place very suddenly. It was perched on the highest crag of the whole red range, more precipitous and cruel than all the rest; and it surveyed a tortuous boulder-strewn ravine on one side, and a steep ridge on the other. It looked utterly impregnable.

And inside the gates it was very quiet. The men were hushed and respectful, going about their business with serious attention. Even the children were not noisy. We moved through the mute streets like a band of mourners.

I heard a little bell being rung, and around a corner came a procession of monks, headed by a high church dignitary dressed in flowing robes of crimson, with a crimson hood and a great glittering cross on a chain around his neck. Two of the monks swung censers, while the rest chanted earnestly in Latin.

I watched with curiosity as they came to the broad stone front of a branch of the Pretorius Bank. There they paused; the crimson-draped holy man intoned a prayer, and another monk sprinkled holy water on the steps of the bank from a little silver vessel.

"What are they doing?" I asked the leader of the patrol.

"Blessing the money," he said.

"What for?"

"To stop it from going bad. There's a city down there on the plains where their money went bad. Now you can buy nothing there, people cannot work, business is finished for ever, and even the food tastes different. We don't want our money to go bad, so the monks bless the banks every day, and the money stays good."

The men of God wound their way around another corner and out of sight, and we walked on.

I was moved to ask him what the city lived on.

"Why should I tell you that? I am tired of answering your questions. You are too curious, and it would be a good thing if Don Alvaro were to have your tongue cut out as a warning to others."

He spoke so sharply that I was sure I had interrupted some unpleasant speculations about what his own fate would be when the fearsome Don heard about the missing guns.

But we were approaching the Magistracy. This was next to the police station, a stoutly-built three-storey fortress of a place on the main square. The Town Hall, where Dan Alvaro held court and simultaneously represented the interests of capital, was decorated freshly with bunting and flowers.

It was clear that we were expected, and that the decorations were for us. A crowd was waiting, and all eyes turned our way.

On a balcony on the second floor of the Town Hall stood Mary, in a dark evening dress; Johnny, quite at ease, in a place of honour; and a tiny man balanced perfectly on a pair of stilts. Behind them was a row of officials, interpreters, secretaries and the like.

The tiny man was clothed in a dark-green uniform with gold braid at the shoulders and cuffs. A military cap was set dead square on his head, looking, although no doubt it fitted perfectly, a trifle large. He looked almost ridiculous; but really he looked terrifying. Or would have done, had I not known of the trick we were playing on him, by the help of Juan.

Where was that faithful unreal friend now?

There was a wooden platform, with a canopy, set a little apart from the crowd. It had the look of a bandstand.

The crowd parted for us; the leader of the patrol, a man of iron discipline, marched us unhesitatingly up to the steps of the Town Hall, where we halted.

He came to attention, and saluted the miniature magistrate.

Don Alvaro nodded, and spoke to one of his aides, who stepped forward deferentially and tapped a microphone in front of the tiny man.

Then Don spoke to the aide, who relayed his words to the microphone, and thence to the assembled populace.

"His Catholic Excellency Don Alvaro Silvestre y Surtidor wishes it known by the inhabitants of Ciudad Segundo del Pueblo

147

Ilusorio that a miracle, by the grace of God and the gracious intercession of our patron saint, has taken place in our midst!

"And that it is a miracle has been confirmed by His Grace the Bishop, who with the Council has been deliberating this very question all night.

"The miracle is this: that supernatural beings have come among us! Standing in our midst in this very square are three visitors from the spiritual world!

"But the question Don Alvaro and His Grace the Bishop have still, in their wisdom, to decide, is this: are these beings angels or demons?"

I saw Mary start. Johnny looked at the little magistrate, who remained perfectly still, only continuing in his whispered ventriloquism through the spokesman. What had gone wrong? We'd need all our wits now, and mine seemed to have vanished.

I heard the drone-like chanting of monks. And into the square, headed by a lavishly decorated bishop, came a similar procession to the one I'd seen earlier. But this was no routine cleansing operation: it was bigger, and more solemn.

"His Grace the Bishop will speak to our visitors. They will make their way to the platform and answer his questions with all the truth they can command."

Johnny and Mary left the balcony. Don Alvaro, the salesman, the commercial agent, the man of law, stood implacably on his stilts.

My two friends came down the steps to greet me.

Mary said "I don't know what he's doing, he's mad! I'm so sorry . . ."

Johnny muttered "Juan gave me the guns. I've got a pistol with me now."

"Keep it hidden," I whispered. "They're still half inclined to think we're angels. Keep it up a bit longer."

By this time we were at the platform. A simple flight of a dozen wooden steps led up to the stage, where the monks were waiting.

"I'll speak," I said.

We went up. The crowd was getting bigger every minute, as the word spread around the town and curious citizens came to watch our examination.

Then the Bishop began to speak. He was a gaunt middle-aged man, with lines of politics on his face. He cast, strange to say, not a clean dark shadow like everyone else, but a shadow of gleaming scarlet.

He said: "We have examined the female spirit, and find her to be truly and in fact spiritual, being made not of gross matter as we are but of condensed light. His Excellency the magistrate informs me that she behaves in all respects like an angel of the seventh order. We have not yet had time to examine the two male spirits, but from a cursory glance at this one—" he indicated Johnny—"he seems to be of the same kind. But whether they are indeed angelic, or whether they are demonic, is still to be established.

"Part of the difficulty, of course, lies in the cunning of the devils. How are we to distinguish them from angels when they mimic them so cleverly?"

He stopped, and turned to me. The crowd had been listening with a dull attention to his sermonic pedantry. What had happened to them, to make them so dull? Even the presence of three supernatural beings, be they angel or devil, made little difference. And I began to wonder if it was curiosity that had brought them to the square, or an insect-like desire to congregate.

I thought the time had come for us to register our presence more effectively.

"Bishop," I said, "you propose to examine us, to decide what our spiritual natures may be?"

"That is so," he intoned.

"Tread very carefully then," I said, "in case you expose your own ignorance and folly to the common people. They will not forgive you as magnanimously as I shall."

He frowned slightly; but I had spoken quietly, and my words had carried no further than the edge of the platform. He was more than a little taken aback, but he recovered quickly, and put his first question to us.

"Name," he said, "the forty-nine angels of the Ark of Solomon, with their attributes."

"Your first mistake, my lord Bishop, for such knowledge would be equally available to infernal spirits. I shall not answer, on those grounds."

"You will only answer questions to which good angels alone know the answers?"

"Yes. Obviously anything else would be a trap."

"But how can we know what to ask? Unless we know the answers as well we won't know if you're right or wrong; and if men know the answers, why then, the evil one has access to our minds, and can read them . . . What questions can we ask?"

"Do you give up so easily? The sort of questions you have proposed deal only with knowledge. Can you think of no other sort of questions?"

He retired to the back of the platform, his red shadow staining the wooden floor, to confer in whispers with his ecclesiastical assistants.

I stood quite still and waited. After a minute or so the bishop returned.

"Your objection has been considered," he said, "and found reasonable. So you will be asked not to answer questions but to perform certain acts, which are only in the power of angels to perform."

"My objection may hold true for those," I said.

"The female spirit has already, in the presence of Don Alvaro and his confessor, revealed her incorporeal nature," he said, taking no notice. "It remains for the two male spirits to do likewise, as a preliminary to moral examination. Therefore the first test is for you to perform a miracle."

But then there came an interruption from the balcony of the Town Hall.

"One moment, your Grace," said Don Alvaro's assistant through the loudspeaker. "A message from Don Alvaro."

A secretary in a black frock-coat and striped trousers hastened down the steps of the Town Hall and across the square to the platform. He handed the Bishop a note, which the prelate read and then showed to his priests. They stood in crimson-shadowed conference for a moment or two, and then the Bishop came to the microphone.

"The magistrate is, as always, correct," he said. "Don Alvaro declares, and rightly, that the spiritual or supernatural origin of our visitors is in no doubt; all that we have to settle, he says, is the question of their goodness or wickedness.

"And as the male angel newly arrived argues, any test based on knowledge or miraculogenic capability that men can devise will be flawed at the source, like all the productions of men. So the only test which will establish their natures beyond doubt is that of martyrdom. Every other answer can be faked, but death cannot.

"We shall be blessed today! Our city's fame shall reverberate long and loud in the celestial kingdom! For we shall not shrink from testing, even to the utmost degree of rigour, until we have proved beyond the veriest shadow of doubt the true nature of our guests.

"Thanks to the genius of Don Alvaro Silvestre y Surtidor, O angels, you will rejoice to know that we shall discover the true depths and founts of your goodness!

"As it is the best thing conceivable, we have on the highest authority, to suffer and die, so the degree to which you joyfully welcome suffering and death will reveal to our eager hearts the degree of your goodness.

"So, my dear visitors, you are to be killed!"

Precisely How Good It is, in Fact, to Be Martyred
A disputable question, but I had no doubt then or before. These people were mad, for all their success in preserving the value of their money, and to silly questions they found mad answers.

But I couldn't fault their logic, obviously.

A monk was sent to fetch the public executioner. I gathered that we were to be killed in the way I was told of by the leader of the patrol, that being their standard method of dispatch. The Bishop was kind enough to inform us that the singular colour of his shadow was a mark of recognition and favour from Heaven for the zeal with which he had thrust heretics to their bloody doom: heretics or false economists.

So we stood and waited, I on one side of Mary and Johnny on the other. She was cold with fright, but stood quite still and straight.

Now was the time to imagine, if I never had done before, so vividly that the world itself changed shape according to my imagining. I thought of a mental pistol, constructed of magic, held snug and heavy and full of bullets, in my right hand.

"Keep your talents hidden," I said to Johnny, and he understood that I meant the real gun that Juan had taken from my captors.

The Bishop was discussing matters of protocol with his committee. The normal procedure on these occasions was some form of religious ceremony, with confessions, repentances, penances, prayers, etc., etc.; but obviously that did not apply in our case, and the committee decided on a single address to the Deity.

I occurred to me then, with a little misgiving, that as according to their scheme the only proof of our goodness was our death, so if we were to come out of this alive they could only consider us evil. What would they do to us then?

But first we had to survive a public execution. I daresay it had been done before.

It had been decided that Mary was to die first. I kissed her, and whispered "You'll be safe—we've got a plan"; at which she breathed deeply and nodded, but kept a fierce grip on Johnny's hand. It was his right hand. He unfastened his fingers, went the other side of her and took her other hand with his left. The gun was in his right pocket, which was where he put his hand.

Guns everywhere. A monk on the edge of the platform was holding a rifle, obviously an ecclesiastical guard or policeman. I thought, I must be careful to put the Bishop between me and that man, if it comes to it.

I took Mary's other hand. I was going to pull her away from the knife and let Johnny shoot at the executioner. What then? We'd have to improvise. The executioner came up behind her. Such things were done with what mercy they could find; he had no knife visible, and when he drew it he did so quite silently so as not to frighten her; the first I was aware of it was when the sun glinted on the blade, held up for the Bishop's blessing.

I braced myself ready to snatch her away, and before I did so, levelled my mental pistol, heavy and full of bullets, at the knife, and fired.

At the crash of the shot Mary nearly fainted. The knife spun out of the man's hand, with a sound like a piano wire breaking. But my gun didn't crash like that . . . .

We were all still, shocked.

There was a stir at the edge of the platform; a monk was remonstrating with his armed brother, whose rifle was still pointing at the executioner.

Then a sharp crackle of static filled the air, and a magnified thud-thud as someone tapped a microphone to make sure it was live.

From the loudspeakers on the Town Hall came the words: "Don Alvaro is satisfied. His Grace and the three celestial beings will be so good as to confer with him."

So we had done it . . .

Brother Juan, the unrecognisable, the genuine unreal among the hooded forms of religious fear, had done it for us. And then slipped away: gone again, and invisible, and forgotten.

No one knew, of course, precisely what had happened, because no one could quite remember. Certainly the commercial plenipotentiary could not; he was in a state of extreme agitation when we reached his office.

Learn from experience, profit by the example of the capitalists who are at the heart of this adventure, and seize your opportunities boldly, I thought. I attacked him instantly, summoning reserves of fury I didn't know I possessed.

"Don Alvaro, it is very good of you to allow us to see you face to face, since your splendour and power are such that even angels have to bow to you . . .

"Miserable quavering fool, you do not even trust the evidence of your senses! May God have mercy on you, who has given you limbs, organs, nerves, for you to misuse and corrupt with the poison of suspicion and fear!

"A vision and a duty has been given to you out of all men. Do you intend to betray that vision by retreating back to the haunted womb of ignorance? And to check the reality of bright daylight by comparing it with the feeble gleam the fire throws on the wall of the cave? If our coming will teach you nothing else, let it teach you to meet the world as it is, and feel the reality of it with bare hands.

"Give me those tongs of yours."

There was a gasp from the officials, who stood in a semi-circle behind their master, a chorus of quaking poltroons. The magistrate was biting his lips, clapping his fists together in an extremity of nervousness.

He was too afraid to move of his own accord, so I went forward and took the tongs myself. I snapped them in two and threw the pieces on the floor at his feet. It was easy enough to do; they were lightly and delicately made, and it was a shame to break them, perhaps, but I was angry.

"Take off your gloves," I said.

He was wearing white kid gloves, another way of not touching the world. I was remembering Mary's expression as she waited for the knife, as he had no choice but to obey me. He took off the gloves and I tore them to pieces.

"Bring me the Bishop," I thundered.

The scarlet-shadowed ecclesiastic was brought in. There was an atmosphere of retribution, judgement, doom, and I was in charge

153

of it. I could have ordered them to commit mass suicide just then, and they would have done it. In a way I think they were half hoping for it; they had a taste for silly extremes in that city.

"O ye of little faith," I began, "neurotics to a man, and you are the worst of them, Bishop! Angels come down from Heaven, and are welcomed with the executioner's knife! It is lucky for your immortal souls that we did not allow this ridiculous charade of yours to go through.

"The doctrine you have conceived, this misbegotten doctrine that suffering is the measure of goodness, is the doctrine of Hell!"

They gasped.

"The true doctrine is that good works alone are the measure of goodness! That is the doctrine they teach in Heaven, and it is the only true one. From today you will preach that from your pulpits, and cause your children to learn it in their schools, on pain of eternal damnation if you do not.

"What is the doctrine of Heaven?"

"Good works alone are the measure of goodness," came my improvised words from the unhappy mouth of the prelate.

"And you may be grateful to Almighty God for the rest of your days, and you may thank Him daily on your knees, that it is I who am dealing with you and not my holy brother and sister, whose power and might as far eclipse mine as mine does yours."

He nodded, as if he understood, and seriously agreed.

"Go, then."

So he went. I turned back to Don Alvaro.

"Send away these encumbrances, and give them some work to do," I told him, indicating the officials.

He nodded faintly, and gestured at the civil servants and town clerks who stood miserably around him. But the interpreter had fled; he had to use his own voice. It was surprisingly deep and well-modulated. I said quietly to Johnny that it might be as well to take Mary back to the hotel and look after her, and he agreed.

But apart from the one moment when she felt the executioner approaching her, she had not faltered. She was magnificent; such an actress . . . I intended to examine my memory of that expression of hers, in that fearful moment, later on.

So I was alone with Don Alvaro.

One or Two Things Are Made Clearer Than They Were
Everything was tricky and risky, I was realising, everything in the world, if you wanted to get anywhere and do anything.

I had to screw some information out of this little man, and yet not reveal the fact that I knew nothing, because that would have shown that my angelic powers and omniscience were less than formidable.

But first I was hungry and thirsty. Explaining that angels, when they assume human form, assume human needs, I commanded coffee and rolls to be brought.

The Don hovered anxiously nearby. I had forbidden the use of his stilts, and he climbed up into his large leather chair and sat behind his desk like a manikin.

I decided to ask him every question I could think of that pertained to my search, and present it in the manner of an examination, to test him in the things he should know.

I began: "How far is the Anderson Valley from here?"

DON ALVARO: Sixty kilometres.

M.B.: What is happening there?

DON ALVARO: They are building a city.

M.B.: For what end?

DON ALVARO: I don't know. But their resources are enormous. It will be very large.

M.B.: What do you know about a woman called Catherine Anderson?

DON ALVARO: I have a great admiration for her. She came here a little while ago, distributing blessings. It is after her that the Valley is named. She has been to every previous settlement of capital in the province. She was last in the First City of the Unreal People, where the money decayed, before she came to us, whose money is still incorrupt, but where we have created no more of it (I confess). And every other place, farm, hacienda, factory, enterprise, where capital has settled. She is like, forgive me, the angel of capital.

M.B.: Where has she gone from here?

DON ALVARO: To the city in the Anderson Valley, which will be called the Perfect City of the Unreal People, when it is completed. And when it's ready, she will rule it as its President.

M.B.: She told you all this?

DON ALVARO: I guessed it from what she said.

M.B.: Now tell me about your city. What do you live on here?

DON ALVARO: On the vegetables we grow hydroponically in the mountain, and on intensely-farmed animals, and on the few goats we can hunt in the mountains, which are my prerogative. Hence the stern measures to protect them from poachers.

M.B.: When was this city founded?

DON ALVARO: Some years ago.

M.B.: For what purpose?

DON ALVARO: In the hope that we should find some minerals in the hills.

M.B.: Why has the Church acquired such power in this city?

DON ALVARO: I invited the Bishop, as the first act of my administration, to set up a commission of enquiry into public morals. I wanted to rule at all times according the the will of God, and clearly the best way, my own (as every man's) conscience and will being utterly flawed by original sin—the best way of ascertaining the will of God was to take the advice of priests; particularly in the matter of preserving the value of our money, which I was very anxious to do.

M.B.: Tell me about your Unreal People. Who gave the city that name?

DON ALVARO: The name came about spontaneously, and is not official. The official name of the city is Santa Teresa de los Montes.

M.B.: And the Unreal People?

DON ALVARO: They are those who have chosen to break the law, and our penalty for that is very simple: slavery, for a length of time commensurate with the gravity of the offence. In other words, for life.

M.B.: Tell me more about them.

DON ALVARO: There is very little more to tell.

M.B.: Where do these slaves work?

DON ALVARO: In the mines under the city.

M.B.: I want to inspect these mines, and see the slaves for myself.

DON ALVARO: But, being omniscient, you must know about it already. You must know all about it.

M.B.: It is analogous to your practice of confession. You must show me, not for the sake of my knowing it, but for the sake of baring your secrets.

DON ALVARO: Is it wrong, then?

M.B.: Very probably. We shall see.

DON ALVARO: You don't know already. You have to wait and see!

M.B.: Don't try to dispute with me, Don Alvaro. Tell me more about the woman who came to see you, Miss Anderson. How was she travelling?

DON ALVARO: By helicopter.

M.B.: Did she have any companions?

DON ALVARO: None; only the pilot.

M.B.: How was her bearing towards you?

DON ALVARO: Friendly and condescending.

M.B.: What did you know of her before she came here?

DON ALVARO: Only rumours, of her unannounced appearance in various places, bearing gifts and blessings.

M.B.: What gifts?

DON ALVARO: For me, a signed photograph of herself; for the city, the promise of immortality soon to be achieved.

M.B.: Show me the photograph.

DON ALVARO: Certainly.

He pressed the button of an intercom speaker, and told the secretary on the other end to fetch the photograph.

"It's in my house," he explained. "Have you any questions in the meantime?"

M.B.: What did she mean by immortality for the city?

DON ALVARO: I assume that it must be something to do with your presence.

M.B.: Quite possibly.

DON ALVARO: May I ask you some questions?

M.B.: Certainly not. That is, you may ask, if you dare, but I may or may not answer.

DON ALVARO: Why, I would like to know, are you travelling on foot and not (say) by helicopter like Miss Anderson?

M.B.: Because we want to study the ways of men, such as the manner in which they greet innocent travellers in Santa Teresa de los Montes.

The magistrate nodded, the serious expression never changing, and said no more. He was so serious and concentrated that he forgot for the moment to be self-conscious about his stature; and he got down from the chair and wandered slowly to the window with great and genuine dignity.

A knock on the door, and a secretary brought in the photograph. My heart beat faster, and my hand was trembling slightly as I took it.

I wanted to be alone with it. I dared not look at it otherwise. My hands became still.

"Don Alvaro," I said as politely as I could, "I would be grateful if you could ensure that my companions are safely installed in their hotel, and if you could see to the preparations for our visit to your slave-mines this afternoon."

"This afternoon?" he said anxiously.

"Indeed."

"It'll be difficult to arrange at such short notice.'

"But not impossible."

"Oh, no."

"Very well, then."

"Quite . . . yes. Yes."

And he nodded, and left the room, and I picked up the photograph.

Daguerre, Fox Talbot, and so on, Thank You

It was a carefully composed studio portrait, evidently the work of a skilled photographer, and it was signed with the name Catherine Anderson in ballpoint in my wife's hand. It was her, not a doubt of it.

I hadn't imagined her capable of such ease and naturalness in front of a camera. I was surprised to see how well it suited her, the studio lights, the muted background, the smile into the lens.

I felt a kind of awe. Was this my wife, and had I held her in my arms? And had she held me, and whispered that she loved me? And had I and this girl touched each other's naked bodies?

The angel of capital, he had called her. She had been in this very room, perhaps, only a few days before, and perhaps the air still held traces, molecules, of the clean smell of her hair.

Had we really lived together? I couldn't remember.

Something had gone badly wrong, to make her go away like that. I examined myself with dismay. Had I contracted a loathsome disease? Or had I gone mad, so that it wasn't possible to live with me?

We had never talked about ourselves or our love. It was as if we'd tried to keep it secret from each other. We came together in silence, in darkness; or if in the light, then in a trance, or a daze.

No! Once we had spoken about it.

It was the night before she left. . . . It was coming back to me in pieces. I had to sit down.

I'd said some tantalising thing; something like "Tell me what it feels like. Talk to me."

She turned slowly to look at me. And we never did that either, naked. We came together like automata, blindly. But in that very will-less movement of ours there was something extraordinarily affecting, as if it illustrated the amorousness of flesh itself, unconscious. And here I was trying to—what? Make us more human?

I forget what she did then, or said, but it ended badly. I found myself reproaching her for acting mechanically.

"You don't know what a machine is," she said.

I remembered her saying that, and not knowing what she meant.

Suddenly that brought back to me my words to the Bishop, for some reason, and my discovery at the tip of my tongue of the true doctrine of Heaven. Good works alone were the measure of goodness, which meant that the way someone acted and appeared in the world was the most important thing, in the end. If in his heart he concealed hatred and evil, nevertheless, if he did good, he would find himself in Heaven when he died. While if a person had great faith, and did nothing, he would go to Hell.

The outward semblance of things the most important? How could that be?

Nevertheless it was. And if we at our love acted like machines, that was what we were.

Though I didn't know what a machine was, she said. Well, no, they were all mysterious to me, like electricity. But I was on the trail of the answer when I thought about it all in this way. And more than ever in love with my wife, and the world was charged with the electric crackle of it. Impulsively I kissed the picture.

Then I felt sleepy, and nodded in the chair; and when after a moment or two I opened my eyes, there was the messenger, she whom I had last seen in that empty bank, standing calmly beside Don Alvaro's desk.

I felt a rush of nerves, adrenalin, if that stimulates sexuality: a universal tingle. But saw that that was not the purpose of her visit. Although the wonderful clean oxygen, fresh air smell, March winds, filled the room. What would she teach me this time?

Her face was calm and ironical.

"You don't learn. Here you are posing as an angel, in great danger of being exposed and forfeiting your own life and that of your friends. Haven't I told you to turn back, to go home and forget it all?

"But we'll have to give you credit for perseverance. That's all you'll get, though. If you go to the Anderson Valley you'll find nothing but disappointment and death, and you won't find your wife."

"Is she there, though?" I asked.

"Not yet," was the answer. "You will not find her."

"But why, for God's sake? Who are you to say? And what is she doing?"

"You're not capable of finding her, because you haven't the imagination for it. What's needed for this is infinite sympathy and imagination, and years of patience, qualities far from yours. You are shifty and dishonest and equivocal. But I admit that you're less of a coward than I'd thought, so you see that things can change, even your nature. Become sympathetic, imaginative, patient, honest, and you'll see your wife again, but not for some time."

There were no ghosts about the messenger, I noticed; only a clear desert-like absence of them. And while that impression was coming to me, she went. She turned abruptly and left the room.

I sank back into the chair and took up the photograph again, with a wild sadness leaping at my heart like a tiger. My wife looked at me, and smiled, but it was really the camera she was smiling at. Perhaps I had not earned the luck I had in winning her.

But I wanted to take the messenger's lips between mine, to press that lithe curved hip, run my cheek down the dreamlike smoothness of her arm. I was torn in half with contradictions.

And I had not the imagination to be patient and realistic, and do as I was bid. *That* is imagination of a strong sort, which I am without.

You think I'm wrong? That the imagination deals with the outrageous, extreme, fantastic? A thousand times no! The subtle powerful strength of the imagination is that it deals directly with the real world. When I met the agents of the Anderson Valley Company in a contest of imaginations, I found that out. Later, later.

I put the photograph down on the desk, turning it away from me. I must not look at it again.

I rang a bell to summon the magistrate to take me to see his slave-mines. Perhaps it would be my fate to liberate these wretches, as it had been my fate to free the imprisoned corpses on Haibel's farm.

The Culture of Mushrooms

Close evil-smelling galleries, rank on rank of them, like the inside of bones, ran in every direction through the interior of the mountain.

When the first settlers plunged inside the many caves that pitted it, searching for gold and silver, they had found only platinum, a difficult metal of no great beauty, and had abandoned their prospecting in disgust.

The citizens of Don Alvaro's administration, keen to improve their chances of eternal salvation by energetically promoting the interests of the Company, extended the first crude workings and tunnelled like moles or termites. only to find that there was not even very much platinum, and that they had a hollow mountain. Scraps and grains and traces and smears of valuable minerals were still found, but nothing worth extracting commercially; and so the empty mountain was given over to the culture of those plants which do not need direct sunlight, and the breeding and keeping of those animals which are suited to captivity: hens, calves, pigs.

The criminals who provided the work force, the slaves, were employed on such elevating tasks as the slaughtering of calves, the strangling and plucking of chickens, the gathering of eggs; the clearing of these subterranean Augean stables being a job for the most despised and hated of the convicts, which is to say the oldest and weakest.

The cleaning of the animal pens was a fearsome task. But nature had provided a waste-disposal system of sorts; a cavern had been discovered in the very depths of the mountain, in the centre of which was a fissure that had no measurable bottom. It had been calculated mystically by the Bishop's committee that shit could be deposited in there with perfect safety until the year 2,000, when the lord Jesus Christ himself would return to earth with further instructions. So a vast chute had been built in this cavern, down which the excrement was allowed to slide into oblivion, helped on its way by old hermaphrodites with poles and rakes. Occasionally the build-up of dried shit became too thick for the rest to move easily, and a kind of dam would form, which could only be breached by desperate courage and the strength of a lion. Young men were usually drafted in for this, but only after a number of ancient lives had been lost.

It was more peaceful altogether in that section of the mountain which was given over to the plants. Mushrooms were the main crop, and it was a fine sight, the fungus gallery, row after row of wide shallow drawers, in tiers like filing cabinets, containing dark earth and the little white heads, like stars or children, of the growing mushrooms.

The main sort grown was the ordinary edible mushroom, round and white. But under the command of their energetic manager, the mushroom workers were experimenting with many other varieties of fungus, from the simply hallucinogenic to the downright poisonous.

Old logs, imported at great cost from the forest and profoundly rotted outside the mountain, were sown with different spores, and kept moist and warm in carefully regulated cabinets. They sprouted grotesque flaps and plates of all colours, horrid distended ears and lips that glowed malignantly in the permanent night of the mountain, and from which powerful drugs were extracted.

Of course, all this was run by the criminal element, the most individualist, original, and desperate of the citizens. Scientists and technicians were recruited by advertisements in European and American journals, but a surprising amount of the research as well as the shit-moving and throat-cutting was done by slaves, trained and experienced in the work.

As for the operations which had been performed on them, they had several purposes, I was told. First, they were a punishment, and a warning to others. Second, they had a definite medical interest. Studies made in the howling caverns of the effects of drugs on tissue-rejection, for instance, had found a keen readership in the pages of learned medical journals in this continent and others.

But Don Alvaro's chief and abiding interest, he informed me, was in the sexual field. The manipulation by surgery and drugs of the sexual desires of the unhappy prisoners was well advanced. Eunuchs, transsexuals, behaviouristically created deviants of every kind twittered and gesticulated with hate as we passed among them.

True hermaphrodites were rare, that operation being both complicated and dangerous. There were many failures, but some advances; attempts were now being made to induce some of the younger ones to breed, but without as yet much success. Meanwhile, they were kept on and even allowed a measure of privilege as a reward for their beauty. They worked as receptionists, secretaries, and the like, and they chatted and flirted very prettily with their small begetter as we went the rounds of his dark domain.

All this activity had an economic end in view. It kept the city fed, as well as producing goods for export. From time to time a

162

large helicopter would descend to the main square opposite the Town Hall and take on board surplus produce, unloading in return such necessities and luxuries as the city could not produce by itself.

These transactions were supervised by a representative of the Church, and all incoming goods had to be blessed, in order to prevent the germs of inflation from entering with them.

So the city managed to live.

While I was learning all this, I was secretly fighting a desperate battle to retain control of the mercurial magistrate.

I had some trouble before we left the Town Hall. I had lunch on my own, while Don Alvaro attended to his gubernatorial business; and then I was sent for, and told that everything was ready for our tour of inspection.

I was taken to the entrance hall of the magistracy, where I found the usual gaggle of hangers-on, and in the centre of them Don Alvaro—on his stilts. Beside him stood, nervously but still, the interpreter, holding the tongs, or another pair very similar; and the magistrate was looking at me with a mixture of fear and sly triumph. My heart sank. I would have to fight this.

"A word with you, Don Alvaro," I said.

He inclined his head.

"In private, if you please."

"But it is time to go."

He stuck there, stubborn as a schoolboy. What could I do? More to the point: what had happened, to convince him that he could get away with is? I was afraid.

But after a few moments he came. Easily and masterfully he walked forward, with an aristocratic slowness, the stilts balancing perfectly on the polished floor. We went into his office.

"Well?" he said, angrily.

"I have forbidden you to treat the world thus. Stand your proper height on the floor like a man, dismiss that dummy who speaks for you, throw away that false hand. And do so now, before I grow angry with you."

"How am I to display myself to the world in such a state? They will laugh at me! No, I shall not do it! Don Alvaro is the essence of aristocracy, he who does not touch the world, he who strides above it like a god! That's how I'm known. And I will not suddenly be diminished, do what you will with me, I will not stand for it."

"Your mind is on vain trappings and tinsels!"

163

"*My* mind is not, but the corporate mind understands nothing else! That's how I'm judged! I can't help it!"

"You can help it very well, you feeble man. Get off those stilts now before I knock you off."

"No!"

I seized him by the lapels and hoisted him into the air, kicking the struts away from him. I held him under my arm, struggling in torment like a wicked child, while I put the struts up against the wall and snapped them in two with a kick.

Then I stood him on the table, and tore the decorations and epaulettes and gold buttons off his uniform, so that it hung ragged and torn from his shoulders. He was still now, quivering with shock.

"Send to your house for plain clothes," I told him. "Or go like this: it's your choice."

His face crumpled with rage and frustration, and he wept furiously. I stood quite still. If he hadn't been intending to watch my execution that morning, I would have felt sorry for him, but I felt simple and implacable, instead.

Finally he gave in, as he had to, and we went off to the mines on foot.

His walking normally, and speaking directly, made a great impression on all those people who saw us. But I constantly had the feeling that he would denounce me, or that I'd betray myself by some foolish carelessness . . . .

So we penetrated the stinking chambers of the mountain, lit by dim lamps and reeking of spilt blood, ages old and rotting, of shit, of human waste. There was no modern and effective ventilation that could overcome such a compound. In the lift shafts, in the galleries, in the remotest internal fastnesses as well as the broad well-lit rock highways, this fetid miasma throttled us. The room in which Gilles de Rais dispatched his hundreds of innocent victims, or the foul chambers where Erzsebet Bathory bathed in the blood of virgins, must have been thick with a similar melancholy reek.

The slaves cut the throats of terrified calves and pigs with great long hooked knives; blood spurted everywhere, feet and hooves slipped in the splashing greasy tide that flowed through the caverns.

They slept down here, apparently, wherever they happened to be; they had no appointed resting-places, they had to lie down in the mire, above it if they were lucky, and sleep as they were, discharging their natural functions into the open sewer of the floor.

They were not fed at all. They had to take what they could eat from the raw meat they killed, or the fungi they cultivated. Naturally they died like flies. But the fittest survived and formed hierarchies, ruling with the connivance of the guards over the fate of the majority.

Thus under the rock the city heaved and boiled. So much for the Second City of the Unreal People.

Back above the ground again, I saw that the city had a haunted air, of doom and retribution. The streets were quiet as if in the aftermath of some particularly violent public execution. Or perhaps they were hypnotised by the spectacle of their own ruin, and half-willed it.

So I thought we would have to oblige them.

The Fate of the Second City. A Conference Among the Angelic Powers

"Chief angel," I said to Mary, "what are we going to do about this place?"

"I'm not the chief angel," she said. "I don't think it's up to us."

"Who, then?" said Johnny.

"The farm was one thing, but a whole city is another."

"The Company won't do anything about it," I said.

"Why not?" said Mary.

"They put Don Alvaro in charge."

"They didn't think he'd do this."

"They haven't stopped him yet."

"Perhaps they don't know. So we ought to tell them."

"But who's them, precisely, anyway?" I asked.

"We need to know about the A.V.P. first," said Johnny.

"Why?" said Mary.

"It's all tied in with it. And Martin's wife."

They both looked at me. I scratched my head; I was baffled, as they both knew.

"She doesn't know about this," I said. I wished the messenger would reappear, and tell me what to do. "The important thing's just to get to the Anderson Valley, in the end," I went on.

"Well then for God's sake let's get on with it, and go there," said Mary.

"And leave the slaves?" asked Johnny.

"I don't want to leave it like this," I said.

"But it's not our business," said Mary.

"Nor were the zombies."

"They were," said Mary, "because Johnny . . ."

There was a silence then, as she looked at him, and then away, embarrassed.

"So if we found we had an interest here," I said, "the slaves would be our business?"

"I suppose so," she said. "Obviously, yes."

"Well, they're your business and Johnny's, because the money that subsidises the city will belong to you one day."

"Oh, really, that's hardly fair—"

"Well, it is in a way," said Johnny. "We've got a responsibility."

"Oh yes," said Mary, unconvinced.

"Mary, we have," I said urgently.

"Well, this is all very moral," she said. "What are you going to do? Kill Don Alvaro, I suppose, and then make a speech to the monks?"

"Mary, for Christ's sake," said Johnny.

"You're both posturing," she said scornfully. "That's all it is."

"He was going to kill *you*, this morning! I suppose you've forgotten—" I said. I was becoming angry.

She shrugged. "You'll never understand," she said. "You're too violent."

And she began to examine her nails. Johnny exclaimed with exasperation, and leant back with his hands behind his head. In my agitation I got to my feet and walked over to the window, and leant on the sill and stared out blindly.

We were on the first floor, and our window overlooked a little square with a dry fountain. This was a loathsome city, I thought. I hated it, and I wanted to see it destroyed and sent to the devil.

There was a movement down below, by the fountain, that nagged at my attention like an itch. Some dry leaves were swirling round and round in a little chase, like ghosts. What was it? The sound annoyed me. The square was empty.

No; it was Juan, trying to attract my attention. So that was how he did it, when he wanted to, by making the world make a noise. Anything would be more obtrusive than he was; it was a good idea.

But the square wasn't empty, of course. Ghosts sat around the edges, or thronged the fountain, or flew through the air; thin, weak creatures, given off by impulses of terror or lust, doomed to last only a few hours, and then fade.

A stone flew up and cracked against the wall beside me. I jerked up angrily. Juan again . . . Of course, I had forgotten. What else could he do?

I waved, and told the others, and went out into the square. We sat side by side on the edge of the fountain basin.

"You are in deadly danger," said the unreal. "Listen to me carefully. I overheard the magistrate talking to the Bishop. He no longer believes you are angels. They're going to separate you and submit you to temptations, to see if you can resist them. Unless you do, you'll be killed. They're coming to get you soon."

"What sort of temptations?"

"Does it matter? Could you resist a beautiful whore? You won't succeed. You'll have to go now, as quick as you can, during the siesta."

I thought. Was it likely we'd get far enough away to be safe? No. What else could we do?

"Tell me word for word what they said," I asked.

Juan had gone openly into the magistrate's office at sat down in a corner to spy. Don Alvaro had summoned the Bishop, and the two of them had plotted our downfall. What had given the game away had been my evident distaste for the slave-mines. It contrasted strangely with the attitude of the previous angel, Miss Anderson, who had regarded all their doings with sublime and benign impartiality. But they weren't sure yet, and so had planned to make us drunk, and then ply Johnny and me with the attentions of selected whores, after showing us certain films in the magistrate's possession. The slightest movement, the Bishop said, claiming good authority for his knowledge, the very slightest tremor of a penis towards erection would be enough to damn us irrevocably, and reveal us for demonic imposters.

No; we couldn't get away. There was just no time.

"Juan," I said, "do this now: the lift shaft that admits visitors to the mines is by the south gate. The lift is kept at the top, and there's no signal at the bottom to call the lift down, so the slaves can't get out . . . Go to the shaft, and and send the lift down below. Just do that, and hurry back to the magistrate's house. We'll be there, ready to go. Bring the horses. And take your gun. If you have to hit the guard at the top of the lift shaft, do."

"What will you do?"

But I forgot to answer him, and ran in to tell the others.

"Get everything together," I said. "Load the pistols and take one each. Get ready to go."

"Where are we going?" said Mary.

"To the magistrate."

In haste we piled our belongings into the rucksacks, and thrust bullets into the revolvers.

I came across my wallet, and caught sight of what was inside it: several hundred dollars, maybe two thousand dollars altogether; and felt for a moment, in the middle of the anxious hurry, light-headed with joy and power.

We left the hotel, and made straight for the magistrate's house, where we found him having tea in the English style, with cakes and toast.

"Don Alvaro," I began, "my patience is at an end. Your stupidity is impenetrable; you still refuse to accept the truth of things! Now you are planning to tempt us, as if that were possible, and to make us drunk, as if any liquors in your possession could cloud intelligences from the courts of heaven! As if any meagre treasure or dull flesh you could find in this town could even cause our eyes to flicker . . . oh, you miserable man! Have you not read in your Bible of the fate of Sodom and Gomorrah?"

He looked the very picture of guilt and shame, caught as he was with his white gloves on, a tiny fork in his hand, with a little triangle of buttery toast speared on the point.

Suddenly he hurled his fork to the floor, and, standing up carefully on his chair so that he was the same height as we were, he struck an attitude of defiance.

"I defy you!" he cried. "Angels you may be, but I defy you still! I am no coward, and if I face Hell for acting with decision, then so be it. I shall order you to be imprisoned, all three, and to work in the mines as my slaves. I am the master here, and I will have no agency subverting my authority! None! Not even God's! The Bishop endorses what I say! It is a bad example to the citizens, to have you behave like this unpunished! Humble ordinary folk cannot be expected to distinguish theological subtleties! I have great experience in politics, and I know! They merely see insolence, bragging, insubordination stalking the streets and raising their mutinous heads even in the courts of the mighty! It will stop now! It will cease! I have given orders—"

"So have I," I shouted, "and you will now have the chance to see how effective your authority is. You are a murderer and a slave-owner, and a maker of slaves, and you deserve nothing better than death. See if you can avert it now, Don Alvaro! See if you can command your distorted slaves to go back to the foul existence below ground, because they are coming, all of them, in a flood from the lowest levels of the mountains, rising like dead men on the day of judgement, all coming to claim their revenge, Don Alvaro! Listen: can you hear them?"

For in the distance, shots could be heard, and cries, and the howling and soft thunder of a crowd running. And then there was the beat of hooves, the clatter of horseshoes on stone, and the shrill whinny of a horse as it was reined in outside the window.

"We are going," I said. "Defend yourselves and your city if you can. And for every innocent person who is killed or hurt today your soul will suffer an added torment in hell."

And we left. Our last glimpse of the little magistrate showed him pale, tottering, his hand to his head and a dreadful fear in his eyes.

We ran outside, and leapt on our horses. Juan swung up behind me, and we galloped away.

The slaves had overrun the place more quickly than I had thought possible. They were pouring into the centre of the city: ghastly, stinking phantoms, clad in rags or clad in nothing but excrement, or dried blood; emaciated, diseased, rotting with a hundred artificially induced poxes; and each armed with a terrible knife from the slaughtering pens, whose deadliness was magnified by the filth which covered it.

The only check to their hideous career was the light, which struck into their imprisoned eyes like swords. They were all blind at first, and staggered about with one hand pressed close over their faces, peering agonizedly through their fingers. More than one fell under the knife of a fellow who took him for a citizen.

We struggled against the crowd, because all the citizens were making for the centre of the town, away from the gates to the infernal regions, which were at the edge. Foremost among those in flight were the monks, a band of whom had been attacked while in the process of cursing a crop of mushrooms for being diseased. While they were calling down divine vengeance on the fungi, and exorcising them of evil, thirteen slaves had burst out of a sewer, and seized the chief monk and two of his minions and eviscerated them where they stood, with practised slashes of their tools.

169

Many people were going to die, and again it would be my responsibility. But all I thought about as we galloped away was the messenger. She appeared miraculously and no doubt vanished miraculously; I wished she were with me. But I had no fears for her safety.

Thus we left the Second City.

Where Next?

The wilderness again; but free now of the game-keeping laws, we shot a goat and had fresh meat for supper, eating in a little cave on the eastern side of the manic range of red mountains. No one said much; we were too overcome by the sights we had seen.

Mary too was disturbed by the thought that if she hadn't invented the fable that we were angels, we wouldn't have made such a mess of things. But Johnny comforted her.

(And secretly the false sexuality of her encounter with Don Alvaro had begun to work, in a magical way, on the trauma of her rescuing of Johnny. She was learning the magic power of pretence.)

It was strange to see, after the storm that had come between the two of them, how they grew closer. No longer did they want to converse through me; no longer did she ignore him, or he avoid going near her. So they sat side by side, and lay down like that to sleep.

The sun struck full into our cave when it rose, and found us cold and cramped and thirsty. With nothing to drink, there was nothing to do but move, so we saddled the horses and rode off straight away.

The mad mountains were no easier on this side of the city, and they seemed to be even higher; certainly we climbed and climbed, and still they rose in front of us, wild bitter crags and bloodstained jutting teeth of rock. We found that by keeping to one meandering ridge, we were being led towards the highest and most involved part of the whole range, but there was no way off it, no way out or down. And at that point we let our horses go; it was harder with them than without.

Where had these mountains come from? They were not on any map. Though on every map I had seen, this area was blank; who knows what might lie there? And why were there no ghosts in the high mountains?

Because I saw fewer and fewer of them as we climbed. Instead, the spirit of solitude brooded over the empty gorges, the granite pinnacles.

Not once did we have the impulse to turn around nervously, to look over our shoulders, which attacks the most thick-skinned of wanderers in the most deserted places. The emptiness was total. And there was a virginal quality in the rocks, as there is in a block newly carved from a quarry or a splinter torn from a plank: the sense that no one has ever seen this particular surface before. But here it was all like that.

No birds wheeled in the deep blue sky; no goats, no sheep, no animals at all haunted the crags after the first few miles. No insects crawled among the dry rocks; no lizards basked in the hot sun.

It would have been frightening, but for that virginal totally empty feeling. It was not dead: it was beyond life and death. It was exhilarating, rare, clean. It reminded me of the other source of that feeling: the messenger from my wife. She had no ghosts, either, and carried the exhilaration of oxygen in the same way.

And from time to time, as we struggled on, there was a puff of breeze from the east, and it refreshed us, being of just the same nature. I was confident that we were going in the right direction.

So the time passed.

Our thoughts became calmer, and we talked little. The hunger and thirst were enough to keep us alert, but not enough to cause us pain. We still had some dried meat and dried fruit; and occasionally on the shadow-side of a mountain we would find a patch of snow, which we could melt for water.

As the spirit of solitude entered us, as we climbed among ever loftier mountains, we found we were hardly thinking at all. I existed in a blue (sky-blue) and white (snow-white) airy region, peopled by thoughts and conceptions too grand, too sublime, to bear articulation, even to myself.

It was in a sort of ecstasy that I surveyed the moon, sailing in the firmament above icy jagged peaks of virgin snow. Delight came to me, responding to the vision of a world that was totally alien, like the God-outside-the-universe of the Gnostics. Nothing of human life! Nothing of time! Nothing of life at all! Nothing of death!

One night I stood alone on a pinnacle of stone, my body rocking silently and tears flooding down my face, unheard sobs racking my breast, as if I was falling in love with the moon and the empty mountains, and lacked the words to declare my passion.

Juan the unseen used to come with me. His nature fitted happily into the cold and the emptiness. I think he came to look after me, sensing that in a transport of ecstasy I might easily fling myself off a precipice, and not know what I was doing.

Johnny and Mary stayed close together, saying little. The world we were in was too large for words and conversation. But still (I noticed dimly) she did not touch him if she could help it; and still he out of courtesy avoided touching her. They slept side by side, but back to back.

All the time we were moving onwards. By my rough calculations we had come by now to a region near the border of the country, where Venezuela ended and Brazil began. Not that borders and frontiers meant a thing in our exalted state. But we had been moving, that was the point; and moving, you cannot help getting somewhere; and at the back of my mind was the thought that one day soon we would walk innocently into a valley that would bear the name my wife had assumed, and that contained people and buildings and the answer to mysteries, and her.

PART THREE

The Anderson Valley

It was a region of permanent snow. There was no rock visible any-where, none of that sterile red. Everything was white. But the snow was fresh; it looked as if it had only just fallen.

One morning, at the top of a high pass that we came to about an hour after dawn, we rounded a spur of rock to see spread out in front of us an immense valley, broad and long and gently sloping. It must have been twenty-five kilometres in length and fifteen in width at its widest point. It looked like a bed, it was so sweetly sloped; and the mountains rose around it on every side, like the low walls of a garden. It was so high up that beyond the walls there was nothing but sky.

It was covered in virgin snow from end to end, and the early morning sun swept across it, gilding everything and washing it with the clearest possible tints of lemon, gold, and pure ethereal blue. And in the middle of the plain, in regions mild of calm and serene air, there was a city under the snow.

At first glance it made me think of the old continent, of the lovely cities of Europe, with spires and gilded domes and green copper roofs. Sparkling in the sunshine, there were towers, domes, chim-neys, glass and ceramic twinkling and gleaming, glinting, shining.

Every horizontal surface lay under fresh snow, so that there were only light colours anywhere to be seen: no black, browns, greys, dark greens, only the lightest and palest and most transparent of colours. It was like heaven, which is made of jasper, gold, sapphire, chalcedony, emerald, etc., etc., sardonyx, beryl, and so on.

The city was the Perfect City of the Unreal People.

It was made of glass and bright alloys and ceramic, all enamelled and glazed for extra brightness.

Mary sighed so suddenly when she saw it that I thought she had been wounded. Johnny drew in his breath; and I sighed, time and time again, wonderstruck, like a little child.

173

And so we set off down the gentle slope into the Anderson Valley.

We were too far from the city to see any details, but the air was so clear that we were aware of details waiting just beyond the edge of sight.

Glittering and twinkling on the near side of the city were a million radio masts, that rose like lines against the sky. An infinite number—necessary hyperbole, like the jasper, chalcedony, and so on—of *lines* were were drawn vertically from the ground up a part of the sky; so slim and naked did the masts seem, which pierced the sky for mysterious electrical purposes. Also on this side there seemed to be a region or estate of factories, oil refineries, gas tanks, electrical transformers, and chemical works.

It was all set about with snow and silence. Could the spirit of solitude reign here as well? Would we be able to walk unselfconsciously down the streets and boulevards, without the impulse to turn and look over our shoulders? As if these created things were as virginal and clean as the sterile wilderness?

Where were the inhabitants, and my wife?

As we trudged through the calf-deep snow we sucked at the city with our eyes, trying to get every bit of knowledge off the panorama in front of us.

The centre of the city was marked by tall elegant buildings, and beyond them was a parklike open space, with large distinguished buildings standing on their own. And slightly to the left of the centre was a small hill, with a building like a palace on top of it.

The air of the valley, and the air all over the city, had the same smell as the messenger from my wife: that profoundly moving scent of fresh ironed cotton, cleanliness, the desert, snow.

Did the messenger come from the Perfect City, then? Not from my wife?

We were moving slowly towards the Parque Industrial (for so I called it in my mind, after the Park in the First City, where I had lost the favour of the Whores); and still nothing moved, no smoke rose from the chimneys, no sounds of traffic came to us across the silent valley.

All three of us drew closer together as we made our way quietly over the snowy meadows. And Juan muttered something that sounded like a prayer. But it wasn't fear that entered us, just wonderment, such as would make small children draw together if they found themselves alone in a cathedral.

The light blue sky and the vigilant rim of snowy peaks around the edge of the valley reinforced the impression that we were suspended between earth and sky, in a region where spirits dwell, angels of the air. So nothing that went on here would be visible to those on earth. As it was; for what had we been able to find out about the Anderson Valley? Nothing.

"I will live here," said Juan.

"Maybe we . . ." I began, but I really didn't know what I was going to say.

The Parque Industrial was fenced in with a single-strand wire fence. It was more like a line on a map than a barrier. The fence-posts, made of galvanised steel, seemed very dark against the bright snow.

Everything shone: the banks of steel-clad transformers, the coral-like clusters of glittering insulators, the tense bright wires that sprang from pylon to pylon like correct guesses . . . Utterly new, delicate, lacy, detailed, clean, all these crystal insulators, blue pipes, red valves, and yellow wires; and the smooth snow they emerged from was like the floor of a gallery full of sculptures, or like the calm foam around the brand-new feet of Aphrodite.

We walked along beside the aerial enclosure. This was fenced off like the Industrial Park; hectares, filled with those line-like masts we had seen from a distance. Johnny thought that they might be a form of radio telescope; Mary imagined that it was not the posts themselves which caught the signals, but the intricate pattern of wire, a cat's-cradle or a mandala, which was woven between them. And I had thought that the wires were merely supports for the posts instead of vice versa, taking the trees for the wood, or the objects for the relation.

Beyond the aerial enclosure we came to the first buildings of the Perfect City. They were four long, low barrack-like structures about five or six metres in height, and without windows. They were enclosed in the area of the Parque Industrial, and obviously housed some kind of machinery. But they were silent.

Beyond them, on the right, we could see a long, narrow reservoir, under snow and ice of course, but manifestly a reservoir because of the railed dam, with iron wheels for opening sluices, that protruded from the snow at the far end of it, a kilometre away.

And then we were among the first houses. It was an ordinary suburban street of the kind painted by Utrillo. But this was Utrillo exorcised of melancholy and lit by a morning light, a clear spring freshness.

At the first crossroads, we looked down each of the streets to right and left. There was nothing; walls about two metres high presented a blank face to the road, while behind them we could see the backs of comfortable houses, of what might have been a school or a church.

But preventing us from entering the road ahead there was a wooden barrier of the sort that is raised and lowered with a counterweight, and at the weighted end of it, there was a stout concrete building about the size of a garage, with windows, brightly painted wooden eaves, and a printed enamel notice which said in four languages:

CUSTOMS POST
HALT
This customs post is administered by
the Economic Security Committee of
the Anderson Valley Corporation. Visitors are asked to ring the bell, and an
official of the Committee will
attend them.

"There's someone here after all," said Mary.

Of all things, the first feeling that flooded into my mind at that moment (and made me blush) was the realization that I had done nothing to let Mary's family, or Johnny's, know that they were alive after the plane crash, and that the pilot and the guide were dead . . . They must have had relatives. Wives and children. I had done nothing.

"Well?" said Johnny. "Shall I ring the bell?"

I nodded. The bell-push was by the door. He pressed it; the bell rang, and the door automatically opened; and we entered the building, and came face to face with the first inhabitant of the Perfect City of the Unreal People.

Computers Beat Holy Water at Its Own Game

The office of the Customs Post was bright and warm. Inside it there were a computer terminal; a desk, empty of paper; and a young official.

He was wearing a dark blue uniform. He was black, but in spite of that he bore an uncanny resemblance to the blonde messenger, because of the angelic perfection and cleanliness of his features. He put aside the book he had been reading, and stood up to greet us.

"Welcome to the Perfect City," he said.

"Are you one of the unreal people?" asked Mary.

"I am whatever I seem," he said courteously. "And so are you. At the moment I seem to be a Customs official."

"Have we left Venezuela, then?" said Johnny.

"Not quite," said the official, "but I don't want to see your passports. This is purely economic."

He explained the function of the Customs Post. The Economic Security Committee safeguarded the money of the city by preventing its adulteration, he said. Just as immigrants to a country had to undergo a health inspection, so money, which in the Perfect City was more thoroughly understood than anywhere else in the world, was subject to a period of quarantine on entry.

During this time the money would be inspected and a record made of its external appearance and serial numbers. Its history would be checked; where it came from, what it had done, how it had come into the possession of its present bearer, and so on. A careful watch would be kept on the current rates of exchange of that particular currency, and on the economic behaviour of the government which issued it.

These records would be added to the computer's memory bank, and a check made on the truth of the story told by the owner. While all this was being done, visitors were advanced free of interest the sum of one hundred sterilised dollars to pay for what they would need; and when their money was cleared, it was returned to them less the amount they had spent.

"It may not seem a great deal to live on in the meantime," he said, "but you'll find that sterilised dollars go much further than the ordinary kind."

"Why do you have dollars and not Bolivars," I asked, "if we're still in Venezuela?"

"Since the Perfect City is administered independently, we might have used any form of currency, or invented our own. But we chose dollars because their name is familiar to many people; and besides, these dollars are different."

So I, as the guardian of our money (that of the son and daughter of millionaires, and I a poor man) handed over every cent we had, and explained in detail where it had come from: so much from the wallet of the dead guide, Joachim, so much from my winnings in the bet with Pretorius.

177

At the mention of that name the official looked interested, but politely made no comment. He gave us each a credit card for our personal use.

"Are we your first visitors?" I asked when the formalities were completed.

"Yes, I believe you are."

"Is the city empty? Where are all the people?" Mary asked.

"The basic services are manned, but the snow is holding things up. We're not quite ready to start yet."

"When you say you are whatever you seem to be," I said, "is that just a form of words, or do you mean it literally? If I said that you seem to be related to someone I . . . met once, even though she was blonde, would it be true to say that you were?"

"Things are always what they seem," he said. "If that's what I seem to be, then pretend it's true, and see how you get on."

I liked the way he spoke. It wasn't formal, but still it was polite; impersonal and friendly at the same time. I wanted to ask him many more questions. But I was anxious to get on and look for Catherine, so I just said "Where do you advise us to go next?"

"If you go to the Palacio de Comunicaciones, on the Avenida de Doctor Faust near the Plaza del Rinascimiento, you will find a Bureau of Information that will be able to tell you anything you need to know."

"Many thanks," I said. "Good morning."

"Good morning."

And we left. He lifted the wooden barrier for us to go through, and we printed our footsteps in the virgin snow of the street.

Except that it wasn't untrodden, I thought with childish disappointment. Someone had walked about on it.

But that meant someone else in the city! It was a double-take.

Then a triple-take, into normality: they were Juan's footprints, and there he stood, beside us.

"We didn't get a credit card for him," said Mary.

"Did you give him my money?" asked the unreal.

"I forgot I had it. But how much was it?"

"Eighty-eight centimos."

That was about twenty cents, an amount which would hardly damage the economy of the Perfect City. So I thought it wasn't worth going back.

The road from there on was perfectly straight, running for about four kilometres into the heart of the city. On either side of it were elegant apartment buildings, shops, stores, and twice as we went along we passed what looked like the entrance of an underground railway system.

And nothing was open. Everything was asleep. Not a scratch marked the paintwork on the beautiful store-fronts, not a light glowed in the wide windows, not a sound broke the silence in the clean white canyon of the street.

Most of the stores were empty, awaiting their owners; but one or two were full of crates to be unpacked, and in another a window display of men's clothing was in the course of arrangement. So there was someone here. And we found another piece of evidence too, the marks of a car's tyres on the fresh snow. They came out of a street from the left, crossed the road, and went on down towards the city centre. It was a big car with wide tyres, and it had been driven slowly with frequent stops.

At every step, our wonder at the place increased.

After an hour or so we could see ahead of us the Plaza into which the street led. And then we saw the second inhabitant.

Business First

It was the first inhabited building we had seen apart from the Customs Post, and it was a bank, appropriately. A branch, large and glass-fronted, of the First National City Bank, and inside it there were lights on and two men in business suits, talking earnestly by a desk; and at the desk a secretary in a blue dress was typing.

We stood in the snow like hungry children outside a confectioner's. The bank was open.

Then a man came out, pulling on a warm tweed overcoat. He had a Russian fur hat, and high thick boots.

He paused when he saw us, and looked back inside; but the two men had gone back to their offices or somewhere and the girl wasn't looking; so he came across to us, doing up his coat. He took off his hat politely when he saw Mary.

I said in Spanish "Good morning. We are travellers. Can you help us find our way?"

But he seemed happier in American.

"Sure," he said. "Where d'you want to go?"

"To the Palace of Communications," I said. "Is it likely to be open?"

"I believe so," he replied. "And you're heading the right way.

But if you don't mind my asking, where have you come from?"

"From the mountains."

He looked dubious. He was real, human, not one of the messenger's kindred.

"You'd better all get yourselves some warm clothes," he advised. "You look half frozen, never mind hungry. There's a few shops open in the Avenida, and a café or two, all you need for civilised living. You better get yourselves all warmed up before you freeze to death."

Mary nodded.

"Guess I should mind my own business," he said, "but there's only a few of us here yet, we all feel like kinfolk. Don't like to think of anyone being without the necessities of life, that's not needful at all."

"It's kind of you," said Johnny, "but we've got all we need, really."

"If you don't mind *my* asking," I said, "what business are you in?"

"I make artificial flowers," he said. "I'd give you a card if I had one, but that's where I'm going right now, to have some printed. Guess I'll see you around, though, if ever you need some of my products."

We exchanged good-mornings, and he went on his way. So business was beginning in the Perfect City. And he would shortly rent one of the new offices, I thought, and have a telephone and perhaps a telex installed, and, with the capital advanced him by the bank, sow the seeds of a profitable enterprise.

On we went.

"I suppose," I said, "that we'd better decide what we want to do. You know what I want to do, anyway. Mary, what about you, though?"

She sighed. "Buy something to wear find somewhere to stay, I don't know, all that sort of thing. I can't think here, it's all . . ." She flapped her hand vaguely. She was tired.

"There's plenty to do," said Johnny obscurely.

Then we were in the Plaza del Rinascimiento, the Square of the Renaissance, Reawakening Place.

It was about a hundred and fifty metres across. Six roads entered it, and in the very centre stood an ornate fountain, with Nereids, Tritons, and dolphins frozen solid. In the clear air I could see icicles bristling like spears, like the prongs of the trident held by the figure in the middle, sharp and glassy. And the bare and level snow stretched far around.

Juan said something. He was almost radiant. It was possible to see him clearly at intervals now, or perhaps we had grown accustomed to him.

"I shall live here," he said.

"Let's find the Information Bureau," said Mary.

Snow and the Balance of Payments

The Palacio de Comunicaciones was an imposing square building entirely covered in glass of a delicate bronze shade. It stood at the corner where the Avenida de Doctor Faust, a handsome boulevard, entered the Plaza.

It looked quiet and empty, but the revolving door was unlocked, and we went in. Inside we found a wide carpeted lobby, warm and light, with climbing plants arranged along a broad marble staircase. The expanse of one wall was covered by a mural depicting the construction of the city, against the immense low rim of the mountains.

A girl sat patiently at a wide mahogany desk. She was waiting for us to speak.

We stood like filthy ghosts borne in on an ill wind. We showed up as clearly as rooks in a field of snow. We conferred in whispers: what should we say?

Mary became impatient and walked over to the desk.

"My name is Mary Pretorius," she said imperiously. "We have been wandering in the wilderness after a plane crash. Can you tell me if my father, of the Pretorius Bank, is in the city?"

"I'll find out for you," she said.

A section of the desk rolled back to expose the keyboard of a computer terminal. She tapped expertly at the keys, and seconds afterwards a glass display screen on the desk lit up and flashed out a message to her. She looked up.

"Mr Pretorius is not here, I'm afraid," she said. "He's in Zurich."

"Is he likely to come here?" asked Mary.

"In the ordinary course of things, not for a month or so. But if the snow doesn't go he may have to come earlier."

"What for?" asked Johnny.

"To decide what to do about it."

"Ah."

This girl was like us and like the maker of flowers, human. The Customs official, and the messenger, were of a different kind, and now as I stood numbly in that great glass lobby they seemed to fade into uncertainty, and the city and everything in it flicker between reality and unreality, as unstable as Juan the ilusorio. But I was going to have to distinguish between several kinds of unreality, and as I thought about it found myself shifting into English from the Spanish we had been speaking, because the Spanish term *ilusorio* was too clumsy. Juan the unreal was illusory, but the Customs official and the messenger, if they were the unreal people of the city, were not. Everything is what it seems, he'd said to us in the Customs Post, not answering Mary's question. Everything here seemed solid and expensive and beautiful. Did that make it real? Another word for unreal was artificial, like the flowers made here.

Like the flowers in the messenger's hair.

Johnny spoke to the girl, and distracted my thoughts.

"We're cold and hungry," he said. "Is there anywhere we can stay? Are there any hotels open yet?"

"The Hilton, further down the Avenida Faust, is open. I think the London on the Calle Gulbenkian is nearly ready, but not open yet."

"Are they very expensive?" I asked.

"There's no doubt that you will be able to pay," she said.

But I wasn't sure what that meant.

"You were given credit cards, weren't you?" she went on, seeing my hesitation.

"Yes, but my money is limited, none the less."

"There's no doubt that you'll be able to pay. You'll find that everything in the city is very moderately priced, but everything has a price. I have to make a charge of one dollar for this information, for example. But that dollar will also buy a map of the city, and a list of the major places of interest."

She took a folding map from a chromium rack beside her. All these appurtenances seemed to spring into being as she needed them. She took my credit card, put it into slot in the front of her keyboard, tapped the keys, and the machine bleeped. She handed the card back.

"The Hilton is on the very next block," she said, "just this side of the Municipal Museum."

"Okay," said Johnny. "Many thanks."

"Thank you," she said, and smiled politely and began to polish her nails, waiting for the next information-seeking travellers from the eternal snows.

So out we went again and headed for the hotel.

"There's plenty of money, for Christ's sake," said Mary.

"Mary, Martin's not rich, and he doesn't want to have us pay for him," said Johnny.

"Well, that's ridiculous. I'll never spend all my money if I live to be a hundred, and nor will you. He shouldn't be so bloody proud. It's just snobbery."

"That shows how much you know," he said hotly. "If you were a man, you'd be a playboy. You know nothing about money."

"And I suppose you're not a playboy when you ride your silly bicycle," she said, equally angry. "You don't earn your living any more than I do."

"Shut up, both of you," I said. "We didn't quarrel about money out there in the mountains. I might have thought we'd learnt not to. Anyway, you're no richer than I am, because we've only got a hundred dollars each. And if you're poor, Mary, you get into the habit of asking what things cost, because you might not be able to pay."

"Oh, I see," she said sarcastically. "*You're* allowed to keep your habits, but we're not, is that it? Penny-pinching's good, and generosity's bad. I must try and remember."

I held my breath and said nothing. Johnny took her by the shoulders and turned her to face him. She shook his hands off.

"If you want to be dumped on your arse in the street," he said, "just carry on like this for a bit longer. You know nothing, Mary, and it's time you bloody well did. . . ."

I walked away and left them to it. It was their quarrel, and I had the feeling that they might be happy with it, in the end.

Auto-erotic Speculations

The great hotel was deserted except for one clerk at the desk. The building had the by now familiar air of immaculate newness, of luxury and up-to-date taste.

I asked the clerk how much it would cost us to stay in the hotel, mentioning that I had two friends who would be arriving in a little while. He said that it would cost us one dollar a night each. I was staggered.

"Only a dollar?" I said.

"A sterilised dollar," he said, and handed me the register. I was the first customer.

"Who do you expect to come to your hotel?" I asked. "Is it for tourists?"

"Perhaps, eventually," he said. "The snow is holding things up."

He led me up to a room on the tenth floor. It had a view over the whole city. It was now nearly midday, and the sun was high and the snow dazzling. Most of the streets were untrodden, and I could see our tracks in the Plaza, leading to the hotel. I couldn't see the other two, or Juan, even if he would have shown up against the snow.

"How long has the snow been lying?" I asked.

"Many months," he said. "It falls freshly every night. It wasn't planned for when the city was built."

"Who was it who planned the city, then?"

"The managers of the Anderson Valley Company."

"Are they in charge of the city? Or is there a mayor, or a governor?"

"The Company administers things now, but when we're ready we shall have elections, and choose a President, so I've heard."

A little radio receiver in his top pocket bleeped.

"Excuse me, sir, but there's someone at the desk. We don't have many staff yet, you see. But the kitchen's working, and the bar's open, if you'd care to eat or drink."

And he left.

I sat down on the bed. That must be the other two downstairs, I thought. The bed was soft and the quilt was warm, and I felt drowsy by suggestion.

But I needed to wash first. I stripped and shaved, and then had a hot shower. Some property of the water invigorated me, or woke me up. I tasted in it a suggestion of that remote clean smell belonging to the messenger. . . . Was there some mysterious mineral that impregnated the waters here, and gave the inhabitants that resolute beautiful cleanliness? Would my wife share it, when I found her? Would we (the travellers) become like it?

Another impulse returned under the needling hot water, as I remembered the strange coupling I had shared with the messenger in the empty bank, smelling of money and this clean water. I felt dizzy for a moment. I gave in to the impulse to indulge my sexuality, feeling savage and happy.

184

And fully awake. If they melted the snow, what a flood of power would be released!

As I towelled myself dry my mind teemed with ideas for concentrating the rays of the sun on to the snowy plazas by means of giant mirrors; of heating air and blowing it through the virgin canyons of the streets; of laying electric cables the length of all the great boulevards, and heating them.

I laid out the map we had been given so as to determine the best order in which to clear the streets, to see where the melted snow would drain away, and so on. I stood naked and damp on the warm carpet, tracing roads, avenues, streets with a finger, and measuring distances with the width of my thumb.

But the enterprise faded; I grew more interested in the plan of the city itself. I couldn't believe it had been created from nothing. There must have been some existing city on the site. Or else they had borrowed the plan of it from another place. It looked organic, that was all, not planned.

The Avenida de Doctor Faust, on which the hotel stood and which I could survey now from my warm double-glazed window, was the main artery of the city, broad and handsome and lined with bare trees.

The main public buildings the map showed, ministries and museums and libraries, were on the Avenida itself or nearby. But there was a Palacio Municipal, a large building, a kilometre or so to the east in a little patch of green. A canal or moat ran round the park in which it stood; and the park was given the curious name of La Colina Tamaño de Hombre, the Hill with the Height of a Man.

There was a lot of green on the map. There was a Parque del Siglo Veinte, in the north-west of the city, with a Zoo and a Jardin Botanico beside a lake; and near the Municipal Palace there was a large meadow-like park with a road leading through it. Off the road on one side was an area called the Ciudad Universitaria, with buildings labelled Medicina, Filosofia y Letras, Ciencias. The great park they stood in was called the Campo de Minerva; and another such meadow, the Campo de Afrodite, stood on the same side of the city, divided by a stream which meandered through it and fed a little lake.

Everything was complete. And the streets had names that honoured, for the most part, great capitalists. Rockefeller, Dupont, Gulbenkian, Vanderbilt, Carnegie; but also Adam Smith, Ricardo, Keynes, and Friedman; and, to my surprise, Marx and Mao Tse-tung. Nor, since this was Venezuela, was Simon Bolivar forgotten. Nor were Byron, nor Shelley, nor Hoffmann.

Someone tapped my shoulder, and I turned absently to see who it was.

"Nice place, huh?" he said. "Good idea, to come here."

"Did you come in with me?" I asked.

"I stayed with them, and watched them argue for a while, then came up here."

He sat down on the bed; I turned back to the map. The name of the hill where the Palace stood rang a bell, but I couldn't think what it reminded me of.

Juan was speaking again. I began to get dressed, trying to listen to him, but it was never easy.

"You know what I think, I think there are no unreals here. This is a place they come to get real again. Where they cure them."

"They might be another kind of unreal," I said.

"How can there be? I bet they could make me real, if I wanted it."

"Maybe so," I muttered. I would have to buy some clothes with my hundred dollars, for these were filthy. Life repeats itself. Juan went on talking.

"With you as my helper I could do a lot here," he said. "No need to be real for it either. Better if I stayed unreal for a bit, maybe. Nobody knows I'm around. I could go anywhere and not be noticed. There's a lot of stuff here they don't need, just lying around."

But I wasn't listening. When I was dressed I called room service and ordered an American meal, hamburgers and coffee. I was in an American mood, keen to use every gadget I could get my hands on, to speak to strangers in bars, to alter the way the world was run and profit by the change. When I remembered Juan again, he was gone, looking for the place where they could make him real.

I ate hungrily, and then reached for the telephone. I rang the Information Bureau.

"Can you tell me," I asked, "why the city was built?"

"For one thing, to provide a social laboratory for the companies underwriting the Anderson Valley Project."

"I don't quite understand."

"A sterile area, sterile in financial terms, where profits, policies, services, and so on, can be tested and their effects measured."

"Is that all?"

"No. The City is also to be an important manufacturing centre."

"What will it make?"

"Various high-quality goods which need an abundance of pure air and water in their manufacture."

"Where will the inhabitants come from?"

"Some people will come from those countries which allow their citizens to emigrate, and others will begin their lives here."

"I see. And whose idea was the city?"

"It developed out of previous ventures of the same kind; the first and second cities, on the plain and in the mountains, were unsuccessful prototypes. But here we think we have it right."

"How much did it all cost?"

"Untold billions. The cost is so vast that it surpasses numbers."

"So the world itself must be mortgaged to pay for it."

"Oh, no. It's only a drop in the ocean of wealth there is in the world altogether."

"Can you tell me something else? I am looking for my wife. Her name is Catherine Browning, but I think she may be using the name Anderson. Is it possible that you might know of her?"

"Oh, yes. I can tell you where she is."

Cash Only

I took a deep breath. "Where is she?" I said carefully.

"She is . . ." a pause as if she were consulting her computer . . . "at this moment, in the Palacio Municipal on the Colina Tamaño de Hombre."

"Can one go there?"

"Yes, if you have a pass."

"And how do I get one of those?"

"It has to be paid for in cash."

"In sterilised dollars."

"That's right."

"Can you tell me what my wife is doing there?"

"Unfortunately no. There are limits to our knowledge, I'm afraid."

"If I want to get to her, then, what should I do?"

"Only the unreal people can see her when they choose. Others have to wait until she summons them."

"But why? And what sort of unreals? Like the Customs official? I don't understand what's going on."

"The unreal people of the city. But I suggest you telephone the Palace. The number is on the list of places of interest sold by the Information Bureau."

"Yes, I've got it . . . I'd better do that. I will. Thanks."

"Is there anything else I can tell you?"

"Not for the moment."

"Then would you please insert your credit card into the slot underneath the dial of your telephone? Face uppermost, embossed end first."

"What's the charge?"

"One dollar, as always."

"Of course. Thank you."

"Good morning."

I slid the rectangle of plastic into the slot; a pip on the line registered its presence. And as soon as the line went dead I thought of a dozen other questions. Next time I'd be prepared, I'd have them all written down and get more information for my dollar.

But what did I mean, next time? I'd have my wife again in an hour or two. As soon as she knew I was here my questions would disappear, and we'd come together like two drops of mercury.

I reached for the telephone again, to dial the number of the Palace. But I put it down; I hadn't digested what I'd been told yet.

The unreal people of the city could see her without an appointment, or whenever they chose, but others had to wait to be summoned. She was some kind of chief or mistress; but the unreals weren't subordinate to her; so they were superior to real people, perhaps. That seemed to be logical.

Juan had said something about unreals, that there was only one kind, his own. But maybe he hadn't seen the official, or the messenger. Maybe I was wrong about everything. Maybe the unreals here were like Juan; maybe there was no difference between the messenger's kind and humans. If the unreals here were of Juan's kind, they'd be able to see her whenever they chose anyway.

I pressed the quilt on the bed, and ran my fingers over the smooth plastic of the telephone, uneasy about the reality of everything. I decided that I didn't believe what the girl had told me about the origins of the city. It wasn't enough to account for all this. An entire and beautiful city in the empty wilderness just to test-market new brands of toothpaste and cornflakes? Ridiculous. And goods needing sterile conditions for their manufacture were made daily in the most polluted regions of the earth, in laboratories and factories.

For the first time, I felt a sense of danger. I had no right here; not only that, but I had been forbidden to come, by the messenger; and I wondered what I would do if I found my wife involved in something I didn't like. I wanted to talk to Johnny, and again reached for the phone, and again took my hand away. It was up to me.

Old Vienna

So I went out alone. I meant to go directly to the Palace and seek entry, in spite of having no pass. That sort of straightforward approach appealed to me just then; it was like telling the truth, I thought.

Unfortunately, I lost my way. The streets were all clearly marked on the map I took with me, but the city was bigger than I thought, and the snow confused me, and everywhere I looked things were so strange, so gleaming-new, and so dazzling in the bright sun, that I became almost hypnotised and wandered loosely around in a circle, tracing a path through the same quarter as the Palace without actually seeing it. It had been designed, this part of the city, in a Bohemian fashion, like a stage set for *The Prisoner of Zenda* or *The Vagabond King*; all new, but made to look old, as false and artificial as Mary in her capacity as a priestess of fashion, and as beautiful. Little squares with frozen fountains, picturesque balconies and shuttered windows, bare lime trees. In the future there'd be the scent of roasting coffee in the air, the aroma of cigars, the hum of conversation in the cafés, the laughter of artists and lovers, and the plangent ring of music in the old Viennese way, violins, zithers, guitars . . . all unreal.

And one café was open already. It was called the Café Florestan, and the sign over the door said it was kept by a man called Ignaz Gruenberg. He was mild and middle-aged, and he received me with great politeness.

I ordered a coffee, and said "You have all the custom to yourself."

"So far," he said. "A little competition will be agreeable. My wife makes the best Sachertorte in all of South America, but who knows about it besides me and her? No one yet. But they'll come before long."

His café was as clean and new as everything else. Marble-topped tables, a polished wooden floor, various large-leaved plants, decorative ironwork, all spoke of the best taste of turn-of-the-century Vienna; and his coffee was delicious.

I told him where I was going and what I was doing, and he said "Easy to lose your way in this little part of the city. It's built like a maze, so that the Palace is hidden. Everyone going there for the first time has to pass a test of initiation, a search, as in the ancient mysteries."

He was speaking seriously, a good solid bourgeois telling an important truth. Very well, I thought, and took it at face value.

"Is it intended to be like that? Or did it just happen to become like it?" I asked.

He settled himself down, leaning on the counter with his arms folded. "You mustn't misunderstand me," he said. "I'm a student of these matters. If you don't see the occult side of things, there's a lot you miss completely. Take it from me, anyone could end up in all sorts of trouble through not understanding the secret forces."

"Is this city designed to an occult plan, then?"

"That's what I meant by misunderstanding. It is and it isn't. Don't think I'm being unhelpful, now, because you've got to see double, so to speak, before you can see straight. So all the great occult masters say, at any rate."

He wiped absently at a spilled drop of coffee on the counter. I could see him searching for the right words, and sat patiently.

"In fact," he said, "I don't know why the city was built, and I may as well admit it. But only a fool would go around in this place and not see the obvious. These people they call the unreals. You must have seen one or two of them, eh? Nothing special about what they do, ordinary jobs, like the rest of us. What do you think they are?"

"I've seen many kinds of unreals on my travels, but none like them. I can't guess what they might be."

"Where have you been travelling, then? Never mind now, there's plenty of time for tales later, we've got all the time in the world. But I'll tell you what I think those beings are. And remember what I told you, I've studied this, I'm not just talking through my hat. This is intelligent speculation. I think the city is a sacred place, and these unreals are a new order of men and women, like angels. It's been foretold. You come back another day when I've got all my books unpacked and I'll show you Nostradamus' very words. The angels are going to set up a state of perfect harmony and tranquillity here in the Anderson Valley, and then it's going to spread all over the world. You can tell what they are by looking at them. Have you seen one close to? I don't mean stare, that would be discourteous, but look. They're finer than us, their flesh is purer. They don't age. I've only been here for six months, but I can see already that they don't grow old. Angels, that's what they are. The city's been built in homage to them."

"I don't find anything in that to disagree with," I said. "What else do you know?"

He told me about the Freemasons, the Illuminati, the Rosicrucians, and other such exotic matters. They were all the necessary forerunners for the climax of all mysteries, which would be the inauguration of the Perfect State of the Anderson Valley. The signal for it to start would be a marriage. Thas was prefigured in such legends as the Chemical Wedding of Christian Rosenkreutz, and in the secret rites of the Templars, where men acted as women for purposes of magic. The marriage he was thinking of, he confided, would probably be between a human and one of these angels.

"I don't say a man and an angel, or a woman and an angel, because it might be both," he said mysteriously. "They have elements of both sexes in them. These mysteries are very deep."

He'd dreamed of it, what's more, so he was pretty certain he was right. He knew what would happen: first the snow would melt, and then more angels would appear, as the first flowers came out in the great meadows and the trees in the avenues put out their buds. Weddings, matings, copulations would take place; the meadows and groves of the Campo de Afrodite would be white and black and brown with the bodies of lovers, and the shores of the little lake at night would see the couplings of men and angels, men and girls, angels and girls, all like animals. Animals when they mated thrust, jerked, panted, became hot, their nostrils flaring; in their ardent movements men, women, and angels alike would all become animal. It was necessary to be like an animal, it was ordained, it was part of the plan, said Ignaz learnedly.

I was in no position to doubt a single word he said. Besides, I liked him; he was honest and serious, and his coffee was excellent. I told him what I had come to the city for, and he nodded gravely.

"I could tell you were no tourist," he said. "It was fate that led you in here. Believe you me, it was manifest destiny."

"Would it contradict my destiny to have the way to the Palace explained?"

"It's not a good idea. But it isn't far away, if you look carefully. How are you going to get in?"

"Knock at the door and ask. I don't know yet."

He nodded and spread his hands. "Well, it may work. You come and see me again, tell me how you get on. One thing we could do: tomorrow they're opening some of the public buildings for the first time, a museum and a concert hall. You and I could go there maybe and see what they've built for us, eh? And you can tell me what you find in the Palace."

So we agreed on that. He was curious and I wanted a sympathetic listener, and his advice would be helpful, even though I had routed a master of zombies and survived a public execution. Then I set off again to find the Palace.

Watch Your Step

I found it in five minutes, by looking carefully as the illuminated proprietor had advised.

A wide snowy park and the gentlest slope imaginable led up to a crystal-coloured little palace, a jewel-box in the baroque style, all encrusted with frost and glittering like sugar. A childlike canal, hardly six metres wide, ran delicately around the edge of the grounds. It was spanned by an ornamental iron bridge. Later on, swans and teal would paddle under the bridge, and beautiful girls would lean on its parapet, waiting for their lovers; but now the snow covered it all like a dustsheet, keeping it clean for them. If our poetical friend, the salesman of the First City, were to see all this, his soul would expand in measured ecstasies, because its poetic value was immense.

I made my way towards the bridge, and I was just about to cross it, when I heard something I hadn't heard at all in the city: the sound of a car engine. It was coming up slowly behind me. I turned and stopped, and the car, a great Mercedes, came quietly to a halt.

A uniformed chauffeur got out, and saluted me.

"Mr Browning?" he asked.

I nodded, on my guard.

"My employer, His Excellency Prince Giorgio Cavalcanti, would like to speak to you."

"Where is he?"

"In the car, sir. Would you care to sit inside?"

He held open the back door. I got in and looked at the man who was sitting at the other side of the great car. The chauffeur shut the door and walked a few paces away.

Cavalcanti was about Pretorius' age; his heavy-lidded eyes looked subtle and melancholy, and his clothes were dark and very formal. He leaned across to shake my hand.

"Welcome," he said.

"Thank you. But how do you know who I am?"

"I asked the Information Bureau," he said, smiling a little, almost apologetically. "They told me what you were looking for."

"And have you come to take me to her?"

"I'm afraid not."

"No, it wasn't very likely. You're going to tell me not to bother to look for her, and go away and forget all about it. Is that right?"

"No, no. As a matter of fact I was going to ask if you'd care to stay in my house, as a guest, while you're in the city."

Silence, while he waited, with a slightly anxious irony, for my answer. I laughed a little nervously, being completely taken aback.

"I've asked your friends too," he said, "who are old friends of mine, as it happens. There's a reason for it. As visitors, you see, you're only allowed to stay three days in the city."

"I didn't know that."

"Unless you're the guest of a resident. Then you can stay as long as you like; or as long as he chooses to keep you."

Was there a tiny hidden threat in that? The Prince's manner was so polite and, without being condescending, friendly behind the formality, that I hardly knew what to make of it.

"My friends have accepted your offer?" I asked.

He nodded gravely.

"I'm sorry to be rude," I said carefully, "and I don't want to be, believe me. It's natural that you should want to have Johnny and Mary as your guests, if they're friends of yours; but you don't know me, and I can't see that your friendship for them need go so far as to take a total stranger into your house just because he turns up in their company . . . Forgive me: but I'm suspicious, and I guess that you want something from me in return."

"Well, I need not, you know; my house is large, and it's not impossible that my motive should be hospitality, is it? But I'm teasing you. You're right. I *would* like you to do something in return, but it's nothing onerous. I'd just like you to suppress your curiosity."

"All of it?"

"In the matter of your quest this afternoon."

"My wife."

"And other matters that concern the city. There's a great deal you may legitimately find out, and please do so; but if at any point you find that your questions are no longer being answered, there you must stop."

"Would I find out all the truth in the end?"

"No one does that."

"That's just a form of words. Would I find out everything I want to know about my wife and where she is, in the end?"

"As to that . . ." He sighed, and looked genuinely concerned and troubled. I believe he was. "I don't know."

"I see. Well, my friends have their own concerns now, but all I have is my wife. You must see that I can't accept your offer? I'll see what I can do in three days."

"Ah well. Today is the twenty-first; you must leave by the evening flight on the twenty-fourth. No doubt we'll meet again before you go; there are only a few of us here, and new faces are welcome, even if they stay for only three days. Good afternoon, then."

He smiled, and nodded ruefully. I got out of the car and waited while the chauffeur started the engine and drove away. Cavalcanti waved politely as the car turned out of my sight.

The Lure of Dissolution

Three days, I thought grimly; well, then, I could break the rules without a conscience. I crossed the bridge and walked up the Hill with the Height of a Man towards the sugar palace. I was in a mood to throw stones and break windows if there was no other way in.

The snow was untouched, virgin all the way round. If anyone was inside, they must have been there all day, unless they had come by helicopter and landed on the roof. I walked through a courtyard where the sun lay and the main entrance was, and found the courtyard bare and the door locked; and I walked along the terraces on the other three sides, trying door after door, and finding them all shut against me.

But when I came into the courtyard again I felt weak with surprise, and had to put a hand on the newly-cut pink sandstone of the wall to steady myself. For there were no footsteps but mine leading into the courtyard, and there standing in the middle of it was a man I thought had died: the red-haired sorcerer and business consultant, Alexander Vrykolakas.

He stood with a broad beam on his face right in the middle of the sunny square, and there were no footsteps in the snow around him.

"Touché, mon vieux," he called out, and strode amiably across to me, his hand outstretched. I shook it weakly.

"I thought I'd arranged to have you killed," I said.

"That's what I mean by 'touché', my dear chap," he said. "The trouble with air crashes is that you can't specify which of the passengers will actually kick the bucket. So you got away from me there. Still, you jolly nearly had me there on the ranch, I must admit."

"What happened?"

"Poor old Felix couldn't resist the fire. But if it weren't for that, he'd probably be chopping still; you know what these zombies are, they can't balance; and every time he swung the axe, he fell over. Shame really. Still, here I am, and it's fifteen all, and likely to remain so. I've got a proposition. Do you want to listen to it?"

"Yes," I said carefully.

"Let's go inside then. I don't like this weather at all."

He strolled over to the door I'd tried myself ten minutes before and found locked, and it opened in his hand as easily as the door of the bank had opened in the messenger's.

"All done by magic," he said cheerfully. "Come along in."

"Are you pretending to be English today?"

"Must be nerves. There's rather a nice little room down this way, a sort of library thing. Yes, I usually pretend to be American, but I thought I'd make you feel at home—I wasn't sure how pleased you'd be to see me, you see . . . Here we are."

A warm sunny room, large, but with proportions that fitted it intimately to the purpose of two people sitting and talking. It was furnished in exactly the style I might have expected; and all the furniture was newly made. I looked around doubtfully.

"Imitation," said the astrologer, "in charming taste. Don't you think?"

"What do you want, exactly?"

We sat down on elegant chairs, like eighteenth-century gentlemen.

"Knowledge," he said. "That's all."

"What'll you do with it?"

"Reflect on it. Don't you find that coming near to death makes you calmer and more philosophical? My previous ambitions seem very paltry now. No, all I want to do is know, and you can help me."

"I don't know why you think that. But how do you come to be allowed in the Palace? Have you got a pass? And when did you get here, to the Valley, I mean?"

"Only a little time before you did. No, Martin, I think you can help me because the boss of this enterprise, old Pretorius, is absurdly prejudiced against me for some quite trivial reason, whereas he's not against you. In fact they're all anxious for you to do well."

"How the hell do you *know* all this? And what do you want me to do? What'll you do for me in return? I don't like any of this."

"I don't want you to do anything dangerous, Martin, put your mind at rest. If there's anything dangerous to be done, I'll do it. In fact I don't want you to do anything other than what you're doing already. You're looking for your wife, aren't you? Well, carry on, don't waste time on anything else. Just tell me what you find out, that's all. I'm genuinely interested, believe me. Now for what I can do for you. Supposing you want to get into a locked building; I'll get you in. Supposing you find you need some extra money; I'll find some for you. Suppose somebody's embarrassing you, preventing you from searching where you think they've hidden her; I'll persuade him to let you go there. There are a hundred things I can do for you, Martin. Don't hesitate to ask, believe me."

He leant forward earnestly and grasped my forearm to emphasise his sincerity.

"And I know some things about this city already," he went on, "and I'll tell them to you. Freely. I'll ask for nothing in return. Take this room as an example. What's the first thing you notice about it?"

"It's a fake."

"Very true. Come and look at this."

He led me over to the chimney-piece, which was an ornate piece of carving in marble. He pointed to a section along the side which was not quite smooth.

"Not hand-carved," he said knowledgeably. "If you look closely you'll see the characteristic marks of machine-cutting, these absolutely regular little arcs, you notice them? And if you come next door I'll show you a little mark in the plaster moulding that—"

He'd been standing there in a lordly manner, one hand in his jacket pocket and the other gesturing authoritatively at these details, but now suddenly he broke off, his eyes widened, he put his head on one side and listened intently. In a second he'd become a guilty schoolboy trespassing. Then he clutched my arm and whispered anxiously "Quick! Let's hide!"

He tugged me to the other side of the room, where a low sofa stood against the wall. Hastily he pulled it out and ducked down behind it, gesturing to me to follow.

"Hurry!" he whispered desperately.

I crouched down beside him, feeling foolish. He grasped my hand; I made as if to take it away, but he clung to it like a child. He was peering around the side of the sofa, wide-eyed.

I heard footsteps, slow and light, a girl's. My wife, I thought with a surge of longing. Then I smelt the messenger-smell. Vrykolakas' hand was gripping mine so tightly that his fingernails were digging into it. I couldn't see the angel from where I was, but I longed to stand up and declare myself; and then the slow steps left the room.

A few seconds went by. The mystic let go of my hand and calmly stood up, dusting down his elegant dark trousers.

"You see," he said in his normal voice, "how careful we must be? There are powerful elements in this city working against us. You and I, we must be circumspect. And daring."

He looked grave and courageous. His changes of personality were difficult to follow; he looked up at me next with a rueful, charming smile, and said "Martin, can you forgive me?"

"What for?"

"I thought you were on *their* side, you see. That's why I put a spell on the plane and made it crash. I misjudged you completely."

"I think you're mad. You'll probably drive me mad before long. If you can help me get to my wife, then I'll go along with you, but I'm not interested in anything else. You haven't convinced me yet that you can."

"Well, I'll tell you where she's not," he said, "and that's in this place. I can show you all over it if you like. It's empty, but for a couple of those . . . like the one who came in just now."

"The angels," I said.

"Is that what you call them?"

"So she's not here, you say? That's too negative. I want positive proof first."

"We might find some," he said, "if we look around the palace."

Now I was here, I could at least look around, having decided to break the rules in the first place. And I could always pretend to do as he asked. And I could always double-cross him later; and I could always kill him, if I could do nothing else; and then I could always kill myself, if I felt like it. Oh, there were lots of things I could do.

So I went around the palace with Vrykolakas. Every door that was locked, he opened by means of magic; and every time we came near an angel, we hid until it had gone past. There was one room where an angel was working, where we couldn't go. So Vrykolakas took a magic mirror out of his pocket, and it clouded over, and showed us the inside of the room, with an angel working at a desk; but no wife.

I felt sick and desperate when I left. I wished Johnny had been with me, because he might have been able to tell me what I hated, the city with its deceptive ways or the sorcerer with his; or me with mine. And I wished I had accepted the prince's offer and kept my curiosity still, but it was too late for that.

How to Avoid the Consequences of Your Actions

"Pride," said Mary resignedly.

"Don't start that again, please," I said.

"She's right this time," said Johnny.

"There's nothing you can do with him, Johnny," she said.

"I'm beginning to think you're right about that too."

"Oh, great," she observed. "You agree with me, then?"

"In this case, yes. But not always."

"Well." She gave a satisfied sigh. "It was worth all the fuss this morning then."

He looked at me coldly, as if sizing me up. "You're not going to change your mind?"

"Johnny, I can't. It's obvious that they're not going to tell me where she is or what she's doing; and I can't stay here indefinitely like a vegetable, not making any effort to find out; I'd die of frustration. So would you, in my position."

"He wouldn't be in your position," said Mary complacently.

Her father had said that, of himself, all that time ago.

"No," I said angrily, "but I am, foolish and proud as I am, and I'm stuck with it."

She was silent for a moment or two, and then said "All right, I'm sorry." She folded her hands calmly in her lap, and looked at Johnny.

"You're not going to change your mind?" he asked again.

"No."

Because I'd pledged myself to the astrologer, about whose presence in the city they were ignorant. I was already too guilty to draw back.

"Okay then," said Johnny.

He stood up. We both felt awkward, and it was Mary who helped us out of it. She got to her feet too and came over between us, taking Johnny's hand and then mine, and smiling and shaking her head.

"Of course you've got to look for her," she said. "They're silly to expect you not to. But you could probably do it at Cavalcanti's as well, if we helped. We'll ask him about it when we're there, anyway, won't we?"

She turned to him, and he looked down at her, the tension going out of his eyes. For a moment they stood quite still, as if they had forgotten I was there, looking like lovers. Then he nodded.

"Yes, of course we will," he said. "We'll probably find her quicker than you will. D'you want to bet?"

So we parted that afternoon in good enough humour, though it was obvious that they were each beginning to find the other more absorbing than any affairs of mine; which I was glad of for his sake. But the only way of avoiding the consequences of your actions, it occurred to me, was to undo them.

Elementary Economics

When they'd gone I decided to go out for a walk. I wanted to look at the sunset from the slopes of the Campo de Minerva and think about something other than myself.

I walked up the straight road that led to the Ciudad Universitaria. The air was clear and cool, and full of the oxygen-smell, which a breeze carried down to the city from the mountain-rim.

The setting sun behind me lit the University buildings with the clarity of a photograph, and gave the snowfields they stood in the delicate colours of artificial flowers. The buildings had all the space in the world to stand in, so none of them were narrow or cramped. I wandered between them, reading their names off the map I carried, wondering about the empty shelves inside them, the clean laboratories, the unopened books; and about the scholars and scientists who would inhabit these temples of learning. Geologists, no doubt, would make expeditions to the mountain rim to ascertain whether the rocks which formed it were igneous, metamorphic, or sedimentary, and collect specimens of quartz, felspar, gneiss, and schist, labelling each with its place of origin and placing them carefully in glass cabinets. Palaeontologists would disinter the stony mammals and reptiles which lurked in the hills, and put them together like jigsaws in the cool light of industrious workrooms. Botanists would walk through the knee-high grass of these warm meadows, when the thaw came, carefully staking out the location of rare orchids and studying the growth of those flowers which fertilise themselves by mimicking a female insect, thus inducing the male to copulate with them, and gratifying their own desires by pretending to gratify another's. A perfect emblem of the Perfect City, and that was why it came to mind, like Mary with the magistrate. The stars would have their servants too, for here was a great green-copper domed observatory, dedicated to the study of those celestial phenomena which require for their viewing the most transparent and ethereal of airy veils, only to be found in the clean high mountains, where spirits walk beside travellers and print their footsteps in the snow as one was doing beside me then, talking steadily.

"Juan," I said absently, in greeting.

"I know how to make myself real," he said insistently.

"I thought you didn't want to?"

"I know how to, never mind if I want to yet. It needs money."

"Well, you can have some of mine."

"No, my money. Yours is no good."

"But you haven't got very much. And anyway, it's not sterilised."

Then my concentration left him, and dissolved into the nebulous airs of the sunset. But presently he plucked my sleeve, and I tried hard to listen.

"Your money is as unreal as I am," he was saying. "My money is real, those coins. You can hold and touch them."

"But they're only tokens themselves; they're not real either."

"They're as real as anything. I know, I tell you. Give me my money back, so I can spend it and be real."

But I was reluctant. I didn't mind breaking the rules of the city in any of the matters to do with my wife, but this had no bearing on

them, so far as I could see, and I felt uneasy about letting unsterilised money loose in the economy, even so small an amount as
Juan's. So I demurred, explaining as best I could that my money
was in truth just as real as his. But he insisted.

"If you are an honest man, you'll give me my money," he said.
"I didn't think you were a thief when I looked after you in the
mountains."

Then I had an idea. Perhaps I could persuade him to take just
one coin at a time; he could hardly do much damage with that.
And with his peculiar advantages, he might be the very person to
help me put up with my alliance with Vrykolakas.

I felt in my pocket for his few coins, as light and nearly as
insubstantial as he was. I put one on my palm and held it out,
closing my hand as he was about to take it; and feeling like a
cheap crook. That was what the astrologer did to me.

"You can have it," I told Juan, "if you spy for me. There is a
man with red hair, a *brujo,* who is planning some evil in the city.
His name is Alexander Vrykolakas. Find him and watch him for
me, and tell me what he's doing, and you can have more of your
money."

"Easy," he said. "But I want more money than that to start
with. I gave you seven coins, remember."

I gave him another one. "Don't let him know what you're
doing," I said.

He scoffed. "Child's work. Do you want me to kill him for you?
I can do that too, if you want. For nothing."

"No, not that. And if you hear where my wife is, you can have
all your money."

He nodded. "All right, then. But maybe when this is all over
and I'm still not real, what will you do for me then, eh?"

"Everything I can."

"Much that will be. Maybe I'll want to stay unreal for a time,
after all. There may be things I'll want to do. Then you'll have to
help me."

He pocketed the coins, and drifted away over the cold snow as
the sun went down.

Levée in the Park
The telephone woke me up. I had slept uneasily, that first night in
a bed for weeks.

"Yes? Who's that?" I said.

"Your partner," said the silky voice of Vrykolakas. "I wondered if you'd care to meet a friend of mine. A friend of yours, too."

"What's the time?"

"Eight o'clock. We've got a busy day, Martin. Coming?"

"Where are you?"

"In the Park. Just the place."

"Have you found out where my wife is?"

"Well, I'm not actually looking for her, Martin," he said, gently, reasonably; "you are. I've found out some things, though. And I've got something for you. Come along and see what it is."

"All right then. Now?"

"As soon as you like. Go to the junction where the Paseo Comercial meets the Calle de Colombia. I'll be waiting for you. See you soon."

He rang off. I sat up and yawned; already I felt the sick, guilty tautness in the stomach that he invoked in me. The morning was bright and clear, as always. I dressed quickly, and went down to the restaurant to have some rolls and coffee. I felt exposed and uncertain in the great warm empty room, with its dozens of tables already laid.

The mystic was waiting, as he'd promised, at the edge of the Park. He was stamping with cold and flinging his arms about himself.

"Oof!" he exclaimed in irritation as I came near. "This is too bad, this cold! The sooner we can move, the better."

"Why, where are you going?"

"No, I meant move in the military sense, move against something," he said. "Come on, let's go and meet my friend."

He led me straight into the empty park. There was an elegant iron gate that looked as if it was locked, but it opened at a touch for him. There was no one in sight, as we went inside.

"Is this where you live, then?" I asked. We followed a snowy path that led between bare trees.

"No," he said. "I'm living in the Unbuilt Slum just at the moment. Until I find somewhere more suitable. But my friends would find it hard to live in hotels." He sniggered.

"You've got lots of friends, then? And what's the Unbuilt Slum?"

"Oh, you must come and see it! A charming place. And yes, I've got lots of friends. Relatives, too, I should say. But I'd value your opinion, Martin. I think very highly of your good sense, did you know that? I don't know what's best to do with my friends for the time being. I've got wonderful plans, and of course I'll share them with you, but for the moment—I don't know. Now let's see."

We were at a bench near a fountain. Vrykolakas swept some snow off the bench, and sat down heavily. His red hair looked very dark against the surrounding whiteness, and his face, with its permanent look of secretive prim enjoyment, was flushed. He fished in his top pocket, and brought out a slim metal cylinder about ten centimetres in length. He set it to his lips and blew.

I heard nothing. But from around the corner of the fountain, running and bounding over the snow, came a dog.

It was a terrier bitch. It leapt up at Vrykolakas, fawning and licking frantically. Mysterious little hacking or mewing noises came from her throat, cat-like, parrot-like noises. I imagined that he had mutilated her vocal cords for some purpose of his own; and the idea of mutilation came to me because she was wounded.

Her ears were torn and bloody. One was nearly severed. There was a patch of hair missing where her shoulder had been bitten. The skin was broken and sore, and her tail was broken about half-way along its length, with a patch of white bone showing through the bare red flesh.

After allowing her to lick his face, Vrykolakas flung her aside, and she lay submissively on the snow at his feet.

"What's happened to her?" I asked.

"Poor little Lulu!" he said. "She's been a naughty girl."

Until that moment I hadn't realised that the dog was the friend he had wanted me to meet. I looked at him with surprise, and he saw it and smiled wolfishly.

"Dear Lulu," he said softly. "But come on, Martin, to business."

"What do you want?"

"Friendship." He saw me start to shake my head, and held up his hand. "No: I want your advice. I've got more friends like Lulu, as I've said, and unless you tell me what to do I'll just have to give them their heads. And I can't be responsible for what happens then."

"That's a threat, is it? And what do I get in return for this valuable advice of mine? What the hell have you got that can interest me? I'm beginning to get tired of you."

"Well, I was a partner of your wife's, you know."

"When?"

"You remember when you came to see me in Valencia? We'd just completed a deal then. Oh, we were very close, Catherine and I."

I hated hearing him speak of her like that. I didn't believe him, anyway, but I knew so little that the most distant scent of a trail, however false I guessed it to be drew me towards it irresistibly.

"What was the deal?" I spoke fiercely.

"We were going to work together on some research I was doing. Astrology."

"I don't believe you. I wonder if I shouldn't kill you now and get rid of you; you're bringing me nothing but bad luck."

"My friends wouldn't like that at all."

"Damn your friends; are you going to help me get to my wife or not?"

"I can't do that yet," he said sorrowfully. "With the best will in the world, I couldn't do that until I knew where she was. But I do feel for you. And I guessed that you might like this, so I got it from the Palace for you."

He took a little ring from his pocket and dropped it in my palm. It was Catherine's.

"Where did you find that?" I asked. I was getting a little light-headed with anger.

"In a filing cabinet, with some other bits and pieces. I left those, though. You must understand my position, Martin; I'm not in command here—" his voice became distressed—"and with other people's unreality to deal with, I've got a fight on my hands; I don't think you realise. But I'm nearly ready for the breakthrough."

He was calm again in an instant, and with the look of concealed joy I had noticed earlier he rose to his feet and smoothed his dark blazer over his hips.

"Keep the ring," he said magnanimously. "I got it for you."

He went over to the fountain, and stood with one hand resting on it, and his legs crossed.

"I can *show* her to you," he said carelessly.

"How?"

"My magic mirror."

Lulu, seeing her master move away, had sat up anxiously. She watched him reach inside his coat, and licked her chops.

The astrologer took out the magic mirror. It was as large as the palm of his hand, and set in a frame of blue plastic. He beckoned me slyly to come close.

"Breathe on it," he said, and held it out.

I did, and it clouded over. When it cleared I saw a portrait of Catherine, done in the style of postcards of the Virgin Mary and the saints which they sell in religious shops, the colours glutinous and the drawing crude. As I watched, the portrait began to move. The eyes swivelled in their sockets and looked out at me, and the lips drew upwards in a parody of a smile, so that she looked like a sister of Felix.

I turned away. I must have moved quickly, because Lulu got up and uttered those mewing, hacking sounds. I turned back to Vrykolakas.

"You can do nothing for me," I said, "and I shall do nothing for you. But I warn you: do anything to damage my friends Johnny and Mary or hurt my wife, and I shall kill you. I know how to kill people now, and I've killed animals too," I added, indicating the dog. "And I guess that Lionel Pretorius might be interested to know you're here in his city."

"Blackmail," he said calmly. "Two can play at that game. Who left his fingerprints all over the Palace? Not me. Don't forget, Martin, I can open doors that Pretorius locks. You'll ask me to, before we've finished. I won't hold it against you that you've spoken so harshly. My motives are absolutely pure. I haven't even got a financial motive. Everything *that* man does is financial, but I'd have thought you'd respect someone with higher ideals than money, someone like you. Ah well, no matter."

"I'm off. I don't want to spend any more time on your mad enterprises."

"I warn you," he said amiably, "you won't get far in this place until you can deal with unreality. All the different kinds of it. But you'll see, you'll see. I won't bear grudges. But remember Lulu and her wounds; I keep her like that, as an example."

He stopped, and smiled.

"As an example of what?"

"Of what's underneath the skin. We're all like that, underneath. Blood and flesh. That's her unreal fate, poor Lulu, to show us what we're like. Lucky Lulu, rather. Such a simple unreality to achieve; all she has to do is suffer."

"*You* keep her like that, you said? How?"

"With my teeth, dear boy!" And he drew back his lips and gnashed his strong sharp teeth together, as loud as castanets.

I turned and walked away. As I moved across the snowy landscape of the Park I heard him shout "No ill-will on my part! I don't bear grudges! Come back whenever you like!'"

Go Home, Go Home

There was a message in the hotel for me; Johnny and Mary asked me to have lunch with them. I had already begun to think of them as having joined the other side, whatever the other side was, or as having gone back to it, and leaving me on my own. Since they had gone off to Cavalcanti's I'd undertaken too many secret enterprises for them to trust me; I didn't want to invite their confidence. So the atmosphere between us was stiff and polite. But half-way through the meal Mary said:

"What's the matter, Martin?"

"The same as it ever was. I'm no closer to her now than I was in Valencia."

"Oh, of course you are. You must be. It's only a matter of time."

"It isn't," said Johnny. He had been quiet and subdued throughout the meal, but I had been so preoccupied with my own feelings that I only noticed it now, because it was a long time since he'd spoken; and now that he did, he sounded unhappy.

I looked at him in surprise. But he was looking down, and said no more.

"Then what is it?" I asked. "Have you found something out?"

"Well, nothing at all," said Mary.

"Yes we have," said Johnny. "Don't ask me what it is, Martin. I can't tell you because I don't really know yet. But it involves us, you see, Mary and me, but not you."

"They haven't said anything about us," said Mary calmly. "Only Martin."

"Well, you weren't listening, then."

She shrugged. She seemed completely happy for the first time since I'd met her, calm, radiant, assured, with a great secret security. I looked from her to Johnny, whom I loved more. He was troubled, and I'd never seen him like that before, as if there was something on his conscience. But in the way he spoke to Mary there was a new feeling, as if he didn't have to strive any more; there was a calmness and authority in his voice, and she didn't protest or challenge it, but accepted it like a cat.

"Is it secret? Is that why you can't tell me?" I asked after a moment.

"No," he explained. "Prince Cavalcanti told us that they didn't like secrets, the Company. They weren't hiding anything from anyone, because no one could copy it anyway. It's not like an industrial secret. He left it to our judgement whether to tell you."

Silence. "So you know where she is, and what's going on?"

"No," said Mary. "Johnny thinks it involves him and me, but I'm not sure. I know it doesn't involve you, though. They didn't tells us where she is, or anything about her. Honestly. Except for what might be going to happen later on."

"It will happen," said Johnny firmly. His voice was neutral.

"Johnny thinks it will happen, but I don't know."

"If you're not certain," I said, "what does it depend on? I mean what would have to come about to make it happen?"

She glanced at Johnny, as if seeking guidance. He remained impassive. Then she said "I don't know."

Another silence. "But it would involve her?"

"Yes," she said. Her voice was quiet.

"And would you want it to happen?"

"You can't ask that," she said.

"Well, why not?"

"I think he can ask anything he wants to," said Johnny. "I don't think we ought to say he can't. But they've told us enough to make me realise that there are some things I can't answer."

"Are they bad? Wicked, I mean? Like the Second City?"

"We wouldn't stay here if they were."

"No. Of course not. But does that mean that you *are* going to stay here?"

"I'm afraid so." He looked as if he found it a difficult thing to say.

"Because you want to?"

"Yes."

"And the matter that involves Catherine, do you want that to stay here?"

"I suppose so. Whatever—"she looked at Johnny again, and again his expression gave no clue to what he was thinking—"whatever I decide, and I might change my mind anyway. For the moment I want to."

"And the matter that involves Catherine, do you want that to happen?" I asked again.

"It might be a good idea," she said equivocally, "for some people."

"For you?"

"It might."

"But not for me?"

"I don't think so," said Johnny.

"Why? Can you answer that?"

"Because you're not unreal," she said.

"Well, nor are you."

Silence. A waiter came, and we ordered coffee. When he had cleared the plates away and gone, Johnny said gently, "Honestly, Martin, it would be better if you went back to Europe."

"I'd never go anywhere, and you must realise that, without a promise that I'd see her again eventually. Or some explanation, or something. For God's sake, you *must* see that, surely? It's not knowing anything that's so frustrating. And you don't help."

I spoke angrily. He flushed a little, as if he felt that my words were just, but Mary shrugged.

"It won't make any difference what you say or how angry you are," she said.

"Doesn't it make a difference to *you*?"

"Well, I don't like being shouted at, if that's what you mean."

"No, it isn't what he means, and you know it, Mary," said Johnny. There was an edge to his voice now. "It upsets *me*, Martin, because of what we agreed back at Mary's ball. It means I'm breaking that agreement, I know."

"What agreement was that?" asked Mary.

"Nothing to do with you," lied Johnny. "It means I'm breaking it, and I'm sorry. But if you trust me to tell the truth about why— do you?" he asked, and slowly I nodded—"then the reason is, because it's best for everyone if you go. Best for you too. Mary said something she shouldn't have said about being unreal."

"About not being unreal," I said. "Me not being unreal, as if that was a bad thing."

"I didn't say it was a bad thing," said Mary. "And it's unfair to blame me for saying something when I don't even know what it means."

"Whether or not she understands what it means, and I'm not sure that I do. But it gives us a protection that you haven't got," said Johnny.

"Oh, you *are* unreal, then?" I said. My anger was rising again, and my hands were shaking. "That would explain a lot. Unreal agreements, for instance."

"I'm sorry about that," he said again.

"Easily said. Do you know, you tempt me to try something I've been holding back from. I don't know whether I will yet, but by Christ you tempt me." I was thinking of Vrykolakas and his friends, and his proposition. If I joined him I'd be revenged on this deceptive city, and vengeance and fury were colouring all my feelings, and making it hard to think straight; and I pushed back my chair and stood up. "Just tell me one thing: what does *she* want me to do? and you must tell me the truth."

"The truth is that I don't know," Johnny answered, "but I guess that she would want you to go."

"And would I ever see her again? Or would that spoil all the plans?"

Mary said "Probably you would. Oh, Johnny doesn't mean it like this; and you shouldn't take it so bitterly. Can't you see that there really isn't any place for you here?"

Johnny ran his hands through his hair and looked at the floor; then he turned his face up again. "I promise I'll tell you one day. I don't know when. But please, Martin, don't do anything to damage the city, if that's what you were thinking of. You'll hurt her if you do."

"I might want to," I muttered. "I don't know if I'll see you before I have to go," I said aloud. "If not—well, I didn't want to quarrel. I certainly didn't want to come all this way to end up like . . . whatever we are at the moment. See you."

I walked away, and they said nothing to stop me.

The Chess-Playing Turk

It was half-past one when I left the restaurant, and I suddenly remembered that I was going to meet the café proprietor, Ignaz Gruenberg, in half an hour's time at the new Museum, so that we could examine its mysteries together.

The thought of the calm and genial Gruenberg acted on me like a cool wind, taking away my anger. He might even have an explanation for it all, and so far as I knew he was under no obligation not to reveal his secrets.

I walked up and down the streets, reflecting on things, like the moon in the bottle-glass in Dog Street. Here it was all different. The sun occupied the glass of the office-blocks, the shops and apartment buildings and embassies, examining itself in the warm air of the afternoon with quite as much devotion as Mary felt, examining herself before she granted her favours to the magistrate; seeking oracular answers in false sexuality, and finding them. The reflections likewise were not the sun, but they lit the dark corners where the sun didn't reach.

The Museum was in a square called the Plaza de Nueva York, which in spite of its name was small and modest. The buildings were like the houses in Amsterdam, tall and narrow and elegant.

Over the door of the Museum was a sign that said *Musuem of the History of Unreality*, and a board by the door announced that it was opening today with a special exhibition on some aspects of deception and entertainment in the nineteenth century. Admission was ten cents.

Ignaz arrived after a few minutes.

"Are we the first to go in?" he asked eagerly.

"I don't know," I replied, "I've only just arrived."

"You don't look very happy, my friend," he said. "You better tell me what you've been doing. Come on, let's pay our money and go in to this famous musuem."

The attendant on duty at the desk was an angel; the third one I had seen. And as with the first it was impossible to tell its sex, but it was just as beautiful, and just as much an individual. Ignaz was scrupulously careful not to take too much notice.

"Unreality," he whispered as we went into the first gallery. "It's all around us. This is a temple to it, and that angel on duty at the door is really the centrepiece, but he's given an unreal function to perform so as to deceive people who aren't aware of all these mysteries. It keeps the pattern true, you see. A temple disguised as a museum, and an angel disguised as a doorman. The beauty of it is that it's so clearly indicated in the name they give the building! There are secrets, and there are no secrets, that's the poetry of it."

"Yes, I see," I said. I looked around. The first gallery was devoted to a number of miniature reproductions of stage-settings from the theatre of the early nineteenth century. Exotic Indian palaces, gloomy Satanic caverns, Egyptian temples, and enchanters' grottoes glowed like jewels in their tiny settings. Ignaz wandered up and down, peering at them all, and explaining the hidden symbolism in each one.

When we had exhausted the depths of that room we went into the next, where a great curtain hung across one end. A notice told us that if we pressed a button we would see a reproduction of Pepper's Ghost, a famous stage illusion invented by a Professor Pepper of London, whose claim to his academic title had never been proved. Unreality again, pointed out Ignaz, and pressed the button.

Slowly the room darkened, and the curtain rose to show a back-cloth depicting a ruined chapel and gravestones. A faint radiance, as if of moonlight, suffused the scene. Then a ghostly figure drifted across the little stage, draped in a loose white garment, and raised it arms. The sleeves fell away, revealing the bony arms of a skeleton, and then the figure turned towards us, pushing back its cowl to disclose a skull. The ghost was transparent, but three-dimensional, so it wasn't projected on to a screen. Then it gave a dismal groan and vanished completely. The curtain fell and the lights came up.

The café proprietor gave a little sigh of satisfaction.

"If he wasn't a Professor," he said, "he should have been a Herr Doctor at least."

In the next room were a number of curious automata, such as the famous Chess-Playing Turk designed by the Baron Von Kempelen, which sat cross-legged at a cabinet too full of intricate machinery to conceal a person, and which had defeated the finest chess-players of its time. There was also a machine called the Temple of the Arts, consisting of an automated view of Gibraltar, with moving warships, a platoon of tiny soldiers marching up and down, and a band of mechanical musicians, playing suitable tunes. There was an orange tree which blossomed and bore perfect painted fruit in less than a minute. There was a duck which quacked, breathed, ate and drank. There was a life-size automaton flute-player made by Jacques de Vaucanson which, according to its label, performed so realistically that many learned men had thought that it was human.

This last figure aroused many different emotions in me. I remembered the words of the Customs official: things are always what they seem to be. Perhaps this poor stiff musician *was* partly human, exactly as human as he seemed to be. Perhaps his playing was as realistic as mine; perhaps we could change places, and he could go out looking for a lost wife, and I could stand there still and unreal, a true citizen at last, and my wife would accept me again.

Ignaz noticed me gazing at the automaton, and discreetly indicated that he would go on into the next room. I nodded, and examined the figure more closely to see whether the mechanism still worked.

"Would you like to hear it play?" asked a gentle voice beside me. It was Vrykolakas, smiling anxiously.

"Shall I make it work for you?" he asked.

"I think it's broken," I said, trying to avoid either encouraging or rejecting him.

"Don't you worry about that," he said. "Machines obey me just as locks do."

"Where did you come from?"

"Through a window. I didn't like the look of that creature at the door."

He stepped up to the figure of the flute-player and ran his hands over its head, and over the place where its genitals would be. There was a faint whirring of clockwork machinery and the hiss of air inside the musician's chest, and then his stiff fingers depressed some of the keys of his instrument and his polished lips blew across the mouthpiece. The first two bars of a minuet came out, breathy but tender, and then something broke inside the mechanism. The music died away on the subdominant.

"What have you done?" I said angrily.

"Old machinery," he said evasively. "They make them more solidly these days. Actually, I was hoping to find you here."

"Have you broken that?"

"I could make it go again, if I wanted."

"That's not the point."

"Oh, it's all useful knowledge. That's what I came here for. There are some wonderful things here, Martin, wonderful historic pieces of art."

He pointed to a clockwork dancing girl, of the same period as the flute-player. She might have been the original for Olympia in the story by Hoffmann, with whom the student Nathaniel falls in love, for she was graceful and exquisitely made. A gauze skirt covered her beautiful thighs; her small feet were shod with dancers' pumps, and her shoulders and the upper part of her breast were bare. Whoever had sculpted her face had given her an expression of happy confidence and innocent charm.

Vrykolakas went behind her and tore off her dress. Then he bent down and, before I could move, broken open a panel in her back. One of the arms stirred feebly; he pushed it roughly out of the way.

"What are you doing?" I said in anguish. "For God's sake stop it!"

"Quite harmless," he said, his voice muffled. "Let me just . . . Yes, that's it . . . Over she goes."

He pushed the dancing girl over on to her face. She fell heavily and her face cracked. Vrykolakas' hands were busy in the mechanism; something creaked, and the joints of the hips and the knees moved, so that the girl slowly thrust her satin buttocks upwards. When she was kneeling, with her face and arms still on the floor, she stopped. Vrykolakas stood up, and grinned, showing all his teeth.

"So now we know," he said. "Very simple. What shall we call her, eh?"

I knelt down, nearly frantic with anxiety, beside the broken girl. I put my hand on her golden hair for a moment, automatically, and then peered inside her open back. But the machinery made no sense to me.

Then the astrologer clutched my arm.

"Quick!" he whispered. "There's someone coming!"

He bent over and with a swift movement tucked the dancing girl under his arm. Her head lolled behind him. It was his turn to be frantic, and in fact he was nearly beside himself with nervousness, as he had been in the Palace. His face was white, his eyes wide, his nostrils dilated, and he made a series of curious hopping movements, looking this way and that. But he didn't let go of the figure.

"Out of the window," he muttered. Then, to me: "Come on! They'll find you! They'll think you did it! Come with me!"

With his free arm he snatched at my sleeve and tugged me after him. And again, bewildered, confused, and unhappy, I followed.

Impurities in the Nuclear Reactor of Economics; the First Coin Strikes Its Target

As soon as we were in the street, his panic vanished as suddenly as it had come.

"Those unreals," he said. "I don't mind admitting, I'll be glad when they're all gone."

He had a talent for deflecting the other person's anger with tantalising observations about something else. I had been about to reproach him for stealing the dancing girl, but I couldn't ignore that remark.

213

"Why are they going? And when? What do you know about them?"

"Oh, nothing's finalised yet," he said, hoisting the broken figure over his shoulder. "We may have to change our plans. We'll see how we get on with this lovely lady."

"Who's we?"

"Well, you and me, of course." He looked astonished that I should have to ask. "Are you coming? My friends will be glad to see you. You might have some ideas for us."

"I wish . . ." I began, and then broke off. Wishing was useless. If I killed him now, in the street where we stood, what would come of it? I'd be no nearer my wife. Better hope that he hanged himself, and give him rope to do it with. Equally, there was no point in being angry with him, for his personality changed too quickly for it to have any effect. But at least I could ask for the dancing girl.

"Let me take that figure back," I said. "I won't mention you. I'll describe someone entirely different. But she belongs in the Museum."

"I'm different anyway," he said complacently. "Besides, I want her. You can't have her. Perhaps we could share her, if you really wanted to. But you don't know what I want her for yet. Wait till you see what my friends can do with her."

"No, I'd rather not," I said. "Goodbye, then."

He nodded, and set off jauntily towards his headquarters in the Unbuilt Slum, with the automatic dancing girl lying unhappy over his shoulder.

I thought of Ignaz Gruenberg in the Museum, finding me gone, and wondered if I should go back to explain. But while no one else knew about Vrykolakas (for as far as I knew for certain, no one else knew he was in the city) my knowledge of him and his doings gave me a slight advantage over other people, and one which I might need to exploit. Somehow. It was all very doubtful, especially the supposition that I was the only person who knew about him, but it was all I had.

So I went slowly back to the hotel, having nowhere else to go.

The great lobby, warm and elegant, with an immense dark blue carpet and wide leather chairs, was empty, as usual. There was a fountain in a marble basin, playing softly in the silence. A gentle afternoon light lingered inside the doors, but most of it was lit by concealed spotlights which picked out features like the fountain or the curving, shallow staircase, dramatising them softly and giving the whole scene an undersea appearance. I liked it; I wanted to sink into it and go to sleep for days.

Except that I wasn't sleepy, I was restless. I drifted up and down inside the enormous room, looking at everything. There were three little shops inside it, a jeweller's, a florist's, and a shop which sold fashionable silk scarves and woollen garments. None of them was open, but their window displays were ready, with artificial flowers in the florist's window. Sparkling diamonds and rubies were lit by pencil-thin beams of light, and the wide crusted bands of gold and platinum (from the slave-haunted galleries under the empty mountain) shone calmly on their gentle beds of velvet.

The only sound in the lobby was the quiet splashing of the fountain, so I heard the clerk's footsteps as soon as he appeared, and turned towards him. I didn't expect him to do more than gravely acknowledge my presence and go to the desk for some purpose or other, but he came towards me, looking morose; almost as if he wanted someone to talk to. This was such a novel expression for one of the citizens to wear that I couldn't help wondering what had caused it.

"Good afternoon," I said. "Is something the matter?"

"Yes," he replied, "but I dare say we're all over-reacting."

"What is it?"

"It's rather a mystery . . . Someone has been arrested for passing unsterilised money."

"Really? Who?"

"A garage proprietor from the suburbs beyond Bella Vista. Only one coin, apparently."

"And he's been arrested? Isn't that rather overdoing it?"

"I don't suppose he'll be charged with anything, once they find out where the money came from. The Economic Security Committee have got a team going over his books right now, so they say."

"But I don't quite see why they're making so much fuss. I know it's unsterilised, but . . ."

It was Juan's coin, and my fault, and I wanted to minimise it.

"Well, the economy of the city is as efficient and powerful as it can be," he explained, "rather like a nuclear reactor. But if you get a grain of sand inside a nuclear reactor, the whole thing comes to a halt, or blows up. And if we get any impurities in the financial system of the city, goodness knows what will happen. Immense damage. Bankruptcies, business collapse, would be only the start of it. Look at the economies of Europe. Look at the economy of the

First City, down on the plain. We thought we'd learnt all those lessons."

"Well, you probably have," I said. "It seems to have been detected soon enough, after all. And I'm sure you've got ways of containing any infection. I shouldn't worry about it."

"Yes, you're probably right," he agreed. "I shouldn't have mentioned it. People are worried, though . . . Did you say it had been detected soon enough? Do you know how long it had been circulating, then? How do you know?"

He was looking at me almost sharply, not quite wanting to challenge me because of my status as a guest, but clearly anxious in case I did know.

"I mean if he'd tried to spend it before, he'd have been caught before," I said. "Obviously it's his own coin, and he just forgot to declare it when he came here."

There was an ironic laugh from behind me, like the wind scattering a pile of stolen money. The hotel clerk looked past my shoulder without interest.

"Come on, Martin," said Juan. "Tell him some more lies, and get rid of him."

The clerk heard nothing, and looked back at me. "Ah well," he said, "our troubles are not yours. I must go. I've got work to do."

I nodded to him, and he walked away.

"Come upstairs," I said to the unreal. "If we talk here, they'll think I'm talking to myself."

"Who'll think that? There's no one about. You don't know how empty this place is. I've been all over it and not seen more than twenty people."

"Well . . ." I looked around doubtfully. The clerk had disappeared. "All right. Over by the fountain, then maybe I won't be heard talking."

"What's the matter with you?" he said scornfully when we were seated on the leather couch that was built around the fountain basin. "You weren't frightened like this in the Second City, when they were going to kill you."

"I had my friends with me then. And I was happy. Now I'm not . . . What have you been doing? Have you found out anything about the man I told you about?"

"He's a werewolf. That's how he controls those dogs, they're all frightened of him, just like you."

216

"Are you trying to become real by making me angry now? Won't money work?"

"Not one coin at a time, like you gave me."

"I gave you two."

"Not two at a time either."

"Do what I ask of you, and you can have them all."

"Even if they smash this precious city up?"

"I don't believe they could. I think he was exaggerating."

"Well, he wasn't. They could ruin the city if I spent them."

"And would you?"

"To become real, I would do anything."

"If two coins haven't made you real, five more won't make any difference. I think you'd better try something else."

"Like what? What do you know about unreality? There's nothing unreal about you. Even that man's dogs know more about unreality than you do. You couldn't tell me anything about unreality to save your life."

"I know more than I did," I said patiently. "But we made a bargain. I paid for some information with those coins. You've told me he's a werewolf. What does he do? Change his shape? How does he do it? How can I defeat him? What's he trying to do?"

"You can't kill him by any means except water. You have to drown him. You can wound him with knives or bullets, but he's too strong to strangle. Anyway, his friends would all help him. They would sacrifice themselves to save him."

"What is he doing? Why does he want my help?"

"Just looking about," he said. "That's all he's doing. He thinks you know where everything is in this place. He's got a great respect for you, fool that he is. He's frightened of you, but not as much as you are of him. He doesn't know you're frightened yet, but I could tell him."

"He wouldn't hear you. No one can hear you except me; no one wants to listen to a phantom who can't even frighten little children on a dark night. You could go and shout in his ear and he'd just hear a buzzing like a fly, and brush you away. You are powerless, Juan. You're scornful of me because I'm frightened, and I *am* frightened, I know, but I'm not powerless like you. You can do nothing, because you're next to nothing yourself, there's as much emptiness in you as there is water in a jellyfish. So don't go boasting that you'll tell him this and tell him that, because the only way you can do that is to become real, or to talk through me. I am your reality, do you realise that? You're only real when you're talking to me, because only I can hear you. So you better do as I ask and find out more about that man, or I'll ignore you completely and you'll fade away and vanish."

He sat still for a moment, and then sprang to his feet and seized a heavy onyx ashtray from the low table in front of us and flung it at the window of the jeweller's shop. The glass shattered, and a cascade of sharp fragments and bright stones fell out, littering the carpet.

Juan hissed "Explain that to the clerk, tell him that's unreal! There's plenty more like that I can do without you to speak for me. You don't need speaking for what I'm going to do. You'll wish you were unreal by the time I've finished, you'll wish you'd never married her, you'll wish you'd never been born."

And he was away out of the door and down the street before I could stop him. Unhappily, I went to look for the clerk.

Night Thoughts
Whether they believed my explanation, I hardly knew; nor did I greatly care. In fact I hardly remember what I told them. But when I was alone again there was only one thing I wanted to do, and that was sleep, so that I could forget everything. I went and lay down in my room and fell asleep straight away.

It was seven in the evening when I woke up, and dark outside. I felt calmer and more resigned. There wasn't much that was in my power, so I could forgive myself for not accomplishing much. When I realised that I felt happier.

I called room service for some coffee, and took out my flute. I hadn't touched it since I had played for the Musical Society in the First City, that night I met the Electric Whores. At one time the idea of going for days without playing music would have made me shrink with sadness; never since I had been given my first wooden fife had I let a day go by without playing, unless I had been too ill to blow. But now my lovely silver instrument rested in my hands like a stranger, and felt unfamiliar to my lips. I played some scales and arpeggios, and they were harsh and ragged.

I drank some coffee, and persevered. There was only one thing I could do, after all; it was a shame to let it decay. I played for two hours, studies, sonatas, exercises, passages from orchestral works, until my fingers and lungs were moving properly again. But

218

it would take many days of practice to make up what I had lost.

I'd started, though, and that was enough to be going on with.

I went to my window, and opened it to breathe the cool night air. I could see right across the city to the Parque Industrial, where the million masts of the aerial enclosure each stood bearing a red jewel of light at its tip. There was so much light in the city, even though there were so few people to see by it. Streets and avenues were bathed in it; whole buildings were lit from within, all their windows glowing warmly as if a thousand wealth-creating enterprises were under way behind them, as if a thousand people, ten thousand, were enjoying each other's company. And all over the city there was silence. Far away in the suburbs a light moved; it was a lonely car being driven through the snowy streets.

Then suddenly things changed.

The lights in one huge section of the city went out all at once. It was a district the shape of a long triangle, its short side beyond the Parque Industrial and its apex in the heart of the city: in fact right opposite the hotel. It looked as if a black wedge had been driven into the city from the outer darkness. And to accompany it there came the thin distant wail of an alarm siren in the Parque Industrial.

Apart from that far-off banshee howl there was silence. I don't know what I expected to hear, but the silence had a different quality now, it was tense rather than peaceful. Nothing else changed. The black triangle remained black. No one appeared.

I found I was gripping the windowsill, and shivering. The air was cold.

I shut the window. I wanted to find out what was happening, but there was no one I could ask. I thought I'd go and find something to eat, and talk to the waiter.

The restaurant was empty, and the food was good, and the waiter knew nothing, and I felt as if the whole city might have been a starship, bearing me to some inconceivably remote galaxy; or as if everyone in the world had died but me and a few courteous and mysterious servants, who were to minister to my needs until I should die in my turn, and then they'd be free to die too.

My thoughts were full of echoing melancholy. Vast impersonal sadnesses reverberated in them; all these issues and circumstances were too big for me, too strange and cold and alien. I began to think that Johnny and Mary and Catherine were right when they said I didn't belong there, and that I'd better go, after all.

I wandered slowly up to my room again after I'd eaten. The room was in darkness; the only light came from the window. The great wedge of darkness was still there. The lights of two or three cars were moving through it towards the Parque Industrial. Some lights had already been set up on various gantries in the Parque, but they must have worked from an emergency generator, for the light they cast was feeble and local.

I sat down in an armchair by the window. The sill was low, and I could look out and see everything. I left the light off. I wanted to think. There was a time, I remembered, in the Second City, when I had almost come across a clue as to why my wife had gone; but something had happened, the train of thought was broken. I wanted to re-assemble it, if I could.

The door opened quietly and shut again. Hadn't that happened before, too?

The clean sweet fresh smell drifted across the room. It was almost like a perfume she wore. I turned slowly to look; then stopped myself, and stared out over the night again. There was little I had to say, after all, and little I wanted to hear.

"May I switch a light on?" she asked quietly.

Her tone was so different from the authority she'd had before that I was disarmed.

"Not the big one, if you don't mind," I said. "What have you come for this time?"

A reading lamp came on behind me, and the image of the room sprang into being in the window, obscuring the light. I let my eyes adjust to it, and then turned.

"Just to see you," she said.

Nothing could have weakened me more than that, and the sight of her, crosslegged and graceful in an armchair.

"This is your city, then, where you behave as other people behave in theirs," I said.

"If you mean this is my home, yes, you're right."

"Then who are you?"

"Do you mean, what's my name?"

"I suppose so. Among other things."

"My name isn't important. I've got more than one, anyway, depending on what I'm doing."

"What are you most of the time?"

"A representative."

"Of my wife?"

220

"Of course, among others."

"Other humans?"

"Well, yes. Who else?"

"Others like you. You're not human."

"I speak like a human, look like a human, act like a human. It's very hard of you to say I'm not."

"You're one of the angels of the city."

"Angels . . ." she smiled. "But I'm as physical as you are. As you know."

She looked plainly at me, and the look was like a statement: we have made love.

"Are you male or female?"

She considered that carefully. Then she said "If you still have to ask, then what I am precisely doesn't matter at all."

"I just want to know, as I want to know your name."

"You want things fixed, and they're not. Everything changes."

It was my turn to consider. "No, not fixed. I only want to know how they're changing."

"Impossible."

She stared at me coolly.

"But you can control your own changes," she went on.

"What do you mean?"

"If you don't like what you're doing, you can stop doing it **and** do something else. You can change yourself. And as you're in command of your destiny, you can change in the way you want to."

I must have looked unconvinced. She made an impatient little movement with her hand, and, looking around, saw my flute on the table. She went on:

"You changed when you became a musician. You weren't born a flute-player; you became one by imitation. Change happens when one state imitates another one, because it desires it. You imitated good flute-players, who practise several hours a day; you acted like one when you had your flute in your hands; and so you became one."

I couldn't see what she was getting at. "Yes, and . . .?" I said.

"Your friends are changing, and your wife has changed."

"Is it always a change for the better?"

"When the change is willed and desired, then it is."

"Well, you're very glib with this word change; I wish you'd tell me what you meant by it."

She raised her hands to her head and slowly ran her fingers

through her fair hair, letting it fall softly back around her face. I was reminded of Mary for a moment. She seemed to be in love with her own body.

"Why do I think of you as a girl?" I asked.

"You're used to the idea that you're physically attracted to girls and not to boys. That's all."

"Why did . . . in the bank, that afternoon . . . do angels have impulses too?"

"Evidently."

"But why that particular . . ."

I couldn't say it. The messenger was so clean, cool, seraphic; I was embarrassed.

"For many reasons. That might have been my desire. Or it might have been to make you feel ashamed, so that you could face your shame and accept it, and go on to other kinds of feelings, complete ranges of them. Many reasons."

"Do you feel shame as well?"

"No."

"You're not human, then."

She smiled, and shrugged.

"I met a man the other day," I said, "who told me about the secret rituals of magic, and the mysteries of Eleusis, and so on. Would that have had anything to do with it?"

She nodded; but then said "There's no magic in the Perfect City. Some things are true in more than one sense, though, and opposite things can both be true at once. If I say there is magic and there isn't magic, the tension which those statements create can be used to find the answers to several questions. If you use it properly."

"So this is all an academy of philosophy."

"Not by design, but philosophical principles lie behind it."

"You never say anything without qualifying it. Everything is equivocal and shifty; it might be this and it might be that, but on the other hand it could be something else . . . Can no one in the city give me a straight answer?"

"There you go again," she said gently. "Forget this mania of yours for the straight answer. Have you learned nothing from your journey here?"

I shook my head. "I was too busy thinking about my wife to notice what I was seeing."

She laughed. "Well, that's typical!" she said.

"If you like. But I need to know things unequivocally. I can't believe them otherwise."

"Then you're contradicting yourself. What you called the true doctrine of heaven, when you defeated the salesman of the Second City, is pure unreal philosophy."

"I dare say. I suppose the Electric Whores dealt in unreal philosophy as well?"

"Of course. The best. Everything they said to you is literally true in the Perfect City, whereas it was only foreshadowed down there on the plain."

"And now I've forgotten what they said . . ."

"It'll come back."

She breathed deeply, a breath of contentment, not a sigh, and looked past me and out of the window.

"Are you an unreal?" I asked.

She nodded, and looked back at me.

"How does it happen . . . is my wife now unreal?"

She laughed. "How could you stand for that?" she said. "But I told you she'd changed."

"Are Johnny and Mary unreal?"

"They were already, in their ways. But we can all work together, as we are."

"For what purpose? What for?"

All this time, as she was gently frustrating me and turning my questions aside, I was becoming more and more ill at ease. And more than that, I was nervous, and I had began to sweat and tremble. Something was moving away from me, as if my life was going out with the tide . . . This feeling wasn't coming to me from the messenger: it was an intensification of the sadness I had been feeling earlier on, but now it was becoming intolerable. I felt a lump in my throat, I wanted to weep. And this ironic, unbearably beautiful messenger sat opposite watching me calmly, and didn't move.

What in heaven could I do?

I was near to tears, and I had to say something. The feeling was deepening. I felt like a swimmer carried into deeper and deeper water by a current, feeling the seabed drifting past below his feet, getting harder and harder to reach, and at last sinking away altogether, leaving him with nothing to stand on in the wild waves. But the sea, the feeling, was inconstant; at one moment it was warm, at another icy cold; it would seem to buoy me up and bear me safely, and then to suck me down into bottomless desperation. Where was the lifeline I needed? I had to speak.

"You mock me," I began, half in a whisper, "because I want straight answers. But they're all I can understand. And I must find my wife, because without her I'm . . . nothing. I need her to tell me what's been happening. I need her, you see . . . I wish I could be part of this city, because it's lovely, but it rejects me, and I don't know why, I can't understand what I do wrong. My wife has rejected me too, and I don't know why. I could put up with anything if I knew why it was happening . . . I thought at first that when she knew I was here, she'd come to me, and together we'd make the snow melt. Can you imagine that? But I don't think that any more. I don't know what I think. And soon I'll have to go."

She said nothing. I had closed my eyes, and now I opened them again, thinking she'd gone. But she was still there, and she'd been listening carefully, because she had a look of serious attention. We both sat still, staring at each other unselfconsciously. Her grey eyes were wide, her mouth held gently shut, her hands folded in her lap. All the close physical details of her pressed at my awareness: her slim thighs in the light-blue cotton of her jeans, her creamy neck with a little pulse in it throbbing steadily, the soft white shirt and underneath it the gentlest of swelling curves, as delicate as the slopes of the Hill with the Height of a Man, the shape of her ears under the soft blonde hair, the clean square fingernails . . .

It wasn't until that moment (in spite of the encounter in the empty bank) that I realised that the messenger had a body, that her body was heart-rendingly beautiful in every detail, and that I longed for it.

The quality of the emotion I was feeling changed as I realised at last what it was. I was in love with the messenger; I loved her more than I loved my wife. The terrible pressure to weep subsided, and the sea grew calm, and I floated quietly in the warmth, dazed with knowledge.

"You know what's happening to me," I said.

She gave a tight, almost nervous nod.

"I want to go out," I said. I stood up. "I'm sorry I'll have to leave you. I want to go for a walk and think about it all."

She nodded again, a deep nod, as if she understood completely.

I longed to be back in the cold mountains, where I had communicated with the moon and the stars with the unnoticeable form of Juan beside me.

I made for the wide spaces of the Campo de Afrodite, beyond the Hill with the Height of a Man, where the celestial bodies glowed like cinders on the velvet sky.

The streets I passed through were silent. A warm yellow glow shone into the darkness from the windows of the Café Florestan, and I thought of going to Ignaz Gruenberg and consulting him about my predicament, but I remembered that I wanted to be alone.

I went across the canal by the Avenida de Amsterdam, past the secluded little lake inside the park, and out into the wide sloping snow-fields of the Campo de Afrodite, there to meditate on the different forms of unreality I had encountered.

Here and there groups of trees, sacred groves haunted by nymphs and gods, stood out invitingly against the snow. I found a fallen tree-trunk, and sat down to stare over the city.

The fault in the electrical system had been dealt with; the city was itself again, I could see all of it.

Far, far off in the distance, the sweeping red light of an aircraft circled the airport, whose glowing blue and green and white dots marked the safest lines of approach. A little closer, on the far side of the city, the philosophical instruments of the Parque Industrial glittered under the brilliant moon. Here and there a powerful light, mounted on the gantry of a crane or at the junction of a system of pipes, cast a local glow over pagodas of white porcelain, or steely assemblies of valves and wheels. Wisps of steam, the only ghosts the city possessed, rose like giant flowers from points in the Industrial Park.

Beyond the frozen reservoir the gravelled enclosure containing radio masts, hundreds of them, bristled with invisible hairs, thousands of miles long, great sensitive whiskers that reached out beyond the stratosphere to the ionosphere, the mysterious layers of air that bent them back as glass might, back to the earth again in a different place.

And silently along these hairs passed words and signals and music. Present in the air all around me were voices from Australia debating the proceedings in Parliament, the strings of an orchestra in Buenos Aires sweeping through a symphony by Mahler, desperate messages in Morse Code from trawlers foundering in the Arctic Ocean, jazzy Latin pop music from the Congo, millions of human signals in a noiseless crepitation; and the long invisible hairs from the Parque Industrial touched them all, pulled them all in; and passed right through my body, almost as I had gone into the messenger's all that time ago.

Then the city itself, at my feet. Clean and glowing and warm, a clean, well-lighted place, containing people who had been my friends and other people whose status was near divine, whose interests I wanted to serve. And the body of the messenger, the memory of which stayed like radioactivity in all the cells of mine, so that I thought I glowed with it, and would be visible for miles, the luminous man lit up by love.

And the sky stayed clear, and the moon sailed on, and the stars swung slowly around the Pole. It wasn't going to snow that night. Had I begun the thaw by falling in love with the messenger?

That unreal being . . .

How many kinds of unreality were there? Many, many. Zombies were unreal, and so were the slaves in the stinking chambers of the red mountain. The Electric Whores were unreal. Hadn't they rejected me, and shouldn't that make me unreal too, like Juan? Or had I put them to flight? I'd have to think about all that again. Then Juan himself was unreal, and the automata in the Museum were unreal, all in different ways. Mary Pretorius was unreal, because she changed herself according to the fashion, becoming the artifice she put on. Johnny was unreal because he had died and been made into a zombie, and had achieved the further unreality of a second life. And I remembered something he'd said to me the night we first met Vrykolakas; talking about his cycle racing and his need to pretend to be poor so as to race well, he'd said then, all that time ago, that he lived an unreal life. The city itself was unreal, from the plaster in the Palacio Municipal to the layout of the streets, borrowed from another place.

Unreality was a mark of distinction, no matter what form it took, or how unhappy it made you. Even insubstantial Juan was a prominent member of the nation of the favoured. I must tell him that, I thought, if I see him again. And the romantic moonlit bareness of Aphrodite's meadow had the look of a stage set, and that solid citizen Ignaz Gruenberg was up to his ears in the concerns of the mystic arts; the catalogue lengthened effortlessly.

Could I acquire unreality? Could I buy it? I didn't want to stay as I was, that was certain.

One or two of the lights in the city had gone out, but still the distant airport glowed, and still the invisible radar swept the sky, searching for aeroplanes, birds, or the flight of angels.

I'd been skirting around the central question ever since I got up to the meadow, but now I reluctantly faced it. What was I going to do about my love for the messenger? Solicit her affection in return? The idea was grotesque. Go away and leave things alone, do no more damage, turn Vrykolakas and Juan over to the authorities. Impossible; that would be a retreat, and I wanted a confrontation.

Then, out of the corner of my eye, I saw a movement over the snow. It came from a little grove of trees not far away, between me and the city. Something was running fast round and round the grove, kicking up the snow. Then it set off at a blinding pace directly towards me.

Other shapes came out of the trees, pursuing it. Or led by it.

I was on my feet, looking around for shelter. The sheer pace of whatever it was made me sweat with fear. There was nowhere I could hide; I put the tree-trunk I'd been sitting on between me and them, and prepared to stand my ground.

Dogs, I thought, feeling sick, Vrykolakas' friends . . .

The bitch Lulu was the one being pursued. As they came closer I heard the hacking, mewing sound they made, but harsher now with the panic or the lust of the chase. My fists involuntarily bunched. I was in a crouch, with wild ideas of seizing the first one by the throat, and swinging it around to beat off the others.

Was she pursued, or leading? I was in doubt up till the last moment. Then she leapt at me, snarling silently, a few metres ahead of the rest. I ducked, but managed a grab a hind leg, and dragged her twisting and thrashing to the trunk.

Blood flicked here and there from her freshly-torn ears.

I stood on the tree-trunk, trying to maintain a firm grip on her hind leg. The rest of the dogs, led by a huge Alsatian, bounded up and snapped madly at my feet and legs. I noticed that whenever a drop of the torn dog's blood splashed on to one of them, it flinched and fell back for a few moments. I'd have to use that, if I could get more of it. How did he do it? His teeth? The Alsatian fastened his jaws around my shoe. I kicked and kicked, and fell heavily off the trunk. The dogs closed in. I pulled Lulu's head towards my mouth, baring my teeth like a wolf. All around me the coughing moaning sound got wilder and wilder. The Alsatian's teeth got a better purchase on my foot; my head roared with pain. But for Lulu's body between them and my throat, I'd be dead already. I sank my teeth savagely into the loose flesh between her ears, tasting the rank salty tang of her blood, and tore at it for the sake of my life. The blood gushed; the dogs fell back. I held her body with trembling arms high above my head, so that I was drenched with the bitter flood. It worked, for there was a space around me now, but Lulu kicked her way out of my hands and fell beside me. I scrambled up again, dizzy, and then they closed in for the second time, making their vile coughing noises as they snapped at my legs and feet, which hadn't been stained by the dog's blood.

I couldn't last for much longer, I thought; that bastard, I should have killed him when I could . . .

Then there was another sound, a full-throated howl, from somewhere behind me. Away across the snow a great gaunt wolf stood, giving voice. It looked up at the moon with its throat wide open, howling like a slave-driver in hell, and its cousins around me shivered, and sat down where they were, as meek as rabbits.

One of them began to lick the flowing wounds of Lulu, finding the blood no longer distasteful. Some began to groom one another like cats. The Alsatian settled down along the ground with his forepaws extended in front of him.

I looked around again. The wolf was nowhere to be seen, but strolling towards me across the snowy plain was the dapper figure of Vrykolakas.

I straightened up, trembling. My fists were still clenched, and I was soaked to the waist in stinking blood. It was hard to believe that it all came from the slight figure of the tame little bitch at my feet.

"Ah, poor Lulu," observed the mystic, as he came near enough to see what had happened.

"Is that all you can say?"

He waved his hand dismissively. "They were only playing. You shouldn't have taken it so seriously. They wouldn't have hurt you, really. We're very fond of you, you know, Martin. Besides—" he lowered his voice—"we need you."

I was shaking so violently I couldn't stand upright. I had to sit on the tree-trunk. I felt sick; a flood of coldness boiled inside my stomach, and my face was cold and sweating. But it subsided; I didn't want him to see me vomit. After I'd sat still for a minute or so, with Vrykolakas stroking and petting his friends, and giving a fresh tweak to Lulu's ears, I felt better. I began to clean myself with handfuls of snow.

"So you're a wolf, among your other accomplishments," I said.

He nodded modestly. "A small talent," he said, "but sometimes useful."

"Why didn't you let them kill me?"

He looked distressed. "We couldn't do that! Believe me, Martin, we're on your side! You're so sceptical. I don't know what I've got to do to convince you, honestly I don't. We want to help you find your wife, don't you realise?"

He'd given himself away!

He'd said that too urgently. His own purpose was plain in it. *He* wanted to find Catherine, and he was relying on me to do it for him, since he couldn't do it on his own. Even with friends.

Another piece a secret knowledge I held, then. Now what could I do with it?

"You really want to help?" I said carefully. "You're not just saying that to try and get out of apologising for this?" I gestured around at the dogs. I couldn't pretend to lose my anger too soon, or he'd suspect something.

"Yes," he said sincerely. "We really want to help."

"You say 'we'," I said. "Those things haven't got any wishes at all, apart from the commands you give them."

"Oh, on the contrary," he said, defending them anxiously. "They share my feelings fully. I know them, you see, I know them like a father. Have you got any children, Martin? Was your marriage blessed with children?"

"No."

"You can't be expected to know, then. A father and his children; that's how I feel about these creatures. But it's more than that, too; friendship, real warm intimate friendship. We can feel it for people sometimes, can't we? Those first few moments, with a stranger, when you know instinctively that you and he are going to be friends. There's a flash of intuition that leaps across the gap between you, and it doesn't matter how little you know about him, it doesn't matter how ugly he is, or how cruel he is. You know you're going to *like* them, and that feeling's just like the feeling I have for my friends, and they have for me. We feel things together, we do things together, we want things together."

"How long have you had them?"

"We met on the way here."

"I don't believe a word you're saying. It's all lies."

"Oh, Martin," he said sadly. "You still don't understand, do you. *That's the thing to do in this city.*"

"To lie?"

He sighed. "I showed you, in the Palace, what a fake it all was. Have you heard any true words since you came here?"

"Not from you."

"No, I won't be provoked," he said patiently. "Have you had a straight answer to any of your questions?"

"Since you mention it," I said cautiously, "no."

"Haven't you seen how everything is artificial?"

"Everything."

"Everything that matters. Pretence everywhere, nothing but lies. If you want to get on in the Perfect City, lie and cheat, that's the thing to do."

"Tell me what else I haven't noticed."

"I can show you . . ." He looked around, though we were a kilometre or two away from the edge of the meadow, and there was no one but his quiet friends to hear us. "I can show you," he went on in a lower voice, "their sexual customs."

"What do you know about them?"

"Oh, I've found out a thing or two. Look, let's go back to my place. I'll show you something there that'll make you think. Besides, it's cold out here, don't you feel?"

"You want us to go to the Unbuilt Slum?"

"That's right."

"I want to go to my hotel first, and get a gun."

"Oh, but I won't allow that. My friends would think you wanted to kill me, and . . . no, that's quite out of the question. Honestly."

I didn't really want a gun, but I did want to establish the idea of myself as suspicious and cross-grained, in the hope that it would divert attention away from the fact that I now knew what he wanted. But I'd have to be careful among all these behavioural subtleties; it was like embarking on a complicated variation in chess.

"All right then, I'll come with you," I said grudgingly.

In order that the Perfect City should lack nothing, it had been provided with a wasteland in the form of the Unbuilt Slum, where things could rot and run wild. It was used as a dump for the city's waste, and resembled a bomb site several hectares in size, set about with the shells of various buildings designed to be partly demolished and left to decay.

Broken cranes and bulldozers and a few ruined cars had been placed at points here and there on the scarred earth. Great ruts marked where the beasts had crawled to their rusty death, and steep ravines, two or three metres deep, had been gouged at random, ending in blank walls of snowy earth or drifting up into shallow oblivion. When the snow went it would be thick with mud and choked with rambling weeds, and there was a shallow pool about a hundred metres in width whose water would be blood-red with decay; but now it was white everywhere, except where a rearing wall of earth showed dark against it, or projecting remnants of a building kept a corner clear of snow.

At the edge of this strange domain, the friends waited politely while Vrykolakas held up the wire for me to get through. He smelt of after-shave lotion, I noticed, and I smelt of dog's blood. But then he might have liked that.

The cold moon glared violently as I stumbled over the decaying bricks and piled-up earth of the Unbuilt Slum. The dogs trotted sure-footedly, and the werewolf clambered with a steady assurance, knowing the way.

We came to a great gaunt leaning wall facing the moon. There were gaps in the brickwork, as if huge machines had been torn out like teeth. The friends lay down, while Vrykolakas sat on a rock and mopped his brow.

"Milord," he commanded, "amuse our friend Martin."

A grey and black mongrel got up and began to dance, leaping elegantly on its hind legs high into the air. Vrykolakas reached grunting into a crevice behind a rock.

"Where do you live?" I asked.

"Oh, here," he said, his voice muffled.

"You sleep here, in the open?"

"I don't sleep," he said more clearly, coming upright again. "I doze a little, on my feet. Now then."

He was holding the nude figure of the stolen dancing girl. Her face had been made up carefully, with heavy black eye-shadow, but her dark lipstick was smudged. The mystic licked a little finger and repaired the damage.

"Complete in every part," he said proudly, displaying her.

He had coloured in two nipples on her satin breast, and a dark triangle of hair further down. He shook her; her hands flapped, and a dismal whirring came from inside her.

How can I describe what I felt? It was as if he had Catherine there in his hands. I forced myself to sit down. Everything he touched, he made vile.

"If you bear the city no ill-will—" I began.

"No ill-will at all," he said, shocked. "I'm an anthropologist, after all. I did my doctorate in anthropology at Leyden University; my word, I'm here to study, that's all."

"Then why did you steal its property?"

"The doll? It doesn't belong to the city. Didn't you read the label? It's on loan from the Musée de Cluny in Paris."

"All the more reason for you not to steal it."

"Ah, well, if we took that attitude, science would be nowhere. Knowledge belongs to all the world, Martin, I'm sure you agree. No damage done, anyway. I'm an expert in these matters."

He took off his overcoat and spread it on the snowy ground. Then he arranged the dancing girl on it so that she was resting on her elbows and knees, with her head bent down submissively.

"Must keep her pretty knees dry," he said facetiously. "Now then. In the so-called Perfect City of the so-called Unreal People, sexual matters are arranged with great circumspection. What you are about to see has been witnessed before by no one except the perverted inhabitants. But I am forced into it, Martin," he said, clenching his jaw and looking clean and strong, like an American President, "by the pressure of circumstances."

He sat down close beside me, shivering with the cold, but rapt with scientific passion. He gestured expansively as he spoke.

"What circumstances?" I asked.

"An unusual condition of the atmosphere, up here in the high mountains. Perhaps it's due to a distortion of the earth's magnetic field. Who knows? But there's a law in the city that face-to-face sexual congress is banned." His voice dropped. "And that's not all. In order to reproduce, the people here have to use artificial aids."

"The unreal people, you mean?"

"Oh, no. Everyone. There's a law about it. But don't talk to me

232

about those unreals. I don't want to think about them, I can't think scientifically if you've got them on the brain. Oh, you've made me lose what I was saying!"

He stamped petulantly, and snarled at me, drawing back his lips. Involuntarily I flinched, which must have pleased him, for he instantly gave a sunny smile and carried on.

"Oh, yes, they all have to use artificial aids. I'm sure you know the sort of thing I mean." He nudged me, and grinned roguishly. "Electrical devices, eh? And the rest. Otherwise they can't reproduce. Simple."

"But why?"

He shrugged. "Nature still has her mysteries, and who are we to try and pry beyond the curtain?" His tone was pious; now it became brisk again. "And I—want—more—friends. I want lots and lots of friends. I can't get any more here, because there aren't any more friends in the city, so—we make some!"

He clapped his hands.

"Max!" he called.

The massive Alsatian walked powerfully out of the shadow of the gaunt wall.

"Go to it, my friend," said the anthropologist of Leyden. "Do your duty; get some children for me."

He leant forward and patted the dancer on her smooth rump. She began to move feebly backwards and forwards. Max padded forward, sniffed at her, and then mounted her with an easy lunge. He thrust a dozen times, his weight pushing the gentle dancer forward on the coat. Then he finished, got off, and licked her flank vaguely before going back to lie down again.

"Good, good," said the werewolf benevolently. "And now for one of the marvels of the mystic arts, known to the wizards of ancient Egypt but lost to the rest of mankind for the last four thousand years. With my help, the dancing girl—what shall we call her, by the way? Mary? Is that a nice name?"

"You'd better not," I said.

"No, no, we'll call her Olympia, that's a nice name, like the doll in the story. Don't worry, I was only teasing . . . Yes, the doll Olympia, with my help, will now give birth!"

He tipped the doll over on to her side and thrust his hand up between her legs. There was a scraping of machinery, and his hand came out bearing a miniature dog-man, pallid and limp. He slapped it; its jaws started to move, it became stiff, and its legs moved briskly. He set it on its feet, upright like a human, and it ran mechanically away over the rocks.

Vrykolakas bent down and picked up the doll. Her satin skin was dark and wet at the side, where she'd fallen on the dirty snow beside his coat. He brushed her down, and snapped his fingers.

"Stürmer!" he called.

A languid Dalmatian strolled from the shadows, and began to perform the act again. And again Vrykolakas assisted the doll to give birth to a dog-like manikin, and slapped it into whirring life, and sent it scuttling off into the moonlit waste.

Then it was Milord's turn, the grey and black dancing dog. The doll's position had to be adjusted, as Milord was rather short. "Fine couple," said the astrologer fondly. "Wonderful talent on both sides; fine breeding stock."

Milord tumbled away, pirouetting elegantly. This time the offspring was female. Vrykolakas held it up for me to examine; sick and curious, I did so. It was about fifteen centimetres in length, a pale colour, and hairless. It had the head and front legs of a dog and the body and legs of a human. It was perfectly mechanical, and its mechanism came to life as he slapped it.

"It doesn't stop, you see, Martin," he said tenderly. "It'll keep going, you'll see, it won't need rewinding or anything like that."

The jaws of each of them had opened and shut like traps, disclosing steel teeth like needles. When they moved about, the other two had gone in straight lines, but Milord's child skipped here and there like a naked demon when he put it down. And its tiny jaws never stopped snapping.

The ritual continued. Each time it happened the dancer's skin got more torn and soiled, and eventually the soft wool underneath was coming through in a dozen places, and being draggled in the mud and slush.

The skilful anthropologist acted as midwife at the birth of fifteen children altogether, and lost only one of them. It was the daughter of Dante, a poodle. She was a sickly child who didn't respond to the life-stirring slap, but hung soft and limp in the mystic's hand. After slapping it four of five times, he smashed it on a rock in irritation; its skin split, and tiny cogs and ball-bearings rolled out and vanished into the snow.

The dancer's child was still skipping and curvetting not far from where we sat, but all the others had gone out into the night. I asked the wizard where they had gone.

"Ah," he said. "Heredity . . . a wonderful thing, isn't it! How sad that you haven't any children, Martin, to inherit your musical gifts. You shouldn't be so parsimonious: these things are meant to be passed on. They flow from generation to generation like a mighty river, deepening and widening as it flows towards the sea . . ."

"I don't understand what you're talking about," I said. "Where have those things gone?"

"I was trying to explain," he said sorrowfully. He shoved the dancing girl off his overcoat and on to her side in the slush, picked up the coat and shook it, and put it on. "My dear friends and I," he went on, "have spent so much time in the last day or so trying to find things out about this precious city, and looking for your wife for you, that all my friends want to do is find her. Isn't it, my lovelies? And what the fathers want, so the children want too. I arranged all this as a present for you, Martin. All my little children have gone out to look for your wife. Isn't that good of them?"

Old Debts and Compound Interest

I was on my feet and running as hard as I could over the tumbled earth. Vrykolakas called out "Stop! Stop! Let me come too!"

But I didn't think he would; he wanted to see me frightened, and he had; and if he really wanted to stop me he'd have set his friends on to me. And I realised even as I ran that he still wanted me alive, for some reason. I was necessary to his plans. I couldn't imagine why, but it gave me one thing to be grateful for.

I had to find all those children, and kill them, if they could be killed. Those teeth . . .

I was lucky; I found the tracks they'd made as they left the Unbuilt Slum, and I caught up with the last one shortly afterwards, in a side-street not far from the Calle de Roma, with its smart shops and bright lights. I ran up to the thing and kicked it as hard as I could against a wall. It broke; the mechanism fell still, and I picked it up carefully. The jaw snapped once or twice, making me start and nearly drop it.

I took it with me and followed the other tracks. They had all gone the same way, it seemed. Another thing on my side was the fact that it wasn't snowing. The night was far advanced, and I thought it snowed every night. Had the pattern changed, then? Had something happened?

But I soon stopped thinking about that. I came to a crossroads, and my heart sank, for the tracks of the dog-children led off in each direction. I stood indecisively; this would take all night, and more. I felt bitterly unhappy.

Should I ring Johnny? Would he help? Of course he'd help, but should I? It was my fault, because I'd done nothing about Vryko-lakas before. And I was ashamed, but I still felt angry when I thought of the way they'd rejected me. No, it was my business, my quarrel, my fight, my wife; nothing to do with him.

I looked up. Juan was standing in front of me.

"What are you doing, man?" he said.

"Not real yet?" I remembered I was quarrelling with him too.

"Not tonight," he said equably. "I've done enough damage for tonight, that'll last me until tomorrow." I didn't know what he meant; I thought he was talking about the broken window in the hotel. "What are you doing?" he said again.

"Have you seen any of these?"

I held out the broken dog-child. He looked at it equably.

"Three or four of them went towards the palace. I haven't seen any more."

"Will you help me find them? There are thirteen left. I want to kill them. They're looking for my wife."

He pursed up his unreal lips.

"I don't know that I've got the time," he replied.

"Please!"

He shrugged. "It's a busy life, becoming real. I've got a lot to do. Maybe I haven't done enough damage tonight, after all. Perhaps I ought to go and break something else, to bring you to your senses. If I help you now, what will I get?"

"Anything I can give you, for God's sake!"

"Thanks are no good to me, you know that?"

"Whatever I can, Juan. All your money, if you want it, and all of mine."

"Oh, well, I might come along for an hour or two. They move fast, those bastards. You're too soft to catch them on your own, you'd get too tired . . ."

So he came along with me. All the time he kept up a stream of insults, laughing at me, taunting me; and once or twice I lost my temper and took a swing at him, which he easily dodged, and then threatened to give up helping me, so that I had to apologise, and promise never to do it again.

236

I was entering a state of unreality myself, I thought. I was numb with tiredness, dazed with various kinds of shock, and the background of my feelings was a general blur of disappointment and hopelessness against which the phantom's insults and the wicked snapping shadows of the dog-children showed up like hallucinations.

As the night went by, we caught more and more of them. They did move fast, but they moved in predictable paths, and if they were trapped against the wall of a building they could no nothing but bite. I kicked ten of them to death before the first light came into the sky. Juan refused to touch them, out of fellow-feeling for other unreals, he said, but he watched quite happily while I finished them off. I was only bitten once; it was a clean wound and soon stopped bleeding.

But although we returned time and time again to the first crossroad where they'd split up, and followed all the tracks we could see, we didn't find the remaining three. One of them was the dancer's child; she might still be in the Unbuilt Slum, entertaining her father and his master, but then she might be anywhere.

As the first light of dawn began to show over the mountain-rim, a change came over the form of Juan, and his manner changed too. His body became even less clear to look at, his outline more flickering and uncertain, and he fell silent and morose, so that eventually I asked him what was the matter.

"You're going to fall asleep soon," he said, "and leave me out in the cold again. I knew this wouldn't last, this dog-hunt."

"But we've nearly finished," I said. "I can't go to sleep until they're all dead."

"I didn't mean that. We won't find the others now, I know that. If you don't believe me, that's too bad, but you're going to fall asleep soon whether you like it or not. Then what shall I do?"

I stopped and yawned; he was right. I was nearly asleep on my feet. We were at the entrance to a park, on the other side of which was the Avenida de Doctor Faust and the hotel. It must have been, I thought as I leant against the entrance, about the only part of the city we hadn't covered that night; our footprints wound through street after street, crossing and re-crossing like threads in a maze.

Was it possible to stay awake till I found the others? No, it wasn't. I'd removed most of the danger, after all. The remaining three couldn't much harm, surely, I thought, setting off across the snowy expanse of the park. They were easy enough to kill . . .

Juan plucked at my sleeve. I'd forgotten him.

"Sorry," I muttered, reaching into my pocket.

"No," he said. "Never mind the money. I want something else."

"What, then?"

"I want to sleep in your bed, by your side."

"Why?"

"To become real."

"But . . ."

I was too tired to think of objecting, or even questioning. I nodded, and plodded on. The pale light of dawn showed us the unreal fauna of the park: mobiles in the form of birds hanging from the trees, too stiff to move for the frost in their joints; and mechanical fish and turtles which lurked in the ice of frozen ponds.

But here and there the snow was melting. The thaw was under way; patches of dark grass showed through. And at one point I stopped, too tired to move for a minute or so, to discover that I was standing on a stone that had been let into the grass. Other stones led away from it, surrounding it in a complex pattern. I was at the centre of a maze. I nodded dumbly, and moved on.

Foxtrot d'Amour

The first beams of the sun were striking into my bedroom as we opened the door. Juan had said nothing. I had forgotten he was with me until he closed the door behind me.

I pulled the curtains across to shut out the light. The room was warm and dry, and I was cold and wet and filthy. Almost in a stupor of weariness I had a shower and stumbled into bed, but sat up quickly when I found something sharp and rustling on the pillow.

It was an artificial rose made of yellow silk.

I was wide awake in a moment. *She* had left it, the only she, the messenger, it was a private token from her to me. I loved her—she knew about it—what did the rose mean? Did it matter what it meant? After all I'd felt, that night, this at last . . .

I smelt it; a faint scent of perfume, and under it the oxygen-smell, infinite cleanliness. I lay back in the bed, and there was a lump in my throat.

"Martin?" came Juan's voice, in a whisper.

"Yes?" I whispered back.

"I want to come into your bed."

"All right, if you want . . ."

238

I put the rose on the floor, and moved up. He was as light and chilly as a mirage; his hands on my body sent me quickly to sleep.

But I couldn't sleep; he kept whispering, telling me things. Or asking me, because it was hard to tell the difference. He asked me about the Electric Whores of his home town: what was it like to make love to them? Was it true that they were both male and female? What had they said to me?

I muttered "I don't know, I've forgotten." But as I said it I knew that I hadn't, and that I'd have to try and remember, because the messenger had said that what they'd told me was literally true in the Perfect City.

So I tried. "Juan, don't bother me," I whispered, and held his hand to keep it still. I had to put off my clothes and be naked; well, here I was, in that state. Put off my flesh and be a spirit, they'd said. Not so easily done, but I felt half-spirit then, with only my heavy eyelids entirely in the physical world.

Not even the closeness of my body, under the warm quilt, could mitigate the chill of his. It was his most real quality. "I don't feel it," he said quietly, when I told him. But it wasn't real enough to make me cold; I was warm all over, no matter where his hands lay. I dozed.

He said "You have to make love to me, before I can be real. I didn't know that before I went to that prince's, where your friends are. He told them about it. They didn't like it. She didn't, anyway, at first. Then he said he wouldn't, because of you. That should make you pleased, eh? He wouldn't betray you, he said. But then she said that she didn't want to either, for that reason, not for any other. If it weren't for you, she'd do it, she said."

"Do what?" I murmured. I could hardly hear him.

"Be married," said the unreal, I think. "Hey, Martin, you know what to do with me, like you did in the Parque Electrico with the male whores. Then come on, I'm getting impatient."

"What did Mary and Johnny have to do?" I said again. Too tired to resist, I let his hands go wherever he wanted. It made no difference.

"Make love, that's all."

I fell asleep then, for the fifth or sixth time. But Juan went on talking, and I went on hearing.

He seemed to be interpreting the future of the Anderson Valley for me. In the city the unreals and humans were to live together in

239

love and friendship. The humans would have closer and subtler relations than those regarded as desirable in the outside world, relations with each other as well as with the unreals. Yes, and? Nothing was immutable, everything was subject to change, including the most private and secret regions of the soul. What did that mean? The outward appearance of people could change, and so could their natures. Businessmen could become musicians, musicians become businessmen, thus illustrating the multiplicity of phenomena and the unity of matter. Everything was what it appeared to be, which was a philosophical advance on the old truth, that nothing was what it appeared to be. The key to this magical and scientific universe was pretence and imitation. My wife, as the presiding genius of the place, would shortly be re-united with me, and my efforts and trials would be rewarded as we came together to the applause of all the free citizens of the Perfect City; and the werewolf Vrykolakas, his villainous parodies exposed, would be expelled in ignominy to the ends of the earth.

I was dreaming. I knew, because I woke up then, and Juan was silent. But his hands were frantic, and I was unresponsive.

"Then you better turn over, you bastard," he whispered. "Let me do it. You think I can't?"

But that was like a dream as well. I rolled over unthinkingly, to find myself looking over the edge of the bed at the yellow silk rose that lay on the carpet.

I woke up properly then, with a start. The rose was torn and chewed. Fragments of silk lay all round it, and the green wire stem was twisted and bare.

There was a tiny intermittent snapping noise from the corner of the room.

I sat up and pushed the unreal aside; he was as light as the quilt. In spite of the drawn curtains, the room was light. In the corner, one of the dog-children was gnawing at something.

It was my flute. I'd left it on the table when I went out the night before, and this thing must have found it there.

I looked for something to kill it with, but there was nothing, and I had bare feet. I heard the tiny screech of steel on silver, and my blood boiled. I was across the room in three steps, and I seized the end of the poor ruined flute and lifted the creature up. I whirled it round and beat it against the table, but it clung on and gave a sound like the rasp of metal on metal. I beat it against the table again and again, and then it dropped off, and I used the flute as a club to crush it to a pulp. Except that it wasn't a pulp; inside the broken skin were wheels and cogs and escapements.

The flute would never play again. It had chewed the pads off all the keys and then set to work on the keys themselves, twisting and bending them and all but breaking them off. And I'd done as much damage in trying to kill the thing. I stood there in a daze, and then put down the flute and picked up the rose, its torn petals fluttering through my fingers to the floor.

The telephone rang.

I blinked. I looked at my watch; it was eleven o'clock. The phone went on ringing.

After a few moments I sat down on the bed and picked up the receiver.

"Hello?"

"Martin? This is Johnny."

Pause; what could I say? I said "Hi."

"How are you?"

"Tired."

"Yeah. Well . . ." We were both embarrassed, and there was a moment then when I could have said so, and we might have admitted it, and been friends; but I said nothing, and the chance went. "We've got some news," he went on brightly. "Mary and me. We're going to get married."

"What? Oh, that's fine," I said. "Good, I'm really glad. But isn't it a bit sudden?"

What Juan had whispered to me in bed, was it true, then?

"Sudden for her, maybe. Not for me . . . But I wanted to say thank you, you see."

"What for?"

"It's your journey. If you hadn't turned up in Valencia, we might never. . . . anyway, look, Mary's father's coming in on the morning flight, and we're having a sort of party to celebrate. You don't feel like coming, do you?"

"I've got to go today, you realise."

"On the evening flight. But you could come to lunch."

"Yes, I could. There's a lot . . . Can I talk to you alone?"

"I don't think so," he said carefully. "Not for a while anyway."

"But I've got to go! How long are you going to stay here?"

"For . . . some time. I've got a lot to do. I spoke to my father on the phone last night; he wants me to set up an office here and take charge of it. He sends you his best wishes, by the way."

241

"Thanks, but . . . I won't see you again, then?"

"Of course you will, man. I'll have to come to Europe sometime, if I'm a businessman."

"Johnny, you're not on my side any more, are you?"

There was a silence.

Then he said "It's not that, Martin."

"Well, what, then? I feel as if I'm being punished, or as if I've caught the plague or something. Can't you see that?"

"It will all come right in the end," he said emphatically. "They've told me that, and I believe them. Unless you damage it yourself, nothing can go wrong for you. But you have to do what they say."

"I don't like doing what people say."

"Nor do I, as a rule," he said, "but we shouldn't have rules. It's bad to do things by habit. Anyway, are you coming to lunch with us?"

Someone else took the phone from him, and Mary's voice came on the line.

"Are you still being snobbish?" she said crossly. "Get over here and stop sulking. We're going to get married now and it's very rude to stay away when you're invited to lunch, don't you know that?"

"Yes, I do," I said. "Congratulations on your engagement. When will you be married?"

"Oh, some time soon. You're coming then, are you?"

"Can I talk to you if I come?"

"What, just me? The time for that's past. You should know that."

"You or Johnny. Or both of you. But I want to know—"

"Well, if he won't, I won't. You should know better than to ask. Are you going to come or not?"

"I suppose so."

"You don't have to sound so grudging."

"You don't have to sound so bossy."

"Good," she said, in a tone of satisfaction. "Back to normal again. We'll see you at twelve-ish, then. You know how to get here? A big sort of Italian-looking house on the Avenida de Amsterdam. It's called the Villa Tedesca."

And she rang off. I put the phone down thoughtfully.

I'd have to buy some more clothes; the others were filthy and reeking. And dispose of the body of the dog-child. Or I could take it with me, and force them to listen. No, I couldn't; I'd behave, they knew I'd behave.

"I know more than I've told you," came a voice from the other side of the room.

Clothes, first. I'd have to wear these stinking things, stiff with blood, to go out in and buy some more. I found my credit card and put it on the table while I pulled the foul garments on. I'd need another shower when I came back. I'd have to hurry.

"What's the matter with you, you bastard?" cried Juan. "You want me to break something else?"

I wondered about the dog-child, and after a few moments stuffed it, with loathing, into a pocket. I'd throw it away when I got outside.

"You know what I did last night?" cried Juan as I went out of the door. "I fucked up the electric factory in the Parque Industrial, and I killed a man! I pushed him into the spring where the electric water comes out!"

I heard him.

"You did what? You killed a man? What do you mean?"

"Ah, you listen now, eh, when I hurt your precious bloody city, but you don't help me to become real in that simple little way I told you about! That's all you've got to do, just do it with me like you did with the other ones. You bastard, you want me to kill someone else? Or maybe tell the werewolf where your wife is, so he can kill her like he wants to? Shall I go to him now, eh?"

"Where is she? If you know, tell me."

"Why should I?"

"I don't know. But why should you want to tell him?"

"So he can kill her. That'll spoil their bloody marriage, those two."

"Why?" I stood in front of him, though I was unsure where exactly he was; and I raised my voice not in anger but out of a feeling that he must be perceiving me as dimly as I was now seeing him.

"And then the whole city'll be fucked up," he said gleefully. "Nothing you can do about it then."

"But what do you *mean*? I don't understand you," I insisted.

"All I've got to do is find out where those unreals come from, and then I can tell the werewolf," he said, as if he was talking to himself.

And he pushed past me, or drifted past me, and left the room. If the others wouldn't listen to me, could I be to blame for

243

whatever would happen? The answer was, clearly, yes, it was all my responsibility, it would all be my fault. But I was happy with that; with responsibility sometimes goes power.

Life in High Society

"So," said Lionel Pretorius. "What do you think of these two?"

"I'm delighted, of course," I said.

There was a party of about two dozen people in the great drawing-room of Prince Cavalcanti's house. Johnny and Mary stood together, talking to a young man with horn-rimmed glasses; a group of four or five surrounded a very old lady who sat on a sofa; the Prince circulated among the other guests, and in the middle of the room, wearing a beautifully cut dark suit with a yellow rosebud in the buttonhole, the mighty banker stood, rocking gently backwards and forwards on the balls of his feet.

"And you?" I asked. "How do you look on it?"

"Marriage?" he said. "An excellent institution."

"This one too?"

"Nature favours it," he said. "So of course I do too."

"Do you mean the snow melting? That's due to their engagement, is it?"

"Of course," he said solemnly, and puffed at his cigar. His eyes behind the tinted glasses were narrowed slightly, as if to watch for my reaction, to see whether or not I'd take it as a joke. I smiled politely.

"When we last met," he went on, "you were looking for your wife. Have you found her?"

He didn't modify his voice at all. Nobody was actually listening, but there were few people there who could not have listened to us, if they chose to. The difference between us was that he was at ease, and I was extremely nervous. But I had nothing to lose.

"Don't ask me that," I said. "You know as well as I do."

"I take it from your savage tone that you've been unsuccessful?"

"I should think that everyone in this room knows more about her than I do. Certainly Johnny and Mary, certainly the Prince, certainly you."

"Weren't you warned of that?"

"How do you know?"

"Well, you assume my omniscience, it seems. Don't you? Of course I know you were warned."

"So you do know where she is. You always did, didn't you?"

"Shouldn't you have taken the job I offered?"

"You'd have known all about me then."

"Actually," he said, having taken a sip of champagne, "there are things about this city that even I don't know. Omniscience doesn't exist."

"I can guess what they are."

"Go on, then."

"How an exhibit can be stolen from the Museum in broad daylight. How an unsterilised coin finds its way into the economy of the city. How a man can be electrocuted. How power failures occur."

"Do you know anything about them?"

"I know something, and I'll sell it to you, as they do in the Information Centre."

"What's the price?"

"More information."

"What about?"

I thought. "About the Unreal People. About what they are, and where they come from, and so on. All about them."

"Too much," said the banker; "I won't pay that much."

An acquaintance touched his elbow, and, with a nod and a smile, he turned away.

A little draught of desolation chilled me for a second. Then the Prince, seeing me alone, came quietly to my side.

"Let me introduce you to my mother," he said. "She's very old; she wants to settle here permanently . . . Call her Madame, by the way. She's Russian, and she's never cared for the Italian title, in spite of . . . And I've told her what you're doing here," he added, just as we got to the sofa where she sat, so that I had no chance to ask him how he'd explained it.

"Mama, this is Martin Browning. Do you remember my telling you. . . .? He came here with Mary and John."

The old lady was nearly blind. The others who had been talking to her rose, acknowledged me politely, and drifted away. I took her frail hand.

"You'll have to sit down beside me," she said. "No good standing up there. You're so tall I can't see the top of you. I can hear all right, but not see. Come on, sit down, that's right. Has the angel given you a drink? Have you got some champagne?"

The angel was the servant, who was unreal, as I might have expected.

"Yes, I have, thank you, Madame," I said. "Tell me, if it's not a rude question: why do you call him an angel?"

"That's what they are," she said stubbornly. "I know all about them. I've got a good friend who brings me the most delicious cakes and pastries that I shouldn't eat at all, but I do, and he tells me what he knows about them. Oh, it's fascinating."

Cavalcanti had gone too; I was alone with her.

"I think I may have met your friend," I said. "In fact we may have another acquaintance in common—that is, if your name is Lydia."

"You want to know my name? Lydia Alexeyevna Cavalcanti. Why does that affect the friends we have in common?"

"Well, when I was in Valencia some weeks ago looking for my wife, I saw her in the company of a man called Alexander Vrykolakas. And Johnny Hamid told me that you had known him once."

"You know him?"

"Yes, a little."

"And do you like him?"

"No. I hate him."

"How sensible of you. I haven't seen him for many years now, but I expect he hasn't changed. Do you know what he told me once?"

"No. What was it?"

"He told me that not only was it possible to make a car crash from a distance, but that he knew how to do it. And an aeroplane too. Is that what you're thinking about?"

She spoke quietly but briskly. She was very old; she was also very sharp.

"Yes, that among other things. I can't believe my wife would have been friendly with him, you see. And in fact now I think I know she wasn't."

"Is he in the city, then? I don't think my son knows about him. Do you think he ought to?"

"For the sake of the city, yes. But I don't know whether the city's interests are mine, altogether."

"You've got to go tonight, Giorgio told me."

"Yes. He invited me here, you know, on condition that I didn't ask any questions. But I couldn't do that."

"Do you still love your wife?"

I blinked. "What an odd question . . ."

"No, it isn't, it's perfectly straightforward. Do you still love her?"

"It is straightforward, of course it is; I meant I was curious why you asked it . . . I think I love her, but it may be a memory I love. It must be, because that's all I have. In any case . . ."

I hesitated. I'd been about to mention the messenger, but I was in enemy territory, more or less.

"I thought you weren't very sure about it," she said calmly.

"And why did you ask?"

"Because I've not nothing else to do, these days, but be curious. And love is always interesting. But you don't seem interested in it."

"Don't I?"

"Well, you're not, you know. You've not very interested in people at all. Are you?"

"I don't think I am, now that you mention it. But I'm interested in everything. People as well as everything else, but not more, perhaps."

"Then you probably don't know if you're in love with your wife or not. Poor man, you must feel very bewildered."

Was she being sarcastic? She didn't seem to be. She seemed to be kind and concerned, and in the Perfect City everything was what it seemed to be.

"Yes, I am," I admitted.

"I thought I was in love with my husband at first," she said. "Fifty years ago; more. Oh, he was very handsome, and I was very poor, but just as well-born as he, if not more so; but my family left Russia after the Revolution, and we had to leave all our property there, of course. So I was a poor girl, and he was a handsome Prince, and we were married and I thought I loved him, and he thought he loved me. But we soon found out that we didn't. So d'you know what we did then?"

I shook my head, and then remembered that she couldn't see. "No," I said.

"We carried on as if ncthing had happened," she said triumphantly. "That's the thing to do in a case like that."

"Weren't you unhappy?"

"Oh, yes, at first. I didn't know how to pretend, you see. But I soon learned. Then I pretended to be happy as well, and that was easy."

"So life in the Perfect City is quite to your taste."

"Oh, very much so."

And then I heard a whisper from my other side. "Say goodbye

to that old bitch and come out of the house with me," said the voice of Juan. "I want to show you something."

Cavalcanti's mother took her glass of wine from the table beside her and sipped it delicately.

"You don't think that my son ought to know about that Bulgarian?" she said.

"Vyrkolakas? I thought he was Greek," I said.

"He pretends to be Greek. He did when I used to know him, but he didn't do it well, so I could tell the difference."

"If he *had* done it well, would it have made him any better, in your view?"

"It depends what else he did. No good being a good actor if you do wicked things. If he acted a good person and did good things, that might be different. But he never did. He thinks pretending is wicked in itself, you see. So he thinks we're all cheats and evildoers, and that all he has to do is be hypocritical on top while he remains wicked underneath, and he'll be one of us. But of course that's no good at all."

("For Christ's sake, leave this old woman and listen to me," said Juan. "I know what's going on now. Do you want to know or not?")

"Do you know," I said, "where my wife is?"

"Yes, I do," she said, "but I'm not going to tell you, because it's secret."

"Can you tell me anything?"

("I can tell you everything, you bastard, and show you too," said the unreal close by my ear.)

"You don't want advice, of course, but I've got plenty of that," said the old lady. "I don't blame you one bit for what you're doing. When I was your age I'd have been asking just as many questions. And I hated people saying 'When I was your age' just as much as you do. But there you are, you get forgetful. I'll give you the advice anyway, whether you want it or not. Fall in love again, with someone else."

"Supposing the someone else belonged to the city?" I asked.

"No one belongs to the city. You make us all sound like slaves!"

Juan was tugging at my sleeve. On an impulse I said to the old lady, "Can you feel this man's hand?" and seized his wrist and touched her arm with his fingers. He pulled back, startled, and she, for her part, trembled and spilt a few drops of her wine.

"That was clumsy of me," she said equably. "I'm too old to be out in polite company."

She mopped at the spilt wine with a lacy handkerchief, but couldn't quite see where it had gone. I helped her, dabbing at the arm of the sofa with my own handkerchief, feeling a flash of anger at myself. Juan crouched in front of me, whispering insults.

"I do apologise," I said. "But listen—can you hear him?"

She inclined her head a little towards him.

("For Christ's sake when are you going to listen to me, you mad bastard!" he was saying. "I don't care if this old whore hears me too, nor all the rest of them. *I know where the unreals of this place come from, I know all about them, and I can show you too if you come with me now!*")

"Yes, I can hear it," said Lydia Cavalcanti. Her eyes were blank, but the loveliest deep blue, and her cheekbones were high and wide; had she looked like the messenger, I wondered? "Who is it? A friend of yours? Where is he?" she asked.

"He came to the city with me. He's unreal, but a different kind of unreal. I haven't told anyone else he's here; they can't notice him, you see, it's as if he's invisible—"

"Why are you telling me, then?" she said. "Do you trust me not to tell the others? I wish I could help you, but you don't understand that I can't. Excuse me, I'm a bit confused now. But listen to me—" she gripped my wrist, and leant forward—"do try not to do any damage, won't you. It would upset your wife so much . . . I won't tell my son about him, this friend of yours, or about the Bulgarian, if you don't want me to, I'm quite good at keeping secrets, and I'd like to see you find your wife again, because I'm sentimental. But if you break anything, I'll wash my hands of you. The best thing you can do is to see my friend the pastrycook. He's a good wise man, and he'll put you on the right track. But this man here is talking violently, and that's a bad way to talk, so I hope you don't listen to him."

"Yes, yes," I said. "You're right . . . In fact, I'll go and tell him to leave. He had no right to come here. Will you excuse me?"

I got to my feet and looked for the phantom. Lydia Cavalcanti sighed, and let go of my wrist.

"I'm sorry," I said involuntarily.

She nodded distantly, looking tired and frail. But then someone else came up on the other side of her and, smiling at me, began to talk to her. With a beautiful wide-awake expression, the old lady turned to her and left me free to wander away in search of Juan.

But his nature was to be come on unexpectedly, not to be looked for.

I couldn't see him anywhere in the room. After I'd gone all the way round it, peering carefully into the corners, Johnny came up to me.

"What's the matter, man?" he said.

"Have you seen Juan?"

"Christ! Juan! I'd forgotten—is he still around? Is he okay? Where's he living?" he said; and I realised that there was so much he didn't know. However close we were, it was a closeness of the past; wedges had come between us since those days in the cold mountains. I couldn't make up for it all now.

"He's—just hanging around. Trying to become real. But he's got worse since we came here." I was looking around as I spoke, but I couldn't see him.

"How do you mean, worse?" said Johnny. "More unreal?"

"Sort of," I said. I looked at him. "Johnny, is there a chance that I'll be able to talk to you some day? I want to tell you about all this, everything I've been doing—I feel like a spy or something, I just want to explain—"

His expression changed, becoming more open, and a flicker of pain crossed it, and there he was again, Johnny whom I loved, the athlete and my friend. But what would have happened then I don't know; something else did. Mary screamed.

She was on the other side of the room, by the window. I heard some glass break, and a curtain swirled out as she grabbed it and fell. The young man with the horn-rimmed glasses slapped at something, and then drew his hand away swiftly. No one else moved; they were all shocked. Mary was writhing on the floor. Johnny and I moved at the same moment.

It was the daughter of Milord the dancer and the automaton, and it was biting at Mary's bare arms. It had bitten the man in the glasses too, and he wasn't quick enough to get it away from her, though he was doing his best. I got to her a second before Johnny, and because I knew what it was, I could deal with it without hesitating.

I took it by the neck and pulled it away. It went on snapping and its legs kicked rhythmically; I'd kill it when I got it outside. Johnny was down on his knees beside Mary, who was sobbing. Her arms were bitten badly, and she was bleeding a lot. Johnny looked up, his expression wide with anguish.

"What is it?" he said hoarsely.

There was a tug at my sleeve. "Come on, now you've got it," whispered Juan.

People were hurrying to see whether Mary was all right. The shocked silence was broken, now that the crisis seemed to be over. "I'll just go and get rid of this," I said to Johnny, and to anyone else who might have heard.

Juan didn't let go of my sleeve, but tugged even more insistently as we went out of the room, wanting me to hurry.

A True Version of the Facts, with No Holds Barred

As we hastened out of the house and down the wide steps into the elegant garden, the little dog fell docile in my hand, and even turned its head to lick my wrist fondly. Absently I stroked its head with my other hand, while trying to keep Juan in sight; for he'd let go of my sleeve by now and hurried on.

Outside the wrought iron gate stood another old acquaintance.

"My dear," said the astrologer, "and you've brought my little pet with you; you are good."

In reply I took the creature, now grown quite playful, and wrung its neck in front of him. He raised his eyebrows.

I flung its body as hard as I could into his face, but it never got there. Juan intercepted it, and tossed it aside. Vrykolakas hadn't moved a muscle. The unreal said "Forget that bloody dog, and listen to me, you bastards. Up in the mountains, an hour's walk away, there's a building where all those unreals come from, the ones they have here in the city. I don't know how they get there, but that's where they come to the city from. Now *you*—" he said, meaning me, "you need him, because the door is locked, and I can't open it. And I need you, because you believe in honour, and you'll protect me from him. And he needs me, because only I know where it is. You understand that, you two?"

"But of course, Juan," murmured the business consultant. "And Martin understands too. He's a little distraught. Perhaps we all are, eh? We've had a long night, haven't we?"

"You know him, then," I said. I was beyond surprise by this time; I wasn't even sure which of them I was addressing.

"Well, I can't deny it," said Vrykolakas amiably. He put his hands in the pockets of his fur-collared coat and shivered briskly. "Shall we go?"

I shrugged. Out of the corner of my eye I caught sight of Juan nodding.

So we set off to walk to the mountain rim, the three of us, all

251

enemies. Juan said nothing. He was dreaming of reality, and he thought I'd help him find it, and so I would, if it was in my power and didn't conflict with what I wanted. But the astrologer kept up a cheerful monologue, disregarding his soft leather shoes that were soon soaked and muddy, disregarding even the cold, disregarding my sullen silence.

"I think I'll tell you now," he said, "what this place is all about. A true version of the facts. I've been holding them back from you up to now, out of consideration, you know. The filthy deeds and filthy plans in this city! They'd turn your hair white, they're so evil.

"That diseased old sodomite Pretorius is at the bottom of it all, ha ha. He hates all simple natural things, like love and friendship, things which you and I value so highly, Martin. Nothing like that's good enough for him. And I'm afraid the good old truths, the good old values and so forth, they count for nothing in this den of perverts."

He shook his head sombrely. The silent form of Juan padded like a shadow beside us as we turned out of the Calle de Amsterdam and into the Campo de Minerva.

"A man like me," he went on, "a simple man, one with the humility of the true scientist in the face of the awesome mysteries of nature—how could I not be shocked at the fearful schemes these men are propounding? When it was first put to me, months and months ago, I could scarcely believe it, and I tried my best, in my humble way, to dissuade them; but now I am confident that they will be visited with the consequences of their folly, in a devastating judgement which their presumption has invited, and their wickedness deserved, the bastards."

He gestured eloquently to add force to his words.

"Behold," he said as we passed the buildings of the University, silent in the early afternoon sun, "a temple of impious curiosity, built to pry into the innermost secrets of the world, which only God is supposed to know about. Do you know, they offered me the chair of Anthropology at this benighted place? I wouldn't take it at any salary you could name, I said proudly. I have more respect for goodness and decency than for my own advancement in the markets of the world."

He smoothed his red hair back from his forehead with a disdainful stroke of his fingers.

Juan pointed to the white rim of the valley, an hour's walk away.

252

"That's where we're going, up there," he said with his frail voice. "Save your breath for walking, you hypocrite."

"Ah, no, my poor friend, you've lived so long among shadows that you don't know the truth when you see it," said the mystic sadly. "Does he, Martin? Hasn't everything I've shown you since you came to this place convinced you of my honesty and truthfulness? Haven't I always been above-board with you, and told you everything you wanted to know, straight out, with no holds barred?"

"Yes," I said shortly.

"Well, then, Juan, be less free with your hard words, my fine fellow. Let me tell you what they're up to here. These unreals we're going to look at, you know what they are? Agents of the devil, in disguise as humans. I can prove it. I will, when we get up there to their Satanic headquarters. Oh, yes. You'll see evidence of demonic rites, Black Masses, you mark my words."

"All talk," said Juan. "You haven't seen it yet."

"Have you taken to insulting him, instead of insulting me, then?" I asked.

"You're as bad as each other," he said. "He likes to hear himself talk, and you like to hear others talk. Both foolish activities. There's nothing there but a great building like a warehouse or a workshop. No devil's temples. He knows nothing."

"How comforting," said Vrykolakas smoothly, "to know that our unreal friend is lucky enough to possess only a third-rate mind, and is untroubled by such subtle considerations as allegory, or metaphor."

"Yes, isn't it?" I agreed. "Whereas you know everything, without having seen any of it."

"My power of second sight, you know. But really it's simple. All this city is quite godless. They've just rejected spiritual counsels altogether, and look at the mess they're in."

"Talking about second sight, what do you make of Juan's aura?"

"Oh, he hasn't got one."

"Nothing there at all?"

"Just a flicker sometimes. He won't last long, you know, poor fellow."

"Can you see your own, in a mirror?"

"Stop asking this man foolish questions," said Juan angrily, "or I won't take you to the Casa de los Ilusorios."

He stood still, but that was all we could see of him, the fact that he was standing still.

"If I ask him questions that aren't about you, will you take us?"

"I don't like to hear him talk. You want to talk to him, all right. I don't. The amount of lies that come from that man's mouth, it would need an army of priests to hear his confession. I wash my hands of you. I shall go up to the Casa and find my own way in. If you want to come, you follow me. I want no more to do with you."

And he set off. We were forced to walk quickly to keep up with him. As we went along, the astrologer continued to discourse authoritatively on the depravity of the city's founders.

"They want to pervert Nature," he said. "They want to stop life in its tracks and substitute lewd dreams for it. Make no mistake. You remember my little exposé of their sexual habits? Every word of it was literally true. They want to make everyone forget their natural instincts and fornicate backwards, upside down and in all sorts of foul ways that can hardly bear to be spoken about in God's good open air."

"Why did the dancing dog-child attack Mary Pretorius?" I asked.

"Oh, it did, did it? Their devilish charms are beginning to work," he said grimly, "and their identities are dissolving into one another. For believe me, hard though it may be to accept, your dear wife is one of them, Martin, one of the ringleaders, close to the top. She and Mary Pretorius have had this planned for a long time. Seduce you, then seduce that bloody Arab, that footballer or whatever he is. Oh, yes, the little dog's instinct was right. Mary Pretorius is your wife now, as near as makes no difference, but you can thank your lucky stars I rescued you from being dissolved into that Hamid boy, nasty piece of work that he is. Why do you surround yourself with third-rate people, Martin? You do underestimate yourself, you know. You should snap your fingers at the lot; not worth a fart, any of them."

I didn't speak any more. There was nothing else I wanted to ask, and I was trying to concentrate on following the transparent flicker of Juan among the snowy rocks ahead of us, because now we were out of the Campo de Minerva and on the broad broken slope of the valley side. There was a great cliff in front of us, great in extent rather than in height, and the unreal was making straight for it. Perhaps he'd lured us up here in order to drop a great rock on us from the cliff top; and in that case, I was going to be readier than Vrykolakas, who kept up his stream of salacious denunciation with no sign of flagging.

But he didn't say much more than he'd already said. It came round again and again, with variations. The most novel aspect of it was his piety; I remembered the little gold cross among the dark hairs below his throat, the first time I'd met him, in the hotel in Valencia. And now he was playing the part of a good Catholic knight, out to storm the stronghold of the devil, exuding holiness like the smell of after-shave lotion.

And in spite of my distaste, I had the feeling that he might well have been right. The city *was* dedicated to the unreal, to dreams, though what part the unreals themselves, the angels, played in it I couldn't guess. Maybe I'd see soon. And I couldn't understand his sexual obsessions either.

I followed Juan, and kept my mouth shut, and he followed me, in high spirits, and talked non-stop.

Into the Factory of Possibility
Hidden from the city by a fold in the mountain walls there was an open, rocky, sandy area. Dominating the open space there was a wide factory-like building, facing the sun. Its walls were bright blue; the sandy earth it stood on bright yellow. Glistening banks of pipes and cables ran into points on the walls, and huge silver vats and tanks stood in rows beside it, their valves monitored automatically by electronic sensors. The porcelain and glass of an electrical sub-station sparkled behind a simple wire fence nearby. A purposeful hum of power emanated from it. The words *Peligro Grande*, Great Danger, gleamed in red on a notice, framed by two painted bolts of lightning. The roof of the factory was of bright aluminium, pitched in sharp ridges, with panels of glass set into them. There were no windows at ground level; but at about three metres above the ground, wide empty panes glinted hotly in the sun. The building was set on a slight slope, so that we had to look up at it. From the walls, the windows, there came the hum and click of machinery, the hot dry smell of electricity.

Electricity filled the air. I could feel the magnetism in my skin and hair and clothes. It came from the metallic rocks, the yellow earth, the dry crackling air as well as from the artifacts of man.

The unreal was sitting crouched on a yellow rock, like a demon. When he saw us he stretched his arms in the air and yawned; at the back of his open mouth I could see the blue air of the sky behind him. Then he stood up. Vrykolakas was explaining the logical necessity for those who thwarted him to be damned, when Juan threw a stone at him.

"To hear you talk," said Juan loudly, "I'm surprised that God doesn't take you up to heaven straight away."

"Not necessary," replied the astrologer smoothly. "He knows I shall be with him eventually; he can wait. Now, where's this bloody door you miserable creatures want me to unlock for you?"

Juan jumped off his rock and led us around to the side of the factory, in the shade. He was jittery and excited; he kept punching his fist into the palm of his other hand, skipping lightly on the spot, and looking to right and left every few seconds.

"Is there anyone else around?" I asked, catching his mood.

"Worried, huh?" he said scornfully. "There's no one for miles."

The only entrance to the building was a small red-painted door. Vrykolakas strolled elegantly up to it and flicked the handle disdainfully with his fingernail.

"You may open it now," he said, in a gracious tone.

Juan seized the handle and turned. The door opened into a narrow whitewashed corridor. There was another door on the left, open, that led into an empty office, and at the end of the corridor, a great heavy metal door with an iron wheel in the centre of it, like the door of a cold safe or a vault.

"That first door was open already, fool," said Juan. "I've been this far before. That's the one you've got to open."

"Ah," said the astrologer, frowning.

He studied it closely.

"Ingenious," he said after a moment or two, "but not impenetrable."

He twirled the wheel with a flourish, and the great door swung slowly ajar. There was a slight rush of air, but whether in or out I couldn't tell. From inside came the messenger-smell, fresh water, the desert, snow. My heart beat faster.

The others elbowed me out of the way, and I followed them inside.

The Caves of Ice

Thus began the contest of imaginations I had with the creatures of the Perfect City. It was one I was destined to lose, because I was unwilling to imagine to the limit, even if I had the power to imagine reality, which I had not. They had already imagined it and laid it out here on the mountain, and with every step I took into the factory, I tried harder and harder to imagine the unreality of it.

It was a large open area extending almost the whole length and breadth of the factory; it contained a multitude of machines, generators or turbines I took them to be, humming with power. High-tension wires sprang from them, leading in the direction of a series of chambers in the solid wall of the mountain at the far end of the great hall.

The glass in the roof admitted the bright sunlight, but the air inside was cold, and full of the clean oxygen-smell.

The astrologer and Juan were off, prowling speedily about, looking and touching. Juan would become visible or opaque at intervals, and was grunting with excitement, while the astrologer's passionate involvement made him change shape without realising it, so that the man would drop to his hands and pad along as the wolf, and the wolf would rear on his hind legs and become the man again, the transformation being effected in the blink of an eye. And when he was in the wolf-shape I could see that his excitement was sexual as well as scientific. Up and down between the rows of benches the great grey creature trotted, shouldering aside the flickering form of the unreal; and then the shape would lunge up and back and there was Vrykolakas, his eyes bright, his teeth bared in a vicious grin of curiosity.

And all around the instruments of science glittered and sparkled in the pure mountain-scented air and the dazzling sunlight that poured through the roof. Test-tubes holding concentrations of powerful chemicals hung in aluminium racks; nearby a retort unsupervised stood over a Bunsen burner, the golden liquid in it bubbling gently. Brightly coloured plastic-covered wires led from junction boxes to terminals and connected banks of switches and monitoring dials to valves and thence to more terminals.

But all the wires and pipes and all the aisles led towards the end of the room and those twenty or so chambers in the living rock. That was where I would have to go, but I felt a tremor of reluctance.

Juan called "Hey, Martin! Ilusorios! Come and see them, man! All these bloody unreals!"

Vrykolakas was by his side in a flash, and a great mocking wolfish laugh rang out in the echoing hall. I came up to join them, trembling, at the end of the factory, where the twenty or so chambers were cut into the mountain.

The entrance of each of them was covered by a sheet of plate glass. They were about four metres deep and three across, and the ceilings were low.

I looked inside the nearest one. It was a cave of ice, with green translucent ice on the walls and floor and ceiling. It was suffused with a sun-like radiance. I was reminded of the paintings of Tiepolo, where radiant beings, gods and goddesses, soar effortlessly in a bright blue empyrean, or rest on the whitest and most graceful of clouds, embodying pure, non-human blisses.

On a bench of ice in the centre of the cave lay a dead angel.

My eyes misted with sorrow as my imagination made its last effort. They were dissecting him, I thought. They'd killed him. Out of their love for humans, the unreals had given their bodies selflessly to be probed and examined; for his chest was cut open, and his entrails lay exposed and pulled aside as if for an anatomy lesson.

That was when the agents of the Perfect City won their victory over my imagination. They were not dissecting him; they were assembling him. He was artificial.

The angels were dolls, automata.

They were machines.

The messenger was a machine.

In a futile effort to protest against this defeat, I fainted.

But Juan the forgotten came and flicked water into my face until I awoke, and then I jumped up in a frenzy and ran from one chamber to the next, ravaging them all with my maddened ice-melting eyes.

Vrykolakas, I hardly noticed, was doing likewise, except that he was strolling, his chest puffed out, little twitches of ecstasy distorting the bland solemnity of his expression.

There were angels in all the chambers. Some were nearly complete; they seemed to be asleep, so that a gentle touch would awaken them. Each one was an individual. And so subtle was the art that went into them that none of their faces was perfectly symmetrical, like a doll's, but each had the slight irregularity of beauty.

They were all naked. They each had the organs of both sexes.

Mocking automata! Vile deceitful toys!

In my rage I stumbled over a wire that led to a terminal beside one of the chambers, and it came away. A cluster of sparks scattered across the floor.

Horrorstruck, I tried to replace it, but was daunted by the potency of the current that flowed through it.

I tried three times to touch it to the point, sparks fountaining brilliantly. Inside the cave, drops of water were forming on the surface of the ice.

"Observe," said Vrykolakas sanctimoniously, "the futility of the intellect."

"Why?" I snarled, sparks leaping around my hands.

"No one can repair that now," he said in a tone of sepulchral contentment. "The mockery of life, intended by the builders of this temple of impiety to animate that artificial corpse on the slab, is snuffed out before it can make an eyelid flicker, or a muscle twitch. Well done, my good and faithful friend, you've given me an idea! Now to put my plan into execution."

He thoughtfully bent down and tore out the corresponding wire from the neighbouring chamber. A similar burst of pyrotechnics cascaded over the floor, but he took no notice.

"My astral body is proof against electricity," he remarked, as he went on to rip out the wires from another, and another. "With the insulation of faith, a true believer may plunge his hand into the very fountain of electricity itself, used by our translucent friend to dispose of an interfering engineer only last night. The man was plainly a rank unbeliever, and is now in hell, as I have it on good report."

Before I could stop him, he murdered a fifth angel before its birth.

Then Juan pushed him roughly away from the next window, and stood in front of it.

"You owe me something, you pig," he said, as clearly as he could, though the crackle of sparks and the hiss of water seeping through the gaps below the windows and meeting them made it hard to hear anything.

"Indeed, phantom?" said the werewolf, and growled. "Stand aside, or I shall damn you where you stand."

"Not in your power," answered Juan. "There's not much you can do, but you can do this. Inside these chambers they are making these dolls real, right? Then if I get in there, and put the wires into myself, then I shall become real as well."

"You don't know," I said.

"Be quiet," said the unreal, in charge of both of us. "Then do this, hypocrite, because you owe it to me. Let me get in there, and see that I become real."

259

Vrykolakas grinned, showing his teeth. "What a very good notion," he said. "Capital. A just reward for all your devoted service. Stand aside, Browning, so that we can bring the fruits of reality to this creature of illusion."

"He'd kill you," I told Juan. "Don't believe him, don't believe anything he says."

Vrykolakas dropped to his hands and a shiver of fur ran all over his body. A howl of rage rang through the echoing hall, drowning even the electric fury on the floor.

Then he stood up again, and wiped his mouth.

"Patience, patience," he admonished himself.

"Yes, fuck off," said Juan to me. "Go and abuse yourself in a corner, you doll-lover. I took you here to help me, not get in the way of making me real."

My chest constricted with rage. I contained it and turned away.

There was the crash of glass as they smashed the window of a chamber, and the sound of a body being tumbled off its bench of ice. Could I come up behind as they were busy and kill Vrykolakas with a blow to the head? But no, because he could only be drowned. Stun him, at least, and hold his head under water. That would do. I looked for something to hit him with; the nearest thing was a heavy metal stand for holding test-tubes, but it swung awkwardly.

I turned back to the broken chamber. Juan was lying naked, as transparent as the bone in a squid, on the bench of ice, which was melting. There was a wild gleam in his eyes, which watched every movement of the astrologer, fixing wires to various parts of his skinny frame. Then he saw me.

"Watch out," he cried.

Vrykolakas turned, his hand on a switch. His expression was preoccupied.

"Here I am," he said, "holding back the awesome power of several million volts. With a movement of my hand I can release it to flood through the deluded body of this glassy person. What a piece of work is man! How contemptible, indeed. Even a block of wood stands up to reality better. Have you come here to engage me in conversation, Browning, and prevent the apotheosis of our good friend?"

"Juan, you will die," I said.

"Take no notice," shrieked the unreal. "He's losing his reality, he makes no sense with his words! Pull the switch, pull the switch!"

"A weapon," observed the werewolf, seeing the metal stand I carried. "Hmmm."

And then he pulled the switch, and a flood of electricity hurled itself at all the cells of Juan's body, seeking a way through. Beneath the transparent skin I saw the nerves curl themselves and thresh like tiny whips, the bones shatter like glass, the blood fling itself against the walls of his heart to escape the pain.

After a moment or two, this anatomical display was over. His skin clouded and became perfectly visible; a smell of burning came from his flesh. The astrologer turned off the current, and Juan stopped twitching and lay still. He was now as real as death; his expression was mildly discontented. That wasn't what he wanted, after all.

"Ah," said Vrykolakas sadly; "so young."

And it was true, he didn't look more than seventeen, he didn't look any older than my angel. Mechanical being, who had duped me!

Vrykolakas stepped over the fallen angel and out of the crowded chamber.

"What are you going to do now?" he asked politely.

"Kill you, when I get a chance," I said.

"Not yet, though," he said, and began to move away towards the door. "You might consider the advantages of becoming my partner," he called over his shoulder. "I've still got one or two scores to settle. And now that I know what their blasphemous little secret is, I can call down all the powers of heaven to act on my behalf, so you'd better watch out."

I followed him. There was little point in staying there; I wanted to be somewhere else, away from all this death and disillusion, on my own.

He was waiting for me outside. He was tapping a little gold pencil against his long sharp teeth, and he held a pad of paper in his hand.

"A contract of friendship," he said. "I've just been drawing it up. To prevent us from killing each other, don't you know."

I shook my head.

"You refuse?"

With a snarl of chagrin he bit the pencil through, and flung the note pad to the ground.

"Then you will have to answer for the consequences," he said, spitting out twisted metal and bits of lead. "And they may be terrible."

He began to tear off his clothes, hurling them carelessly in all directions.

"Now," he said, "I change for good! No more shall the full power of my spirit be compromised by the feeble frame it was condemned, by circumstances, to inhabit! Now I begin my war upon the world! Humanity, farewell!"

And he dropped to his hands, which, the instant they touched the cold ground, were transformed into the hairy paws of a great wolf. His forearms sprouted grey hairs, his shoulders narrowed and his chest deepened, and the snarling mask of a wolf replaced the impassioned features and red hair of the astrologer. In a second or two the change was complete.

With a howl, he turned towards the peaceful city, and moved off towards it at a run, with the bone of knowledge clamped firmly between his teeth.

I followed slowly, full of apprehension and dismay.

Night on the Electric Lake

The little lake in the Campo de Afrodite had in its waters an unusual concentration of the salts of electricity, which coloured the water all the tints of the rainbow and bit, as if with little teeth, the flesh of anyone who put his hand in it.

At night, tiny glowing sparks would drift and circle in the depths, where electric crystals were forming. Every so often one would suddenly be extinguished, and a moment later the faintly glowing skeleton of a fish would flick its tail and swim away, lit from within by the spark it had swallowed.

Someone, and I hoped I knew who it was, had summoned me there by a note. I was to wait by the boathouse at about nine o'clock. The plane I had to catch left at midnight. Could I ask her everything I wanted to know in three hours?

I found the note on my bed when I got back to the hotel. I'd glumly trudged down from the factory trying to exorcise my memory of Juan; while he was alive I'd never been able to remember him, and now that he was dead, he was impossible to forget. Guilt got in the way of everything. And I tried, too, to account for the influence Vrykolakas had over me, that made it impossible for me to kill him. His shifting madnesses, like his shifting shape, were vertiginous and hypnotic. Perhaps I could link the two obsessions by means of magic, I thought, and make the cold young corpse of Juan remind me insistently to kill the werewolf wherever I found him.

The note was in a plain white envelope, written in a graceful italic hand. Not my wife's. Machines can write, then, I thought unhappily, but I pressed the paper to my face to catch her clean scent; and then lay down and slept dreamlessly.

All the stars were out when I woke up. The night was fresh, the air had the taste of spring, as if all the plants in the valley were waking up. It wasn't warm yet, but it was no longer cold. Everything had a different quality; the silence over the city was gentle and expectant now, instead of tense.

A variety of elegant trees grew around the shores of the lake. I couldn't see the boathouse at first, because the only light came from the stars and from the drifting sparks in the water. Then I saw a little jetty, and half a dozen rowing boats tied up, and a square shape in the darkness beyond, under the trees.

I moved around the edge of the lake towards it, slowly and quietly, smelling the spring in the air. My heart was pounding. I was eager and nervous, as if I was in love for the first time. As if I was in love, indeed.

Everything there was graceful. Two colonies of swans, one black and one white, nested on the shores of the lake, providing fixed poles for the chromaticism of the water; and the little boats tied up at the jetty were ornamented with carved and gilded dolphins. On the moonlit side of the boathouse there grew a slender and lovely silver birch, all its twigs terminating in tiny buds.

I stroked its bark, as cool and smooth as the moonlight, and leant against it to wait.

Not far away, in one of the other trees, a bird began to sing in the pregnant darkness. I listened to it carefully: how could I play those notes on the flute? Though in that city, the bird was as likely as not to be made of wood or metal; or like the messenger, more than a bird, not less.

"Hallo," she said quietly.

I took a deep breath to cover my surprise.

"I didn't hear you coming," I said.

She inclined her head to avoid a branch, and stopped in front of me, about a metre away. Her blonde hair gleamed like silver, like the bark of the tree. Beneath the sweet smell of cleanness, the first thing I'd known about her, I could smell something else, and I was touched to my heart when I realised what it was. She was wearing scent for the first time, just the slightest hint of patchouli.

"I don't know what to make of you," I said. My voice was unsteady.

She reached up and plucked gently at a twig, just as a human might have done. But she didn't pull it off; it was more as if she were stroking the little thing to make it come alive, like her.

"No," she agreed. "It's just as well you don't have to."

"You know what I did, today?"

"I've heard."

"Why don't you denounce me to the authorities?"

"I told them what would happen days ago. They know what's best, no doubt." But she didn't sound convinced.

"I don't want to talk about that," she went on. "That's not why I asked you to come here."

"Why did you, then?"

"It's a good place for an assignation at night, isn't it?"

"But why the assignation?"

"I wanted to see you again."

I felt as if some powerful and haunting dream had begun, one filled with that kind of miraculous and total happiness that sometimes comes in dreams. It was under way, and I was living it.

"But I don't understand how you can want anything," I said doubtfully.

"Do you understand how *you* can?"

I shook my head. She smiled.

"You're not yourself tonight," I said.

"In what way?"

"You're less stern."

"Ah, well . . ."

She let go of the twig and turned away slowly. I followed her down to the jetty.

She took off her white tennis shoes and socks and rolled up her jeans. She stood on one leg to do it, and I watched her with a blend of incredulity and suspicion and hope: surely she was human! Surely no creature of metal and plastic could move so lightly and adjust her balance with such supple grace!

The calves of her legs were slender and white. Impulsively I sat down beside her on the wooden boards and stroked them. They were soft and warm. She sat down too, and let me continue.

264

"Those poor figures in the Museum," I began, in a low voice, "no one could think they were real, in a million years. But no one would think . . ."

I couldn't finish. She looked at me, and brushed some hair out of her eyes.

"Techniques have come a long way since then," she said.

"Is that all it is?"

"No need to sound so bitter. Without technique, you couldn't play the flute."

She let one of her legs, the one I wasn't touching, down until her foot was in the water. She moved it gently this way and that, making ripples in the moonlight.

"You're perfect," I said involuntarily.

"This is the Perfect City."

There was no irony in her tone tonight. Everything was gentle and serious.

"Why did men make you?" I asked.

"Do you know why you were made?"

"We weren't made. We evolved."

"Same thing. Evolution above all doesn't just happen. But you're right in a way; that's how our growth feels to us. If all the humans died today, we'd be in your position, not knowing why we were created."

"But you're . . . mechanical. You can't reproduce."

"Yes, we can. We can create others like ourselves; we know how to build them. That's as good as reproduction."

"But why? What for? Is that what the Anderson Valley Project is?"

She nodded, and leant back on her elbows.

"I don't know why. Perhaps because we're useful; we make good servants—and messengers; perhaps for our wisdom, for we forget nothing, unlike people; and perhaps for our beauty. Our creators fell in love with us. Don't you know that the city is in love with us?"

"Didn't you know that I was in love with you?"

"Well, yes."

"And you? Does your race have feelings too?"

"You're only asking that out of sarcasm. You know we have. We haven't your talent for dissimulation."

"So if you seem to be in love with a human, you are."

"That's right."

That having been said, a silence fell over us. Enormous feelings circled in the air like the condors of the Andes.

"Can you tell me something about my wife now?" I asked after a minute.

"I don't want to keep it back any more," she said.

"Can you choose, then?"

"Yes, better than you can, because I can see more clearly."

"What's happened to her, then?"

"She's going to be the partner of Johnny Hamid and his wife."

"Johnny and Mary's partner? In business? I don't understand."

"Their marriage was inevitable, but without your wife it wouldn't work. And then the city would fall apart. We all depend on them, and her."

"But what's she going to do? What do they need her for?"

"To act as a . . ."

She sat up and lifted her foot slowly out of the water. She flexed the toes, and set it down beside the other.

"Yes?" I said after a moment.

She bit her lip, and then looked at me.

"As a messenger. A go-between. A lover."

It was my turn to lean back on my elbows. I looked up at the stars, and then back to her.

"Who—" My voice was hoarse. "Who knows of this?"

"The city."

"It's going to be—public?"

"For want of a better word."

"A triple marriage . . . Is that what it is?"

"Not in name."

"And who—whose idea—who thought of it? Was it her?"

"I don't know; that's how it came about. Perhaps the idea just came into being, as we seem to have done."

" 'We' meaning you and me?"

She nodded.

"But why her? She didn't know them, did she? She didn't know anyone like that, I thought . . . I don't understand. She's left me for good?"

"I think so. She belongs to the others now. They all belong to each other."

"Do they . . . love her?"

"Do you think they would fail to? Or she fail to love them?"

"So . . . I'm on my own."

266

She said nothing, and didn't move.

"Doesn't she want to explain it herself?" I asked.

She still said nothing. She hung her head and looked down into the water.

"Well, perhaps she doesn't need to, after all, since we've got you," I went on. I was feeling so thoroughly betrayed that I was beyond bitterness or anger; all I felt was a kind of jaunty contempt.

"*She* hasn't got me," said the messenger quietly.

And that switched me back in a moment into the dream-mood: pretending she was a real girl, pretending we were in that state when one or the other of us would say the word 'love', pretending with all my heart, as the Electric Whores had told me to do.

"Who has, then?" I replied, in the same tone. "Has anyone?"

"You asked me before about my feelings. Aren't they clear?"

"Mine are. Do you want me to tell you about them?"

She nodded, and looked up at me, her grey eyes wide and shining, and her expression apart from them impassive, held back.

"When I thought you were an angel, I was in awe of you. Then when for a moment I thought you were real, a girl, I was in love with you. Then . . . now that I know what you are, I still love you."

"How can that be possible?" she said, with the gentlest of mockery in her voice.

I shook my head. "Now you. You must tell me what you feel, too."

"First," she said, "tell me what you think of me as. What am I?"

"If you're a . . . machine, of metal and plastic, then I'm a machine of flesh and blood. Or if I'm an animal, then you're an animal of metal and plastic and . . . whatever. If spirit and matter are different, I suppose spirit can live in mechanical matter as well as organic matter. And if they're not different, if spirit and matter are the same thing, well then. That's unreal philosophy, if I'm not mistaken. Isn't it?"

"I love you," she said.

Another gust of unreality entered the world, like the wild breeze from the Andes that lifted the scattered leaves and dried paper in Dog Street. She loved me. It was Dog Street, the lovely decayed Calle de Perros, which rose like a vision in my mind as she said it.

I must have sat musing for a minute or so, because eventually she said, almost diffidently, "Does that make you want to go?"

I wanted to seize her and hug her tightly to my breast. Knowledge of what she was held me back. The Electric Whores urged me

267

on, and because I'd resisted them last time I obeyed them now. I kissed her as we'd kissed in the hot streets of Valencia, and in the cool dark money-smelling corridor of the bank, greedily and without conscience.

Then I remembered something else, and broke off.

"What is it?" she whispered.

"The . . . angels I saw in the factory," I said.

"Yes?"

"They were hermaphrodites."

She took a deep breath, and nodded.

"Was that why . . ."

"Yes," she said clearly.

I sat still, in a state of doubt.

"What are you, then?" I asked.

"An angel. One of the unreal people. That's all."

"For God's sake . . . Are you male or female?"

"Both. Whatever you aren't. I'm your complement, don't you realise? You don't think you're entirely masculine, do you?"

"Physically," I muttered.

"Your body isn't a prison," she said.

"More unreal philosophy?"

"If you like. But now your wife has become a lover of two sexes, too."

I sat up slowly and looked out over the lake, up to the sky and the stars.

"What will happen to us?" I said.

"Us?" she said after a pause. "Does that include me?"

"Yes, of course you as well. All of us. I feel unreal too, just like everyone else. We're all unreal. What'll happen to us?"

She leant against me, and rested her head lightly on my shoulder. I stiffened for a moment; it was a machine . . . But it seemed to be the most beautiful girl in the world, a purer being, an angel, and that good man Ignaz Gruenberg was convinced of the angels' holiness and grace; and everything was what it seemed. I relaxed and held her close.

"You should say, what shall we do?" she murmured. "We can make things happen, as well as wait for them to happen by themselves."

"All right then," I answered, drifting into happiness again. "What shall we do?"

"Let's take out one of these boats," she said.

"Why?" I asked curiously.

"I'd like to."

"Do you mind my asking questions like that?"

She laughed. "I don't mind any signs of interest, as long as they aren't malicious. You want to know how I can want things, and like things, and have wishes?"

"Yes," I said, getting up to untie one of the little boats. "I want to know everything about you."

She nodded, as if that was what she had expected. And I was watching her with half an eye, all the time, for anything that would betray her nature, a stiff mechanical movement or a rigidity of posture or an unnatural stillness; but she was more graceful and aware than I was. And by that time, if I had seen anything like that, I'd have hugged it to my heart as being something particularly her own, and hence something I loved.

She stepped into the boat, holding my hand for safety but keeping her balance perfectly as the little vessel dipped with her weight, and sat down and got out the oars from under the seat.

I took them, and sat down facing her.

"How do you want things, then?" I said.

She pushed us gently away from the jetty.

"I see things, and think, that would feel good to me, or would give him pleasure. So I try and bring them about. That's all."

"You seemed—you know at the beginning, when you first came to me?"

She nodded, and looked at me clearly. She was lying back in the stern of the boat now, with her arms along the sides, looking as comfortable as a cat.

"You were in charge then. You told me what to do, you were distant and . . . in command. Why was that?"

"Wasn't that what you missed, since your wife had gone?"

I thought. "I suppose it was."

"I guessed," she said, "that if you were going to fall in love with anything, it would be that."

"You wanted me to?"

"Yes."

"Tell me again."

"I wanted you to fall in love with me."

"But why, why?"

"I was in love with you."

269

"Oh, this can go on for ever—why were you in love with me? You'd never seen me before that afternoon."

"Oh, yes I had. I was at Pretorius' ball."

"But you didn't—it seemed as if you weren't, and everything is what it seems. You can't have it both ways."

"I was pretending. Doing the best I could, don't you see? That was all I could think of."

It was almost as if she was pleading. She looked away across the silvery water.

"I had to tell you how to get to your wife," she went on in an undertone, "so as not to—put you off. Otherwise I might not have seen you again, because I had other jobs to do, you see. . . . But I had to warn you at the same time. And I had to make it all up on the spur of the moment, because of course you can't programme—" and she looked directly at me, almost in challenge—"for that sort of situation. The machine has to be independent of any programme."

"Are you independent, completely?"

"No. There are some things I have to do. Some of my nature is programmed."

We were in the middle of the lake. The world was utterly silent. All around us the green growing tips of trees and flowers forced more life into the universe; there was a powerful current of it flowing in my body, too, making me feel sharp and keen and strong.

I stopped rowing, and looked up at the starry sky, breathing in deeply.

"Don't," she whispered, "ask me any more about myself."

I looked down in surprise.

"Why?" I said. Our voices were quiet, because all the night was listening and urging us gently on towards each other, and it would be unseemly to talk with loud voices in the presence of so much concentration.

"It puts me in a dilemma. There are some things it might be better if we didn't talk about."

"No, surely. If I'm in love with you, whatever you are, I want to know everything. That's inevitable. How can it make any difference?"

"It will," she said.

I didn't reply. The scent she was wearing, and the oxygen-clarity-desert-snow-fresh-wind smell, combined to bring a lump to my throat; the way she lay back in the stern, with her knees up and

270

her beautiful square hands resting on the sides of the boat, taunted my heart and crushed it at once; I was overwhelmed by love, just as I'd been in the hot streets of Valencia, dizzy with longing. I bowed my head.

"You're trembling," she said. "What is it?"

"You," I said. "Are there other angels who love humans in the city? Other people who are in love with you?"

"Not with me, but with us all. The city's in love with us, as a whole. And there will be others like us, other lovers."

"That's planned for?"

"It's inevitable."

"Is that what the city's for? A city for lovers?"

"And for business, and for science."

"Have you ever seen my wife?"

"Why do you ask that? Yes, I have, once."

"I just wondered. Did you speak to her?"

"We spoke, yes."

"What did you say?"

She hesitated a moment, then said "We talked about you."

"When was this?"

"Yesterday."

"What did you say about me?"

"She told me about your life together. And about her life with Johnny and Mary. You know how clear she is about everything. She was so clear-sighted, it was a privilege to talk to her and to hear her explain things."

"What did she say, though? About me?"

"You want to know why she went away," she said, as if she were explaining it to me instead of asking. I nodded. "She said she loved you, she'd grown to since you were married. It was difficult for her to leave, but she wanted to help the Anderson Valley Project. She was needed, you see, and her clear-sightedness. She knew what she'd be doing; keeping the marriage of Johnny and Mary together by making it into something different, a three-cornered thing, more rich and stable, you see; and that would keep the city and the Project together, because their families are so bound up in it. She couldn't do that while she was married to you. She knows that you'll think it a terrible betrayal, to walk out on your husband just to keep some business thing from falling apart, but it's more than that. As you know. This isn't a business thing only, is it?"

"Since I've . . . realised about you, no, it isn't."

271

"And it would have been very painful for her to think of you on your own. So when I . . ."

"I found that I loved you more than I loved her," I put in absently. "Yesterday, that was. And it's easy to understand why you could be loved. But why do you love me, as you say you do?"

"For the same reasons as your wife did," she said, tonelessly.

I looked at her sharply.

"Why do you say it like that?"

She put her hands to her head.

"I feel apprehensive," she said quietly. "Don't go on. Don't ask any more."

"But I want to know!"

"You want straight answers, and they don't exist, as I've told you before."

"Don't you see that if I don't know why you—love me, I . . . it's very much harder to believe?"

"Let it be hard, then," she said. She sounded as she had done the first time I'd seen her, authoritative, like a sybil. But her hands were still pressed to her cheeks. "It's not easy for humans and us to love each other. Why should it be easy to believe in if it's not easy to do?"

"Easy! What do you think love is, then?"

She put her hands over her eyes.

"What I've been told," she muttered.

"What is it, then?"

"Wanting," she said. "Wanting to be with and share and have . . . And a pull like a magnet towards the other person, his body . . . And admiration, for all his qualities, all his good qualities, and his gifts. It's conditional, always."

"Love, conditional?"

"Oh, yes. Of course it is. If you changed your character and became greedy and lazy, I'd stop loving you. What else would you expect?"

I shrugged. "I don't see what I have that attracted your love anyway."

She said nothing.

"Can you tell me?" I went on.

"Please," she said. "I can't help it."

"What do you mean?"

"Just accept it. *Please.* Does it make you happy, to be loved by me?"

272

"I . . . Happy's not the word. Oh, of course it does, or it would if I knew why . . ."

"I can't help it," she said.

Suddenly, I realised what she was trying to say, and trying not to say.

"Were you *made* to do it?" I whispered.

She nodded. Her lips were compressed. Her hands pressed tightly on her cheeks.

"They made you like that? Programmed you to?"

I was appalled to see tears, artificial tears, come to her eyes and glitter brightly in the mocking moonlight.

"Yes," she said.

I set the oars carefully down in the bottom of the boat. I was as weak as a baby; my hands were trembling. I dared not look at her.

"It's all false, then," I said, my voice harsh and uncertain.

She shook her head emphatically, so that the boat rocked gently with the movement.

"No, no!" she said, and for the first time there was passion in her voice, by means of a delicate arrangement of crystals and electrons. "There's *nothing* false about it, Martin! Don't believe that!"

"What am I to believe, except what you've told me?"

"Your wife loved you in exactly the same way."

"Oh, yes! And you'll be telling me next that all I've got to do is pretend, and everything'll be all right, just like the Electric Whores said! Pretend, pretend, live in a world of lies, is that it?"

"You're wrong, Martin, *it's not lies . . .*"

How we would have finished, I don't know, I can't imagine; rather, I can imagine false endings, but not the real ending, reality being too far from my imagining powers; but at that moment we stopped talking, and with a single impulse we were in each other's arms, tasting each other's tears, the real and the unreal, indistinguishable.

And that too might have been a kind of ending, but something happened.

The silver birch tree under which we had met was suddenly covered in a blaze of lights. Fierce little flames appeared on every twig, and the voice of the astrologer whispered over the water "Hello, young lovers!"

273

How to Relax Among Friends

That very tree! The demon must have seen and heard everything we said ...

Very well, I would kill him. In his tree-shape he wouldn't find it easy to get away, and I wouldn't be distracted as poor Felix had been.

The messenger, the angel, my loved one, sat still and anxious as I lifted out the oars and set them in the rowlocks. But before I could start pulling for the edge of the lake, she sat up and pointed to the boathouse.

I turned; and saw, trotting neatly out of the blackness, all of Vrykolakas' friends, from the dainty Milord to the abominable Max. They sat down around their master the birch tree and licked their lips, making not a sound.

My arm faltered. I was afraid of them.

Then one of them, perhaps out of eagerness, gave that mewing, hacking sound which was all they could produce.

"Ssh!" came the voice of the birch tree. "An idyll on the lake, my pets! Don't wake the two sweethearts from their perverted trance! If we keep still and quiet, my darlings, we might be able to watch them *fornicate!*"

And with that he gave all his branches a flick, so that the flames went out; and in the momentary darkness that followed the shape of the tree shrank into itself and became a man again. There was a short yelp of pain as he tore quickly at Lulu's ears, and then he was scurrying out on to the jetty and untying a boat.

My heart leapt. Doesn't he know I can drown him?

But he wasn't going unguarded. He called "Stürmer! Nixon! Max!" and three of the largest dogs lounged obediently on to the jetty, and leapt into the boat.

With the greatest of care, which included brushing the seat before he sat down, the werewolf joined them, and supervised the arrangements for rowing the boat. He directed Stürmer the Dalmatian and the other dog called Nixon to take an oar each in their powerful jaws, while Max sat in the bows in order to demoralise us with his pale eyes.

"What are they going to do?" whispered the angel, my nameless one.

I shook my head, and sat still. They weren't starting yet; Vrykolakas was unfolding something. I thought it was a newspaper at

274

first, until he put it over his head and began to blow into a nozzle. It was an inflatable lifejacket.

I laughed loudly, so that he could hear me. He looked up, bared his teeth, and gave a howl of rage before bending his head and continuing to blow. Max grinned, and licked his lips silently.

At last the lifejacket was full, and tied safely under his arms. He gave the order to move; the two rowers pulled awkwardly at their oars, and the boat clumsily moved out from the jetty.

"Have you got anything sharp?" I whispered.

She looked frightened. "No," she whispered back.

"Can you swim?"

She shook her head.

"Would you drown? Can water damage you?"

"I'm human enough for that. I'd drown, yes."

"If the boat turns over, cling to it. I don't know about the dogs, but I can drown that bastard if I make a hole in his lifejacket. You . . . better keep out of the way."

The movement of the other boat was so erratic that I thought we might be able to avoid it altogether, by rowing around all night if need be; but I was angry. Vrykolakas was haranguing us vigorously, his hands gripping the sides of the boat, his tongue lapping furiously around his lips after every fresh burst of rhetoric.

"So *that's* your filthy little game, is it! Deceiving your fair wife in this vile and unnatural manner! Little did I know, when I went into partnership with her only a short while ago, that I would be defending her honour from him who should hold that honour dearer than his own life! My God! You bastard!"

Max howled briefly, agreeing with every word.

"And you, you tin bitch! You rubber fetish-queen! Complete with every aperture, and lifelike movements! You give yourself a fine set of mechanical airs, don't you, eh, you piece of sex apparatus! My word, I shall let some of the steam out of *you*, make no mistake!"

I looked in the bottom of the boat for anything I could use to puncture his lifejacket, a nail, a splinter of wood; but the boat was too new and too carefully built. I'd have to use my teeth and nails, if I could get close enough. Just like a zombie.

The boat sat high in the water. It rocked easily; it was going to be difficult to keep a balance. And I mustn't tip her into the water . . .

"Take one oar," I whispered, "and use it to hold the dogs off."

275

She picked up one oar, and I took the other. Vrykolakas' invective continued.

"The curse of Sodom lies in wait for you, beyond a shadow of a doubt. Oh yes, I know all about it, I've seen them at it, these catamites of Satan. Didn't I tell you about it before, you guilty man? Didn't I generously expose their concupiscence before your very eyes, with no charge? Didn't I let you in on the secret, with no questions asked? Then you and that deluded magic-lantern slide of a refugee from justice go off and abuse yourselves together, doing it backwards and inside out and all sorts of dirty ways, no doubt! Oh, the stark ingratitude of it makes the heart reel, and the brain perspire! And your poor wife sitting weeping in your little home, while you gad about the night with this creature of the mail-order bordello, and her lubricious expertise, so dearly purchased, my goodness!"

The two dogs stopped rowing when their boat was just out of reach. Under the direction of their mad captain, they shipped the oars and turned around. The mastiff Nixon took the place of Max in the bows. Vrykolakas paddled, using both hands at once, until their boat was pointing directly at us. He was gasping and blowing with the effort, and the cold of the water, and the biting of the electricity.

Little by little the two boats came together. Nixon was gathering himself for a spring. I waited.

Then, when I guessed he was about to leap, I swung the oar at him.

I was lucky. It took him on the side of the head and tumbled him into the water. The astrologer gasped with shock; Max and Stürmer took no notice.

"I say, steady on," said the mystic, looking anxiously into the depths, where the furious kicking of the dog had raised glittering clouds of phosphorescence. "Can't you understand a manner of speaking? Let's not get hasty, now. Terms for negotiation, that's what I've been setting out. Don't believe in mincing my words, I'm a blunt man, and I can be a tough man if you cross me. But we're all men of the world, or two of us are, and you know how it is, everything's a manner of speaking in this place, isn't it? Let's sit down and talk this thing out, man to man, with no hard feelings."

The force of my swing had pushed our boat out of reach of the other. I paddled it carefully back into range, pausing only to bring the oar down on the skull of Nixon the mastiff, who was circling his boat completely ignored by its crew. He sank.

"Now now," said Vrykolakas mildly.

An expression of benignity settled on his face. He was still seated comfortably among the cushions at the stern, gripping the sides of the boat so that his knuckles stood out like a skeleton's.

"I've been thinking," he said. "Why don't we form ourselves into a limited company? With my brains and your daring, and the inside knowledge of this plastic trollop, we could clean up in this place. The only thing we lack is money, and I bet you know a thing or two about that greasy little Hamid that we could turn to good account, eh? What about it? Is it a deal?"

He looked like a bishop. Stürmer the Dalmatian stood up, his tail slowly swinging, and began to growl in a harsh whistle. It made me frightened; and there were still so many of them on the shore, if we got that far alive . . .

Our boat was drifting gently sideways. I didn't want that, because it meant that the stern, where she was sitting, was the closest part to the dogs. I dipped the oar into the water to try and turn it back, and that was when he leapt.

It was a huge jump. It pushed their boat back a couple of metres, and the great spotted beast seemed to get longer as he flew through the air, his forepaws extended straight in front and his teeth bared in a greedy snarl.

But she wedged the handle of the oar against the seat, and raised the blade at just the right moment to meet the dog full in the face. It broke the force of his leap, but the momentum carried him on and over the side of the boat, which rocked heavily.

He twisted and scrambled up, snarling and mewing, his claws scrabbling on the wood. He was after her, teeth bared, going for her throat. I dropped the oar and grabbed his tail, bracing my feet against the seat in the middle of the boat and tugging hard. He lashed and flung himself this way and that, like a python. She sat unmoving, her hands on the sides of the boat, her eyes closed.

But I had a better purchase than the dog did, and after a few moments of bitter struggle he turned on me, snapping and growling madly, while his master howled encouragement from the other boat.

I had no other weapon; I used my teeth. He sank his into my arm, and I sank mine as far as I could get them into the flesh around his ear, and ripped it away.

What was I turning into? What was he making me?

I spat the ear out. The Dalmatian loosened his grip on my arm, and went for my throat. I just got my hand there in time, and dug at his eyes with the nails of the other. His head was shaking, thrashing, flinging from side to side, in all directions, and my hand slipped time and time again in the flow of blood from his ear. But then I got a thumb into his eye-socket, and he let go of my wrist; and I darted my head forward and seized his throat with my teeth, feeling exultant, tasting the blood, and tore and tore at it until he was dead.

I looked up, dazed, to see the other boat two or three metres from us, the astrologer looking judicious and concerned in the stern and Max on his feet, greedy, joyful, in the bows.

I tipped the dead Stürmer over the side and scooped up a handful of fresh water to wipe my bloody face.

She (and why hadn't she told me her name? I might need it) sat huddled opposite me, her hands to her mouth as if she was praying. Her eyes were wide open.

"Did they teach you how to fight?" I asked, my voice hoarse.

She shook her head.

"Just keep your balance, then," I said.

My eye caught a movement from the other boat. Vrykolakas had changed shape; a great gaunt wolf now sat on the seat in the stern, still with the inflatable lifejacket around its chest. Its eyes glowed red, and it howled impatiently. Max swung his tail, and looked half round and then back again at us; and then the wolf-shape melted into the suave form of the astrologer, and he settled himself again on the seat.

"But a foretaste," he muttered, "of what is to come in the future, when I have had my revenge . . ."

"Revenge for what?" I called across the water. He was always ready to talk, and I was genuinely curious.

"Deceit, my dear," came the reply. "I was cheated by the one woman to whom I had given everything; my heart, my riches, my body, and my formidable influence in the land of the spirit."

"And who was that?"

"You cannot guess? You poor simpleton!"

"He means your wife," said the messenger quietly.

"When did you give her anything? What did she have to do with you?" I asked angrily.

"Mind your own business," said Vrykolakas sulkily. "I'll tell

278

you, but I don't have to. We were going into partnership, of course. She cheated and ran away, left me, jilted me."

"Do you want to know the truth?" said the messenger.

"If it's the truth he wants, he won't get it from you, you clockwork floozy," the astrologer shouted. "You're nothing but a great big lie from your head to your painted buttocks."

"What is the truth, then?" I asked her.

"Lionel Pretorius asked her—"

"Lies!"

"To go to this man—"

"Your tongue will turn to ash!"

"And find out what he was planning to do—"

A violent howl, disturbing small birds at the edge of the lake.

"To disrupt the Anderson Valley Project. He and Pretorius were old enemies, you see. And it was a kind of test for your wife."

"She passed it, no doubt," I said. Well, it was all coming clearer, at least.

The astrologer raised his arms, making the lifejacket squeak. His fists beat at the air in fury.

"False, false, false, every letter of every word of every sentence! I am betrayed! She loved me, I had the proof of it in my arms! Oh, yes, she could hardly contain her love for me, she said so herself! She was no more a spy than my good friend here is a Persian cat! She was seduced by the evil of that millionaire with the tinted glasses, that impotent voyeur who establishes his daughter in a menage à trois for his own perverted delectation! She loved me!"

"Is that why you go about murdering people?" I asked.

"Revenge, mon ami! Simple. I may not enjoy the rewards of love, so I take those of hatred. Little else is open to me these days."

His tone had become, in a second, maudlin. I began to see that it was because he had no substance, because in his mind he was as empty as Juan, that he had no momentum; his headlong rushes in one emotional direction were easy to stop and reverse, because they had no weight behind them.

The thought of Juan brought my resolve to mind; I would kill him. Simple magic.

"When I have killed your friend," I called, "I shall kill you, and rid the world of you. I shan't let you go this time."

He laughed carelessly. "You let *me* go? What about all those

279

times I let you go, ungrateful boy? But you'll have to catch me first."

He dipped his hands in the water, tutting and shivering at the sharpness of it, and paddled the boat around towards us for the last confrontation.

"Now, little Max," he muttered tenderly. "Kill the lady first."

The fearsome beast stood up, and licked his lips.

"Martin," she whispered. I looked around, suddenly weak.

"My name is Galatea," was all she said.

She was sitting upright, calm and happy, smiling with love. For a second I thought she had gone mad; now I know she hadn't, I know she'd already planned what she was going to do, and wanted me to see her like that again.

A scratch of claws from the other boat made me look away from her. And then Max leapt.

Our boat was sideways on to theirs, and he leapt straight at her. I swung my oar, uselessly; for when he was in mid-air, too late to turn or change direction, Galatea the angel slipped over the side of the boat and down into the electric water, to drown.

I cried out: a great "OHH!", wrenched from my heart; and clubbed and clubbed at the huge dog, who'd fallen clumsily, since his target was gone, half out of the boat. I think I broke his back, for his front legs were working, and his jaws grated and slavered, but he couldn't move his back half. Again and again I struck him, head, back, neck taking all the burden of my hate, until he lolled dead and harmless, and I tipped his carcass into the water and off the seat she'd sat on.

Then, my heart cold and fixed like an animal caught alive in the ice, I turned back to the designer of all these deaths.

Blazing Water

The water around the boat was glowing, the electricity being excited by the violent movements of the dogs and the splashing of the oars. Little sparks burst out of the surface here and there, firing themselves through the air like tiny rockets and expiring two or three metres above the water.

The werewolf sat drumming his fingers on the sides of his boat, eyeing the water with apprehension. I looked around for my oar, to hit him with, and found that it was drifting away, out of reach.

"Vrykolakas," I called, "I'm going to kill you!"

And I dived into the water. It was bitterly cold, but what hit me more than the cold was the succession of jarring shocks that slammed into my flesh. The lake was alive with electricity. I trod water, shaking the hair out of my eyes, and tried to see where his boat was.

Vrykolakas stood up unsteadily.

"Foolish youth," he cried, "prepare for the consequences of your folly!"

He checked that his lifebelt was safely in place; and then his boat caught fire.

In a moment, without warning, it was blazing from stem to stern. The gilded carvings on its prow bubbled and cracked, the planks split, the sides burst open, and with a howl that should have been heard in the secret places of the moon the astrologer changed shape one final time, became a wolf again, and leapt like an arrow at my throat.

I was full of pain. I didn't know what to do; but I held my breath, and sank. He crashed into the water above me. His claws raked my shoulders and chest, and his snapping muzzle, fiercer than a crocodile's, thrust down into the water to tear out my throat.

I shook my head; I couldn't hold him off. The electricity jarred me convulsively several times a second. I didn't expect to live; the most I could do was take him with me. I seized his ears and tugged him down.

His mouth was wide open when it went under. He swallowed gouts of the flashing water, thrashing in panic, flinging his head from one side to the other to get out of my hands. But I had a lucky grip, and thought of Galatea, down below, where I'd soon be; and he must have had empty lungs when he'd gone under, and swallowed a lot of water, because his struggles lasted less than a minute, and for the last part of that I'd managed to lift my head out of the lake; and then he was dead.

I let him go, and slowly, with infinite reluctance, he sank into the radiant depths.

I turned on my back, oblivious to the currents of light and pain in the water, and floated like an angel in a thundercloud. I'd won; and I felt a great healing emptiness, as dear as the scent of Galatea or the cold landscapes of the mountain wastes, enter and possess my soul.

There was nothing else to do now, except go home, and there was plenty time for that.

I looked at the stars, and at the moon, and at the deep cool spaces between them; and all around me the electric turbulence of the water gradually subsided. The shocks grew less painful and frequent, the little sparks left the water less eagerly; and after a minute or two, the water was dark and still again.

I turned wearily over, to swim back to the shore. Now that their master and their three champions were dead, I cared less for the other dogs; and in any case I forgot them in a second, as I stared transfixed through the water.

For there on the bottom of the lake was the vision I had seen after I had left the Electric Whores of Dog Street; the body of my loved one outlined in stars across the dark firmament. Only this time it was the messenger and not my wife, and the electric crystals had begun to cover her lovingly in pinpoints of fire. I looked down at her for a long time. The sharp water brought tears to my eyes.

Hospitality, for the Second Time

The sound of a car came to my dulled attention before I saw its lights. It drove into the Campo de Afrodite and followed the curving road that led to the lake. By the time it got there I had reached the jetty, but I was too weak to climb on to it. I hung there with one arm hooked over the side of a boat, breathing deeply.

The lights of the car swept across the patient friends sitting under the trees. None of them moved. They didn't even turn their heads.

The engine stopped. A door opened and closed; footsteps crunched on the gravel path.

"Over here," I called feebly.

He came on to the jetty, paused uncertainly, then leant over the side and helped me up.

It was the young man with horn-rimmed glasses, who had been talking to Mary at the party all those hours ago.

"Everyone else is dead," was all I could say.

He nodded seriously and took my arm over his shoulder, half-carrying me to the car. He opened the passenger door and took out some neatly folded clothes.

"I haven't got a towel," he said, "but these'll fit. You've worn my clothes before."

"You're Mary's brother," I said.

He helped me undo the clothes I had on, sodden and torn, and put on the ones he had bought. I was shivering violently, and my arm was still bleeding from the bites.

The headlights of the car were directed out across the silent lake. In their path sat three of Vrykolakas' friends, as still as statues. They were only a few metres away; I wanted to see them. I walked carefully away from the car and stood in front of Lulu, whose ear had bled copiously from her master's last fond gesture.

She was as still as papier mâché, as still as Felix the zombie. I touched her gently and she fell over, rigid and light, like a model. The others were all in the same condition. Everyone was dead.

Again I felt the easy tears come to my eyes. Mary's brother touched my arm and I turned to go back to the car.

"I think I've got everything," he said as he started the engine.

In the back were my rucksack, my passport, my wallet, and the case my flute went in.

"We've had the . . . flute, is it?—mended," he said.

"I didn't think it could be," I said. "Thanks." My voice shook.

"That's okay," he said.

The clock dial on the fascia showed eleven-thirty as he turned out of the meadow of Aphrodite and put the car on the road towards the airport.

"What do you know," I said after a minute or two, "about all this business?"

"Mary's told me all she knows," he said. "Was it Alexander Vrykolakas who was involved? Johnny thought it might be."

"Yes," I said.

"What happened then, at the lake?"

"I killed him, as I'd promised to do. But it's a long story."

He nodded. "Was the angel there as well?"

"She drowned herself, to save me."

He looked across at me, and then back to the road. I sat and clutched the flute-case I'd taken from the back of the car, as a baby might clutch its mother, and stared at the unfolding road ahead.

We were silent again for a while. Then I said "Why didn't they stop him before? Or catch Juan, the one who died up at the factory? It was him that killed the man in the generating station. But no one seemed to take any notice of—of any of us."

"That was Catherine," he said, and her name came easily to his lips. "She told them to leave you alone. She wanted you to find your own way of doing things, I expect. She implied that that was

283

the price of her being there, you see. No one . . . well, no one would dream of arguing. She commands . . . no, that's too cold and formal . . . I don't know how to put it, but the whole of the Anderson Valley is hers, it's her creation, now that she's here. She *is* the Anderson Valley; it's all hers, and Johnny's and Mary's . . . I may be telling you things you know; sorry."

"No," I said. "Please go on. I know nothing about her any more."

"I don't know much," he admitted. "She's like a queen; she's magnificent. It's almost as if she can see into the future; everything's so clear and calm . . . I'm rhapsodising. I really don't know anything about it."

"Well, you're one of the family."

"Mary's the important one; I'm only a lawyer."

We left the last buildings of the city behind, and the car picked up speed on the long flat road across the valley floor.

"By the way," he said, "my grandfather sends you his regards."

"He thought I was you."

"Oh, they tried that, did they? What did you do?"

"You mean they've done it before?"

"It's a game they play. They tried it with Johnny too, but he didn't join in."

I could imagine; he'd gently insist that he was who he was, and they'd give up and laugh. El Cambista de la Realidad couldn't buy *him*.

After a drive of ten minutes or so, on an empty road, we were at the airport. A huge deserted passenger terminal, clean and brightly lit, and off to one side an even larger freight building. Two vast transport planes were being unloaded on the floodlit runway; a Boeing airliner was being fed by a fuel tanker beside the passenger terminal.

David Pretorius handed me an envelope when the car was parked.

"Your ticket," he said.

"Where am I going?"

"Madrid, initially. After that, anywhere you like."

I took my things out of the back of the car and stood there, feeling dizzy, on the tarmac. He hesitated, and then held out his hand. I shook it.

"Thanks for the lift," I said. "Where shall I send your clothes?"

"To my father's house in Valencia. Will you be all right?"

"When I've slept for a month . . . Give my love to—my friends."

"Yes, I will." He turned the car, and then looked back. "I don't really know," he said, "what you've done, or what's going on in the city. But I know about the angels. I wanted to say I was sorry about it, that's all, really."

"Thanks. I don't know what it means, either."

He smiled sympathetically, and nodded; and then he drove away.

Later, on the plane, I looked through my wallet to see how much money I had left. There wasn't much. I began to fear for the future; but then I found, tucked away at the back of the wallet, a torn handbill advertising a cycle race. And then I remembered what was written on the back of it, and put it carefully away again, and went to sleep.

Night Thoughts

The king of Cyprus, Aphrodite's island, carved the statue of a beautiful girl, and fell in love with it. The goddess took pity on him and made the statue come to life, giving the artificial girl the name of Galatea; and she married the king, and they lived happily ever after.

When I got back to Valencia I found my partner Benny in the position of Pygmalion the king. Having made models of his machines and patented the designs with the money I had lent him, he could not bear to choose a firm to entrust with the business of actually making the things: he hoped they'd come to life on their own, I guess, or by the intercession of the goddess of machinery.

So the sleeping partner woke up, and began to organise the business. I sold the design of an improved derailleur rear-wheel gear change to a large French cycle manufacturer. I sold the design outright, preferring immediate cash to distant royalties; but one of the carefully negotiated conditions of the sale was that the manufacturer should never refer to the gear-change without using the name Hagen, which was Benny's name. If the firm of Hagen-Browning was to prosper, it needed to be heard of.

With the cash from that sale I filed several more overseas patents and set Benny up in a workshop. Then I began to sell in earnest. Everything I sold had the name Hagen as firmly attached to it as lawyers could manage, so that before long the Hagen derailleur, the Hagen bearing, the Hagen automatic gear-change were all advertising each other's excellence.

Then we moved to Switzerland, borrowed some money, and set

up our own factory. Benny became interested in materials, especially in the possibilities of carbon fibre, and with the resources of a whole laboratory at his disposal, his powers of invention took fire. A little while after that, the company went public; and that was the beginning of our fortunes.

Benny's talent was rare and inexplicable, like oil or happiness. But he needed me to do the wheeling and dealing, the selling and the bargaining and the shaking of hands; and where my talent for that came from was just as much of a mystery. It may have been that I'd given up music. I was never a composer, any more than I was an inventor like Benny; but I was good at bringing music that already existed to life by playing it. Similarly I could bring Benny's inventions to life by orchestrating their appearance in the world. And I enjoyed it.

Benny owned three-quarters of our original company, and so he grew rich to begin with three times as fast as I did. But he wasn't interested in money, and merely allowed it to accumulate. The more I worked with it, on the other hand, the more fascinating I found it, and I began to speculate and invest my share of the profits. My money grew and grew. So did Hagen-Browning. All the possibilities for growth were there, but I didn't want to move too fast, having seen what happened to firms which over-reached themselves. We kept our manufacturing base, and diversified carefully.

I am a millionaire.

If I wanted to go back to the Anderson Valley, I could fly there today in the Lear jet that waits at Zurich to take me anywhere in the world. Alternatively, I could lift the radio-telephone in the back of my Rolls Royce and ask to speak to the Vice-President in charge of Communications and Air Transport, the Hamid Corporation, and the telephone operator would search him out in Beirut or Caracas or New York or London, and I could speak to my old friend Johnny, the winner of the cycle race advertised on the back of the original Hagen-Browning agreement that now hangs framed on the wall of my office.

Or I could do nothing, and let rumours of the Valley come to me, as they've been doing for some time now. Mary is expecting a child, I hear. News of interesting developments in the field of electrical engineering comes from Venezuela. In Rome, a face of unusual beauty catches my eye in a busy square, and I can't be sure that I haven't smelt the snowy scent of oxygen. Someone at a party in Paris tells of the strange quiet gifted assistant he's just engaged. Sexual habits delicately change.

I write down the story of it all, and think about the unreal people. The cities we visited on the way, the city on the plain with the Electric Whores and the city in the mountains with the mad magistrate, were early ventures of the same kind. They failed because, as the messenger would have said, techniques were not sufficiently advanced. But, more important, they had an uncomfortable attitude to their unreals. The true doctrine of heaven, which the messenger told me was what they believed in the Perfect City, is more fruitful: If a thing appears genuine in all its parts, then treat it as genuine, and see how you get on.

Nothing is natural any more, and nothing is artificial. It's a false dichotomy, and we should forget about it.

We all show false faces to the world, and a good thing too, for a hundred reasons. We should be consistent with our friends and lovers, so as not to be unkind. But if in your heart you are not kind, it's better to be false, to act kindly even if you don't feel it, because the deed is important and not the reason for it.

That kind of falsity is the triumph of our civilisation.

What are the unreal people? They've always been with us, as angels or nymphs. Not gods, but beings less than gods, like us but better than us, cleaner and more radiant. Poets have written about them too, Hoffmann, Homer, Shelley. We can't aspire to being gods but we can be a little more like the unreal people. Civilisation has made us more like them, and can make us more so still if we want it. We are more powerful, more healthy, cleaner and kindlier than people of fifty thousand years ago. The unreal people are part of evolution.

And I think often about my vision in Dog Street, and about what the Electric Whores said to me before they vanished. I couldn't see it then, but it's all around me now, all kinds of success are due to it. Electricity, and finance, and sexuality, and happiness, and evolution, they all come about because of the amorous inclinations of matter.